Praise for the no

Third

"Witty, whimsical, reflective
should tickle your funny bone, as well as touch your heart."
—Tanzey Cutter, *Old Book Barn Gazette*

"A screwball comedic romance that stars several interesting characters. Claire Cross writes a warm, witty, and often wild novel that shows the expanse of her talent." —Harriet Klausner

"This book is hilarious. [Cross] has a unique and quirky style all her own and one that will leave more of an impression behind than just a proverbial mental footprint." —*The Romance Reader*

"Do you feel lucky when you get more than you expect? If so, I strongly recommend this book. I rarely laugh out loud while reading, but this gave my smile muscles a good workout while engaging my brain. The writing is snappy and refreshing. . . . This was my first Claire Cross and I plan to pick her up again when I need a good laugh." —*All About Romance*

"Laced with a good deal of humor, Ms. Cross creates characters that will alternately have you laughing and sniffling. [She] makes the transition from writing historical romance to contemporary romance seamlessly and without apparent effort. Writing with a completely different style, [her] creative voice still shines through. I thoroughly enjoyed this emotional, riveting tale." —*Romance Reviews Today*

continued . . .

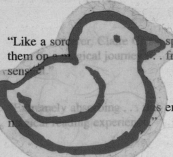
The Last Highlander

Double
Trouble

CLAIRE CROSS

JOVE BOOKS, NEW YORK

DOUBLE TROUBLE

A Jove Book / published by arrangement with
the author

PRINTING HISTORY
Jove edition / November 2001

Visit our website at
www.penguinputnam.com

ISBN: 0-515-13178-4

A JOVE BOOK®
Jove Books are published by The Berkley Publishing Group,
a division of Penguin Putnam Inc.,
375 Hudson Street, New York, New York 10014.
JOVE and the "J" design
are trademarks belonging to Penguin Putnam Inc.

PRINTED IN THE UNITED STATES OF AMERICA

10 9 8 7 6 5 4 3 2 1

Subject: what to do dating blues

   Yo Aunt Mary -

   Ancient uncle kicked, Mom says all 2 go 2
   funeral FRIDAY NIGHT! =8-o
   lame.com - I could be meeting Mr. Right
   instead. Wah! :-(
   Yr advice?

   Hot_Chic

Subject: re: what to do dating blues

   Dear Hot_Chic
   Go . . . in something sleek and black.

   The heir might need solace—and yr Fri night
   might not be wasted after all.

   ;-)

   Aunt Mary
***
Uncertain? Confused? Ask Aunt Mary!
Your one-stop shop for netiquette and advice:
http://www.ask-aunt-mary.com

I propped my chin on my hand and stared at the message.
Maybe I was getting bored with this gig. Aunt Mary certainly had lost a bit of her sparkle—she was sounding more

like a cranky old bitch than an irreverent livewire these days.

But then, it was only nine at night and I was just waking up.

I saved the response without posting it to the board—just in case lightning struck in the wee hours of the morning—yawned, and stretched. The truth of it was that I shouldn't even have been out of bed yet, but I hadn't slept well. Something had kept me awake today. Guilty conscience, maybe. Ha. Hole-digging types in the street below, more likely.

I was still warm and fuzzy, halfway between sleep and wake. But there were lots of messages for that sage of netiquette, Aunt Mary. Time for some rocket java to fuel the keyboard merengue.

The phone rang when I was elbowing some space on the cluttered counter for the coffee-bean grinder. You've got to grind your own if you want a decent cup of brew.

"Auntie Maralys? Is that you?"

It wasn't such a weird time for my nephew to be calling, but something about his tone made me forget my coffee. I would have bet my last buck that this ten-year-old kid was never uncertain of anything, but he sounded . . . lost.

He had my attention but quick. In fact, he was giving me hives. I don't do kids. Don't handle dependence and vulnerability real well. The only reason I can deal with my nephews is that they're getting older—I think of them as very small adults and it's okay.

Mostly.

But now Jimmy was doing a "make my boo-boo better" voice and I felt my bile rising.

"Sure, Jimmy, it's me. How's it going?" Maybe I sounded a little more cheerful than necessary, but it seemed to reassure him.

It certainly reassured me.

"Houston, we have a problem," he said, slipping into a routine we often used. In this scenario, I was NASA control and he was captain of the intrepid space voyager *Calypso*. To say that Jimmy was a space nut would be the understatement of the century.

It worked out all right—kind of a meeting of the minds in technogook land.

"Roger, *Calypso*. I copy." A problem to which I was the solution. I was already making a good guess as to what the deal might be. My sister, in case I haven't mentioned it, is a selfish harebrained idiot. "What are your coordinates, *Calypso*?"

"Um, at the pool."

"You have swimming lessons tonight?"

"Roger, Houston. Exercise maneuvers have been completed."

A long pause followed. Time for those latent psychic abilities to kick in. Sadly, they missed their cue. "Can you describe the nature of your problem, *Calypso*?"

"Um. Auntie Maralys . . ."

His voice quivered and I shivered right to my toes. Just having clutchy, needy people on my phone—well, one person really, but it was enough—made me want to break and run.

I closed my eyes and forced myself to guess what was up. Eenie meanie jelly beanie. "Have you made contact with your shuttle, *Calypso*?" I was thinking that my twin and I were going to have to have a serious talk if she couldn't even remember to pick up her kids from swimming.

"Uh, no, Houston. There is no sign of the shuttle. Rendezvous may have been aborted."

Now I was mad. This was typical Marcia, imposing on everyone else and scaring the crap out of her kids, just so she could . . . what? Get her nails done? Probably something stupid, feminine, and frivolous like that.

"And your backup shuttle, *Calypso*?" I tried to keep the edge out of my voice because we all knew that James worked more hours than any human alive. "Do you have its coordinates?"

Jimmy faltered. "California, I think."

I bit back a scream, then took a deep breath. It wasn't Jimmy's fault that morons were allowed to breed. "Okay, *Ca-

lypso, I copy. Let's review the checklist—are you currently at the scheduled rendezvous point?"

"Roger, Houston."

"How long have you been at the rendezvous point, *Calypso*?"

"Since eight-thirty, after class ended."

"At my mark, your shuttle is precisely thirty-two minutes late. Please confirm, *Calypso*. Mark."

"That is correct, Houston. Thirty-two minutes and counting."

"Please confirm, *Calypso*, whether you are on a solo mission. Your mission orders are inaccessible to me at this juncture."

Marcia's boys are just two years apart, spitting images of their father, and practically joined at the hip. I always thought it was weird for them to be so close—Marcia and I nearly murdered each other when we were kids, after all—but maybe my sister found it more convenient to keep them at the same place at the same time.

Maybe they secretly did hate each other's guts in healthy sibling fashion. The prospect always cheered me.

"No, Houston. Lieutenant John is also aboard this mission. His class is done, too." Jimmy's voice dropped with uncertainty, and he sounded like a lost little boy again. "Auntie Maralys, everyone has left."

I damned my sister silently to hell and back, then wished that there really was something to the psychic bond between twins. At least then I could make a guess as to what Marcia was up to.

On the other hand, I really didn't want to know more than I already did about how she thought. My very own twisted sister. I must have beat her to the line when they were handing out common sense.

Which was why she was married and had two kids, while I wasn't and didn't . . . and never would. These periodic crises were enough to keep my biological clock from ringing its alarm.

Along with a lot of other things, now neatly buried in my paleolithic past, and destined never to be exhumed.

"Roger." I really had only one good choice, even though it was incredibly inconvenient. Almost as if Marcia planned it that way.

Hmm.

"Hold your position. Repeat: Hold your position, *Calypso*. We have a technical complication on this end—there is no vehicle available for immediate rendezvous. Do you copy, *Calypso*?"

"We copy, Houston." There was Johnny. I guessed that the boys were sharing the receiver.

"Mission control suggests you enter low orbit, *Calypso*, from which you can watch your designated position. In the event that your shuttle does appear, please hold your position until the second vehicle arrives to rendezvous. Repeat your orders, *Calypso*."

Jimmy did, then Johnny whispered, "The janitor's office is right over there, Auntie Maralys."

"Roger, *Calypso*. We will rendezvous ASAP at your selected alternate coordinates."

"Roger, Houston."

"Over and out." I flung on my battered leather jacket, ran for the door, and vowed to break every bone in my sister's body when I found her. Maybe I'd snap those perfect nails one at a time. I flagged down a cab, and the cabbie thought he'd died and gone to heaven when he discovered I was going all the way out to Lexington.

Might as well be Canada. Or California. Haha. I could pick James up myself and give him a telling-to about the responsibilities of parenthood. That would be fun.

As if I knew anything about it.

The fun would have to wait, though. The boys were my first order of business. I rummaged surreptitiously through my pockets and hoped like hell that I had enough cash on me for the fare.

One thing was for sure—Marcia was a dead woman.

Marcia wasn't dead, just AWOL.

I took the kids back to Casa Coxwell, and they gabbled the whole way, their confidence that the world was their oyster evidently bolstered by this return to routine. It wasn't as if I could have them in my place. Perish the thought.

Oh, look, another hive.

Actually, my theory was that some forgetful someone would be at the house, but every light was out in the place when we arrived. Some kind of crummy security system the lofty Coxwells had installed. Between us, we had two keys, Jimmy knew the security code, and I was only short a nickle on the fare. The cabbie decided to be generous.

In case you aren't sure, I don't do kids really well. I'm not particularly domesticated myself and at least have the good sense to keep my bad habits to myself. I let the boys manage their own nocturnal routine—the world was hardly going to end if they didn't brush their teeth this once, and they were already too excited to listen to sense. They'd probably be awake half the night, but that wasn't my problem.

At least, I hoped it wouldn't be. Ewwww, queasy gut. A night alone with the kiddos. I immediately looked for clues in the case of the disappearing sister.

There was a big clue on the fridge. An envelope, addressed to my brother-in-law in my sister's neat girly-girl script.

I eyed it for five entire seconds before I decided that under the circumstances a loss of privacy was the least of James's troubles. After this adventure, he owed me. Not that I expected him to agree with me about that, or anything else.

But he would never know I'd read the letter anyway.

Unless I got caught. I popped the flap, kept an ear tuned for the reappearance of the boys, and read.

Dear James—

I've had enough of you and your problems. Pick up the boys at the pool tonight after swimming—I won't be there and I won't be back.

                                        Marcia

Breathtaking originality. Marcia made Auntie Mary look like a literary genius. And she still signed her name with a little heart for the dot over the *i*. I shook my head, marveling that a thirty-eight-year-old woman could cling so desperately to sweet sixteen.

Keys turned in the front-door lock, and I replaced the letter in the nick of time, managing to lounge in the kitchen doorway just as James stepped into the foyer.

He stopped and stared. I smiled, the proverbial cat who swallowed the canary, and enjoyed the rare sense of having surprised him.

Now, my brother-in-law is a good-looking guy, always has been. He's tall and lean and chestnut-haired, although now there's a bit of silver at his temples, and I've caught him with reading glasses once or twice. He can appear to be concerned and sympathetic—or he can show the feral watchfulness of a predator with one eye on lunch, especially in court. He's always given me the impression of a calculating machine, zinging through the combinations and permutations and probabilities before he responds to anything.

As much as I can relate to the math-favorable part of that, I find him a bit unnerving.

(Tell him that and I'll have to hunt you down and hurt you.)

James has that ease that only men raised with money have: For example, he looks completely relaxed in his custom-made Italian suits. A man of the world or something like that. He wears his clothes with an indifference to their cost, pushing up the sleeves on the cashmere sweaters my sister buys as though they're sweatshirts from the Gap. He plays soccer with the boys without a thought for his imported leather loafers.

This drives my sister bananas, she who worships designer labels and wants all garments as perfect as the day they were acquired—even if it means only wearing them for twenty-minute intervals. I don't know how she survived two sons and a husband with a perspective like that.

Come to think of it, maybe that was why she was gone.

Or maybe that's why she started looking like hell while her "men" were turned out to perfection.

Huh. Maybe *that's* why she left.

James's manners are impeccable, a legacy from private schools, and his thoughts are characteristically tough to read. He's one of those types who always says the right thing.

That drives *me* bananas.

I don't think he has any emotions. He's always struck me as the kind of man who eliminates excess baggage—like feelings. Yearnings. Hopes and dreams. Anything that doesn't contribute to his own ongoing meteoric rise to success.

I never could figure out why he married my sister. Unless a wife and kids were necessary accessories for the lawyer-destined-for-Great-Things—and she was as good a choice as any. They never seemed to have much in common, but maybe it was something basic between them. Like lust. Marcia used to be quite a looker, and I say that with the undue modesty of an identical twin.

Tonight, James looked surprisingly haggard and annoyed for a man made of granite, and as I mentioned, that expression didn't improve when he saw me.

"What the hell are you doing here?"

Oooh, a vulgarity. Of course, the strumpet sister had invaded the last bastion of propriety in the Free World. That, at least, conformed to our usual script. His job was to make sure I didn't feel welcome enough to hang around too long and taint the precious boys. I knew my lines by heart.

Too bad I hadn't worn something really skimpy, just to tick him off. I slouched harder, knowing that perfect posture was a household holy grail. "You should be more gracious to the one doing your dirty work."

The man glowered at me. "What are you talking about?"

"Your kids called me from the pool when no one picked them up."

James flicked a glance up the stairs, some parental part of him clearly reassured by the ruckus coming from the bathroom. "Where's Marcia?"

"Where were *you*? Takes two for the fun part. Why should one be left with all the work after that?"

See? There is some residual instinct to defend your other half when you're a twin. Probably more of it was due to his assumption that someone else—someone *female*—would pick up the details of his life.

As if his kids weren't his problem. Grrr.

But the man of stone surprised me. James shook his head and ran a hand through his hair, leaving it uncharacteristically rumpled.

His next words were just as uncharacteristically emotional. "God, you two are exactly the same. Who would have guessed. Now I'm to blame for airline traffic stacking up over Logan."

James didn't wait for an answer. He just chucked his coat in the general direction of a chair and dropped briefcase and suitbag on either side of himself. The overcoat slid to the floor and he didn't pick it up.

Marcia would freak.

Well, if she had been here, she would have freaked, but she wasn't so I guessed she wouldn't.

James didn't look like he cared. It was unlike him not to put me right in my place—i.e., elsewhere—but he seemed to be out of steam. "But what the hell—blame me for the cloud cover and the delays out of LaGuardia, too." He flung out his hands. "Everything else is my fault around here."

He shoved past me, loosening his tie as he headed into the kitchen. He still wore the same cologne and I still liked it, though I'd die before I admitted such a weakness.

I thought he looked as down as a guy could look, until he scanned the empty counters in the pristine kitchen and his face fell a little further. "I don't suppose there's anything to eat?"

I shrugged. "I dunno. I just got here. Maybe the caterers are late."

He fired one of those quick incisive glances my way, the ones I always forget are in his arsenal. I jumped a bit, just like I usually do, and he shook his head. The steam seemed to go out of him then, as though that one glance had emptied his stores.

James really must be running low. "Sorry you had to pick up the slack, Maralys." The edge was gone from his voice. "It's a long ride out from the city."

Sympathy? From *James*?

I blinked and stared at him, wondering whether this was some kind of joke.

He sighed and shoved his hands into his pockets before meeting my gaze steadily. "I know the family shtick isn't your thing. Thanks for stepping in."

It seemed harmless to soften a little bit toward him. I'm not the kind of person to kick someone when they're down, after all. Well, not often. I've been there, seen the view, and know it's a bitch. "Sorry you had a bad travel day."

We eyed each other warily, then he reached for his wallet. "What was the fare?"

For a moment I considered the merits of being proud and shrugging off his offer. James must have guessed the reason for my hesitation, because he almost smiled when he offered those twenties to me.

"Take the money, Maralys. You wouldn't be here if it wasn't for my kids, and I know you work at night. I can't give you back the time, so at least let me cover the fare."

It was not the kind of understanding I expected from the courtroom shark. His tone, too, was suspiciously compassionate. I wondered which particular aliens had seized my real brother-in-law and left an overwrought decoy in his place.

"You feeling all right?" I demanded as I took the cash and squirreled it into my pocket.

"No, but since when does that matter?" James didn't seem to expect an answer, which was good because I didn't have one to that. He turned away, then straightened suddenly.

Obviously, he had spotted the note. This would have been a tactful moment to disappear, but then, disappearing would have proven that I knew what the note said.

I strove to look innocent. Not that it mattered—no one was looking at me. James pursed his lips and stared at the envelope, without making any move to cross the room, much less to read it. He didn't seem to need to open it to know what it said.

Okay, so things had been really bad around here.

He didn't even look at me when he finally walked to the fridge. He opened the envelope with resignation, clearly not surprised by its contents, then chucked it on the counter.

Like scrap. "You read it?"

"Me? What kind of a person do you think I am?"

James laughed then, though it wasn't a merry ho ho ho. "I *know* what kind of person you are, Maralys. Of course you read it." He winked at me so unexpectedly that I jumped. "I would have read it, too. Do the boys know?"

After that it seemed pointless to lie. "I sent them straight upstairs before I saw it. They're doing the wash-and-jammies thing."

James nodded once, crisply, a man who had made his decision and was seizing control of his universe once more. "Right. Thanks for stepping in. I appreciate your trouble. Why don't you call another cab and get back to the city?" He reached into his wallet and tossed me another couple of twenties, then left the room.

Maybe it was because I was used to the kind of men who expect you to fix everything for them that this dismissal annoyed me so much. Maybe it was because I liked what I saw and my sister didn't, yet he was waiting for *her*. Doesn't matter. I said it anyway.

"Be still, my foolish heart," I muttered as I folded the money. "All this appreciation is going to go straight to my head."

I didn't think James would hear me, but I was wrong.

He whirled in the hall and I took a step back. Raptor on the attack. His eyes were flashing and his jaw was set. "What the hell do you expect, Maralys? A monogrammed thank-you note hand-delivered to your door?"

He strode back to the kitchen before I could say anything—which is a feat, in case you aren't sure—as ticked as I've ever seen him. The man was definitely on a roll, or had come to the boil. He was seriously pissed off and looked, if you must know, a lot more virile than when he was in command of all the variables.

Oh, and I got another whiff of that cologne. Something in me that had been asleep for a while woke up but quick.

Then it roared.

James, however, didn't notice that.

"In case you missed it," he said with crisp enunciation, "my wife—and your sister—just walked out of here, destined for points unknown. She's left me, my kids don't know and won't understand, and, oh, yes, I still need to go to work in the morning and try to save some twice-convicted crack dealer from a third conviction. Don't expect me to fall on my knees in gratitude here, Maralys. I don't have the time or the inclination."

I faced him down. "You chose your profession, sport. Don't look to me for sympathy."

His eyes narrowed. "Do not go there, Little Miss Bleeding Heart. You can't begin to know—"

"Oh, cry me a river, James. Why don't you hire someone to fix your troubles? Isn't that the usual solution around here? Someone to clean, someone to cook, someone to garden—book a hooker and you won't miss Marcia at all!"

His features set. "Not funny, Maralys."

"But true, all the same. You're not defending a crack dealer, and I know it as well as you do. What would you be—the number-three criminal lawyer in the city? You've got to be making what, seven figures? Eight in a good year? You've got all sorts of fancy clients paying big bucks for your silver tongue and oh, boohoohoo, you're not having everything go your way today." I clutched my chest. "It wounds me, it really does."

"You don't know what you're talking about. . . ."

"Oh, but I *do*. My dipshit sister has left you, a bonus no matter how you slice that pie. You've got two, great, healthy kids upstairs, somewhat against the genetic odds, I might add. This house is big enough to house a family of twenty, and wait, I forget, are there three or four German luxury sedans in the garage?" I patted his arm even though I knew damn well that he was seething. Talk about tickling the dragon's belly. "Poor baby. I don't know how you drag yourself out of bed in the morning."

His lips thinned. "You made your choices, too, Maralys."

"But you'll notice that I'm not the one looking for a pity party."

"Fair enough." James leaned in the doorframe, so suddenly relaxed that I didn't trust him. Not at all. I took a step back. "Sorry to break your record, Maralys, but this time you've got it all wrong. Your sister did the only sensible thing I've ever seen her do—she bailed out of a sinking ship."

I made no comments about rats. You should be proud of me.

I did laugh, though. "Sinking? This? Don't tell me you haven't been prudent with your assets, James. What kind of a moronic investment banker do you have?"

James shook his head. "No banker, no bad investments." He shoved his hands into his trouser pockets and surveyed me, daring me to figure it out. I was trying, but no luck.

What the hell was going on here?

He spoke quietly, but his eyes were still too dark. "Just bad blood."

"Bad blood? Where? Not my sister—our genetic strings are perfect, if I do say so myself."

"Nope, not Marcia."

"You?" I snorted. He was pulling my chain, there was no doubt about it. "You're the straightest shooter I've ever met in my life, every mama's dream for her little girl." I tweaked his lapel, knowing he had more bucks invested on his back than I had in my closet. Maybe more than I'd ever owned. "Check out the suits and the Italian shoes. Lalala. Bad blood, my ass."

"Wrong, Maralys." That exhaustion claimed his features again, and I felt more sorry for him than I should have. "You've got it all wrong."

"Bull. You've got everything going for you. You're not going to make me feel sorry for rich and successful James Coxwell." I picked up the receiver to call a cab.

James put his thumb on the rest, breaking the connection. I could feel him right behind me, the heat from his skin pressing against my own. It was tough to take a breath. He was close, too close, and smelled too goddamned good.

And truth be told, I was enjoying myself. It's not often I meet someone who gives as good as they get. Nothing like a worthy sparring partner. I was all tingly for more than one reason.

Lust, my cookie, is not just about physical stimulation. Engage the mind and oh, boy, things get mucho hot. They were toasty right about now. I could have wrapped my tongue around this boy's tonsils and enjoyed it thoroughly—from the heat wave of tension emanating from him, I guessed that I might not be alone in that urge.

Interesting.

"Well, how about this?" James's face was right beside mine, his eyes glittering. "My father is ousting me from the partnership in his own subtle but effective way. I'm losing it all and your sister knew it. That's why she left."

It wasn't just his proximity that shut me up. This was a choice bit of news.

I stared at him, incredulous, noticing all the hues in his eyes. He has hazel eyes, James does, and they change from gold to green to gray. Right now I could see all the slivers of color, the star of dark gold around his pupils, as well as the thickness of his lashes.

He was looking at me, hard, challenging me to challenge him, and it just about stopped my heart. My brain, mercifully, kicked into gear and ran.

Everyone knew that James was the pride and joy of Judge Robert Coxwell, as well as his hand-chosen successor. James was partner in his father's legal practice and had benefited from his father's connections. He'd also worked damn hard to get to where he was—I knew that because my sister had bitched about his long hours for years. And he'd played to his daddy's rules for as long as I could remember.

Despite myself, I wanted to take his side on this one. "No."

"Yes, Maralys." James bit out the words, his bitterness

clear. "Oh, yes. I really am defending two-bit hoods these days." He shook his head. "And oh, I have the pathetic billings to show for it." He walked back across the kitchen, peeled off his jacket, and slung it over a chair.

I went after him. "But that's nuts. You are good at what you do—whatever value to society it is to get big-time crooks free."

James chuckled and leaned against the counter, looking more relaxed for having spit out the truth. "Thank you. I think."

"So, what gives?"

"Luck of the draw," was what he said, then looked away, but I knew even then that there was more to it than that.

"Bullshit."

James looked me in the eye then, considering. "My father's brought my brother Matt into the practice."

"But I thought Matt did real-estate law."

"He did. He's changing specialties." One brow lifted as if daring me to believe what he was going to say even though he spoke with deceptive mildness. "Matt's going to be the new courtroom star."

"By winning those big nasty cases?" I rolled my eyes. I'd met his bookish brother and couldn't see it happening. "I don't think so. Matt could never be a shark like you."

James's lips quirked. "Two almost-compliments in one evening. You're losing your touch, Maralys."

I smiled at him, I couldn't help it. He has a nice dimple.

Not that it mattered to me. "Hey, well, you know how I like to back an underdog. Looks like you've joined the ranks."

He sobered and sighed, frowning again at the kitchen as if he could conjure food by will alone. "Don't I know it."

James needed a good hard kick, and I was just the one to give it to him. I leaned on the counter beside him and sighed. "You poor bastard. Is this what I have to look forward to at the ripe old age of forty-two? Hey, you might as well chuck it in. Drive that big ol' sedan right into the Atlantic and call it quits. Leave me the Cuisinart, would you?"

He looked down at me and smiled then, a teasing smile

that didn't last nearly long enough. "You really are a little pit-bull, aren't you?"

"Live and learn. When life gives you lemons and all that." I nudged him, enjoying this unexpected moment of conviviality. "I've got to tell you that I make a mean jug of lemonade. Experience is the key."

James grinned and that dimple took my breath right clean away. "I bet you do," he murmured, and there was something other than animosity in the air.

"Whatever doesn't kill you makes you stronger," I chattered. "That's my theme song."

"No wonder you're so tough." There was admiration in his voice, unexpected admiration, and I felt myself blush.

Blush! It was a bit too cozy for me, thanks. I was having palpitations but knew damn well that the last person on the planet I needed nookie from was James Coxwell. Talk about losing my pointer. The man was wrong for me in just about forty-five thousand ways.

Each and every one of them independent of the fact that he was married to my sister.

I stepped away and put my hands on my hips, just to show that my shields were up. "But this thing with Matt and the partnership. It's not fair."

James watched me, his voice hard and his expression inscrutable. "But that's how it is."

I understood that there were a lot of things James wasn't going to tell me, because telling them to me wouldn't change their outcome. For whatever reason, James wasn't the star rainmaker at his partnership anymore. Maybe he lost one too many big cases, maybe it was something else.

Either way, he was no longer the apple of his father's eye. Well, I could relate to that, even if I might have preferred otherwise. Thing was, I had never been the apple of my father's eye but had the bonus of being able to contrast his response to my twin with his treatment of me.

James was right in saying that the exact reason for his fall from grace didn't matter.

I didn't know what to say. We stared at each other, a whole

lot of understanding telegraphing back and forth, at least when it didn't get choked out by the sizzle. I swallowed and he watched my throat move.

"Maralys . . ." He took a step toward me, then chaos erupted from the stairs in a most timely fashion.

The boys had realized that he was home. They descended upon the kitchen, and much family mayhem ensued. It got a bit cuddly for me, but James noticed that I was starting to twitch. He called me a cab and watched from the doorway until I was safely inside, in that old-fashioned protective male way that isn't all bad.

My gaze slipped over the trophy house as the cab pulled from the curb, and I thought that maybe I understood why my sister had left. The goodies were going away—and James Coxwell without his money hadn't been enough to persuade Marcia to stay. She'd always liked good things and good living, and a man who couldn't supply them, well, just didn't interest her.

It was that simple. We slipped through the affluent neighborhood, past the horse farms, past the long winding driveways with distant lights partly obscured by trees, and I wondered how many other tasteful entries hid similar stories.

I had a funny feeling that Marcia, not atypically, had it all wrong. Even though he wasn't my type, James Coxwell's bank account wasn't his only asset.

See? I'm a sucker for a dimple.

But what I didn't realize then was that the exact reason for the change in James's circumstances *did* matter, it mattered a lot.

Which was why, of course, he kept it to himself.

```
Subject: this must be love!

  Dear Aunt Mary—

  I'm in love! I've found my PURRfect
  soulmate in a chatroom!
  :-D

  Any advice on that 1st live meet? Or
  ::ulp:: on moving across the country?

  Smitten in St. Paul
-----
```

They do say that curiosity killed the cat.

This would have been the perfect opportunity for me to just shut up and get on with my life, such as it was. Certainly no one was asking for my help.

But then, they also say that satisfaction brought that cat back, right? That's one of the major scores of my life.

That night, back in what passed for my cozy, safe haven (i.e., a drafty warehouse in a wicked bad neighborhood), I couldn't let it go. Now, I'm not going to tell you exactly where in Boston this warehouse is, because I don't want to be responsible for keeping you up nights, fretting yourself senseless over l'il ol' me.

Trust me—I can take care of myself. I've been doing it for thirty-eight years.

Maybe we should take a moment to set the scene, now that you think I'm living in a former pickle factory with broken windows and gang members doing dastardly deeds in the dark streets hereabouts. It's actually a nineteenth-century candy factory, the windows aren't broken because they're made of glass bricks, and the graffiti from the gangs has a certain artistic flair. If nothing else, it decorates the outside of what is otherwise a breathtakingly functional structure. As far as I know, they limit their expressions to calligraphy.

That's all I want to know.

Okay, it may not be precisely legal in terms of the zoning for me to be living here, but that's immaterial—I live in my office. Why not? I work a ton of hours, live, eat, and breathe my sweet code.

Besides, with two-thousand square feet of brick walls, twenty-foot ceilings, and ancient hardwood factory floors, it's not as if there isn't room for me, too. I have a lot of stainless shelving on wheels—an assembly of that in the vicinity of the sink passes for my kitchen. I sleep on a futon, which makes for a "reception area" by day and offers no privacy whatsoever.

Maybe there's something paranoid deep in my psyche, some forgotten trauma which left an indelible scar, but I need to see all of my surroundings all the time. This place gives me that. I can see all the way to the walls in every direction from any position.

What's beyond the walls I can ignore. How's that for a trick?

There's only one entrance—a big steel sucker that rolls up like a garage door. You don't trot too fast over that threshold—the freight elevator shaft is on the other side and some industrious soul once saw fit to remove the safety grate.

There's a fire escape, too, but the door is bolted down hard and rusted. So, yes, I need to duck not only the zoning inspector but the fire marshal. It adds a certain spice to life.

The place is cheap, for how big it is. And the windows are amazing. Rows upon rows of glass bricks, stretching all the way to the ceiling. They have just a little ripple in the glass, not a pattern, so the world beyond looks like a reflection of itself. Or a Monet painting. The light is awesome—not that I'm often awake to see it.

It's a great space and one that took me half of forever to

find. I have half of the second floor of the building—the first floor is more showy, but I had security concerns. I can lock down the door and disallow access to my space from the elevator—there's another smaller elevator at the back of the building to service the other part of this floor.

Perfect security.

See, there's nothing domestic about my veritable wall of old monitors and televisions hot-wired to play computer screen. Or about the mounds of computer cadavers, their hard drives and CD-ROMs plucked like the choice morsels of roadkill and the rest left to gather dust. People give me old boxes, I buy my share, and I get some hot stuff in for beta testing. Beta testing doesn't pay that well, but it gives me a revenue baseline, and with everything powered up all the time, I log enough hours to find some bugs.

It also gives me some fearsome juice bills.

The tubes are particularly impressive, I think. On a slow day I hook them all up to one source, and with a flick of the wrist I can animate the wall that they're stacked against. Only a geek would appreciate how cool it can look to have umpteen versions of your code dancing in unison—especially in the dead of the night.

It's also a mind-boggling way to play games.

On this particular night it didn't do a thing for me. Even a pot of primo Jamaican dark roast did little to make me want to get to work. I swiveled in one of my borderline antique chairs—acquired for peanuts at the university property disposition department, like most of my decor—then slung my legs over its arm.

I was thinking about James. Not a healthy preoccupation and I knew it, but I couldn't stop. He'd looked so defeated, that must be it. And who knew the man had a killer grin? I was certain I'd never seen him smile like that. But worse, I was used to seeing him in total control, commander of the universe or something like that.

Just how bad were the finances of the Coxwell household? How broke was broke, in my sister's estimation? Even James seemed pretty stressed about the cash, but then, we were from different worlds, the Coxwells and the O'Reillys. He might be down to his last five million or so and feeling the pinch.

And Marcia had a pretty high burn rate—coming from nothing teaches you zip about the language of money. I'd come by what fluency I had the hard way, and she'd never been to that part of town.

I prowled around, like the proverbial feline on the hunt, unable to concentrate on any of the questions sent to dear opinionated Aunt Mary. I was trying, if you must know, to persuade myself to forget about it. My mother always said that my need to know other people's business would get me into trouble—not so far, but there's still time. And I had a feeling that once I started to dig into this, it would be tough to stop.

Curiosity won.

Wondering was getting me nowhere, and nothing done, after all. James wasn't the only one who needed billable hours to make the math work.

The cost-effective solution was to ferret out the truth, then get back to my diligent labor. Of course, it had nothing at all to do with James, or even with Marcia. I couldn't have cared less whether I ever saw her again or not.

I just like to know stuff. What makes people tick. What triggers them. What it takes to get something done. My sister had crossed a little threshold of no return. I wondered—quite naturally—just what it took to push her that far.

After all, if she ever came back, I might need to give her a nudge myself.

I got on the phone and you know how it is. You know someone who knows someone who knows someone and sooner or later, you've got the number of the secured line for some guy somewhere who can negotiate a black market one-time-use fee for a password to a big credit bureau.

Is this legal? Don't be ridiculous. But it's there, and hurts no one other than the mega-corporation that keeps the database.

This is incidentally the same mega-corporation which has tried to ruin my life on several occasions, through absolutely no fault of my own. It's not as if I have a vendetta against them, but defrauding them of a hundred bucks here and now wasn't even going to make a bleep on my moral radar screen.

See, I made a bad marital choice, but am hardly the only one who ever did that. Why should it cost me for the rest of my blessed life? Okay, the guy was a loser—I should have insisted in the divorce papers that he have an *L* tattooed on his forehead, as a warning to all my unsuspecting single sisters— but enough is enough. The last drop of blood I had to pay to be rid of him forever was coming up due in a few weeks, and I had the cash coming in, right on time.

Amnesty from the IRS would be mine shortly. Finally. Monkey off my back and all that. It's been my holy grail for what seems like most of my life, but has really only been about six years.

Only. Ha.

I tell you, I should plan a major celebration. It's got to be worth a bottle of the good stuff to get your life back from them. It's not as if anyone's going to reclaim my gray hairs.

Anyhoo, defrauding this corporate entity who blew the whistle and got this steamroller going in the first place is a zero guilt decision—in fact, it's a matter of principle.

I like bucking the system, after all, *and* backing the underdog. Conveniently, in this case, I happened to be the underdog, so it was a double-bonus plan.

Once I had the magic number, I knew I couldn't wait. In for a penny, in for a pound. I snagged my leather jacket and one of those prepaid phone cards, then headed out to a doughnut place with a reasonably private public phone.

Do I worry about heading into the evil city in the middle of the night all alone? You bet. But I don't let fear stop me. You can't when you're single. You'd end up living in a box with three deadbolts on the door, eating cat food, and waiting to die.

Stay home and the crooks win. They get the night, by default and concession, the night which should rightly belong to all of us.

That doesn't mean I'm stupid. Keep your head down, walk

purposefully, and stay where the lights are. Doesn't always work, but there you go. It's not as if the world hasn't always had its crop of bad types who prey on others.

And oh, yes, I have a set of brass knuckles that I always slip on under my gloves, a little insurance just in case. Surprise is one helluvan advantage.

You will, of course, have the good sense to not ask where I got them.

The doughnut shop has terrible coffee, but such is the price of no one minding your business. Double-double-dreadful in hand, I snagged the booth by the phone, poked the phone card in the slot, and dialed. Jeez, forgot my secret decoder ring and everything.

"Hey."

"I'm looking for Dennis."

"You got him."

I could just imagine this guy. He had a slight wheeze, which reminded me of every geek I'd ever known who lived on Doritos and never came out of his cave. Full beard because shaving takes time away from writing code.

Or worse—a soul patch. I shuddered. Next time I go to a computer conference, I'm taking a bucketful of razors and will volunteer to shave those miserable things off. Dennis—if that was his name—probably had skin the color of milk, wicked fast fingers, and was dangerously clever.

"I need a credit report. I heard this was the place to call."

He chuckled. "You live at Donut Paradise in Boston?"

I let scorn drip from my tone. He had caller ID, just as I had suspected. "Yeah, well, their chocolate crullers aren't all bad. And I don't have to go out to get them."

"What's your name?"

Fat chance I'd confess to that. You learn a lot about what can be tracked from a phone call in my business—let alone what can be divined from surfing around—and no one was getting me that easily. I love prepaid phone cards, keep a drawer full of them, all bought at different convenience stores and kept for at least six months before use.

I cut to the chase. "You selling or not?"

"Sure, but I want to know what you've got to exchange first." Before I could try to interpret that, he continued. "You know that microbrewery down by the harbor?"

"I know it. Westphalian Lagers."

"That's the one. How about a twelve of their wheat beer?"

"Are you nuts?" I was outraged. "This area code is for *Utah*! Do you know what it will cost me to ship a twelve pack of beer there? They use glass bottles! They're PINTS!"

"Overnight," he added mildly.

I fumed. "That's unbelievable. That's extortion!"

"That's the price."

"Beer. You want *beer*. What kind of wacko are you?"

Now, did I really want to know that? Probably not, but the damage was done.

"I like beer." I could almost hear him shrug. "They don't ship out of Massachusetts, and I need the bottle for my collection."

I swore and didn't care what he thought of that. I did a little math and swore again. The overnight charge could make legal ways and means look good. "Six," I countered, ever hopeful.

"Twelve. Take it or leave it."

"I could just call the company. Do this legit."

"Ah, the forms." I heard his chair squeal as he leaned back to expound on his theme. I rolled my eyes, which fortunately makes no sound. Wouldn't it be a drag to have the rattly eyeballs of cartoon characters? There'd be no privacy left in the world at all.

And there already isn't nearly enough.

"Have you seen the forms?" ol' Dennis asked. "They need to know who you are and why you want to know and what purpose you have for the information in question. You fill them out in triplicate and sign them in blood. Yeah, why don't you call them?"

"Twelve it is," I agreed, growly and disgruntled. "I hope you choke on them."

He laughed, then gave me a URL—which is a Web site address, in case you don't know—and a password, along with the warning that it would only work for a single unauthorized access to the database. Then the charming, if inevitable, warning. "I'd better get those brews on time. If you screw with me, Ms. Donut Paradise, I'll find out where you live."

"Oh, I'm scared," I whispered, then gave my best maniacal laugh and hung up the phone.

I'd send him his brews—another matter of principle—but he'd never find me. Once you understand how this stuff works, it's relatively easy to thwart.

Like the phone cards—no one gets my name and address on their caller ID when I do this. They get the address of the doughnut shop. Big deal. The phone is used here so much that it's pretty unlikely that anyone could hook me up with any specific call. I left the booth, and someone else slid in to use the phone, proof positive of that.

Because you see, once someone has your name and city of residence, they can get your address very easily. Phonebooks are great resources and readily available. You can get them at the library for all kinds of places and, even easier, snag them online.

And speaking of the Internet, every time you log on and surf, my little pumpkins, you leave a trail of breadcrumbs. Those little snippets of code prove where you went from where, and tell interested souls a great deal about your particular habits. Marketing types feast upon this information, the better to deluge normal people with spam and direct mail.

But I'm not normal people. I duck spam and dodge direct mail.

Worse, your e-mail address gets logged everywhere you go. Equipped with that e-mail address, any junior-league hacker can bust into the Internet service provider and get a name, home address, telephone number. If that's not bad enough, oh, goody, he or she can snag that credit card number to which your account is billed every month.

Are we having fun yet? See, you don't even have to shop online to be vulnerable. We won't even talk about the so-called cookies that various sites slide onto your drive when you aren't looking, little spies inserted into your own hierarchy where they flourish away, undetected. Just *being* online puts you in the sights of all kinds of bounty hunters.

On the other hand, so does walking down a city street at night. You choose your risks, we all do, and you live with them.

In my business, I deal with a lot of people who could be professional class hackers. They're good. They know how things work, they know how to find a weakness. There's a big screwball factor out there in the wide wacky world of the World Wide Web. You never know what's going to set some-one off.

Maybe it's the role-playing games to which we're all ad-dicted. Maybe it's spending too much time solo, maybe it's the lack of a sexually integrated culture, or maybe it's just too many people who were labeled too smart too soon, so never learned their social *p*'s and *q*'s. Doesn't matter. As more-or-less a female lone wolf in a den of horny men, I cover my own butt, thanks just the same.

It's not that I'm doing anything out of line—you're proba-bly thinking I run drugs out of this place or something—but it's a point of pride that I learn from experience. I was stalked once and lived to tell about it. It's never going to happen again.

So I have one computer which is not hooked into my of-fice LAN. It's a little island of its own, isolated and breath-takingly stupid, a laughably antique box. It chokes on most sites these days, its meager memory just incapable of dealing with all the data. Suits my needs well. It has nothing on its hard drive except applications as pure as the driven snow. Any poke from a remote site gets nada. I programmed it to wipe the cache constantly, so they can't get that, either.

It has an e-mail account which is prepaid. I change the ac-count name and mailing address—always a P.O. box some-where that isn't really mine. Who cares? All the mail that will result is promo junk from some direct mailer who bought their mailing list—whenever the prepay runs out. I change the ISP at intervals, too, sometimes a big one, sometimes a little one. They never see me, and no one knows that all those pre-paid people are the same person.

So let ol' Dennis hack away. He's welcome to that so-called information.

Back in the cave I used the dinosaur PC, logged in with the magic password, and searched for the illustrious Coxwells.

I choked on my java when the report came up. The screen scrolled and scrolled, listing debt after debt after debt.

Oh, baby, this was major credit card meltdown. Someone had had some huge fun. Those cards had to be so hot that they imprinted their little numbers on everything within a two-inch radius. I imagined James with his Amex number burned right into his tight butt and took a hot swig of joe.

To distract myself, I tried to imagine even having that much credit—this made my historic financial woes look like nothing—then went back and looked again.

The initial cards—the usual platinum assortment, one from each company—were jointly held. My sister had a companion card, or whatever the company called it, and James clearly paid the bill. The credit report showed that he was the only one making a dime. He made a lot of dimes, but not nearly enough of them to support this, and if his billings were lower this year than last, well, any idiot could do the math.

There was a whole suite of new credit cards, only in my sister's name. Department store cards, the kind that the clerks will give you on the spot if you can produce any other major credit card. A wave of a platinum card obviously got my sis-ter a $500 to $1,000 shopping limit for the day, and she used it all. Yee-haw. They were all maxed out, probably chucked in the bottom of her purse once she was done with them.

Some stores had been fool enough to give her two.

It was interesting in a way, to see the hands of each of them. On each joint account one card was used for gas. Just gas. Sunoco, Exxon, Shell. Twenty bucks here and twenty bucks there. Maybe once a month, there was a charge from a restaurant. Not a fancy place and not for a lot. Fifty bucks. Client lunch, no doubt about it. Expense form probably submitted that afternoon in duplicate. James was a detail kind of a guy.

The other card was chock-a-block with charges. Shoe stores, department stores, chocolate shops, hairdressing salons, and spas. At least three lunches a week and not cheap ones, either. I looked at all those shopping charges and wondered whether my sister even knew what she had.

Then I wondered what she did with it all. She never looked that good anymore. Maybe she bought stuff for her friends. (And yes, I did think that hell, she could have bought something for me once in a while if she was so determined to spend.) Maybe some of these charges were for the boys. I'd have to check out her closets, if I ever went back out there.

Just to know, you know.

Okay, I felt a bit of gleeful anticipation that the little hate mail message now appearing beside my name in banks everywhere would be showing up on a credit report of the Coxwells real soon now.

Realizing that I was taking forever and that there had to be a clock ticking somewhere, I printed a summary of the sucker, then detail reports of a couple of the cards. What the hell, I wasn't paying for this access again—in fact, I ground my teeth right then as I imagined the courier bill for the beer—so I printed every detail report they offered. The dinosaur's print buffers must have been bulging, but the printer dutifully began to chaw out the copies.

Thank goodness there were no graphics.

Then I couldn't resist temptation. Sure, it could blow my cover to Dennis, but I rationalized that my tracks were covered well enough. I had to know. I searched on my own name and shouldn't have been surprised to see that I was still in credit purgatory.

It still pissed me off.

I damned Neil to hell—again—logged off with a flick of the wrist, and checked the pile of output from the printer. There were the cars—Marcia's SUV was leased. Who knew? The big sedan was almost paid off.

Here I thought that rich types paid cash for everything—

clearly James financed the hell out of everything. I suddenly understood a bit better the concept of making your money work for you. He had borrowed this money when they didn't need to borrow, when there was cash rolling from their fingertips, and now he had enough credit to weather out a fairly sizable storm.

Seemed as if I could learn a few turns of phrase in the language of money from James.

If this had been a short patch of trouble, they could have coasted through it with no one knowing the difference. I gave credit where it was due—haha—and noted that this financial strategy had kept the house of cards standing longer than it would have otherwise. Now, though, it was doomed to collapse in an ill wind of my sister's making.

The house had been refinanced two months before to such a point that if it hadn't increased in value—oh, those desirable neighborhoods!—then they wouldn't have had anything in it. And the money was gone gone gone. There were a couple of whopper payments to the cards, but the charges just kept on coming and the checking account was empty.

Then I saw that thirty days ago, James had liquidated a bunch of 401(k)'s. Ouch. Mr. Longterm Security must have hated that.

My sister had had some serious fun.

I felt a weird sense of having something in common with James. We could write a book together—*How Marriage Ruined My Credit Rating*. Too strange. I actually felt sorry for him, finding himself unexpectedly in the same inhospitable place I had visited. No wonder he looked so glum.

I had an even weirder urge to call him up, offer consolation and advice.

Right. There I went, confusing my career with my life. No one at that house wanted to hear from Aunt Mary. I could just imagine James's patrician tone as he told me to mind my own effing business.

It wasn't my business. And he could probably sort it out more easily than I could suggest, what with his connections and all.

But there was one wrinkle.

Two eruptions in the earth's crust, actually. I leaned back in my chair and worried about the boys. Not my department, you know, but I wondered whether James would blame our whole family for my sister's foul deeds. Not for me—I don't care. If I never saw any of them again, it would be too soon. I certainly didn't intend to get any more involved than I had been already.

But there was one problem with that. See, my dad adores his only grandchildren. They do the mutual dependency thing really well. Regular little Norman Rockwell scenario to see them together every second Sunday.

Surely James wouldn't take that away from my dad?

I worried that he would, if it would serve his advantage. That's what he did for a living, after all, he played the odds. He was a shark. He was cold. He manipulated people to get the results he wanted, and he was good at it.

And what other way did he have to coax my sister to come back, than denying her own father what he wanted most in all the world?

Truth be told, I felt a bit sick.

Subject: re: this must be love!

Dear Smitten—
Call me a skeptic. Maybe it's love, maybe
it's not. Face the fact that the Net is a
great place to live out fantasies of all
kinds.
Run a credit check on your newfound
soulmate before committing, meeting, or
moving. The truth (or part of it, at least)
is in the math.
The rest may be in a criminal record.
Good luck.

Aunt Mary
***

Uncertain? Confused? Ask Aunt Mary!
Your one-stop shop for netiquette and advice:
http://www.ask-aunt-mary.com

When I typed that cynical little reply, I had another brain-storm. James played games for a living. What if this credit meltdown was all an elaborate game of manipulation?

It was hard to believe—no, *impossible* to believe—that he wasn't making as much money as he had been. I mean, he is good at what he does. I couldn't imagine that any family turmoil at Coxwell & Coxwell could make either James or his father turn off the tap that kept the bucks rolling.

I mean, you don't get rich and stay rich by not understanding where money comes from. It had to be a joke to try to make James's brother Matt into a shark.

Which meant that maybe James wasn't making less. Maybe it was a lie, God knew why. Maybe it was a way to make sure Marcia couldn't get half of the bucks—by pretending there weren't any.

So where was the incoming moolah going?

I spun in my chair. Nowhere legal, or it would have shown on that credit statement.

Lawyers. The Caymans. Numbered bank accounts. Some of these things belong together. California, my ass—James had been dropping off cash, I bet, and had been doing it offshore. What business did a criminal defense lawyer called to the Massachusetts Bar have in California?

James was an opportunistic rat, and Marcia had run from him in a fit of sanity, losing everything in the process.

This was even more scary. I had commonality with my *sister* of all people. Before I could get too comfortable with that concept, the phone rang.

"I suppose you've forgotten again?" my father demanded, in that shrill tone he'd taken on lately.

"How could I forget when you remind me twice a day? You'll have to give me a *chance* to forget to find out whether I do."

He snorted. "As if I'd risk that. It's seven o'clock already. Where the hell are you?"

"Obviously, I'm at home, since I just answered the phone here." I noticed belatedly that it was getting lighter. Mingled shades of gray and blue made their way through the glass bricks. Where had the night gone? "Your appointment's at eleven, Dad."

"Oh, so we're going to rush in there at the last minute, like the last time."

He was in a mood and I was tempted to agree that I had forgotten, just to make him gleeful again. There was nothing my father loved better than recounting my failures and missed opportunities. It always cheered him up.

But I was a bit cranky myself. "It wasn't the last time," I corrected with remarkable forbearance. "It was 1996. I was getting divorced at the time, if you recall, from the guy who you thought walked on water. Remember him? Neil something or other. Good-looking bastard. Charming."

He chose to ignore this, typically. "If you weren't too stubborn to admit you were wrong and find another man, then you wouldn't be living in that hellhole, Mary Elizabeth, eating cat food for your dinner."

"I don't eat cat food, Dad." I paused, then gave him some bait. "Not anymore, at least."

He didn't take it. "If you married a decent man, you'd have a normal life, friends, and a family. Instead you're living in the dark alone, like you're afraid of the world outside."

"Uh-huh. And when was the last time you met with all your friends, Dad? Having formal dinner parties for twenty-four again, are we? And right after we sold the ten-piece silver flatware table settings, too. It's a damn shame."

"Don't give me your cheek, Mary Elizabeth," he huffed. He was more reclusive than I am and we both knew it. "Do you have the time to take me to the doctor's today or not?"

"Of course I have the time. I told you I would do it." I cleared my throat. "You did ask me to go with you, you know."

"You had best believe that I do know! It's not as if I'm forgetting things, and you had best remember that."

Oh, this was going to be fun. "It's seven in the morning, Dad. I'm still working." A lie, but who was to know.

"As if you knew the meaning of the word. At least your sister had the sense to marry well."

Oh, I bit my tongue hard hard hard. Want to see the scar? I think there's a permanent notch left as a little souvenir. All the same, there was no question of me telling him about Marcia.

Hey, let her do her own dirty work.

"So, what is this? A breakfast invitation? I like my eggs over easy, you know that."

He harumphed, but I knew he was pleased. "If you take too long and it's cold when you get here, I won't hear any complaints."

"Deal."

"Well, hurry it up, then." He hung up the phone with a clatter loud enough to make me wince. I brushed my teeth and washed my face and headed out.

I was going to need sustenance. This doctor's appointment was not going to be fun. They never were.

Subject: butterball city

Dear Aunt Mary—

Ever since I moved in with my honeybun, my own buns have been spreading 4ever and 4 days. What should I do?

Fat in Fresno

Subject: re: butterball city

Dear Fresno—
Body Fat Index, thine enemy is contentment. Misery, in marked comparison, is a tested and true means of melting away those unwanted pounds . . . and maybe a few wanted ones. Think of that, the next time you look at those fashionable waifs. Wouldn't you be miserable, living on half a grapefruit a day?
OTOH, a layer of subcutaneous fat is a good way to minimize wrinkles.
So, choose from the doors that lovely Carol Merrill is showing us:
Door #1: dump him, B miserable, and waste away to zip.
Door #2: join a gym and GO to it. Buy moisturizer.
Door #3: get over it and buy bigger jeans.

The choice, my little dumpling, is all
yours.

    Aunt Mary
***
Uncertain? Confused? Ask Aunt Mary!
Your one-stop shop for netiquette and advice:
http://www.ask-aunt-mary.com

It took my father about two seconds to start scowling when he opened the door and found me on the step. "What in the heck are you doing here?"

I pretended to swoon. "How could I resist such a greeting?"

He would have shut the door in my face, but I'm faster than he is now. I got my boot into the gap between the door and the frame. He glared at it, glared at me, then shuffled back into the house, leaving me there.

No, you didn't miss anything. This was the same man who had invited me for breakfast not three hours before. And no, he hadn't forgotten. He was just in a mood. He's become kind of a capricious, ornery leprechaun in his sunset years—well, since my mother died. He can be as funny as hell, but he's changeable and unpredictable.

I think it's his way of dealing with being alone. It's no secret that husbands usually go first, but my mom's been gone more than fifteen years.

I think it ticks him off, as if all those years of falling on his knees got him nothing. God pulled a fast one on Connor O'Reilly, and he doesn't appreciate the joke.

Used to such receptions and his many moods, I shut the door behind myself and followed my dad into the kitchen. He was always particularly snarly about going to the doctor.

I refused to pander to him. Rudeness got rudeness. I gave as good as I got, which usually ticked my father off enough to laugh.

Eventually. First came the tirades.

"Trouble is what you are, Mary Elizabeth, trouble is what you've always been." He sat at the table and poured himself a cup of strong tea before giving me another look. "Your sister, now, there's a girl who gave your mother and me no grief at all, none at all."

Ah, dear sainted Marcia. She who never took my father to the doctor, she who never called, she who seldom sullied her angelic reputation by actually showing her face at the ol' homestead. Be amazed, oh, gentle reader, for I gritted mine own teeth and said naught.

It just about killed me. Look, Ma, I'm Hercules. Maybe Atlas is more like it, holding up the world and all its woes. Haha.

My dad had tried to leave no hint that he was making breakfast, but the skillet was on the stove and I could smell bacon. I was not offered a cup, so I got my own, then poured my own tea.

I was late and I knew it, but I had had things to do.

"Some kind of crappy service you've got in this restaurant, Mr. O'Reilly." I took a healthy swig of very strong tea—four teabags per pot in this house, the expense be damned, it's not made of gold and a man's got to have some pleasures—and got a lightning bolt of caffeine.

Oh, I needed that. I had to send off that beer this morning, and the brewery shop hadn't opened until nine.

Besides, these family doings were going to screw up my routine if they kept up. I was getting a major rush, just from the demands. Call my delay a mental health break.

"Always complaining, too." My father waved his cup at me to punctuate his criticism. "That's another thing different between you and your sister."

"Maybe you should hire some staff." I pretended I hadn't heard him. "A waitress, you know, to greet people with a smile, pour tea, that sort of thing. It would give this joint some much-needed ambiance. If she was cute, she'd lift your spirits, too."

He glared at me, spoiling for a fight. He was more wizened every time I came here and seemed to get shorter by day, but age certainly hadn't mellowed my dad. Nope, he looked like a gnome ready to go to the mat.

It was probably what kept him going—and what kept my sister away. O she of the faint heart. I kind of looked forward to sparring with the old guy.

A habit, if you will.

"Look at you!" he said with scorn. "Nearly forty years old and you look as grubby as a penniless student! Has no one told you that you've grown up, Mary Elizabeth?"

"It's a lifestyle choice."

"So is washing your jeans."

I grinned, unrepentant. "Ah, but that's why I buy black ones. They don't need to be washed until I can write my name on them with my nail."

He snorted. "The smell would give you away in a crowd."

Don't be getting the wrong idea here. I'm clean. It's the choice of clothing that annoys my father. He'd prefer that I came à la Doris Day, with little gloves, spectator pumps, a perky hat, and one of those dresses with the cinched waist and ballerina skirt. Polka dots, maybe. The man got lost in the fifties. Can't blame him entirely—they had some awesome shoes.

"Here we were, your mother and I, doing our best to raise our girls right, and look what happened. You look like a bit of trash left behind by a biker gang."

"Now, don't be sweet-talking me."

Amazingly, he became even more belligerent. "You didn't come over here for a cup of tea, I know that."

"Can't a woman visit her doting father once in a while?"

"Ha! You've got a scheme, or my name's not . . ." He shook a finger at me in sudden outrage. "If you think you're going to take me to the doctor, as though I'm no more fit than an old woman, then . . ."

I feigned surprise. "You've got a doctor's appointment today?"

"As if you didn't know it." He sipped his tea, a man disappointed in the world.

"I know it because you told me."

"You would have found out anyway and insisted upon coming along. I know how you are."

"Jeez, this is some kind of invitation you offer."

"You would have had to escort me, just as you always do," he muttered unhappily. "As if you didn't think I'm too feeble and too old to be going just two blocks to the doctor, that's what you're thinking." He roared fit to rattle the dishes in the cupboards. "I'm not dead yet!"

"Of course not." I leaned forward. "Corpses are silent." I clicked my tongue. "Bloody hell, but you make a lot of ruckus. You're going to give me a headache, and that before I've had my breakfast."

He snorted, pleased, though he tried to hide it.

"Not only that, dead people are easy to push around. God knows you don't have that problem."

He actually smiled before shaking a finger at me. "I'll be late just because I've had to entertain you."

"Then let's go right now."

"Ha! You don't trust me to take care of myself. I knew it, I did."

"Hardly. But now that I'm here, I might as well go along to protect the doctor."

Nosehairs bristled at that. "What?"

"If you terrify him, he may need trauma counseling. It's my family obligation to ensure he gets it quickly." I wagged a finger at him. "And you always said I wasn't the responsible one. Try not to be too disappointed. Is there more tea in that pot?"

"It's no wonder I'm suspicious, then. Why the sudden concern for a doctor you don't even know?"

I sighed and cast my eyes heavenward. "I'm trying to reform my wicked ways before I go to meet my Maker."

"Your Maker lives the other way, Mary Elizabeth O'Reilly," he said with great delight. "And don't you try to tell me different."

I laughed, then looked pointedly around the kitchen. "I distinctly remember being bribed with a promise of breakfast.

Don't tell me you've gotten so old that you forgot how I like my eggs?"

He snorted again, then pushed to his feet. "Don't begin to think it. I forget nothing, *nothing,* you hear!" He tapped his temple. "Everything I ever saw, everything I ever heard, everything I ever thought, is as clear as crystal, and don't you be thinking otherwise."

"Well, that's a relief. I can't remember anything, and if I had to remember all your stuff as well as all of mine, we'd be in serious trouble."

"Cheek. Nothing but cheek," he muttered. He pulled a carton of eggs from the fridge and popped some bread into the toaster, moving with the swift economy I remembered. My father never wasted energy getting anything done—he might bitch through Tuesday about it, but usually the job itself took a lot less time than his complaints beforehand.

"Suppose it's my job to be feeding you, as a parent and all," he growled as he cracked two eggs into the skillet. "Have you eaten since the last time you were here?"

"Just caviar and champagne."

He scowled at me over his shoulder. "Don't be giving me that. You're too skinny, Mary Elizabeth, and that's the God's honest truth of it. You should be more like your sister, a woman with a few curves." He turned his back on me, and I knew what was coming. "A man likes a bit to hold on to. If you weren't so thin and you didn't look as though you'd had a fright, you might not be scraping by on your own."

"Wow, breakfast and counseling, too." I poured myself another cup of tea. "I thought advice to the lovelorn was my department."

"And that's another thing." He kept a careful eye on the eggs. I've never had eggs cooked more perfectly than my father's. He even manages to get the yolk almost exactly in the center of the white every time. "If you had a real job, you might meet a decent man."

"I have a real job, Dad."

That won me a boffo snort. He said nothing more, certain all that needed saying had been said. He slid the plate in front of me a moment later, and I refilled his tea, noting that there was only the one plate on the table. "What about you?"

"You took so bloody long that I already ate."

I dunked a piece of toast in the yolk and cast a glance at the clock. I had to say it. "If I had a real job, I wouldn't be able to have breakfast with you at ten on a Tuesday morning."

"And there would be a loss," he snapped. "There I'd be, an old man, knowing that his daughter has enough to eat, that she's happy and healthy and raising a family while she lives in relative comfort. I can have my breakfast alone, thank you nicely."

He turned his cup in the circular mark it made on the linoleum tabletop. He watched me eat for a minute, his lips pursed, his eyes still that robin's egg blue. "You're not going to tell the doctor that I can't live alone anymore, are you?"

"God, no!" I rolled my eyes. "Then you'd have to move in with me. I couldn't put up with you all the time. And if I ate breakfast like this every day, my arteries would choke up with cholesterol. I'd be a dead woman in no time flat, and I've got contracts to deliver." I pointed my toast at him. "If anything, I'm here to insist that they let you stay loose in the world."

He chuckled to himself then, well and contented to sip his tea and watch me eat.

"It's good, Dad," I said as I practically licked the plate clean. "Thanks."

We shared a smile and he got to his feet, hunched over like the old man he wanted so desperately not to be. He hunted down his other glasses and his cardigan, then his better shoes and his cane "just in case." I finished my tea and put the dishes in the sink, then gave them a rinse.

Thing is, he *is* getting older. He's not so quick as he used to be and not so observant. And I like having him around. Conceptually at least. He was not walking even two blocks in this city's mad traffic without me and that was that. He was right—I do come over and examine his calendar once in a while to make sure that he isn't holding out on me. He's stuck with my escort service, like it or lump it.

My sister, you know, could never have been so casual

about this. If she had ever bothered to accompany my dad, she would have hovered and fussed and made him completely paranoid about walking out the door. He was already worried enough about how much the world had changed without her assistance. I was sure that my own no-big-deal approach was better.

Even if I had some major doubts about his independence. He was getting older and more frail despite his tough talk and yes—don't miss this rare soft moment—I do worry about him.

What if he fell? My nightmare is of that commercial, with my dad in the starring role. "I've fallen and I can't get up!" Oh, boy. Hang on a second here, my gut just had a convulsion.

Because no one would even know that had happened, because he would never have one of those alarm beepers in his house. And he gets mad if I call or drop by "too often."

On the other hand (OTOH in netspeak), losing his independence would kill him even more quickly. Break his spirit. Since I didn't know what to do for the long term, I kept doing what I was doing in the short.

"Too bad it's not Marcia who came," he said so innocently that a casual observer wouldn't have guessed it was a jab aimed right for my heart. A practiced one at that.

I sauntered, indifferent as only a biker chick in a leather jacket can be. You'd think I'd be used to this crap by now. I flicked my silken tresses over my shoulder, insouciance squared. "Why's that?"

"Ah, she's the one with the lovely manners, always was. You were the one with the devil in your eye, right from the day you were born. I told your mother that you would be nothing but trouble, and she didn't believe me until you began to talk." He shook a finger at me. "Nothing but sauce from you. Like those two princesses, remember that book I used to read to you? One who had pearls fall from her mouth when she talked and one who spewed frogs."

"Frogs are cool."

"There's no hope for you, then, and never will there be."

He sighed, then shuffled out onto the porch. I took his keys, locking the door behind him.

"I didn't hear the deadbolt," he complained. "Do it again."

"I heard the deadbolt."

"Well, I didn't and you'll be doing it again and not giving me any trouble about it for once in your life."

I unlocked the door, opened it, shut it, and turned the key once more. The deadbolt shot home audibly, and I gave him a look. "Got to make sure no one steals that television."

He squared his shoulders. "It's a perfectly good television."

"It's the only thing in that house of any value, and that's only because it's old enough to be antique."

His chin set. "I'll not have some young hooligans in my home."

I looked at those single-pane basement windows and knew that it was only ten thousand coats of paint holding the frames together. Anyone armed with so much as a butter knife could break into that house in nothing flat.

But there was no point in arguing about it. If he believed in the power of a single deadbolt to defend his fortress against the wickedness of the world, well, so be it. I'd tried and failed at all other arguments. Everything was "perfectly good," including those windows. A person could only hope that any would-be thieves would case the place, see how little there was to take, and shop elsewhere.

We started down the sidewalk, and I surreptitiously matched my pace to his slower one. "Oh, yes, it was Marcia who always spoke so lovely and polite," he said, getting even with me for challenging him. "It's Marcia who knows the right thing to say and to do, Marcia with two handsome sons and a successful husband. It's Marcia I've no need to worry about."

"Marcia who has the morals of an alleycat," I muttered.

"What was that?"

"Nothing."

"You said something, I heard it."

"Then why are you asking me to repeat it? I thought your hearing was perfectly good?"

"Cheek!" he accused, then lunged forward. A good rant would propel him halfway to the doctor's, so I let him have at it. "It was always cheek from you, no matter how many tastes of the soap you had. Marcia, now, Marcia might have been born with a gilded tongue."

"Dear sainted Marcia," I growled, sorely tempted to blow my sister's cover.

Dad spun. "What was that?"

"Nothing."

"You said something and I demand to hear it."

"I said that Marcia was such a dear."

"You did not!" He scowled at me skeptically and I shrugged.

"You'll never know."

That ticked him off. He rapped his cane noisily, making sure he walked a step ahead of me, shouting loud enough that people in Hawaii would hear him. "You'll not be telling me that I need a hearing aid, no you won't. And you'll not be tricking me into getting one, no you won't."

He shook the cane at me when he paused at the intersection, proving he didn't really need it and nearly decapitating me in the process. "I won't have one!" he roared. "I don't need one!"

He marched across the street, oblivious to the traffic, and I nearly put my hands over my eyes. But he strode with such confidence that two cars squealed to a halt.

He was apparently unaware of them, though even I didn't believe that. I shrugged to the two cursing drivers and darted after my father.

Just as I suspected, there was a mischievous twinkle in his eye. My own demented leprechaun.

"Damn fool drivers. It's time enough they learned to keep a slow pace near a school."

"Self-sacrificing as always."

His twinkle disappeared. "How many times have I told you

that it's not polite to mock your elders? You shouldn't be trying to trick me by lowering your voice so."

"Who me?" I mouthed the words, making no sound at all,
and thought for a moment he would slug me.

Then he laughed, a real witch's cackle. "Wicked, wicked
girl! You'll not fool me, no, you won't."

I might have thought that was the end of it, because he
practically bounced up the steps to the doctor's office, but he
spun on the top step with unexpected agility. "When are you
going to get married again?"

"I'm never, *ever* making that mistake again. Don't hold
your breath."

He shook his head and smiled a sly smile. "Ah, then you
have found a man. You make sure you invite me to the wedding." He darted away with all the agility of Fred Astaire.

What?

I was hot on his heels through the glass doors, ignoring the
people who paused to stare. "What in the hell are you talking
about?"

He was as delighted as a child with a new toy. "You usually say that you're not the marrying kind."

I paused and realized it was true. "Well, so what? I've
changed my line. No big deal."

"Ha! I knew your mother was going to marry me when she
said she never, ever would." He fired me a sharp glance, enjoying my discomfort a little too much. He jabbed his finger
at me. "Mind you get married before I'm dead, you hear?"

I propped my hands on my hips, not caring that we were
entertaining the locals. "I thought you were so young and virile that you were going to live for another fifty years or so.
I've got time. *Lots* of time. Maybe even time to figure out
what you're talking about."

"Ha!"

He bounced into the elevator, and I nearly abandoned him
right then and there. Instead I followed, then slumped against
the back wall and watched the numbers light up, considering
that if my father could see what I was thinking, then I was in
trouble.

God damn that dimple.

"He's a she," my father reported as the doors slid open.

I had no idea what he meant. "What? Who?"

"The doctor. He's a she, so mind your manners for a change."

Dr. Wendy Moss greeted my father with a bemused smile. She was about fifty and looked sufficiently no-nonsense to fend for herself. To my relief, she was a general practitioner, not some kind of specialist whose involvement I had heard nothing about. My father was in reasonably good shape for his age, a vigorous seventy-nine.

"What happened to Dr. Havermann?"

"Retired," my father said with dismissive scorn. "He's *old*."

"Or maybe he'd rather play golf than deal with the likes of you. It has a certain appeal, and you know how I feel about golf."

"Women are nothing but trouble," my father announced to his new doc by way of greeting. He jerked a thumb in my direction. "She's always following me around."

"Please, Dr. Moss, don't suggest that he can't live alone," I begged, determined to get even. Eyes widened in the waiting room. "He'd have to bunk with me since he's so destitute, we'd have to eat cat food, and I just know that he would eat all the best kinds on me. One day I'd have to kill him to keep my sanity." I sighed. "I'll spend the rest of my life in jail, and for what? Let him get his own cat food."

His eyes were dancing now. "Nothing but lip, that's what I get from this one."

Dr. Moss bit back a smile and beckoned to her patient. "Lovely to meet you, Mr. O'Reilly. Would you like to come in?"

I sat down to peruse dog-eared magazines that had been pretty dull before they became office origami and weren't much better now. *The Economist.* Oh, joy.

Where do they find this stuff? I have a mental image of

doctors rabidly raiding Dumpsters and recycling trucks, trying to find the most deadly dull discards for their waiting rooms. "Ha," they must chortle to each other, "*this* will make them feel as though they've been waiting forever. This will make them understand what an incredibly important physician I am."

The only thing worse are the selections in dentist's offices. Maybe it's an insecurity thing. I mean, why would anyone become a dentist? Tough to think of it as a first choice. Imagine a lifetime of having your fingers in other people's mouths. Imagine having to pretend that bicuspids are interesting. It's got to be a fallback decision.

Like running an Internet advice column instead of writing cutting edge code. Hmm. Bet dentists make better money. Oh, yeah, there goes Aunt Mary with her untold millions of Internet advertising revenue. Hahaha. Cruising to the Caymans without a care in the world.

I don't think so.

My father wasn't gone that long, but when he came out, he was wearing one of those knowing expressions. You know, the smug kind that says "I won't tell" even more effectively than words.

Those looks freak me out—they make me think evil words like *cancer*. Oh, yes, that is an evil word.

I wondered what he wasn't telling me. "Well?"

"Well, nothing."

"Bullshit. Something's up. What did she say?"

He walked onward, looking straight ahead. "It's none of your business."

"I think it is."

"I think it's not."

"Too bad, I win." I stepped in front of him, and he came to a stop. He stepped left, then right, but I was there before him, blocking his path. Like I said, he's slower than I am now and being reminded of it makes him mad. He swore at me, muttering the curse between his teeth so that it wouldn't taint my virgin ears.

"Trouble, from start to finish. Uppity, too."

"Tell me."

"Or we go no farther?"

"Something like that." I looked left and right. "Sadly, no one is serving tea and I could use a cup. Let's have the truth, then head home to put the kettle on."

He heaved a sigh of exasperation. "If you must know, she wanted to touch my balls." He leaned closer to whisper a confidence, his eyes doing that merry mischief thing. "They all do, you know."

"They?"

"Women. Women doctors especially. Oh, they make some excuse, but I know what they really want. It wouldn't bother me if she just did it, but these modern women, they're all talk." To my shock and dismay, he began to fumble with his fly.

"Dad, what are you doing?"

"I know it bothers you to miss out on anything . . ."

"I am not going to touch your balls!"

I yelled without meaning to, my father's smirk telling me that I had stepped right into his trap. "What kind of a man do you think I am?" he crowed triumphantly.

I did not call him a demented leprechaun whose every choice is utterly unpredictable. He would have been insulted and that I can do without.

"Not as bold as you'd have everyone believe, are you, daughter mine? You, too, are all talk." My father smiled for the world at large—most of which was watching with open interest—then chuckled to himself.

Dr. Moss shook her head and retreated to her office, and my father bounced into the corridor.

"Mary Elizabeth, it must be love," he murmured as we rode the elevator back to the lobby. "I cannot remember the last time I saw you shocked twice in an hour. I can't wait to meet this man."

"You're wrong," I told him, and it had about as much effect as I expected.

In fact, he began to whistle.

"You're wrong, Dad. You are so wrong."

My father ignored me. And even if (if! IF!) I found myself in a relationship with a man with a dimple, my father would not be happy at all. No sirree. That would be an ugly little encounter, which was all the more reason to make sure it didn't happen.

There was that sick feeling again. In fact, I was ready to barf a Twinkie—despite the fact that I hadn't eaten one.

I tried to change the subject. "I take it this means that you had good news from the doctor?"

"She says I shall live to be a hundred."

"And what's the good news?"

"Cheek and more cheek," he charged, but there was no mistaking his relief.

And yes, okay, it relieved me, too, even if he wasn't keen to let me in on the details. Having him around is a habit. "So, what else have you got going this week? Any more appointments?"

"One." My father's chest puffed with pride.

"Hot date?"

"I'm going fishing with the boys on Sunday." He walked a little quicker in anticipation. "You see, one daughter did the right thing and gave me grandchildren to spoil. You might take a lesson there, Mary Elizabeth."

"Or I might not."

He chuckled. "Talk to your new man. Maybe he wants children."

"Oh, that's encouraging. The opinion of a nonexistent person outweighs mine, just because the fictional person is a man. Hello, Dad, welcome to the twenty-first century."

"Some things, Mary Elizabeth, never change."

There was nothing I could say to that.

But I was going to talk to James. In fact, I was going to hunt him down right now and make sure my dad's interests were defended.

My father adored his grandsons, and nothing, *nothing* was going to stand in the way of his right to see them. Not even my sister's abandoning them. I had to get to James's office and straighten this out between us *toute de suite*.

God bless Marcia for screwing up my day. Hey, maybe I'd be able to get some sleep this afternoon before working my night shift.

A woman can dream, can't she?

My father just about bounced up the steps to the house, but I declined a cup of tea and headed back downtown to the offices of Coxwell & Coxwell.

And no, it wasn't just a mercy mission executed unselfishly. It wasn't even a rationalization. Daylight is dangerous stuff. Handle with extreme care. Maybe James wouldn't look good at all. Maybe that dimple would be in remission. Maybe seeing him in his lawyerly digs doing lawyerly things would make me hate him on principle, just as I had for so long.

It was worth a shot.

Even if the very prospect of seeing him again made me break a light sweat o' the palms. I even said a small prayer—first time in a long time—that my dad wasn't right.

Subject: no good loving

Dear Aunt Mary—

My SO and I used to have a great sex life—
now nada. I'm worried that he's shopping
elsewhere.
What should I do?

Chaste and hating it

Subject: re: no good loving

Dear Chaste—

Variety is the spice of good sex. The
thrill of discovery is gone, so you need to
add another thrill instead.
There are lots to choose from. Do it in an
elevator. Swap fantasies and act them out.
Be playful. Be indulgent. Don't be daunted
by the occasional failure. And be sensible—
adding new partners, for example, should
include condoms and blood tests.
Sadly, you don't get a lifetime of great
sex for free. You have to work at sexual
fulfillment, even with your soulmate and
significant other.
A rotten job, but someone has to do it. ;-D
Enjoy!

Aunt Mary

***
Uncertain? Confused? Ask Aunt Mary!
Your one-stop shop for netiquette and advice:
http://www.ask-aunt-mary.com

The man did his best to help with my mission to find him un-attractive. James glanced up when I was shown into his office, his expression quickly turning frosty.

That was not a change for the better. In fact, he looked royally pissed off even before he saw me, and my appearance did zip to improve the view.

So far, so good.

James's brow was furrowed and he was wearing his reading glasses. He had been scowling at a document and nearly flattened me with his cutting glance.

"Well, this is an event." He didn't take off his glasses, which I assumed was a more upscale way of saying "Don't let the door hit you in the ass."

"Yeah, not my usual territory." I took the seat opposite his desk, mostly because he looked as if he'd rather I didn't.

James sighed with such forbearance that I couldn't miss it, then nodded minutely at his hovering secretary. She hesitated before she left, a subtle combination of clues to let me know that I—and my kind, whatever that was—was unwelcome here.

You'd think she'd have seen enough streetwise disreputables around this place.

I wondered what that prim-and-proper miss would have done if I had lunged across the mahogany acreage of James's desk. Attacked him. Or kissed him, depending on my mood.

There is something wicked in me, just as my father maintains, something that prods me to challenge people's expectations.

The problem was that this particular array of expectations prodded me to be gracious, to outgrace their obvious expectation of vulgarity. Dull, dull, dull. Suspicious people are zero fun.

"Your hair is even the same color as the last time I saw you," James continued, with no improvement in tone. "That's got to be a first."

"I only change it once a day." I smiled sunnily, and he watched me, wary. "You lucky beast, you've seen me twice in a twenty-four-hour period."

James did not look as if he felt lucky. He sat down. He templed his fingers so that his fingertips touched his lips and assessed me in silence. He was as well dressed as he had been the night before, and only looked slightly tired. A few lines around the eyes, but otherwise good enough to eat. A Ralph Lauren ad in 3-D. Zero dimple action, but it mattered less than I'd expected.

Must be the cologne. That stuff shouldn't be legal. I inhaled and enjoyed. Hugo Boss Number One, unless the ol' nose was losing it. Yum dee yum.

James studied me, his eyes slightly narrowed, as if he would compel all my dirty secrets to come spilling out with just that look.

As if.

"The question is, why?" He spoke softly, probably a deliberate ploy to encourage the ready exchange of confidences. I was tempted, for the barest moment, to confide something, anything.

Maybe it would make him look away.

Or make me feel less like fidgeting.

What? You're *surprised* that I have secrets? Come on! Doesn't everyone? And yes, I had a few that I didn't want Mr. James Coxwell to know.

The really primo ones.

So I smiled, as coolly as I could—which is pretty damn cool, in case you aren't sure—and held his gaze unswervingly. The thing was, my Caymans theory wasn't holding up well to my own scrutiny or the cruel light of day, though it had sounded perfectly plausible in the wee hours.

If James had been going, he would have gone. And if he had been the one behind the scheme, then why would Marcia have left? We both have enough Irish scrappiness in us to fight for what's ours.

If anything, she would have snagged his plane ticket and dragged him along to withdraw goodies from those bank accounts.

But what the hell.

"It's this Cayman thing," I said conversationally. Truth was, he looked like an icon of respectability in this mahogany-paneled and book-lined cave. A pillar of the community and all that jazz. But then, weren't they usually the ones with big nasty secrets?

James blinked, a telling sign that the theory stank.

I leaned forward and tapped a finger on the desk. In for a penny, in for a pound. Surprising him might yield an information bonus or two. "You're not going to get away with it. If you think I can't outsmart you on this, then you're dead wrong. . . ."

An indulgent smile crossed his lips. "Am I supposed to know what the hell you're talking about?"

"I've figured out your big plan."

"I've planned nothing lately." He grimaced. "I'm just slugging along, dealing with everyone else's expectations."

Fact was, the man looked too tired to have planned lunch, but like a dog with a bone, I wasn't ready to let this go. I liked this scenario. It appealed to my taste for melodrama and plot twists. I wasn't going to abandon it without a fight. Doesn't everyone want to live a Grisham movie? I'll be Julia Roberts and you be Denzel Washington. Or Tom Cruise. You choose.

"Poor baby," I tut-tutted. "I suppose I should feel sorry for you and cut you enough slack to make a run for it."

"A run for it?"

"A great escape to the Caymans, with all the cash and without my sister. Boys in tow. I'll bet you've got a cabana booked on the beach, and a fridge full of fruity drinks."

He pinched his brow and leaned back in his chair. "God, that sounds good." He closed his eyes, and I briefly saw just how stressed he was.

Before I could feel sorry for him, he abruptly opened his

eyes, and if I hadn't known him better, I might have thought there was a twinkle lurking there. It's official that the man has no sense of humor. "When am I going?"

"You're the one with the answers. I'm the one with the questions." I let my tone turn patronizing, because I guessed it would drive him nuts. "I understand that's not your usual way of operating, so let's keep the rules straight."

A whisper of a smile touched his lips. "Okay, shoot."

"Where'd the money go?"

The smile was banished immediately and he got that hawkish look. "What money?"

"*All* of the money. The cashed-in 401(k)'s. The windfall from refinancing the house. Your income for the past eight months. Where'd you stash it? I'm sure you stuck some on the cards to make it look good, but where's the rest?"

He sat forward, eyes snapping. "How the hell do you know about that?"

I shrugged. "Maybe my sister told me."

"Fat chance. She never knew." James knew instantly that he had acknowledged something, because he sat back in evident disgust with himself. He spun in his chair and clicked his tongue, choosing his next move with care as he studied me and tried to decide how much I could possibly know.

This *was* interesting.

"If you know about the money, then you know where it went."

I nodded, feigning confidence in my theory. Worst case, he'd correct me and I'd know the truth. "Numbered bank accounts. Cayman Islands. High-profile lawyers. Some of these things belong together." I snapped my fingers. "Hey, isn't it time for your annual sojourn to the Caribbean?"

To my astonishment, James laughed.

I stared. I've never seen him laugh, and this one came right from his gut. He howled. It was not at all encouraging that when he started to compose himself, he glanced at me and started again. He even wiped away a tear. I wondered whether it was my imagination that there was a tinge of desperation to what should have been a merry sound.

Then he turned on me, dead sober. "If only it was that easy."

"Everything's easy for a man in your shoes."

"Is that right?" He spoke with remarkable calm, a warning if ever there was one. To my surprise, he flicked the document he was reading across the desk to me.

I blinked.

"Read it."

I did. It was the paperwork for a divorce.

His and Marcia's divorce.

Ooooh, the plot thickens. "So what?" I flung it back on his desk, but he didn't move to touch it. "That's hardly news."

"Check the date. And the instigating party."

I hate when men do stuff like this. When they know something you don't and make you look like a jerk when you find out. I had a feeling that that was what was going down, but figured I might as well find out the worst.

I looked.

Marcia had made the petition. Good golly me. And her signature was dated eight months ago. Eight months. The ink was apparently still wet on James's signature, neatly dated this very day.

"That's more than you need to know," he said, clearly ready to brush me off like a fly. "Isn't it time you left?"

I don't brush off like a fly. "No, it isn't." I settled in. "What took her so long?"

"Thank you very much," James murmured and I blushed.

"That's not what I meant. She just left yesterday."

James sighed and spun in his chair. I waited. "We've been living under the same roof for years," he said finally, his voice tired. "Marcia wanted to end it. I thought it would be better for the boys if we held on for a few more years." He shrugged. Although he spoke dispassionately, he looked like a guy who had had the rug pulled out from under him and didn't like having fallen on his ass. I tried really hard to not feel sorry for him. "I guess Marcia didn't agree."

"Maybe there's someone else."

"Maybe." James didn't appear to care, but then, I was start-ing to see that he was as good at hiding his feelings as I am.

"And the money?"

"I think you know enough of my business." James's gaze turned steely as he retrieved the document, folded it precisely, and placed it into the breast pocket of his suit jacket.

His expression was grim and formidable, and he held my gaze as if I was the one challenging him. It was done, his mar-riage was over, and his wife was gone, and he looked as if it was no more troubling than having loaded up the dishwasher for the day.

And that made me mad. For better or for worse, my sister had spent eighteen years married to this guy, and when she wanted out, he wouldn't listen, because it wasn't convenient.

"No. No, I don't know enough. And I don't believe you, documentation to the contrary. It doesn't add up. Where were you yesterday? I may not know much about law, but being a member of the Massachusetts Bar can't get you anything in California. Where were you, really?"

James assessed me carefully, clearly deciding how much to tell me. He evidently concluded that he'd have to cough up a bit more to get rid of me. "Not officially, but connections can help."

"Is that supposed to answer my question?"

He sat back, eyes narrowed. "Did you ever meet my brother Zach?"

"No. Wait. Isn't he the one that Marcia didn't want alone with the boys?"

James nodded. "That would be Zach, the family black sheep."

"I thought he went off to Europe or something." It was coming back to me now. "To be a photographer."

"He did. But he ran out of money, fiscal responsibility never having been one of his strengths, and came home just long enough to touch us all for a contribution. Matt and Philippa and I only realized that we'd *all* been hit after Zach was gone."

"Isn't that what family is for?"

"To Zach, at least. He went west and found trouble in record time. But then, that seems to be his gift."

There was something important here, but I was going to have to do the math myself. "Why didn't Marcia want him near the boys?"

"Zach has a taste for pot," James said matter-of-factly. "He's not only a user, but he often deals in a small way. He's done it for years but has a gift for landing on his feet. He's unbelievably good at escaping the consequences of what he does. Marcia and I agreed about him not spending time alone with the boys."

"But California?"

"An unusually close call for Zach. He was busted in a speed trap with a goodly stash. But again, he's lucky. Turns out that the DA presiding over that jurisdiction was in my graduating class."

"You went to bat for him." I was impressed by this, by the way, as I didn't think James Coxwell did much of anything that wasn't to his personal advantage. It wasn't logical to do favors for your blood, it was sentimental. His next words proved my suspicions that he had mixed feelings.

"Against my better judgment." James sighed and frowned. "I don't think he'll change. In fact, one of these days, he's going to run out of lives. But he is my brother, for better or for worse."

"The same way that Marcia is your wife, for better or for worse."

"Not for long now." James was doubly grim and I couldn't resist the urge to needle his sanctimonious self. Enough of the "surrounded by sinners" shtick.

"Oh, did my sister hurt your feewings, and weeve a boo-boo on your heart-ums? Poor Jimmy wimmy. What about *her* feelings? Maybe you failed her by not being the guy of her dreams, hmm?"

I got a glare for that impertinence. "Marcia broke a covenant."

I raised my hands skyward. "And the divine vengeance of Coxwell and Coxwell, and the entire legal system of the state

husetts, must be unleashed upon this Jezebel who
fy the authority of her man. How dare this witch
disagree with the spoken word of her husband?" I leaned
back, crossed my legs, and wished I had a cigarette. It would
have looked so good in this moment. "Give me a break."

James regarded me with displeasure. "Trust you to make a
joke about something as important as this. Is there anything
that matters to you, Maralys?"

"Yes, but I can put my ego aside once in a while, unlike
some people we know." I bounced my booted foot. "You
don't like being tossed back, is that it? Hurts your pride to be
chucked out like old fish? Or is it just that you always get
your own way—except this time?"

"This has nothing to do with me!" James was on his feet,
chucking aside his glasses and jabbing a finger through the air
at me. He was mad and it was quite a sight. "I couldn't give a
shit whether we were married or not!"

Whoa! The man knows an obscenity.

I sat up, but he was on a roll and not paying much attention to me.

"Our marriage was a parody of a relationship from the very
beginning, but I was prepared to put up with it, for the sake of
the boys and only for the sake of the boys."

"Then, why—"

"Marcia broke the covenant she had with our *sons,* that's
what's important here. Yes, marriage is important, but we
both knew years ago that ours was a sham. We still had a deal,
Marcia and I, a deal we reconfirmed when she realized she
was carrying Jimmy. We both agreed that children deserve a
stable home. We both agreed that we were bringing them into
the world and had a responsibility to put our own interests
aside for their good."

He sat down, hard, and his voice dropped. "We agreed that
I would work and she would stay home, that she would raise
our children and I would ensure that she had nothing to worry
about financially. We made that deal for the boys, for their
sense of security, for their self-esteem, for their futures. I kept
my part of that deal . . ."

"That's not a whole heck of a lot to expect from a marriage," I interjected, but he ignored me, rolling full steam ahead.

". . . but she didn't. She made a selfish choice. She not only abandoned those kids, but she jeopardized everything we intended to give them with her wild spending. She left them, she's cast their future security into doubt, and you're damn right that I will hold that against her."

"She could hardly have known that you'd be late."

"It doesn't take a psychic to consider that flights coming into Logan might be delayed. She should have made a contingency plan."

James sat down, shoved his hands through his hair, and looked older than he was. His voice was thick with emotion. "My God, Maralys, what could have happened to them, alone there at night? A thousand things, none of them good. How could she have done it? I don't understand."

He was incredulous and genuinely upset. I could hardly say anything to defend her.

Because we agreed.

I watched him, amazed that Mr. Looking Out For Number One was actually more interested in looking out for his kids. It's a noble objective, no matter how you slice it. He was really torn up about Marcia's irresponsibility, and I was touched by his concern.

James shook his head, then took a steadying breath. He stared me right in the eye. "Okay, before you say it, I know that I haven't been the most dedicated parent, and it's true that I expected her to pick up too much of the slack, but this, this . . . I can't forgive it. I just can't."

"So you're saying that I'm a crummy backup plan?"

"No. Marcia didn't call you. It would have been fine if she had, but she didn't. That's a critical distinction." He stared at me, as if he could see right through to my heart, and his words softened. "You talk a lot of garbage, Maralys, but if you had known, you would have been there. Thank God the boys have some initiative. Marcia just trusted their welfare to fate, and that's not nearly good enough for me."

"You're going for custody."

His gaze was withering. "Of course. She's proven her indifference."

I withered back. "What's the difference between the boys waiting an hour for me one time, and them being alone for eighteen hours every single day of the rest of their lives?"

"I have to work!"

"So who's going to parent?"

To his credit, James seemed to consider the merit of what I said. It was a fair question and he knew it. He stared around his office, as if looking for a target. "I'd never be sure that they were okay if she had custody."

"Well, you won't be sure, anyhow. Not if you're here and they're somewhere else." Here I went, defending my sister again. I really had to cut this out. "Besides, it's hardly fair to hold one act against a person forever."

"One act?" He almost laughed under his breath. "If you know about the money, then you know about the bills. By that orgy of spending, Marcia cast everything into doubt. One bad break and the house is lost."

"Shame about the trophies."

"Shame about the boys," he snapped. "They need to be with their friends and in familiar surroundings. A divorce is tough on kids, and they need every bit of stability they can have. Marcia's put all of that in doubt. It's bad enough that she left, but everything hangs on a thread now. I don't care if I live in a garden shed, but I will not forgive her if those boys are thrown more curveballs than they can handle."

He was so fierce about it that I believed him. "A garden shed?"

James sighed and rubbed his temples. "They have to stay in their school. They have to have the connections to their friends. They have to have the chance of going to college, if that's what they want. Whatever changes I have to make personally to ensure their welfare are immaterial."

"Oh, it can't be that bad!"

"Not yet," he said so softly that the hair prickled on the back of my neck.

"What does that mean?"

James was done confiding in me. He stood up and gathered his paperwork, filing the divorce agreement away. His tone, when he spoke, was carefully neutral. "Mind your business for a change, Maralys."

"But this is my business." I stood up, needing the advantage of height even if it was just an illusion. "I want to know exactly what you plan to do."

He was on his feet in a heartbeat, spoiling for a fight and wrecking my fleeting height advantage. The veneer of civility was certainly thin today.

Fact is, I kind of liked him this volatile. At least I knew that he was alive in there.

"Why? Because you're *curious*?" he demanded, then flung out a hand. "Because this is all some game for you? I assure you that it is not a game for my sons." His voice rose with every sentence, and I was sure Ms. Prim was listening intently at the door.

I would have been.

"This is no game, Maralys! I owe you nothing, do you understand? Nothing! I owe you no explanation at all. If I don't know your sister anymore, then I certainly don't need to know you."

"That's where you would be wrong," I insisted calmly. "You've got to know by now that one faulty assumption can skew all your results."

"There is no faulty assumption."

"Wrong-o."

"Let me put matters in very simple terms." He leaned his fists on his desk, intent upon intimidating me. It was classic male body language, but I'm no classic female. I smiled at him, uncowed and unrepentant. "This is none of your goddamned business. Get out."

I sighed, a lady of leisure with no intention of leaving. I settled back into my chair and smiled at him. He was seething. "You should at least ask which of your assumptions I'm questioning."

Again, that brow shot up.

"We may not be blood, James, but we're family, like it or not."

James sat down, sighed, and shoved one hand through his hair. Presto chango, he was an overburdened lawyer again, his tone so temperate when he continued that I was startled. "Excuse me. I should not have raised my voice. You are indeed still my sister-in-law, at least until this paperwork goes through."

He visibly gritted his teeth and his eyes flashed. "Now get out, Maralys, before I do something or say something that I'll regret." His brow darkened. "And I say that in the most *familial* of ways."

I deliberately crossed my legs. "I don't respond well to threats."

James looked as if he'd like to throttle me. "Surprise, surprise."

I let my smile broaden.

And something changed. The charge in the air took a different tone, one less adversarial but no less electric.

James took a good long look, and I wondered what he saw. I mean, I know what I look like, but I wondered what he saw beyond the surface detail. This was a man who read people for a living, and he was known for being particularly perceptive.

And inscrutable. His assessment was lingering, and I couldn't read a thing in his expression. I got one vibe though—his was a look of the male-female flavor, the kind of look that makes a person want to preen a little.

Did James see my sister, his runaway wife, in me? There was a thought to take the sparkle from the situation. Marcia and I don't dress the same way, and Marcia's carrying a few more pounds than I am—all that swish living had its price—but there's a certain amount of identical twinness that can't be hidden.

Did he see a potential advantage? Did he know that I agreed with him about Marcia's choice being irresponsible? Would he expect me to damn my sister in court to help him get custody?

Or did he see a woman who had decided not to grow up? My father's accusation was still rattling around. I certainly was incongruous in that place, with my bottle-red hair, black jeans, black leather boots and jacket. We're tall, Marcia and I, due to some kind of weird mutation—everyone in our family is short, short, short except us—and people notice us.

James's gaze lingered on the silver ring on my right thumb, for some reason. I would have expected a glance that hot to land on the blue lace of my bra peeping at the neck of my white tailored shirt.

Did he know about the tattoo on my bum? My imagination went wild then and there, and my mouth went dry.

When in doubt, change the subject. "Was it always bad, really?"

James shook his head and spoke with the frustrated tone of a man who had not had any in a long, long time. Gad, something else we had in common. This was getting eerie. "We *must* have done it twice."

"Jimmy and Johnny." I laughed under my breath. "They look enough like you that they must be yours. Twice then."

We stared at each other across his desk, and things started to simmer. Johnny was eight, I remembered. Nine years? Even I hadn't been celibate that long.

"None?" I whispered and he looked pained.

"I've worked a lot of hours."

And spent many hours at the gym. I recalled a prize theory of my pal Lydia that only the chaste can truly be fit. She insists that it's the unsatisfied urge to mate that drives them— that getting any, any at all, makes us contented and complacent and plump.

Ms. Prim tapped gently on the door. "Mr. Coxwell?"

"Everything is fine, Mrs. McCready," James said with firm, dismissive authority.

Now he looked at the bit of blue lace, then met my eyes again. He smiled, not a lewd smile, more of an appreciative male "oh, Maralys, you shouldn't be so tempting" kind of a smile.

I felt my face heat.

James's smile widened, very slowly. It certainly was warm in that office. Have I mentioned that the man has a particularly prize dimple? Oh, yes, and elegant, capable hands.

I know enough of lust to recognize its arrival, sirens blaring, crimson feather boas flicking. Lust, I suspect, wears red patent stilettos, that feather boa, and not much else. Maybe glossy red lipstick.

Oh, yes, I was in trouble with a capital *T*.

"*Semper ubi sub ubi*," he murmured, as though I wasn't supposed to hear it.

"What's that supposed to mean?" I bristled, half certain that he was waving his educational pedigree under my nose, mostly to show my lack of one.

"It's just a bit of Latin."

"A legal term for what exactly?"

"I don't mean to interrupt, Mr. Coxwell." Ms. Prim cleared her throat, a little flutter of unwelcome sound, her tone making it clear that she did indeed intend to interrupt. "Mr. Coxwell senior will see you now, sir."

"Thank you." James fixed me with a look. "Your cue to leave, I believe."

"The Latin?"

"Forget about it. It really wasn't important."

I folded my arms across my chest, disliking how accustomed he was to calling the shots. "I'm not going anywhere. I want something from you first."

He leaned back and toyed with a pen, his posture relaxed. "That sounds interesting." Oh, yes, he had another look at that lace.

James flirting. I had some troubles wrapping my mind around the concept, but that's certainly what he was doing.

And I, to my astonishment, was enjoying it. I felt warm right to my toesies. Gave him my coy smile before I could catch myself.

I supposed that it was harmless, especially as I was about to leave for good. I promised myself an extra-long workout next time, a special prezzie for my clearly overwrought hormones. "A promise, that's all."

"What?"

I leaned on the desk, deal-time. My heart was all a-flutter and I knew I was giving him a prime view of the prime acreage supported by that bra. "My father still gets to see the boys, no matter how nasty things are or get between you and Marcia. Unimpeded access." I paused and gave him my most challenging glare. "They're supposed to go fishing on Sunday."

"I know."

"And what are you going to do about it?"

"What kind of person do you think I am?"

"I *know* what kind of person you are."

"Do tell."

"You're the kind of person who uses every situation to his own advantage." Even as I said it, I realized that I wasn't quite so sure of that anymore. "You're a manipulative, clever, and experienced lawyer who plays life like a game of chess. You wouldn't leave this chance to get what you want."

"I'm flattered that you think I'm so thorough."

"Well?"

"Well, what? What do you intend to do to break my sons free from my dastardly clutches?" James didn't smile, which just made me distrust him all over again.

Ever seen a cat, one that hunts, mess with its prey before killing it? It's a good-natured batting around of the wounded mouse or sparrow, a predator looking for a little amusement before the inevitable end. The victim, of course, doesn't get the joke, just keeps trying to escape, much to the cat's amusement.

His watchfulness made me feel a bit like a wounded sparrow, if you must know. I had a definite sense that I was just a pawn in a much greater game, and that his flirting—which admittedly came and went—was just another way to get what he wanted in the end.

Ms. Prim rapped again. "Mr. Coxwell?"

"Yes, I'm coming." James shoved to his feet, interview over. "Fine, Maralys. Sunday is a go. Anything else?"

"What about the long term?"

He sighed and his voice lowered. He held my gaze steadily, and I found myself wanting to believe whatever he said. "I'm not going to deny the kids a chance to be with their grandfather, Maralys." James's soft tone was very compelling. I believed him, and I'm a tough sell. Or at least I used to think I was. "They're crazy about your dad, and it's good for them to have one decent grandfather."

Ouch! Before I could make too much of that, he turned and opened the door. "You'll excuse me, of course, and see yourself out."

"Of course." I indicated the adjoining washroom. "Mind if I use the facilities first?"

James gestured general approval, then left. I had spied a Latin-English dictionary on the shelf and meant to make use of it. At least I would understand his insult.

Thank God I have a good memory. I heard him tell Ms. Prim that both he and Papa Coxwell would be unavailable for a few moments. But I was in the john with the dictionary before you could say boo.

Semper. *Always.*

Ubi. *Where.*

Sub. *Under, beneath.* Ah, like sub-marine and sub-way. Cool.

Ubi, again. *Where.*

Always where under where.

I looked the words up again, but there it was. I said it under my breath, and then the light went on. *Always wear underwear.* And the man had been looking at my bra. Now, if I'd imagined that he had a sense of humor, I might have thought that had been a joke.

But James had no sense of humor.

He must have just conjugated the verb wrong. That was vastly encouraging. Maybe he wasn't so smart after all.

Ha.

I flushed the toilet for show and ran the taps, then replaced the book in his office. As I made to saunter out the door, I couldn't have missed his father's greeting.

"What took you so goddamned long?" that man roared, as

though James was a bad child. "Do you imagine that I have so little to do that I can idle away the hours, waiting upon you? You have never understood the value of time and the merit of efficient billing."

James apologized in a way that seemed perfunctory to me.

And that was when I realized why I could hear them so clearly. There were two doors in James's office in addition to the one leading to the land o' Ms. Prim. One led to the elegant little half bath. The other apparently led to his father's office.

As luck would have it, that door was ever so slightly ajar.

Well, well, well.

Subject: what's up with that?

Dear Aunt Mary—

I'm new to the Internet and don't
understand so many things. Why are there so
many punctuation marks in e-mails and
posts? What does <g> mean? Why isn't
everything just in plain English?

Puzzled

Subject: re: what's up with that?

Dear Puzzled—

Be confused no more. Tilt your head to the
left—those are little faces, meant to show
the writer's attitude.
:-) is a happy face, or a "smiley."
:-(is an unhappy face, etc., etc.

Pointed brackets are used to enclose stage
directions, most commonly:
<g> means "grin."

Double colons can also be used as an aside,
as in:

::chuckle::

Similarly, a number of acronyms have become
popular shortcuts in netspeak, such as:
fwiw   for what it's worth
otoh   on the other hand
rotfl   rolling on the floor laughing
so   significant other
btw   by the way

There are vast numbers of permutations of
these signals, all intended to either give
tone to the written word or to save typing
time in chatrooms. Type "emoticons" into
your search engine to find out more.

*/8-)
Aunt Mary, who has her glasses on today as
well as a new hat
***
Uncertain? Confused? Ask Aunt Mary!
Your one-stop shop for netiquette and advice:
http://www.ask-aunt-mary.com

So, having been dismissed by God, I dutifully took my departure and went on home to mind my own *p*'s and *q*'s. I
knew whatever the senior Coxwell had to say to the junior
was none of my business. The sad truth is that I have no idea
what was said, what happened next or how the story ended.

Ha! AS IF!
Serves you right, if you believed me even for a moment.
You think I haven't heard all your self-righteous sniffing out
there, but I have, oh, yes, I have.
You haven't been very subtle about it, btw.
Now, it's all very well and good to say someone should be
doing this that and the other, but when you want a story, you
need the *facts*.

Face it—without me and my healthy sense of curiosity, there'd be no story here. No middle, no end, no resolution of conflict. We'd just all drift along, getting nothing done. I am your source of information. I am woman. I am shit-disturber.

I am CATALYST.

I suggest that you keep that in mind. Remember how disappointed you just were the next time you huff and puff at my unconventional choices.

Okay, lecture over. Of *course* I listened. What red-blooded American, reasonably normal human being *wouldn't* have listened? It was KISMET, I tell you, raw fate turning in my favor that:

1/ the door was ajar

and

2/ James felt some compulsion to speak to Ms. Prim, who should have known that (duh) they wouldn't take any calls when they were sequestered. Otherwise, he'd have gone through the connecting door and I would have been S.O.L.

Maybe I should call her Ms. Prim & Dim.

I did wonder, briefly, whether James had expected me to eavesdrop and had deliberately engineered matters so that I could.

But why, *why*? There was no motivation for him to do that, or so I thought at the time. It was just pure, untrammeled luck. Luck o' the Irish. Haha.

Not one to spit in the eye of good fortune, I got down on my knees and hovered close to the opening, just so I wouldn't miss a syllable. I knew deep in my bones that this would be good, and oh, baby, it most certainly was.

Though I wouldn't have missed a word even standing in the hall. The old man was in an ugly mood that made me appreciate my father even more.

"What the hell kind of nonsense is this?" the senior Coxwell snarled. "You demand a meeting with me, then you make me wait. I'm a busy man, as you ought to know by this point in your life. I'm due in court in an hour and have reading to do. Make it fast."

"I want to know what's going on." James sounded calm

and reasonable, but then I was starting to wonder how much of that was an elaborate façade. Takes a poker face to know one.

"What is that supposed to mean?"

"Tell me about Matt."

"Tell you about your own brother? Tell you *what* about your own brother?"

I heard a squeak of leather and guessed that James was playing my game of getting comfy just to annoy. I smiled.

"Oh, maybe why he's here." James spoke casually, making me smile in a more Cheshire fashion. Cat, that is.

"He's here because he always should have been here," dear Daddy spat. "It's not my fault that he took so long to realize what choice he should have made in the first place, nor is it my fault that he has a great deal of work to do in order to be effective in the role he was born to play."

"That's really the essence of it, isn't it?"

The old man sounded cautious now. "What do you mean?"

"You must have seen the paternity test results."

Oh, illegitimate babies in the illustrious Coxwell clan. I'm so there! This promised to be really sordid. My ears must have been the size of Saturn's rings.

"Of course I *saw* the test results. I ordered the test, didn't I? I paid for the test, didn't I? You had no right to pick them up yourself."

"I had every right and you damn well know it."

Things got very still. Hostility exuded from the office next door, a little cloud of thwarted testosterone sliding through the slightly open door.

Then James cleared his throat and spoke quietly. "I had thought that we might be reasonable about this." He certainly sounded as if he was trying very hard to be reasonable.

"Reasonable?" his father demanded. "What the hell is *reasonable* about living a lie? What is reasonable about being shamed in front of an entire community? Of seeing your entire life thrown into shambles? Of knowing that you have lived your life, the victim of a cruel deception and the butt of a thousand malicious jokes because your wife hid the fact that she was pregnant with another man's child at your wedding. I have worked hard to build something, to make something of myself, and I will not see all of it squandered upon a bastard child—"

James interrupted his father tersely. "Who just happened to have worked just as hard as you to build this partnership—notice I said *partnership,* which is the legal status of this organization, and one that implies that those partners each have a stake in its future."

"It's called Coxwell and *Coxwell,* not Coxwell and God-Knows-Who-His-Father-Was."

Ouch! Silence followed, which was good because I needed a minute to chaw that one down. James was not his father's son. Huh.

Could have fooled me.

Evidently Robert had been fooled for a good, oh, forty-two years.

"You really intend to cut me out," James said softly.

"I have no choice."

"You have every choice." Now James's voice was hard. "You are the senior partner. You have the choice of acknowledging nearly twenty years of effort, you have the choice of acknowledging that a man is more a product of forty-two years of experience than of five minutes of cells colliding. You have the choice of crediting talent and perseverance, and you have the choice of ensuring that your grandsons are provided an education."

"They're not my blood!"

James ignored the interruption, but his voice hardened. "Alternatively, you have the choice of cheating me of everything I've owned, destroying my life, and then destroying Matt's for good measure."

"It will not destroy Matt to follow his destiny."

"He never wanted this and you know it. You let him live his life before as he chose to do so, but now you're choosing to ruin it, just for the sake of your own ambition."

"I am a judge!" Robert Coxwell roared. "I was the foremost criminal lawyer in this city for years. I am running for reelection on a conservative platform, which is the bedrock of my beliefs. Surely even you understand that a divorce and a bastard heir would compromise my position."

"As opposed to compassion and acknowledging merit independent of birthright. Yes, I can see that would be problematic."

Go, James, go! There was a hit for the good guys.

"Do not try to turn this around on me! Your disrespect is as clear a mark of your illegitimacy as anything else could be."

"Whereas you would stand aside if you were to be cheated of everything you had worked to gain, and that on the whim of an old man more interested in his pride than his morals?"

"Audacity!" the senior Coxwell bellowed. "Get out of my offices!"

"You can't afford for me to leave. Consider your point made and let's get back to work."

"I will not have you in this office any longer."

Silence again, then I heard James rise. "Give me the Laforini case."

"Not on your life!"

"You won't win it without me." James spoke calmly, though with heat. "Matt won't win it. It's unfair of you even to make him try. The stakes are too high and the case is too high profile. It's not a reasonable case for him to take on first."

"It is. He will win and he will make his name."

"And what if he doesn't? What will your lofty partnership be worth, if you can't win the high-profile cases? What will your firstborn son be worth if he cracks under the pressure?"

"He won't."

"He might. We're very different, Matt and I, though I wouldn't expect you to have noticed."

"Your difference is exactly the point. Matt is my son. You aren't."

"Funny." James made a sound akin to laughter. "Most people might have argued the very opposite on the basis of personality."

"Most people are not my concern."

"No, I see that now. I'm still asking you to reconsider claiming carte blanche to trash Matt's life."

"It's none of your business. Get out."

I heard a rustle of paper and the sound of someone sitting down. The senior Coxwell cleared his throat. He'd probably picked up his reading to dismiss James by body language.

"Do you know that Marcia has left me?" James asked.

"I couldn't care less."

"I see. And since I am not your son, then *ipso facto* the boys are no longer your grandsons. They're worthless to you, too, aren't they? It's quite a flattering self-portrait you paint, Judge Robert Coxwell."

"Matt will win the Laforini case," the father insisted. "He will win it because I will coach him. Don't you forget who taught you everything you know."

"But you haven't taught Matt everything you know. And I don't think he even wants to know what you know."

"You will not challenge me!"

"Yes, I will." James spoke firmly. "You've made sure that I have nothing left to lose, after all. Why shouldn't I challenge you? Why shouldn't I defend my brother? Isn't that what big brothers do?"

"You're not his brother!"

"Half-brother, then. Matt and I have discussed this, by the way. We've decided that since we grew up as brothers, we'll continue to be brothers. An accident of conception isn't that important to our perceptions of each other and of our relationship."

"It's critical. I always knew that you couldn't be my son. You're not sufficiently respectful of authority."

"While everyone else says I'm a chip off the old block."

"They don't know what they're talking about."

"You have even said as much."

"Before."

"Yes, before the results were in." Silence carried to me and I figured they were eyeing each other. James continued softly. "Here's a thought—why don't you ask Matt what he wants?

You've never asked me, you've never cared, but maybe it's time to try a kinder, more gentle approach."

A book slammed. "I don't need your advice, counselor. Clean out your office by close of business today, or I'll have it cleaned out for you." A chair squeaked as someone got up, no doubt the judge. "I don't want to see you again, and I expect at least this small courtesy from you."

"I'm not going anywhere, not yet."

"Then I shall call the authorities and have you forcibly evicted."

"And I will tell them that I bought into this partnership with cash and created value in that investment with sweat. I will tell them that I have sacrificed and my boys have sacrificed and that we will have reparation for that sacrifice. And if they will not listen, then I will call the press, Judge Coxwell, and you may be sure that they will run a nice story about your family values in advance of the election." James spoke tersely, but I believed his threat. "You will give me a fair price for my stake, and then I will leave."

"Forever?"

"You don't need to worry about seeing me again."

"Just like your father," Robert Coxwell sneered. "Everything has its price. You can be bought and sold, like cheap chattel."

"I wouldn't have been so harsh," James said quietly. "But yes, in many ways, I am exactly like you. What great luck it is to have the chance to change that now, before it's too late."

The older man inhaled so sharply that I thought the carpet might be pulled from the floor. "Mrs. McCready!" he called. "Bring me the checkbook and bring it now!"

"Not that fast," James said in a dangerously low voice. "First, we get this practice assessed."

I took advantage of the moment and scampered through the foyer once Ms. Prim had taken the books into the other office. Wowie, kazowie. James had been fired from the family biz because he wasn't technically family. That was some kind of shocker.

But, of course, none of my business. No sirree. It was

about time that I got down to some serious code. I did have one contract, you know, and it was a bite technically. My client was going to be getting twitchy about delivery, and I wanted more work from them in the future. Or at least a referral. I also wanted their payment on delivery to appease the IRS.

The thing was, that although I'd had enough of the family stuff, I still couldn't push it entirely out of my mind. Big cogs kept on turning, working over what I'd learned.

I guess, given her objectives, Marcia got out just in time. I had to wonder how James was going to adapt to this. Talk about being born with a silver spoon in your mouth—and here he'd found out forty-two years later that the spoon wasn't his, after all. When somebody ripped it out of his mouth, no less.

I land on my feet, but I've been doing that all my life. It would be kind of a shame if Granite Man shattered into a thousand shards as a result of this.

Don't even go there, Maralys. With Marcia gone 404 and James going cuckoo, I could end up with kids after all.

Wait, I feel a nervous breakdown coming on.

I stopped cold in the street, feeling decidedly queasy. No doubt about it, I was coming down with a bad case of dependencies.

This called for sushi.

Nothing soothes the troubled mind better than a few hours in the kitchen, such as mine is. And I was in need of some serious soul sustenance.

The root of the problem here was that James wasn't his father's son. It was hard to believe, you know, because the two of them really did seem to be cut from the same cloth.

At least I'd thought so up until now. The last twenty-four hours were making me reassess James's Jerk Quotient. He certainly had nothing on the old man in that department.

Not just the dimple, then. I liked that he was more worried about his kids than himself. Probably because it surprised me.

I like unpredictability, and I'd thought this guy was as predictable as milk curdling two weeks past its Best Before date.

I was getting curious. A dangerous proposition.

And okay, I liked that he could hide his thoughts like a pro. Danger, danger, hormones on full alert.

Time for sushi.

Yes, it's a huge pain to make your own sushi. It takes eons to get it just right, but it's soothing in a way. Nice repetitive, detail-oriented gestures. Not unlike writing code, come to think of it. Two things I do well.

Very well.

I like sushi, like it a lot, but am always a bit leery of buying it already prepared. You do not want day-old sushi, or at least I don't. If it's not prepped right, the nori becomes soggy city once it's all assembled. Yuck.

Fresh would be the point of sushi, right?

So I put on some tunes and set to work—if the sushi didn't perk me up, then the soundtrack from *Cabaret* and that box of Passionate Persimmon haircolor ought to do the trick. I'm blessed with thick and healthy hair, though I've tried my best to mess with it over the years. I can't bear to cut it, so I color it. Often. Wildly. It's a hobby.

It was perhaps the fourth time I had belted out the soundtrack with Liza, and I was just realizing that, as usual, I had gotten enthused and bought too much fish, when the freight elevator clattered and groaned into action. I listened, fully expecting that one of my neighbors was arriving, but naturally suspicious all the same. Here's the problem—I'd been so excited about getting to the fishies that I hadn't locked down the hatch.

There are a few disadvantages to my living circumstances. Here's a big one—the isolation-lack-of-personal-security combo-pak. I don't worry about it too much, but when that elevator goes in the night, my pulse certainly picks up. Usually I'm the only one in the building after six or seven.

This is not a good feeling.

The elevator made the unmistakable sound of halting at my floor. I hadn't invited anyone—as if!—and a quick glance at the glass bricks revealed an impressionist interpretation of a night sky. All I could see through the industrial-grade mesh surrounding the elevator was a silhouette tall enough, broad enough, and male enough to be a serious problem.

Don't tell anyone—*anyone*, you hear!—but this kind of thing scares the living crap out of me. I have far too vivid an imagination, and in moments like this I think it should be against some law for me to live alone.

Fortunately, the moment of potential dependency usually passes and leaves few discernible scars.

And even more fortunately, the elevator door takes a few weeks to open. I grabbed my trusty fourteen-inch cast-iron skillet and assumed position. The grate groaned open, I lifted the skillet over my head, and a man stepped into my loft. He moved cautiously into the shadows, as though uncertain what he would find.

I had a surprise for him.

"Hey!" I shouted, then swung the skillet. It's not sporting, after all, to just bash someone on the head from behind.

I like to see the whites of their eyes.

He turned, swore, and I saw in the nick of time that it was James. I averted my swing just as he caught my wrist.

"What kind of greeting is that?"

"Security system," I said, my heart still going like a trip-hammer. "Crude but effective."

He exhaled, the epitome of skepticism. "As long as there's only one person. Why don't you live somewhere safer?"

He didn't let go of my wrist. His grip wasn't tight enough that I couldn't have squirmed free, but he was warm and I told myself that a little human touch was welcome post-crisis.

Assuming for the moment that James wasn't pure predator of some genetically distant class of reptiles. He could probably feel the race of my pulse, smell my blood and all that. That would explain the glint of his eyes.

"Because it's cheap space and I'm impoverished. Sadly, I don't have your array of choices for real estate." I pulled my wrist out of his grip and headed back to the kitchen zone. My heart was still racing only because of the shock, I was sure.

It had nothing, *nothing*, to do with James Coxwell standing in my place for the very first time ever, looking around
with undisguised curiosity. There was someone in my cave
and that was bad enough.

I chopped with a vengeance, but forced myself to stop
when I tore the nori seaweed in my frenzy. I took a deep
breath but couldn't dispel my incredible unease with having
James in my loft.

Probably he wanted something. Sadly there was no good
way of tossing him out, at least not without his cooperation.
He's a lot bigger than I am, and stubborn enough not to leave
before he was ready. Even rudeness wouldn't scare him off.

I looked through my lashes, just checking, and noticed
only now that he had changed out of his suit. His khakis were
too perfectly fitted to be off the rack, his casual shirt was open
at the collar, and his leather jacket was brown. He looked utterly suburban.

And surprisingly good. I was definitely losing my edge.
Celibacy was adversely affecting my judgment.

More time running the stairs was definitely in order. I'd
double up tomorrow.

James was watching me, as if he could read my thoughts
or at least gauge my attraction to him. Sick, sick, sick, to even
be thinking of my sister's husband in any sort of sexual terms.
Sordid. Tacky. Beneath my status as a reasonable and sensible
individual.

Even if . . . but never mind that for now.

So the strategy obviously was to give James whatever he
came for and do so ASAP, thus to restore my precious privacy.

"Any particular reason for this unexpected pleasure?" I
asked, infusing my words with about as much warmth as he
had greeted me with earlier.

He smiled, shoved his hands into the pockets of his khakis,
and sauntered closer. "Is that a payback for the way I wel-
comed you today?"

Caught. I shrugged, sheepish, and made a fuss over my
fishies. "Something like that."

"I'm sorry." He leaned against my counter-on-wheels. Fortunately, the wheels were locked down, saving him from a graceless tumble.

But then, maybe it wouldn't have been graceless. He'd probably checked the brakes before leaning. I had to remind myself that James was more observant than the average bear. Calculating.

God only knew what he was concluding on the basis of my agitation. In self-defense, I gave him a double dose of attitude. "What do you want, anyhow?"

"Advice."

I laughed, I couldn't help it. "Be serious."

"I am. You're the only person who knows the whole deal."

Wow, there was a frightening assertion. I feigned ignorance. "Me? I know nothing . . ."

"Be serious, Maralys." He dismissed my act with a flick of the wrist. "You listened to the whole thing today and I know it."

And here I thought I'd been so stealthy. I snuck a glance, but he looked more amused than angry.

"What kind of person do you think I am?" I demanded, but couldn't summon the right tone of indignation.

"The same kind of person as I am. You listened. I would have listened. Case closed."

Well, what could I say to that? I chopped.

"Go ahead," James prompted, almost teasing. "Tell me that you were just curious."

"Well . . ."

"Well, I would have been surprised if you'd done anything different."

Liza began "Farewell Mein Leibenherr" one more time, and I considered that it wasn't perhaps the most sensitive choice of music. I hit the remote and cycled the CD player on to the next disk, an Ella Fitzgerald greatest-hits compilation. Cole Porter stuff. A bit more intimate than I'd like, but I wasn't going to go change the CDs—then he'd know that it bothered me.

James seemed to be content to wait for me to say something. He was studying me closely, the kind of carefully assessing look that makes your hair prickle.

Oh, yes, lots of that male-female vibe. Hawk on the hunt for lunch. Or at least a good romp in the nest. I was a bit too aware of the proximity of the futon.

"Don't you have kids?" I demanded.

"Karate night. I have"—he checked his watch, which was a nice elegant piece of machinery, you've got to love the style of a man who doesn't flaunt his bucks with gaudy junk— "forty-five minutes before I have to start back."

"And you came all the way into the evil city, just to see me. What's wrong with this picture, James?"

"You're suddenly very modest."

I spared him a sharp glance, but his expression was all innocence. "Is that a joke?"

"What do you think?"

I glared at him, suspecting that he was messing with my mind and not knowing how to prove it. Yet. "It can't be a joke, because you have no sense of humor. This is an established fact. And a man without a sense of humor cannot make a joke, at least not intentionally."

"Res ipsa loquitur."

I gave him a poisonous look. "If you're trying to make me aware that you enjoyed some eight years of post-secondary education, while I copped out after one, your point is made."

"I'm not. It means 'the matter speaks for itself.'"

"Do lawyers all speak gook?"

"Not so much anymore. But I really liked Latin."

"Because it's logical and tough to learn?"

"Because I loved classics." He picked up a slice of cucumber and ate it. "Given my choice, I would have been a classics major, maybe taught Roman history somewhere and deciphered old inscriptions."

I stared at him. This did not jive with what I knew of him, but then a lot of the things I'd seen and heard regarding James Coxwell in the last twenty-four hours didn't jive with what I thought I'd known about him. That sentence is not nearly as troubling as its import, btw. "Get out."

"It's true."

"Then why didn't you do it?"

"I said given my choice." He arched one brow, daring me to challenge him on this. "I haven't had choices ever. It's kind of a novelty."

"You could have made choices anyhow."

James chuckled and I knew what he was thinking. I'd heard his father. How could a kid have defied that? And I suppose that sooner or later, doing what you're told becomes a habit.

Just like *not* doing what you're told does.

"Was he always that way?"

"What way?"

"Bombastic. Judgmental. Furious. Choose a negative attribute—your former father seems to have them all in abundant supply."

James winced. "No, I've only seen him lose it a couple of times, and that's been recent. He was always old stoneface, the king of self-control."

"At least you came by that honestly."

He laughed.

I didn't. I chopped, and James looked around. What more could I say?

Well, I did have one question. "So are you a victim of your father's parenting?"

"How so?"

I had his attention but good, and trod carefully. "Well, is that why you give away so little and make such tough calls?"

Subtext being—is that why your marriage tanked?

James thought about it, considering the question before he replied. "No. I'm a product of it."

"Explain."

"More accurately, I've experienced that parenting. What I make of that experience is up to me. I don't have to, for example, parent the way he did, although the instinctive reaction is often the one I experienced."

I remembered Marcia saying how annoying it was to be

sounding like our Mom when she scolded the boys. I nodded, then looked at him. "Do you follow that instinct?"

"I try like hell not to."

"You don't seem to have done much with that experience yet. I mean, it could be said that you're living a shadow of your father's life."

"It could have been," he corrected softly. "But I'm just getting warmed up. Maybe the real test is seeing what I do with it from here."

Our gazes met and held and things definitely headed to the land of toasty. I could imagine that learning that Robert Coxwell wasn't really your father might not entirely be a bad thing. I looked away, feigning fascination with my prep work, and James looked around, the silence stretching between us.

"What do you do here, anyhow?" he asked finally.

"I write code." I checked, but James was still waiting, my answer clearly having been deemed insufficient. "Besides the advice column, which was an idea that has yet to generate the advertising revenue I'd hoped for, I design Web sites and Web-interactive business solutions."

"Like?"

"You don't really want to know."

He pulled up a stool and shed his jacket. "Actually, I do."

I looked again, looked hard, but James really did seem interested. "In forty-five minutes?"

He grinned. "Forty. Give me the executive summary."

I put down my knife and gave it to him from both barrels. He'd asked for it, but I didn't expect him to survive. "Okay, right now I'm doing a remote human resources solution for a software company with telecommuting employees and freelancers all over the world. They don't want to ship forms all over the place, so we've created a secure Web portal for employees. They can log in and update their records and request forms and modify their coverage. They have a cafeteria-style benefits plan that people can change as their needs change, and their single office person was drowning in paperwork. This way it's streamlined and the single person can still keep on top of things."

To his credit, James didn't so much as blink. He was making short work of my cucumber slices, though. "How secure a portal?"

Trust him to cut to the beast at the core of the thing. "As secure as I can make it."

He looked me dead in the eye. "How secure is that?"

"Not nearly enough." I shrugged. "It'll be as tight as a drum when I deliver, but anything can be hacked with time."

"You have a contract with these people?"

"Well, duh."

James put out his hand.

I knew what he wanted, but I shook my head. "My business is my business, thank you very much."

"And you can't afford a sufficiently experienced legal counsel who could firewall you from the kinds of liability claims you could face from this."

"Excuse me, but—"

"Maralys, you're talking about Social Security numbers, and tax-withholding data, and income and addresses and God knows what other personal information, all in one handy database. You'd be in deep trouble if someone hacked into this and used the data illegally."

"Anything can be hacked!"

"And they probably know that."

"They should. I told them." I sliced with unnecessary force.

"But if the worst case happens, they'll have to do something to make it look good. You're a freelance contractor, Maralys, and the best candidate for scapegoat."

There was an ugly little bit of reality, and one I couldn't argue. He was right and we both knew it. "Thing is, I assumed they had an intranet, but they don't."

"*Intra:* within. As opposed to *inter:* between." James toyed with a cucumber slice. "You thought they had a private network, but they don't. You're having to move this data over the public data freeways. Even worse."

I nodded, impressed despite myself. "Who says Latin is dead?"

"Wasn't me." He met my gaze. "And this has given you a huge security problem."

"Enormous," I admitted, because there didn't seem to be a lot of point in being cagey. "An intranet is controlled much more easily, because there are only a certain number of portals and you know what and where they all are. Using the Internet . . ." I shuddered. "It's filled with pitfalls. I'm logging tons of hours to try to plug the holes. I'm good, but I won't be baby-sitting this after delivery. They're not paying me nearly enough for that."

"Why wouldn't they have an intranet?"

"Cost. Their workers are few and far flung." I put down the knife. "But I assumed that since they're swapping all this proprietary code back and forth that they'd have a more long term view and bitten on the cost."

"To protect their investment."

"Uh-huh." I sliced with undisguised disgust. "But they're a bunch of cowboys. I should have known better. Now I'm paying bigtime for a lack of due diligence on my part."

"Or a lack of disclosure on theirs," James mused.

I looked up, like a dog hoping for scraps.

"You could call it a breach of the understood *t*'s and *c*'s. Terms and conditions," he amended when I looked blank. "You could certainly use it as a justification to amend your *t*'s and *c*'s, if not your price. That's a big variable. It could be argued that it was incumbent upon them to make that clear to you at the outset."

I wagged the knife at him. "Careful, Coxwell. I'm starting to like you."

Again with the killer smile. He flicked his finger at me, as if that would summon the paperwork into his hand. "Give me the contract."

"Isn't there some saying about the Devil arguing Scripture?"

"Maybe there is. Think of it as a favor. I'll sleep better knowing that your butt is covered in Teflon."

"Why? I'm a source of cheap daycare?"

"Hardly. Call it an attack of conscience."

"A likely story," I muttered, but I got the contract. I was pleased, but you probably already know that. I take care of myself, but there's a limit to how many specialties a person can have.

A pet shark has its appeal. Especially one who works for free.

James pulled out his glasses and flicked through the contract, his gaze sharp enough to leave slice lines on the paper. I winced when he glanced my way. "Who wrote this?"

"Me. I mean, who else?"

"Don't give up your day job, Maralys. Any two-bit lawyer could steer an ocean liner through the holes in these clauses."

"I don't think so—"

"I do. Maybe you and your clients can gather around together and sing *Kum Ba Ya*."

"Why does that sound like an insult?"

James chucked his glasses on the counter. "This contract's got no teeth, Maralys. You might as well not have a contract at all." Decision made, James folded it up and tucked it away in his jacket pocket along with his glasses. "I'll get you a new one in the next couple of days. There's so much to revise that it won't be legible by the time I mark it up."

I don't much take to people making decisions for me. Helping is one thing, this was another.

And you ought to know by now that I wasn't going to be shy about making my feelings known.

```
Subject: thanks for the brews

   Hey, querida—

   Nameless maid of silken voice and keen wit;
   Thine beer arrived without nary a slip.
   I'd share with thee a divine sip
   If you'd come my way, upon an airship.

   ;-D>

   What do you say?
   Dennis
-----
```

I propped a hand on my hip and gave James my best glare. It's a pretty good one, but he didn't even flinch. "Who asked you to play God? I didn't hire you and I don't need your hand-outs."

"Wrong-o," he said, no doubt deliberately echoing my earlier challenge. "You can't afford me, and you do need me. This contract is proof enough of that."

James grinned and braced his elbows on the counter, clearly making an effort to charm me into agreement.

It damn near worked, but what he said was the ticket. "Let's just say that I owe you for the other night. You trust people too much, Maralys. It's no wonder you get stung. Let me build you the kind of firewall that I understand. Let me do this for you."

I was touched—and weakening—though I'd be damned if I'd let it show. "It's signed already. Too late for you to play superhero."

"Not at all. Say you don't deliver until they sign my addendum." He winked. "Don't worry. It will be in perfectly good faith and a natural clarification of the standing agreement given the change in the understood situation." He paused for a heartbeat. "Tell them that your prick lawyer made you do it. They'll believe you."

I laughed at that, and we both relaxed a little. "I guess you do owe me," I mused.

"In more ways than one."

I left that one alone. All alone. It was getting a bit convivial for me. "But you didn't come here to fix my contract."

"Nope."

"What, then?"

James got up and paced around the perimeter of my loft, then came back to me. "You know, I'm starting to have a certain empathy for salmon."

I laughed, because it wasn't what I expected him to say. "You're going to have to watch yourself. Some uninitiated soul might think that was a joke."

"Well, it isn't. Every time I turn around, things look worse." He dropped onto the stool again and folded his elbows on the counter. "Every morning I get up and have to swim harder and faster just to get through the day. Every day I think it can't get worse and it does. Every day I think there's nothing more that can go wrong, and I learn differently." He studied me, apparently puzzled. "How the hell do you do it, Maralys?"

"What do you mean?"

James snorted. "You've been poking adversity with a stick for as long as I've known you, and every day you go out and do it again. You never waver in your defiance."

"Call it a weakness."

"No, it's a strength and one I need to work on. Look, we both know that Neil left you in a huge pit of debt." James glanced around. "You seem to have done all right digging your way back out of that hole, and now I'm looking at a hefty one, too. Let's just say that I could use a few tips from a professional salmon."

So he had spied the financial commonality, too. I toyed with the wisdom of pitching my joint-authorship book idea to him, but James didn't look as if he'd see the humor in it. "Six years it's taken me. You'd better be ready for a long haul."

"But you're doing all right now?" There was concern in James's expression, concern so unexpected that it shook me up all over again. Not that I was ready to count on anyone or anything wacko like that, but it's not all bad to know that someone gives a crap.

See? Fix loopholes in my contracts and I'm an instant mushball. I really am getting old and vulnerable. Next I'll be buying those chocolate-covered almonds at the door to help send Bobby's choir to Spain.

"Yeah," I admitted. "Not exactly picking up properties on the Riviera, but I'm okay. Thanks for asking." We exchanged a glance that heated the loft up a few degrees more before I turned hastily back to my sushi. "Want some?" I offered, without intending to do so.

James looked and grimaced. He composed his expression quickly, but not quickly enough. "Thanks, but no."

Aye, and the devil himself had hold of my tongue, lairds and lassies, and I wasn't going to let him mosey out of this one.

"Already eaten?" I asked with perfect innocence.

James visibly squirmed. "Uh, no. Thanks very much."

Clearly, he didn't like sushi but probably had never tried it. I enjoyed pushing him just a bit too much to back off. "But?"

"But I'm really not hungry."

"But you see, the first thing you've got to do when facing adversity is keep up your strength," I said with a charming smile and offered the platter once more. "And seize all the free meals you can. Please, there's plenty."

James looked away.

"Come on. It's good." I waggled it right under his nose.

He recoiled. "Uh, no, thanks."

"Just one, just have one, so I know I didn't slave over a cold tuna for nothing."

"I don't eat bait!" The back of his neck colored then, and

James made a quick recovery. "But thanks just the same, Maralys. Oh, look at the time."

"You jerk." I dropped the platter on the counter, took a piece of sushi, and tossed it back. "It's delicious. All the more for me."

"Well, you just go ahead and enjoy it."

I had another and made a show of savoring it. "I'll bet you prefer a big steak with all the trimmings?"

"Well, yes." James looked suddenly hopeful, as if I might be hiding half a cow somewhere.

"Hope you've got your room booked at the Cardiac Arrest Hotel. The way you work, the way you live, and the way you eat, you'll be visiting there real soon."

He looked at me hard, daring me to continue.

Well, I'm no shrinking violet, especially when it comes to telling hard truths. "I'm not joking, James. Your life is cardiovascular hell, and you've just trebled your stress." I counted it off on my fingers. "You're a desk jockey, living off fast food, stressed out to the max. You're a health meltdown waiting to happen. The machine can only take so much."

"I don't eat junk. And I work out."

"And you're over the big four-oh. Who's going to cook now? You three will be living off pizza and deep-fried God knows what while you sweat your income. You're absolutely primo."

James sighed and frowned. "Don't I know it." He gave me that searching look. "Tell me it gets easier."

"Can it get worse?"

He laughed then, a good hearty laugh right from his toes.

If you can laugh at your troubles, you're halfway home, in my opinion. James eyed the platter of sushi. "Just promise me that there's no karaoke in this joint."

"None."

He sat back down. "Then you've got a deal. Someone told me that anything that doesn't kill me is supposed to make me stronger."

"Obviously a wise, wise woman," I retorted and we shared a grin.

I set the table with some dishes I'd brought back from Tokyo. James asked what everything was and even though I warned him off the wasabi mustard, he gave it a try. We both laughed when he nearly choked on the considerable chunk he had taken.

He ate reasonably well and admitted that it was better than he had expected. I hadn't bought saki—too many bad memories of painful mornings—so we had soda water. It was a remarkably amiable if hasty meal.

"You must have been in Japan for a couple of years." James took a neutral tone so deliberately that it couldn't be an accident.

"Three."

"Marcia was always disappointed that you missed our wedding."

"Please. You're breaking my heart here."

James grinned. "Seriously, it was an odd time for you to go."

"Because twins are supposed to be joined at the hip? What? Was I supposed to get married the same day, in the same dress, to a guy with the same name? Please!"

"Weren't you right in the middle of your degree?"

"What degree? I never finished. Barely started, actually."

"Really?"

"Really. College was not for me. One year was plenty for me. I wanted to do something."

"So you went to Japan."

"Um-hmm. Taught English to the innocent."

James chuckled. "What kind of English did you teach them?"

"Oh, all the legit stuff. We went over the slang and vulgarities in saki bars at night." I smiled at him. "Extracurricular classes for extra credit."

He smiled back at me. "Trust you to make sure they had a rounded education." For once, I didn't seem to have come short of the measure—if anything, he seemed amused by what I had done.

Time to divert his curiosity. "So what did you want advice about?"

"Fixing finances."

"Right. As if you don't know how to manage money."

"It's easy to manage when there's a lot of it. It's the lack of it that's throwing my game."

Another almost-joke. But he looked so exasperated by his circumstances that I figured it was an accident and took the comment at face value. "Make a list of what's critical, what you can't live without, and cover it first. Lose all the rest if you have to, and keep only what's essential to your survival."

"Is that what you did?"

"Oh, yes, with some encouragement from my pals at the IRS."

Sympathy crossed James's expression. "He really left you in a bind, didn't he?"

"Well, yes, but I was dumb enough to believe him a lot of times when I shouldn't have."

"You were young."

"Got over that, didn't I?" I put down my chopsticks. "The worst thing was that it kept coming. Just when I thought I was getting it covered, another debt would pop up. It was pretty discouraging."

"You should have asked for help."

"As if!" I was indignant.

"We could have afforded it, then."

"Oh, yes, and the check wouldn't have come with a little lecture on what a miserable wretch of a failure I was. Oh, and Marcia could have told my dad that she had to support me because of my stupid choices yada yada yada. I think not."

"It wouldn't have been that bad." Our gazes caught and held. I lifted one brow in a parody of his query, and he smiled. "Maybe."

"Thanks for the thought, but I prefer to owe no one anything. No expectations, no dependents, no chance of letting anyone down. Keeps life clean and simple."

"That's a tough code, Maralys."

"It's a learned response." I gathered up the dishes and

started to put them in the Rubbermaid bin beside the sink. "Gotta clean up now. Your forty-five minutes must be about up. Advice has been given, dinner has been consumed. E-mail Aunt Mary if you need more advice and let the world have a look at your troubles." I gave him a challenging look. "That would be your cue to exit stage left."

James folded his arms on the counter and didn't move. His eyes were gleaming in that way that I was learning meant trouble. "Just when things get interesting? I don't think so." He was watching again, looking for clues. "So how did you learn this response?"

"That is none of your damn business."

He unfolded himself from the stool and strolled closer, his gaze locked with mine. "Isn't it?" he whispered, and I was afraid then, really afraid, that *he knew*.

Panic City. Fight-or-flight response was in serious overdrive.

"None," I insisted, a little too breathless to be truly emphatic.

James halted, not a step away from me, and lifted one finger to my cheek. His touch was warm, gentle. It should have been nonthreatening, but my heart was thumping. My mouth went dry and I wanted nothing better than to bolt. I was thinking far, the Sahara might be good. I could smell not just that cologne but the musk of his skin, I could feel the weight of his gaze as he sought my secrets.

I knew the one he wanted.

I tried to bury it. Fast.

When James kept watching me, I closed my eyes and averted my face, about the best I could do.

"Maralys, you are so full of it." His whisper was soft yet compelling. There was unexpected affection in his tone. His fingertip slid down to my chin, urging me to face him again. There was absolutely no air in the loft, a remarkable thing. "I didn't tell you all of the truth."

That worked. I glanced up in surprise and couldn't look away from his intent gaze. I couldn't even come up with the

obvious question. His thumb slipped across my bottom lip,
gently tugging the flesh and making me tingle in anticipation.

"Because I came for something besides advice."

Danger danger. Four-alarm fire in the hold. I found myself
leaning forward, knowing damn well what James had come
for and wanting a bit of it myself. His finger moved south,
down my neck and to the lace edge of my bra.

I didn't step away—quite the contrary, I unfastened the
next button on my shirt. He swallowed, then his hand eased
inside my shirt so slowly that I could have stopped him if I
wanted to. I didn't, though I caught my breath when he
cupped my breast in his palm. His thumb moved across the
nipple, which was already pretty enthused about what he was
doing.

We stood for an eternity like that, cloaked in the shadows
of the loft, serenaded by Ella and the distant rumble of traffic,
staring into each other's eyes while his thumb moved back
and forth, back and forth. Oh, yeah, Ella, in Boston even
beans do it. I could have sworn that I could hear James's
heartbeat, almost as loudly as I could hear my own.

It was one of the most achingly romantic moments of my
life. There was yearning in the air, yearning and admiration
and the unfurling of dormant desires. It was a moment of possibility and promise. It was a moment that I didn't want to
end.

Or that I only wanted to end in one way.

James bent his head slowly, giving me lots of room to escape if that was what I wanted. You know that I didn't. I
tipped my head back to meet him, closed my eyes and was
sure that I was tasting heaven when he kissed me.

His other hand landed on the back of my waist, urging me
closer, and I felt the heat of his erection against my stomach.
He kissed me slowly, lingeringly, as if acquainting himself
with my unfamiliar territory.

Then, by some kind of silent mutual consent, we started to
dance. I put my hands on his shoulders and knew where I
wanted this dance to end. There was nothing but James, his
kiss and his teasing thumb, his tenderness and heat.

This was dangerous stuff, a dance with the devil, a kiss that compelled me to forget every principle to which I'd ever pledged allegiance. In that moment, on that night, I didn't care.

I slipped my tongue between his teeth. He groaned and caught me closer.

And that was when the alarm went off on his watch.

We parted, breathless, and discomfiture set in with record speed. James stopped the alarm and gave an apologetic shrug. "I guess timing really is everything." He sounded breathless, his voice a bit husky.

I took a deep breath, appreciating only now how close I had come to making a Big Mistake. Another big mistake in a long list of big mistakes. I had serious experience at BigMistake.com.

"Probably for the better," I said firmly and pivoted. I marched back to my dishes. I quickly refastened my shirt and realized that my cheeks were burning.

James was right behind me, irk coming out of his ears. "What the hell is that supposed to mean?"

"It means that I won't be a surrogate for my twin." I squirted dishwashing soap over the mess with unnecessary force. "So don't try getting your rocks off on me again."

"Is that what you think that was about?" His outraged tone told me that he thought otherwise, but I know when I'm right.

I was right. Except that maybe I was getting my rocks off on him. Either way, it was plain old lust dressed up in fancy glad rags, lust that came with a whole heap of trouble fast on its patent heels.

"Obviously!" I turned and glared at him. "What else could it have been about?"

James smiled then, a sphinx smile that made me remember that hapless hunted mouse. He leaned closer, eyes shining, looking damn near good enough to eat. "I have a theory, Maralys, one that I've been wondering about for a long, long time."

That was worrisome, but I brazened it out. "Oh, great, a

science lesson. Don't you need a hypothesis before you can have a theory?"

James continued as if he hadn't heard me, an annoying choice. "That theory is the real reason I had to see you tonight."

"What kind of a theory?"

But James was leaving, deliberately leaving my curiosity unsated. As well as a few other things. He walked toward the elevator, snagging his jacket en route.

"I asked you what kind of a theory?" I shouted, well and truly worried. I hate being ignored, but that wasn't all of it.

The stupid elevator was still there, giving me no time to get answers. James pivoted in it, offering no more than a smug smile before he hit the button. "You'll see. But, in case you're interested, I'm pretty sure I'm right."

"What in the hell is that supposed to mean?" I roared through the grate, but the only answer was the sound of James's chuckle echoing in the shaft.

He wasn't going to tell me. He was banking on my curiosity, on my following him to find out the truth. It wasn't going to work. I wasn't going after him. I'd done my bit, more really than anyone could have expected of me, and wasn't getting further involved. No way, José.

I am an island, I exist devoid of ties and dependencies. I am independent woman, a rare breed but one in need of no mate, no herd, no offspring. I am Amazon. I suck men dry and chuck them back. I need no protector. I hunt alone.

I raged back to the dishes and punctuated each of my conclusions with the banging of something substantial.

I was *not* wading into the mire of their divorce.

I was *not* going to keep James warm while he got over Marcia's leaving.

I was *not* going to stand substitute for my twin. Never. Nonnegotiable. Uh-uh.

I was *not* going to bolster his ego, which probably was long overdue for a reality check. Not me. I had work to do. Yes, and advice to give.

Sounded pretty thin in comparison to a wild night between

the sheets and/or knowing what the hell his theory was. James knew me too well—not knowing what he meant would indeed drive me nuts.

Not for the first time, I felt the urge to murder James Coxwell, and to do it slowly. I was sure I would enjoy it. I was sure that he deserved it.

There was one small fly in the ointment here. I was not entirely innocent. I had lied to him tonight. My conscience twinged, even though it had been a perfectly permissible white lie.

I hadn't hated college. I had loved it. But quite suddenly I hadn't loved Boston. I had had to get out, to shake off everything and everyone I had known. The teaching slot in Japan had been a godsend because it had offered a timely escape. I went because I was on the run, not because I wanted to travel or even that I particularly wanted to go to Japan.

The most important thing about Japan had been that Boston wasn't in it.

That was why I had stayed an extra year. The contracts are for two years initially, and only the hardy stay on. At the end of two years I hadn't been ready to come back. Only my mother's final illness brought me back in the end, and even then, I dragged my feet all across the Pacific. It's not as if there was much of a reward for me doing that, anyhow. If I had any sense, I'd still be there, speaking Japanese and living in the smallest, cleanest apartment ever known to mankind.

The reason for my hasty departure all those many moons ago? Oh, it's simple. People are rats. You put your trust in one, you count on one, and sooner or later, he's going to let you down. I've learned that lesson twice and I'm not going back for more. I depend on no one and let no one depend on me.

I added that to my list.

The annoying thing about James was that he thought he had my number, but I could outwait him, I knew I could. He might have baited a trap, but unlike most of the members of class rodentia of my acquaintance, I would not take that peanut butter.

Not me.

James could wait to hear from me for the rest of his everloving life. I had done all that I could to help him out— no, I had done more than any mere sister-in-law could be expected to do, and that out of the goodness of my wizened little heart, and what had it gotten me?

He'd copped a feel in gratitude. Put like that—which wasn't exactly how I remembered it but was how I was going to choose to remember it—my choice was clear.

The gates were closed, the barricades were up, the moat was filled. Call out the dragons and dragoons, no one gets in here alive. Let James have all the theories he wanted, I did not care. I would not care. I was going to color my hair Passionate Persimmon and then I was going to bed alone.

Again.

Hmm. Captain Vibrator would have another busy night, I could just tell. It's never as good as the real thing, which isn't usually an issue for me, but on this night the realization made me grind my teeth. No, although Cap'n V has his charms, there's nothing as good as a man, filling the bed and warming it, growling at you in the morning.

Among other things. I hadn't been this zinged up in years, which should have been a warning. It was just a healthy impulse to hope that someone had dragged their keys along the side of whatever fancy sedan James had parked on the street outside.

Cap'n V was the man of my dreams, for that night and every night. And for your information—those of you intent on seeing things that aren't there—Cap'n V has always had hazel eyes with kind of a gold crown around the pupil, so don't go making a big deal out of nothing.

I checked my e-mail on the dinosaur, just to see if anything had shaken out since my unauthorized acquisition of financial data. There was a bit of inevitable spam, and that ghastly poem from Dennis.

I had the urge to tell him to stick to piracy and forget the swashbuckle, but knew I had to do better to be rid of him for good.

Subject: re: brews

Great idea! The twins are dying for a
fresh start—Utah would be perfect! No
trouble with school—they've both been
expelled. I'm sure that a note of support
from you would persuade the judge to let
them out of the state. And don't worry—
they're old enough to know when to turn a
blind eye.

::nudge, nudge, wink, wink::
I'll bet you're a guy who has a few bucks
to show a girl a good time—unlike the snake
I checked out the other night. :-P Grrr.

All show and no go.

Just send three one-way tickets, Dennis
querido, and we'll be there. (I can hold
the baby on my lap, so don't worry about
her.) Oh, better send me one for first
class. Those coach seats are just too tight
for me, esp on such a long flight. (btw,
it's so *NICE* to meet a guy online who
doesn't ask for pix first.)

ttys—no, SEE you soon
your querida, the doughnut queen

Ha. That ought to do it. And now, Cap'n V, baby, I'm all
yours. I deserve a reward, after all, for a job well done.

Subject: LIFE!

Dear Aunt Mary—

There are so many things I want to do with
my life, but I'm afraid to screw up. How do
I get over my fear of taking risks?

Or should I?

Timid Tess

Subject: re: LIFE!

Dear Tess—

Contentment, comfort, and conformity are
the dreams of sheep. Fulfillment, fortune,
and fame are the dreams of people. Unless
the IQ of livestock has vastly increased—
and their manual (hoofial?) skills—you must
be of the latter genus. You only get one
life, so dream big.
Dream bold.
Dream in color.

Aunt Mary

***

Uncertain? Confused? Ask Aunt Mary!
Your one-stop shop for netiquette and advice:
http://www.ask-aunt-mary.com

Of course, you know that I got suckered into supporting the Sunday fishing adventure.

I should have seen it coming. My father doesn't drive anymore, a favor to the life-loving people of Massachusetts, but I had foolishly expected James to manage the transit issues. Dad was hardly going to take the bus from North Station, not at his age.

First Jimmy hit on me, then Johnny, then my dad called, all three of them singing the pathetic male chorus. Their lives were in ruins without me and my driver's license and my entire effing Sunday.

Grrr.

I've got to get better at saying no. Otherwise I'll end up with a chronic case of psychosomatic psoriasis. I already had serious twitchies from all these people depending upon me. Ewww.

James was notoriously silent—James, notorious? I know, I know. I'm having trouble with that myself. Seems like an oxymoron. This man is too much of a straight arrow to make much of a pirate king, but still his lack of involvement seemed portentious. Maybe I'm getting even more neurotic.

If so, I suspected that it was because of that kiss. Or more likely, because of his strategy to tempt my curiosity. He was counting on me to buckle. And he had set this up, set *me* up, on that you can bet your last buck, just to tempt me a little closer.

I might have gotten suckered into doing the duty run, but I'd go down swinging.

In fact, in honor of my new orange—ahem, *persimmon*—hair, I decided on the swinging vintage zone of my closet. What to wear was a definite issue (isn't it always?) because I didn't want to look either inviting or indifferent. Just casual. But good. I needed to look really, really, really good.

I like men to salivate when I turn them down. It's a power thing.

The chartreuse boots were a definite. They're buttery soft leather, smooth and thin, and fit like my second skin. Spiky little stiletto heels, but only two inches high. Ha. I like the mixed message there.

Pointy toes, naturally, and they zip up tight, ending mid-calf. They are truly wonderful "come bite me, baby" boots. We called them go-go boots when I was a kid—well, we did when they were white—but these I call my Nancy Sinatra boots.

As in "made for walking." Ticka boom ticka boom ticka boom.

Which incidentally, they're not. A couple hours hiking in these puppies, and I'd be soaking my feet for a week, but that's not the point.

They make me feel good. Women stop me in the street to ask where they came from and how they can find a pair. They are conversation-openers in the arcane feminine language of Shoe.

Well, the flower-power zip-ankle slim pants were an obvious choice to go with the boots, as was the chunky funnel-neck yellow sweater. A pair of St. Laurent-ish frames that had yellow-tinted shades and I was ready to rock. Little Miss Psychadelic Citrus.

Worked for me. By the way, I went with the Jockey sport-bra, just to short-circuit any ideas the man might have. You and I both know that those things are about as sexy as support hose. Going without, well, I've enough kazunga that it would hardly go unnoticed. Support is not an optional accessory, and lack thereof might be construed as an invitation.

It was a great day in early March, the first clear day of spring, all sunshine and blue sky, and I was even glad to be awake for it. I took public transit to my dad's, because I was too cheap to spring for a cab and not anxious to be on time.

My father still has a car, don't ask me why. It's a gray K-car in mint condition. I suspect he has a secret dream that he will regain both vision and response times in a miraculous moment and take to the highways again with a vengeance.

It is a frightening prospect. But on this day the K was handy if not elegant.

I was almost early, but my father still insisted that I was

late, neglectful, and a pale shadow of my sister's shining light. He was prepared to pick a fight, probably just for something to do. Sadly for that plan, I was prepared to forgive him much, having finished a butt-kicking firewall for the client the night before and having heard James's dad have at him.

That lasted until Dad started on my driving.

I took 93, because I like to go fast and it was more or less heading in the right direction. I fully expected him to take issue with that—which he did—and to blame me for the traffic jam at one exit—which he did—but not to criticize my flawless execution of the passing technique which *he* taught me all those many years ago.

"Jesus, Joseph, and Mary! You've nearly killed those people!"

I was remarkably temperate in replying. "I don't think so."

"Well, I most certainly do. You've nearly killed us!"

"Thereby depriving you of the chance to one day live on cat food." I glanced his way. "You should be thanking me."

"I will not be thanking you for risking my life!" He was indignant and started jabbing his finger toward me. It was somewhat distracting as the silhouette kept appearing and disappearing in the rearview mirror. "You are not fit to be driving my car. You are not fit to be driving any car. In fact, you clearly *cannot* drive a car!"

I slapped my forehead with my palm. "Oh, my God, you're right! I forgot that I can't actually drive."

"Do not be taking the name of the Lord in vain, Mary Elizabeth!"

"All these years I've been living a lie!" I wailed, then snapped my fingers. I knew it drove him nuts when I took either hand off the wheel.

I took them both off. The K has perfect alignment—I know because I took it in to have it checked just two weeks before.

I surveyed the long empty stretch in front of us, then turned to face him dead on. His eyes boggled. "In fact, I'm going to stop driving right this minute. You're right. I shouldn't be doing this. I'll just turn off the car right here." I reached for the keys.

"Don't be touching the ignition when you're on the highway!"

"Oh, right. Silly me. I forgot, seeing as I don't know how to drive and all."

"Cheek!" he huffed. "That's what you're giving me . . ."

I pretended not to hear his muttering. "Think I should pull over? No, the road is really straight and we'll be late for your fishing trip if we stop. Tell you what, we'll just switch places. It'll be just the easiest thing, thank heaven for bench seats. Come on, slide your leg over here while I squeeze mine over there. . . ."

I chucked my right leg toward him, and the car slowed immediately with my foot off the gas. I deliberately knocked the engine out of gear and steered a bit jaggedy with my left knee. There was no one near us and we were in the right lane anyhow.

My father began to roar. "Mary Elizabeth O'Reilly, you stop these shenanigans this very moment!"

I looked at him, all innocent. "I could only stop if I was going to drive. Which I could only do if I knew *how* to drive."

He inhaled half the planet's atmosphere as he glared at me, then let it out in a long slow wheeze of concession. "Just don't be passing anyone like that again."

I whistled once I got my foot back on the gas. I waved cheerfully at the guy who honked and gave us the finger as he passed us, those gifts in return for the unpardonable sin of daring to slow to the posted speed limit.

We rode almost the rest of the way in silence, my father hunkered down in his coat, glowering like an old sourpuss.

He cleared his throat when we were getting close, and I braced myself. This is his way of ensuring he gets the last word and wins the argument—he launches his last salvo as you park, then bounces out of the car, leaving you no time for return fire.

We turned down the street of the Coxwell residence and he began. "Your sister would never have given me such a fright. Your sister would never have willfully stolen a dozen years from her father's life."

And I had finally had enough. "Shame she didn't pick you up then. It's not as if I had anything better to do today than play chauffeur."

"You've an impertinent tongue in your head."

I tried, I really did.

"Not like your sister . . ."

I interrupted him. "And why was it exactly that she couldn't pick you up today?"

My father gave me a wary look. "I don't know."

"Didn't you talk to her?"

"No."

"And didn't you think that was a bit odd?"

He sat forward, suspicious now. "What is it that you're knowing that I'm not?"

"Oh, look, we're here." I pulled into the drive, turned off the K, and smiled brightly for him. He opened his mouth, but this time I got out of the car and had the last word. I heard him sputtering behind me all the way to the porch. I rang the bell and waited.

"What are you knowing that I am not? What has happened to your sister? Why couldn't Marcia pick me up today?"

I shrugged. "It's not for me to tell you."

Johnny opened the door, his gaze flicking from me to my father. The boy could smell conflict a bit too well, which was a shame at his age. I guessed that he'd had a few good whiffs of it in this house.

"Johnny, my boy, where is your mother?"

My younger nephew's face crumpled, before Jimmy pushed him aside and took charge. "Open the door, you dope. You can't leave people out there all day. Hey, Grandpa, we going to catch some big ones today?"

It was what my father always asked the boys, and I appreciated that Jimmy was truly becoming a small adult. I saw in his eyes that he had not only heard my father's question but had deliberately deflected it.

He was going to have to get a lot better to play that game with my father, though.

"I asked you a question, young man, and I'll be waiting for my answer. Where is your mother?"

"She's gone," Jimmy said flatly. "And no one knows where."

"What is this?" My father's reply was mingled horror and disbelief. "Well, she must have had an excellent reason. What is the story here? What has happened?"

Johnny sniffled, averting his face when his older brother rolled his eyes. Jimmy was showing the insouciant indifference that would have marked a truly cool fifteen-year-old in my day—and he was only ten.

How times have changed.

Neither answered my father, probably because they didn't know the answer. My father began to sputter.

"Connor! Good to see you." James strode down the hall, making a timely arrival, greeting my father with a smile and a firm handshake. "I apologize. I was on the phone with the realtor."

Realtor? I glanced back and only just then noticed the FOR SALE sign on the lawn. Well, would wonders never cease. I hadn't really expected James to make any tough choices or changes in his life. I hadn't expected him to listen to me, or take my advice.

Seems I had underestimated Mr. James Coxwell one more time. I looked back and noticed immediately that the chinos had been chucked in favor of faded Levi's. He was wearing a T-shirt that was tight enough to reveal that investment at the gym and red enough to make his hair look coppery. He had thrown on a plaid flannel shirt and shoved his bare feet into Dockers. His hair was rumpled as if he'd been running his fingers through it in exasperation.

Most of this did nothing to explain the way my mouth went dry, much less why I had nothing to say. He was watching me, though, those eyes twinkling as though he could read my thoughts.

Okay, it wasn't just my boots that were biteable in this vicinity.

"You're not selling this house?" my father demanded.

"Yes, I'm hoping to." James frowned. "Marcia has wanted to move into the city for a long time."

"Is that where she is? Looking at houses?"

"No, Connor." James sobered and held my father's gaze. "She's left us. The choice of living in the city versus the country was just one of our many disagreements."

My father blinked and leaned more heavily on his cane. It was a bittersweet moment for me to see him finally disappointed in one of Marcia's choices.

I was pretty ticked with her, actually, for letting him down.

"She left you? And the boys?"

"All of us."

"But, but—where has she gone?"

James shrugged. "I don't know. She didn't tell us that part."

"She must have had a good reason . . ." My father visibly faltered, but James stepped out onto the porch. He gripped my father's elbow, supporting his weight under the appearance of just escorting him into the house. It was a nice gesture.

And James spoke with quiet assurance. "She must have one, and I hope she comes back to tell us what it is."

"But . . ."

"What's done is done, Connor, and I'm certain that she'll call. It's only been a few days. Why don't you come in? Johnny will make a pot of tea, just the way you like it, and we can all have something to eat before you boys head out to your favorite creek."

James's words were low and soothing, coaxing everyone to follow along. My father was over the threshold probably before he thought about it and didn't halt until he was halfway down the hall.

Then he pivoted and glared at me accusingly. "You knew! You knew the truth and you didn't tell me."

I shrugged. "You've spent my whole life telling me to mind my business. You can hardly blame me now for doing just that."

He turned away so quickly that he almost fell, but James was there to catch his elbow. Jimmy chattered to him of fish and lures and bait, smoothing the moment over with the expertise of a much older person. He actually coaxed a response from my father in short order: a correction, not uncharacteristically, of which lure would work better on a sunny day like today.

I didn't realize right away that Johnny was still standing beside me. "Auntie Maralys?"

A shudder danced over my flesh at the raw need in his voice, but I smiled down at him all the same. The kid was hurting, you could see it in his face. I had the weird urge to ruffle his hair. "What's up, Johnny?"

His gaze flicked to the front lawn, then back to me. "I don't understand. . . ."

I sighed, then crouched down beside him. He watched me carefully. "None of us understands, kiddo. Maybe not even your mom. But she'll turn up; she loves you guys too much to do otherwise." I thought that was a pretty good bit of bull, but he didn't look reassured.

"But we'll be gone. If Dad sells the house, she'll come back and we won't be here." His voice rose slightly. "What if she can't find us? What if she tries to come back and can't find us?"

"Oh, don't be a dope," I said, my tone more teasing than his brother's had been. "She'll call me and I'll tell her where you are. Or she'll call your grandpa. No biggie."

He chewed on his bottom lip, studying me with all his father's intensity. "Do you really think she'll be back?"

I held his gaze. "Yes. I'm sure of it."

She'd come for her half of whatever was left if nothing else, but I didn't tell the kid that hard little reality. Maybe she'd come back for the kids. It wouldn't hurt for him to believe it, even if I wasn't going to bet on it.

He smiled then, a thin smile, thanked me politely, then headed for the kitchen. God damn Marcia, I thought with a vengeance as I followed him, then wondered whether my sister knew or cared what wounds she had left behind her.

"Is Auntie Maralys coming fishing with us?" Jimmy asked with a pointed glance in my direction.

Before I could say anything, James shook his head. "You don't want her to come." He dropped his voice to a conspiratorial whisper. "She'll eat all the bait."

"I heard that!" I cried, even as the boys made faces and groaned. I shook a finger at James, liking very much how his eyes were twinkling. "You better watch it. You keep saying stuff like that, and someone's going to think you have a sense of humor."

The realtor worked that Sunday afternoon like nobody's business. I was impressed by how many couples she trotted through that house after the fishing expedition had departed. I hung out in the kitchen, drank fierce tea, and house-sat. She chirped the house's assets by rote, danced up and down those stairs, and flicked on every single light in the place despite the relentless sunlight.

James was dropping the threesome off with his cell phone at an undisclosed Truly Awesome Fishing Place. It wasn't long before he sauntered back down the hall and tossed his keys on the counter.

"Couple Number Six," I said and took a glug of tea. "Got some kind of fire sale on here?"

"I told her I'd sell for twenty-five thousand less if it closed in two weeks."

"She'll push you to thirty."

"I know." He poured a cup of tea, saluted the passing threesome with it, sipped, and grimaced. "This is terrible!"

"Just the way Dad likes it. Strong enough to walk on, he says."

"Strong enough to peel the lining from your stomach." He stared at me, incredulous. "You're actually drinking it."

"It's an acquired taste."

"Like your dad?"

"What do you mean?"

"He's pretty tough on you, but you keep helping him out. I've never heard you two go at it before."

"That was nothing." I dumped my tea down the drain, unprepared to confess anything more than that. "So, when should Maralys's limousine service be back?"

"Why don't you stay?"

"Because I might go insane in this bucolic suburbia in the next four hours." I was cranky and James had the misfortune to be within range. "Why do people live like this anyhow?"

James smiled, clearly untroubled by my mood. "What's wrong with it? I always thought it was kind of nice. Peaceful."

"Complacent, more like. Smug. Is this the American dream? It's frightening that anyone could aspire to live like this."

"Why?"

"I can't imagine anything more sad than an eighteen-year-old, flush with possibilities and youth, clasping hand to bosom and declaring that he or she wants nothing other than a golden retriever and a riding lawn mower, four bedrooms, and two-and-a-half baths."

James looked bemused. "Do you insult everything, Maralys, or just what you don't have?"

I ignored his question. "Did *you* dream of this?"

He looked away, playing evasive, and I was more interested in his answer than I wanted him to know. "You could say that I'm here because of a dream."

I was disgusted. "That's sad. In fact, that's pathetic. I'll send you a sympathy card. The world was your oyster and you dreamed of *this*."

He gave me a sly glance. "I didn't say I dreamed of this."

Oh, lawyer games. I was wishing for the Latin. "You more or less did."

"But not exactly." James smiled a little and my heart skipped a beat. Oh mousie, I know how it feels to be toyed with. "It doesn't say anywhere that I got my dream." He pushed away from the counter, but I was right behind him.

"Did you or did you not dream of whiling away those golden years, playing golf and wearing chinos?"

"What's wrong with chinos?"

I shuddered. "They're unsexy. Almost as unsexy as golf

clothes. Really. If God wanted a scheme to keep Americans from reproducing, golf clothes and chinos would be critical ingredients."

James chuckled. "Golf as contraceptive."

"Think about it. The true fiends play on weekend mornings, when they could be doing other procreative things, and watch it on television on weekend afternoons."

"Also good times for procreative things." James had a definite gleam in his eye, but I wasn't going to drop the subject and let him know that I had noticed.

"It's the only sport that fat men can play well."

"Ah, there's that unsexy factor again."

"Exactly. And it's the only sport that seems to require men to look like dorks."

"Chinos?"

"Or baggy shorts with knee-socks. All those goofy colors and patterns. Argyle. The single-glove syndrome." I shuddered elaborately. "Go ahead, make my day. Tell me that you love golf."

James grinned. "Never played. I'm beginning to be glad of that."

"What's that supposed to mean?"

"That I wouldn't want you to think that I'm unsexy. Obviously."

James dipped his head and scored a kiss before I knew what he was up to. It was quick but effective, leaving me simmering in my socks. He lifted his head just slightly, whispering as the sound of the realtor's patter carried from the basement stairs. "Because I think that you are very sexy, Maralys O'Reilly."

Oh, danger, danger. I backed away, one hand up in a paltry defense. "Don't confuse me with my sister. Don't even go there, mister."

James's smile broadened and he flicked an appreciative gaze over me. "That's not likely to happen." He leaned back against the wall, arms folded across his chest as he watched me. "So, what should kids dream of?"

I waved my hands, grateful for the distraction, and tried to pretend that his kiss had left me cold. "Fame. Fortune. Glory. Dreams shouldn't be about what you can buy—they should be about what mark you leave in the world. Compared to changing someone's perspective or making the world a better place, a two-door silver sport coupe is a pretty paltry substitute."

"And your dream would be?"

I was tempted to blow James off, just because he looked as if he already knew the answer. But I knew he didn't have it right, and it was too tempting to surprise him. I lifted my chin. "Digging out the truth and setting it loose."

James looked skeptical. "You dreamed of that as a teenager?"

"Don't be stupid. I dreamed of fame, fortune, a two-door silver sport coupe, and the whole materialistic enchilada. Truth is a distant second to that grand-prize package, but it will have to do."

James arched a brow. "No riding lawn mower?"

"Never. I never even wanted a lawn."

He chuckled, then stepped away, catching my hand in his as the realtor and company appeared on the stairs. "Come on, I'd like your advice on something."

"Wait a minute." I realized belatedly that he had redirected the conversation. "You didn't tell me what you dreamed of."

"It doesn't matter. Not now, anyhow."

"And what is that supposed to mean?"

James pivoted on the landing and looked me straight in the eye. "That I'm not going to tell you," he said firmly. "Duh, as the boys would say. Now, come on." He gave my fingers a squeeze, then headed for the master bedroom, me in tow.

I put on the brakes as soon as I saw his destination. This particular goal was easy to name. "Oh, no. I'm not going in there."

"Has anyone ever told you that you have a nastily suspicious mind? I just want you to see something."

"Oh, there's a great line." I folded my arms across my chest and parked in the upstairs foyer. "Come meet Mr. Wiggly. Like I haven't heard that one before. Got an etchings collection, too?"

James laughed and the change in his expression nearly made me change my mind. "I'm not nearly that devious, but if you insist . . ."

I swatted him, to no visible effect.

He continued on without me, knowing damn well that I'd be curious enough to follow. I lingered as long as I could, then peeked. To my surprise, he was nowhere near the bed.

Maybe that was to my disappointment. The realtor was in the house somewhere—the possibility of discovery adds a certain spice, don't you think?

But James had other, more pragmatic things on his mind. He had flung open one closet door and was staring at its contents. It was the walk-in closet that my sister used, but you'd only know how big it was if you'd been there before. Now, it was full to the doors with boxes and bags. They were literally stacked to the ceiling. Three tumbled out when he opened the door and, oh, yes, my need to know got the better of me.

I followed him into the room and was impressed. My sister had redefined the verb "to shop."

Subject: with friends like this

Dear Aunt Mary—

I'm getting married to the greatest guy,
but my pals aren't impressed. Some of them
won't even come to the wedding! Okay, he's
divorced, and okay, I met him when he was
still married, but why can't they be happy
for me? I might not be the First, but I'll
be the Last.

sad bride

Subject: re: with friends like this

Dear blinded Bride—

Puh-leese! Face the fact that you may be
neither First nor Last, but just NEXT.
Your friends may know—or see—something that
you don't. Sure, you could be headed for
sunshine and happiness 4ever, but people
are creatures of habit. Changing partners
doesn't change the steps to a guy's
favorite dance.

Aunt Mary
***
Uncertain? Confused? Ask Aunt Mary!
Your one-stop shop for netiquette and advice:
http://www.ask-aunt-mary.com

I stopped beside James, got a good waft of the scent of his skin, and decided that there is nothing sexier than a man barefoot in beat-up old loafers. "What *is* all of that?"

James shrugged. "I found it this morning when I showed the realtor around the house." He eyed it with something that could have been awe, or could have been disgust. "She says it's got to go to show the house to advantage. This closet is big, which I'm told is a great asset."

I picked up one of the fallen boxes and opened it. Brand-new shoes. They were nice Italian leather pumps and absolutely unworn. Not my taste, too conservative, but I can appreciate quality when I see it.

The next box held a jacket and skirt, fully lined, beautifully made, price tag still hanging on the cuff. The next one had the receipt for the silk blouse still in the box alongside it.

Well, here was the evidence. You heard about women shopping just to hoard things, though my sister had had a better reason.

"The shopping spree," I concluded, looking up at James.

"I'm thinking so." He nodded ruefully. "The closet must be full of it. Do you think a charity would pick it up?"

"Are you nuts?"

"I thought you would approve of me giving it to charity. . . ."

"All of this? That would be insane. It's brand-new. And you need cash, don't you?"

James pinched the bridge of his nose. "Don't remind me."

"Then charity begins at home. Take it back."

"What?" He looked truly horrified.

"Don't you take things back?"

"No!"

"You can take things back to the stores," I explained as if he was a slow child. "It's called making a return. They give you your money back. Normal people do it all the time."

"Not me."

"Well, think about it. It's all in the original packaging, it's clean and unworn. Have them put the credit on the hottest cards."

James narrowed his eyes, thinking as he considered the teetering packages. "If this whole closet is full—"

"—then you'll wipe out a ton of that debt. Let's find out." I started digging, then cast him a considering glance. The man was innocent in so many ways of the world, and I was feeling particularly helpful for some odd reason. Couldn't have been that fleeting kiss, no sirree. "You do know the protocol of returning things, don't you?"

"What do you mean?"

"You're not going to walk in there and say 'my wife left me and I'm bringing back all of her stuff for credit.'"

James watched me warily. "Then what *am* I going to say?"

"You're going to lie, obviously. You're going to say that you bought this lovely blouse as a gift"—I shook the silk at him—"but your wife didn't like it. No, she hated it."

"Wrong size?"

"You can't say that, because then they'll want to exchange it for the right size. You can't even say that it's the wrong color, because for all you know, this blouse comes in sixteen delicious shades. No, you'll say she loathes it. You'll say it wasn't what she really wanted, that what she really wanted was a Bolivian cockatiel."

James seemed to be fighting an impulse to smile. "A Bolivian cockatiel?" He folded his arms across his chest and leaned against the wall, watching me as though I was some unpredictable, unusual, and fascinating life-form.

"It's very simple," I said in my most pedantic tone. "You have to pick something that they don't sell. There has to be no chance of them giving you an exchange or a credit slip or a gift certificate. And department stores have so much unexpected merchandise now—you have to go right out there to Weirdland."

"Are there such things as Bolivian cockatiels?"

"I have no idea. But on the off chance that they do indeed sell cockatiels, dollars to doughnuts no one will know whether they're Bolivian or not. You can pretend that you do know." I mimicked James being disappointed by a clerk's paltry offering, doing his upscale accent to perfection. " 'Oh no, the genuine Bolivian cockatiel is distinguished by a fiery red spot upon its tail. Clearly this is not such a bird. I'm sorry, but this simply will not do.' "

"I can't lie just to get a few bucks back." James gave me a disparaging look. "I'm not you, Maralys."

"What is that supposed to mean?"

"That I wouldn't be able to pull it off."

"Right!" I propped one hand on my hip. "As if lying would be something new. As if you've never lied before or persuaded, oh, maybe twelve citizens that the truth is somewhat different than they had thought."

"I don't lie."

"Bull! You've made a career out of it."

His eyes flashed. "I have not!"

"Oh, every single person you've ever defended has been utterly innocent? My, my. Who would have guessed?"

James had the grace to look a bit sheepish. "Well, it's all in the way you present the information."

"Exactly! You're a natural for this."

James grudgingly pulled out a receipt from a bag with a new purse and scrutinized it. His tone was matter-of-fact. "It's not going to work, Maralys. This is Marcia's number from one of her store cards. They won't put a credit on my card. They'll need her card to do the return."

I wasn't nearly that ready to admit defeat. I examined the purse and found the store price tag on it. I waggled it under his nose. "Look at that. Store, price, and SKU number." I plucked the receipt out of his hand, crumpled it, and chucked it over my shoulder. He looked alarmed and I widened my own eyes in dismay. "What a shame you lost the receipt. At least you know where it came from and how much it was since the tag is still on it. Phew! That's a relief."

That smile made a valiant attempt to curve his lips again, but lost one more time. "But I can't say it was a gift then, because any idiot would have taken off the price tag."

"As if. Lots of men wouldn't have because they *are* idiots."

"So now I have to be a lying idiot who misunderstands his wife. Thanks a lot."

"Okay, you can say that she changed her mind about her own purchase. Or that she's gained ten pounds, or maybe had a bad nose job, and won't come out of the house. Be inventive! You're a defense lawyer—you must make shit up all the time."

"But . . ."

I turned on him, exasperated with his determination to find fault. "If you need to look good, say that she's had surgery, poor peachie, and you're running her errands. What a swell guy." I patted his cheek while he glowered at me. "Remember that the customer is always right, ooze some of that charm that you're keeping in reserve, and you'll do pretty well."

One brow arched. "You're acknowledging that I have charm?"

"Well, you keep it stashed away, but I've seen you in action. Butter wouldn't melt and all that."

"Don't make it sound so attractive."

"Sorry, but I'm immune to charm." I shrugged and smiled. "Your loss, I guess."

I shouldn't have said that. I should have known that it would just tempt him to prove me wrong. "You're all talk, Maralys," he said quietly.

"In your dreams."

"How did you know about that?"

I blinked, momentarily at a loss, but it was enough.

James took a step closer. "I can tell just how immune you are." His fingertip landed on my shoulder, and I swallowed as I stared up at him. He probably felt me shiver, because he smiled ever so slightly. That damn dimple was back.

I realized then that the funnel neck was a mistake. It was far too easy for him to touch my cheek, then let his finger wander south as he had the other night. Goose pimples awakened at his touch, and I knew, I just knew, that Mr. Keen Observation had noticed.

"Nice sweater," he mused, then bent and brushed his lips

against my jaw. I was melting. It felt so good that I didn't want to step away, even though I knew I should.

"Should I be flattered that you broke out of the black?"

"Black's a city thing. I didn't want to frighten the locals."

He flicked a look down the sweater neckline. "Is *that* also for the benefit of the locals?"

Clearly, he could see the industrial allure bra. Big trouble, Maralys. BigMistake.com was coming up in my browser. Who knew it was on my list of favorites?

I stepped away, but fast, and nearly tripped when my stiletto snagged in the carpeting. I talked just as fast and one glance told me that James wasn't fooled. "Look, you've got a chance to seriously undo a lot of the damage Marcia has done. Unless, of course, you're chicken. . . ."

He watched me, having way too much fun. "Now, let me get this straight. Who's the chicken here?"

I flipped open another box, ready for a diversion. "Oh, look, these shoes cost $469. Imagine that, for a pair of quite average-looking black slingbacks. And look, they're in pristine condition and the original packaging. Not a scratch. Isn't that funny. I doubt Marcia even tried them on." I waggled them under his nose. "I bet she just bought them because of how much they cost. I bet she just bought them to piss you off."

"A family talent, obviously."

"Does it work?"

"You're better at it than she was."

I was perversely delighted by this. "Is that a compliment?"

"Don't count on it." James snatched up the shoe and carefully snuggled it back into its box. He fitted the lid on top and set the box against one wall. "All right, we make a pile for each store, and I'll get rid of it all this week."

I was aghast. "You can't take everything back at once."

Now he was really exasperated. "Why not? How many rules does this have? How complicated can this be?"

I sat on the puffy chintz chair and shook my head at him. "Think! You can't say that you bought her five thousand dollars' worth of gifts and she hates them all. They won't believe you. They'll think it's hot and call in all sorts of managers. They'll think you're a shoplifter. A particularly well-dressed thief, perhaps, but not a very trustworthy individual."

James sat down, shoved a hand through his hair, and fought for strength. "This is too complicated. It can't be worth it." He scowled at me, and I'm not entirely sure he was talking about the returns.

"It won't be that bad. You just want to do this quietly, one or two items at a time."

"You could help me."

"Not on your life. Lots of department store clerks work four-hour shifts, so you could make maybe three returns a day to the same department without attracting attention."

James looked at the bulging closet. "This will take forever."

I laughed, determined to give him a prod when he needed it. "You're unemployed, sport. You've got nothing but time."

"Isn't that a stroke of luck?" he muttered, eyeing the lot of it.

"And fear not, whatever you can't return, you can take to a consignment shop. A pal of mine runs a good one in the North End: Twice Loved."

James watched me for a long moment. He didn't look angry, though I certainly deserved a snarl for that shot about being unemployed. "Does anything get to you, Maralys?" he finally asked.

"Lots of things, but I do my damnedest not to let it show."

"You do a good job." James shoved to his feet and came back to the closet. He sighed and considered the stack, before glancing quickly my way. "That's one of the things I admire about you."

My heart skipped a beat, and I acknowledged that what might be going on here was genuine attraction, not any kind of surrogate nookie.

Truth was, I was becoming less adverse to the idea of a little action from James. But I'd be damn sure that he was in the clear emotionally before I stepped over the line.

"You're losing your edge, Coxwell. Keep talking like that

and someone might think you liked me." James laughed, then I laughed, then we got down to work.

We were having a beer in the kitchen, much pleased with our efforts, when someone flung open the front door. I assumed it was the realtor, back with another happy couple, and braced myself for her chipper greeting.

"So, when exactly were you planning to tell me?" a woman demanded imperiously, her tone so different from the realtor's that I jumped. I turned from the table to see Beverly Coxwell sailing down the corridor.

I'd met the grande dame of the Coxwell clan once or twice before, but only briefly. My sister never got on with her, and was certain that was because she had never fit with expectations.

It made sense. Beverly's a classic Old Money type, used to wealth and privilege, oozing perfect manners and poise. She's gorgeous, too, even though she's been stinko most times I've seen her. Marcia's issue was that Beverly never forgot or forgave that my sister wasn't from one of the right families. I know that Marcia bitterly resented her sense that the Coxwells didn't think her "good enough" for their prize boy.

On the other hand, I always got the sense that Beverly—unlike the old man—kept more of an open mind than most. I sensed that she was prepared to reevaluate her assessment of anyone who gave her a good reason to do so. Guess Marcia never bothered.

Maybe she just had issues with Marcia, period, not with who Marcia's daddy was.

"Tell you what?" James asked. His words were calmly spoken, but his smile disappeared and that wariness was back in his eyes. I guessed immediately that he hadn't told his mother either about my sister or about his job and that he wasn't going to tell her more than he had to.

Beverly halted on the threshold of the kitchen, doing a double-take when she saw me. Then she shook her head and waved me off with a flick of her fingertips. "Oh, you're the other one." She looked again. "You look younger than she does."

"Thank you. You look pretty good yourself." I had heard, of course, that she and the old man were getting divorced. The change seemed to suit her. I'd never seen her so perky.

Or so sober.

Beverly smiled briefly at me, then glared at James. "I suppose this is Marcia's doing?"

James was perfectly impassive. "What?"

"What do you mean, *what*? What else? That sign on the lawn! Didn't you think I'd be interested in knowing that you were moving? And where are you going to go?"

"I don't know. I haven't looked yet."

Because whatever James got for the house would determine how much was left and thus what he could afford. From the tightness of his expression, I guessed that he wasn't figuring on much.

How like him to solve one problem at a time.

Beverly dropped into another seat at the table and stared fixedly at her son, as though she would pry out his secrets and spread them out in front of us all. "What's going on?" she asked in a quieter tone. "This isn't like you."

"Who's to say what's like me and what's not like me?" James stood and collected the two beer bottles, setting them neatly by the back door.

Beverly glanced at me, maybe smelling easier prey. "What are you doing here? I've never seen you here." She looked between the two of us. "What has happened?"

James stared fixedly out the window into the backyard. Clearly, he didn't want to talk about any of it. I thought his mother had a right to know about my sister's departure. "Marcia's gone. She ran up a lot of debt to try to persuade James to divorce her, then booked when it didn't work."

Beverly pivoted to stare at James's back. "Surely you can still afford the house?" I found her priorities interesting—the status of the real estate, not my sister's location, was what she wanted to confirm.

He shook his head. "House or tuition for the boys. That's the choice."

"Because you have to give her half."

James almost laughed. "She's already spent more than half."

Beverly opened her mouth and closed it again. She looked around the kitchen as if it would supply her with comprehension, as if it would help her decide what to ask and what not to ask. The doorbell chimed and the realtor called from the foyer, as cheery as a sparrow.

I took the last swig of my beer. "If she keeps that up," I muttered as footsteps sounded on the stairs and her patter began for the thousandth time, "I might have to hurt her."

Beverly exhaled mightily. "Yes. I could use a drink." She raised a brow at James, who didn't move, then turned that look upon me.

I shrugged and started to get up. Another beer wouldn't hurt me, either. "Name your poison."

"Sherry, please. And not in a small glass."

"I thought you were quitting," James said quietly when I was halfway across the kitchen to fetch a glass.

His mother looked a little embarrassed. "It's not that easy."

Oh, complications. I stopped to watch. James turned and watched his mother as avidly as she had watched him just moments before. His skepticism was evident, though he didn't speak as harshly to her as he might have. He just wanted the truth. "Have you tried?"

"I'm easing into it." Beverly lifted her chin.

"How many have you had today?"

"Just two. Small ones." She smiled a social smile at me. "But I've had a shock and need a restorative. Be quick about it, M-not-Marcia-girl."

James gave me a look that stopped me cold. He then went to sit with his mother. "You promised," he reminded her gently.

"People break promises all the time, James. I'm old, I'm surly, I'm getting divorced, and I need encouragement."

"Did you go to the AA meeting?"

"You must be joking."

"That's where you're supposed to find encouragement."

"From whom? From average people? I don't think so, James, I don't think that's appropriate at all."

"They're in the same circumstance as you, but they're trying to change."

She flicked her fingers impatiently at me. I pulled out a stool and sat down, a move that clearly didn't thrill her. Her nostrils flared, but she set her sights on James, identifying that he was the logjam here.

"I don't see any reason to change," she informed him. "It comforts me. It hurts no one but me. It makes it easier to face the day."

"You're not facing the day; you're avoiding it."

Good shot. That sounded like something I would say. I was impressed.

Beverly was not. "You've never spoken to me with such impertinence," she charged. "You've ignored me, that's for certain, all of you have, but you have never spoken this way to me. I think maybe it's better to be ignored."

James didn't even blink. "Maybe it's time someone did talk to you this way. Maybe it's time someone showed you the truth."

"You want some truth?" Beverly sat up straighter and her eyes snapped. "I'm not surprised that Marcia left you. I didn't like the girl, she had no class, but you didn't do her any favors. You lived your life in a perfect echo of your father's life—"

"He isn't my father."

"But he was your model all the same. He might as well have been your father—you two are two peas in a pod and always have been. If I'd ever had any gumption, I would have left him. I would have left all of you, all of you men who could never look me in the eye, all of you men who pretended I wasn't even there. If I'd been a stronger person, I would have walked out that door and never looked back."

If she'd thought to shock him, she gambled against the odds.

James returned her challenging glare impassively. "So the sherry is a crutch then," he said quietly. "It's a way to face the bitter reality of your being ignored by your family."

"Don't you mock me, James Edward Coxwell."

"I'm not mocking you." He hauled out a chair and sat down beside her, his expression intent. "Let's toss some truth around, since everyone seems to be in the mood for it. I don't know why the others ignored you then, but I know why I did."

"Because you were ashamed of me." Beverly blinked rapidly, as though clearing tears from her vision. "Obviously."

"No. Because I didn't know you."

She bristled. "What is that supposed to mean?"

James shook his head and took her hand in his. He spoke quietly, as if chiding her. "You're forgetting that I'm the oldest."

"I'm not forgetting anything of the kind. I'm not that much of a lush that I forget the order of my children's births! Don't you dare say that I'm losing my memory because of the sherry. . . ."

"You're forgetting that I'm the only one who remembers you not drinking."

Beverly opened her mouth, then shut it again. She stared at him, shocked to silence.

James's words were low and soft when he continued, and I was amazed at the tenderness in the way he held her hand. "You're forgetting that I remember having a sober mom. The others probably don't."

Beverly blinked. "So what?"

"So I remember you reading to me. I remember you teaching me the names of things, of boats and plants and vegetables. I remember you introducing me to new tastes and new wonders, teaching me new skills, helping me get up that first stair. I remember venturing out in the world, which was a big and frightening place, but knowing that everything would be fine because my mom was holding my hand." He squeezed her fingertips and Beverly looked away. "I remember all the things you did, and all the ways you loved me. Those memories are helping me learn how to be a good parent."

"But, but . . ."

"I remember how much it hurt to see you change," James continued, his voice husky and urgent. Beverly stared at him, one tear easing down her cheek. "I couldn't look at you then because it hurt too much. It wasn't just seeing you that way— it was knowing that I couldn't help you. It was fearing that some part of what happened to you every day might be my fault."

"Never! It was *never* your fault, nor that of your brothers and sister."

"But I was the only one you had mothered that way. How could I not imagine that something I had done sometime, somewhere, something I didn't even remember, had made you not want to be that kind of mom anymore?"

"That's not true."

"I know that now, but I didn't know that then. I was just a kid, just a kid missing his mom."

I thought of Johnny, worrying about Marcia finding them if they moved, and the parallel was pretty evident. Guess Johnny didn't get his sensitivity from his mom.

Beverly was crying openly now, though she didn't seem to care. She leaned forward and kissed James's cheek, then wiped away the residue of her lipstick with a fingertip. "I'm sorry. I'm really sorry. I know I cheated all of you, but you're grown up now."

"People don't grow out of needing a mom."

"Well, they do, in many ways."

"Not the most important ones." James squeezed her hand and obviously tried to coax her smile. "Come on back to us. We'll make it worth your while."

Beverly took a deep breath and her tears welled again. "But it's so hard." Her voice broke and she looked away, then shook her head. It was amazing—now she was going to try to make him smile. "You know, these AA people, they actually expect you to quit drinking. Totally."

Her attempt at a joke fell completely flat. James said nothing, just held fast to her hand, and Beverly rummaged in her purse for a tissue with her free hand.

The realtor bounced into the kitchen, a grim couple in tow. "Now you see the wonderful light in this room. It needs to be completely gutted and renovated, of course, but you could live with it like this for the short term. Imagine, French doors there to a patio, marble counters, new cabinets. The flow into the family room is just fabulous, and if you moved this wall . . ."

It was startlingly offensive to have her talking about the inadequacies of the house that James and Marcia had obviously thought more than adequate. She and her prey continued on to the family room as Beverly sniffled.

"I'll go with you," James said with sudden intensity.

His mother seemed as startled as I was by this offer. "What do you mean?"

"I'll go with you to the AA meetings. I know it won't be easy for you, so I'll go along." He gave her hand a little shake. "Remember when you used to say that I was your pillar of strength?"

She smiled through her tears. "You were *four*!" She turned to me, anxious to let me in on the story, probably because it would give her a chance to think about what he was saying. "Whenever we did something daunting, like crossing the street for the first time, I pretended that I was afraid and told James that he had to be my pillar of strength. He took the responsibility very seriously, that was my boy." She smiled at him with undisguised pride. "How can you remember that?"

"I remember everything. That's why I want to help you. We'll go together, Mom. It will be easier for you."

"You haven't called me Mom in years."

"Maybe it's time I started again."

Beverly traced a circle on the kitchen table, uncertain but encouraged. "But you can't have time. With Marcia gone and the boys, you have so much to do. . . ."

James laughed, then glanced at me, though it was more than the sight of that dimple that made my heart skip. "I'm unemployed, Mom. It's a matter of record that I've got nothing but time."

The barracuda had a heart. He kept it well hidden, but I was touched that he would do this for Beverly. We were having a certified Disney moment. Bring back Bambi's mom, let's have a song and a rainbow over the whole scene.

Then James blew it.

"Any chance you could help us out, Maralys?"

I did my best Jack Frost. "I beg your pardon?"

"The boys aren't going to be going to any AA meetings with us."

Just a few words and I saw red. An endless stream of weekday nights camped out with the small adults stretched out before me and I snapped. How many years do people go to AA, anyhow? I didn't know and I didn't want to find out.

How *dare* he expect me to take my sister's place?

How dare he expect me to leap in, as a convenient babysitter?

I hauled out one of my business cards and snapped it on the table. I have them printed on thick stock just so they make a nice crisp sound in moments like this.

"Maybe you don't have one of my cards," I said coldly. They both looked at me, Beverly with incomprehension, James with wariness. "Pick it up. What does it say?"

"Maralys O'Reilly. Web-based Solutions," he read without intonation.

"Does it say Registered Charity?"

"No."

"Does it say Baby-sitting Services? Daycare?" My voice rose with each question and I didn't care. "Chauffeur? Incidental housekeeping services? *Surrogate?*"

"Hmm," said Beverly and looked at her son.

James was getting red around the back of his neck. "Maralys, I just asked—"

"I know what you asked. I heard what you asked! You asked what you've been asking ever since my sister left. Would I pretend to be her for the time being as it would be just so much easier for you. No! NO! How many times do I have to say it? These are not my kids. This is not my life!"

"Look, I just asked—"

"I've stepped in to help, but that's *enough*! This is not going to become some cozy convenient little habit: 'Oh, we can just call Maralys. It's not as if she has a life.'" I cast my hands skyward, something I've always wanted to do. "I will *not* be convenient! I will not be *useful*! I will not be *needed*, especially not by you."

"Especially?" James asked, catching the one word of importance in my tirade.

You have to know that I covered my slip as best as I could. I stepped forward and shook my finger under his nose. My voice was lower now and shaking. "All these years I've been *persona non grata* in this household. How's that for some Latin, my friend? I've been insulted, by you, I've been disparaged, by you, I've been judged, by you, and I've been shunned, by you."

"Maralys, I'm sorry—"

"How timely of an apology is that?" I snapped. It didn't help that James looked genuinely contrite. He probably got that mail order—in his former job, he'd need a lot of it. "You apologize right when you need a regular sitter. Well, guess what, this isn't going to follow your script."

"If you'd just give me a chance to explain—"

"No, I won't. I've done what I've done so far for the boys and for my dad, but that's it. I made a resolution years ago that I wouldn't be taken for granted ever again." I shook my head. "If you think I'm going to back down on that for you, you've got another thing coming."

I scooped up my keys and turned to leave.

"Maralys!"

"Sorry, this offer has expired. Look—best before last Tuesday. I'm fresh out of family obligation."

"How about *listening* for a change?" James shouted. "How about finding out the truth?"

I glanced back, big mistake. He was really, really angry with me. I very nearly went back and listened, but the timing was too opportune for him.

His mother was watching the exchange avidly, and I felt myself begin to blush. Just what I needed.

And I was really, really angry with *him* anyhow. "You

don't know what the truth is," I said. "And you wouldn't believe it if you heard it."

"Try me." His eyes were bright with challenge as he began to walk toward me. He was goading me and we both knew it. The air crackled between us, but I held my ground, waiting for him to get to me. He stared down at me, and we were definitely thinking the same thing.

"Don't go," he whispered with urgency.

"I don't play the rebounds," I whispered back just as urgently, then I pivoted before I lost my nerve.

"It's not over, Maralys."

"It never started. There's nothing here to *be* over." I spun and glared at him through the storm door, tears unexpectedly blurring my vision. "All I've ever wanted is to be left alone. All I've ever expected of people is that they solve their own problems. All I've ever wanted was to live my own life and pursue my own dreams. Is that so much to ask? Is that so impossible for anyone to allow?"

James shoved his hands into the pockets of his jeans, his expression inscrutable. "No," he said quietly. "It's not."

I hadn't expected him to agree, or least to do so as readily as that. I floundered for a moment for my footing, then came up fighting. "Good. Good! Then you can drive my father home. I'll leave his car where I found it."

I marched back to the K, a splendid chariot if ever there was, feeling like an ass every step of the way.

"Oh, my," said the chirpy realtor, and I didn't even look to see who she had in tow this time. "It looks as if I might be able to get you two a bargain on this house. You know, you can often make a good deal in the instance of a d-i-v-o-r-c-e."

I squealed the tires, delighting in how many neighbors came to look, and was back at my dad's in half the time. I felt sick, but I really didn't know whether it was because I had lost my temper, because I had said too much, or because I had just done the wrong thing.

I told myself that I didn't care.

Okay, it was a lie, but we're going to live with that one. Get over it now. I'm going to.

I had my dream that night.

Well, in the wee hours of the morning actually, since I didn't crash until around four A.M., that is.

The dream always starts the same way. I've had it for years, over and over and over again, and I still can't explain it. I'm in an airline terminal. It could be Logan or just about anywhere else. They all look so similar, although there's something not quite right about this one. It's a dream thing.

When it starts, I'm at the baggage claim, where the conveyor or carousel or whatever brings the luggage from the plane. This one's a conveyor and it's not moving yet. There are no bags. There's a crowd of people though, standing all around me, and it's a crowd that keeps getting bigger.

It also keeps getting more anxious. You can feel the tension in the air, the unspoken worry that the bags really aren't here. Or that one particular bag—yours—is lost. Maybe gone to Shanghai instead.

So, I'm standing there, staring at the opening that the bags first appear from, thinking that it's like a dark little mouth to who knows where. I always think that at the beginning of the dream, and I always think what a weird thing it is for me to think. I, too, am skeptical and a little tense about the arrival of my luggage.

The conveyor starts and the crowd pushes forward, jostling for position. The bags start to appear, and people snatch them off the belt, claiming them before they can disappear into the dark little mouth at the other end of the conveyor. Maybe they won't come back. The anxiety changes flavor. Speed is key.

I see a familiar bag and shove through the crowd, claiming it victoriously. It is, oddly enough, the impossibly pink suitcase in which my sister kept her Barbies when we were kids. (I did not have Barbies.) My name is on the tag, though, and no one seems to think it strange that a grown woman has checked a bag emblazoned with "Barbie," complete with little cartoons on the side.

I carefully check the latch and am always struck by the oddity of this gesture. It's a kid's toy. The latch is a cheap flip latch that wouldn't stop a goldfish, but I'm always ridiculously relieved to find it still closed. It's one of those round bags that would be a hatbox if there wasn't a hinge on the lid and a loop handle at the opposite side.

And pink, as I've mentioned. Pink!

Meanwhile, people have been snagging bags and claiming carts, and the area is beginning to bustle. I look up just in time to see my backpack from the Japanese adventure lolling on the conveyor. It's black canvas and beaten up, wearing the mark of the miles it's logged like a badge of honor.

It's also pretty round because there's so much junk in it, as well as heavy. I drag it off the conveyor, checking that its Boston Bruins crest and rising sun flag are both intact. It has a dusty footprint on it, a man's bootprint, presumably from some guy on the ramp. I try to brush it off, with no luck.

Next is a big plastic tub with a snap lid—like an oversize Tupperware dish—that I got at Ikea and use to store files in my office. God only knows why it's been checked onto a plane, but no one finds this remarkable, either. It's similarly full to bulging, but fortunately is equipped with wheels. I wrestle it off the conveyor myself, load the backpack on top of it, and carry the Barbie case separately.

And here's the weird part. I don't know whether this is all my stuff. I can't remember. I don't have the ticket with the luggage claim tags stapled into it, so there's no way to be sure. I stand there, stupidly uncertain, waiting until the conveyor brings no new bags forth from its shadowy maw.

This part of the dream worries me a great deal. I know that I toss and turn at this point. In fact, I often wake up even now, a conditioned response from Neil jabbing me in the ribs so many times when we shared a bed.

This time I slept through it. That's happened once or twice before, but knowing what will happen doesn't make it any easier to bear.

I'm very anxious as I leave the luggage claim area, very anxious. I'm constantly looking over my shoulder, worried that I've forgotten something. Classic travelers' paranoia—where's my ticket passport wallet key—but multiplied a hundred times. I even look back through the glass, from the corridor outside the secured area.

And that's when I see it. It's a Bonnie Cashin bag, the kind you wear under your coat like a secret pocket. It's made of red leather and it's mine, I know it's mine, and there's something making it bulge and it's on the conveyor all by itself. A late arrival. It's mine and I'm on the wrong side of the security barrier. The terminal is empty now. There's no one else coming out of the claim area, no chance to sneak back in and get my bag.

I can't claim it.

I press my face to the glass as it disappears into the other dark hole, filled with terror until it comes back around. I pound on the glass as the bag slides effortlessly past me, I shout and scream but there's no one there to hear me. And the bag goes around and around, appearing and disappearing, a glorious prize out of my reach forever and beyond my control to retrieve.

And on that night, that's when I looked up and saw the sign over the conveyor that I never noticed before:

EMOTIONAL BAGGAGE CLAIM.
PLEASE ENSURE THAT ANY LUGGAGE
YOU CLAIM IS YOUR OWN.

I woke abruptly, my heart pounding, my eyes bugging out of my head. It was eleven in the morning, and my sheets were knotted around me, wet with sweat.

I fell back and closed my eyes, trying to stabilize my breathing even as I wondered what the hell it all meant.

Me? Emotional baggage? I think not.

Or at least I think it completely stowed under the seat in front of me. Surely I couldn't be wrong.

Subject: all show no go

Dear Aunt Mary—

All my boyfriend wanted was sex, sex, and
more sex! I used to say to him, "Is there
something wrong with wanting to talk?"

Yes, there is! Now I know. Suddenly all he
wants to do is talk. Yap yap yap and no
action.

:-/
Do you think he's getting the rest
somewhere else?

Worried

Subject: re: all show no go

Dear Worried:

What is it with you people? Sex, sex, and
more sex—it's all you ask me about. Talk
about a fixation.

As for you, there's an old proverb, my
dear—be careful what you ask for, as you
might get it. You've just proven it right.

Maybe he's mucking around. Maybe your
relationship has gone to a new level. Maybe

you ought to be glad you got what you
wanted.

Aunt Mary
***
Uncertain? Confused? Ask Aunt Mary!
Your one-stop shop for netiquette and advice:
http://www.ask-aunt-mary.com

Oh, yes, I didn't miss the irony in that particular little post
turning up at this particular moment.

Thing was, it was quiet, vewy quiet, in my life and had
been since I lost it in James's kitchen three weeks before.
Three weeks. That's a long time. He'd mailed me the new
contract—nice personal touch there—without so much as a
scribble from his own pen. It was a thing of beauty—of a particularly nasty, legalistic kind of beauty, but one designed to
protect me. That was a nice thing.

It might not have been all bad to have a pet shark.

I spun slowly in my orthopedically correct chair and
launched paper airplanes around the loft. Spring has sprung,
the grass has riz, I wonder where the Coxwells is.

You see, I'm not really used to people getting on without
me. I had pretty much expected James to call again, begging
me to reconsider. Not immediately, but in a couple of days.

He hadn't. By now I'd figured out that he wasn't going to.

I am not used to men who can actually resolve anything by
themselves. Not just my dad, either. There was what's-his-
name, Neil, the original cowboy and perennial six-year-old,
the all-time master of offloading responsibility. He wasn't the
first and he wasn't the last, but he gave me a major lesson in
fixing it myself. Anything and everything, that is.

But enough about that.

I had spent my entire life trying to defend my privacy and
my independence, and done so without a whole lot of success.
Now that I had utter solitude, I didn't much care for the view.

And yes, I wanted to *know*. Bring on the details and the

gossip. Had Beverly gone to AA? Had James gone with her? I could easily imagine him virtually dragging her there—surprise sentimentality aside, he struck me as the kind of guy who would make you eat your broccoli because it was good for you. Had they moved? I found it daunting that I might not even know where the heck they lived.

And not just because my sister might suddenly turn up and need redirection. It was starting to look unlikely that she was going to do that.

In fact, I was a bit worried about her, too. She wasn't exactly the queen of keeping in touch and we weren't close, but three weeks is a long time. I have a very good imagination, and in the middle of the night, I came up with all kinds of dire fates for her. No one seemed to be sounding an alarm though, so maybe she had called in.

I spun and chucked another airplane, trying desperately not to feel as if I'd been left out of the loop.

What's that? I'd asked for it, hadn't I? Thanks for the reminder.

Had James really taken Marcia's shopping spree back? I would have given a buck to see him in action, that's for sure. I would have bet that he did do it—he seemed pretty motivated to get stuff done. Yeah, he'd had that gleam in his eye when I showed the price tag of those shoes. Marcia had succeeded in pissing him off, though a bit later than she'd hoped to do so.

Which made me think of another gleam that had been in his eye, and that on more than one occasion. Ah, yes, the one that made Captain V seem a pale shadow of his former studly glory. I knew I shouldn't want any part of that.

But then. But then . . . I felt as Eve might have felt if she'd taken a pass on the apple. Probably not a good idea, probably better to have walked away, but jeez, what would that sucker have tasted like? She'd never know.

And who could stop after one bite? Wouldn't she have wanted another?

It bugged me.

This did not mean, however, that I was going to call anyone up and confess as much. No way, cowboy. My sister and I have one thing in common—we believe that when the going gets tough, the tough go shopping.

Besides, there was a celebration coming up, and I needed something wow for Amnesty Day. I knew just where to get it, too—my pal Meg runs the best vintage and used clothing store in Boston—which is saying something, and not just that I have a biased opinion. Not only would I find something unique and possibly outrageous, but it would be a bargooneroo. I might not find it on the first try, though, and should give Meg some warning as to what I was after.

The prospect of social contact cheered me enormously, but then I'd been working too hard lately. Time for a break. I'd been good, I'd worked hard, and I deserved a treat, at least.

A latte that I hadn't made myself.

It was raining cats and dogs, but I skipped through the puddles, in a huge hurry to get to Meg's.

What? You're suggesting that I might be lonely?

Bite your tongue. I think NOT. Dillydallying only means that the good stuff might be gone.

But true confessions time—I actually spoke to someone on the T and that without provocation. Something banal about the weather. A perfect stranger. And I initiated the conversation.

Maybe I really was losing it.

I scored an extra-large fancy java, reassured myself with a sip, and bopped on. Meg's shop is small, on a knotted little street in the North End, nestled between a bakery and a place that offers almost-ready-to-eat Italian food. If nothing else, her shop always smells great.

I stopped cold outside Meg's crowded display window, my double mocchiato steaming. It wasn't the dress that stopped me—it was the man's suit beside it. It looked vewy familiar.

Could it be?

Had to be. I was sure it was a dead ringer for the suit James had been wearing the day I stopped at his office. My heart did that stupid skip-dee-diddle thing, but that was ridiculous. How much do I know about men's suits?

I knew enough about men to heartily doubt that James had even heard my suggestion, let alone followed it. Give up the toys and trophies? Not a chance. Let the brats starve first.

My heart was still beating too fast when I marched into the shop. To say that Meg looked giddy would have been an understatement. She was glowing and when she saw me, she hooted for joy, then gave me a hug so tight that I nearly spilled the divine nectar.

"Hey! This is the good stuff!"

"Sorry sorry sorry." I should warn you that Meg talks without taking a breath. It's dizzying at first, but you get used to it. "It's just so exciting so perfect and I can't believe it's true you won't believe what happened a week ago Monday. . . ."

"What?"

"I was worried about my rent because it's been slow you know too slow really too *too* slow and I was wondering whether I should move to Cambridge but then I wouldn't have the money to move as they'd want first and last and I don't even have any to cover my rent here so I was feeling really glum. . . ."

"And?"

"And this guy this *guy* this hunk of guy who is just a bit taller than the norm very good-looking by the way brought in a ton of stuff just tons of stuff *designer* stuff in perfect condition and he brought it here *here!* and it's perfect just perfect all of it perfect. Look!"

She dived into a rack of menswear and started touching the sleeves of an array of excellent men's suits. She stroked them as though they were pets, her fingers straying over the fabric, tweaking labels, then occasionally rising to her lips in awe.

"This one's Gucci and this one's Ermenegildo Zegna and this one's a Boss and this one oh *another* Zegna just too wonderful—feel this!—silk and wool blends and pure wool and European craftsmanship and exquisite condition all dry-cleaned and oh!"

She caught her own flushed face in her hands and sat down hard on a stool. She actually took a deep breath. "I was so sure he was in the wrong place I had to tell him that he'd probably get a better price from Keezer's but he was insistent oh yes very insistent and I put such prices on it oh how could I not because it's in such good shape and he was so nice that I couldn't get him less than he should get from the consignment and oh Maralys I've sold more than half of it!"

Tears glittered in her eyes and she clutched my hands. "It was so lucky so perfect that I knew I just knew that someone was looking out for me so I went and had my cards read and guess what guess *what*?"

Meg bounced a bit, as she always did after a good tarot card reading. I smiled and sipped. "What?"

She spread her hands and looked at the ceiling, carefully recalling the fortune verbatim. I was struck by how much she resembled the Madonna in the church we had gone to every Sunday as kids. Her hair was long and blond, kind of kinky and spread over her shoulders like worked gold. Meg's face is a little round and very sweet, and she has the biggest, most soulful brown eyes in the world.

Well, except for those of the Madonna.

"A man will sweep into your life," she recounted with awe. "Your fortunes will change dramatically for the better as a result of his influence. You will ride into summer's abundance ripe with possibilities." Her smile flashed. "Isn't that great? Do you think he's The One do you do you? I could be pregnant by the summer!"

I laughed a bit under my breath, then began to browse. "Meg, they're all The One, at least you think so at the beginning. You've got to get over this idea that your life isn't complete without a man."

"Not just a man not just any man but *the* man The One Maralys aren't you listening?" She trailed behind me, including opinions on everything I touched in the midst of what she was saying. "Not just a guy in my bed but a lover in my life—oh Maralys surely not that dress—a partner a soulmate—it's not your color—my divine soulmate and better half—the zipper's out of that I can fix it but it's not worth the price she insists upon—my *destiny*!" She sighed rapturously. "He's gorgeous in kind of an uptight sort of a way kind of auburnish hair—you can't wear green we've been through this a thousand times it's your complexion—and tall definitely tall I've had to shorten the pants for one buyer but the most marvelous eyes . . ."

"Hazel."

Meg blinked and looked at me, astounded to comparative silence. "How did you know that?"

"He's my brother-in-law. My sister walked and he was cleaning out her stuff. A lot of it was new, so I told him to take it back, then bring the rest to you."

Her features lit again. "Maralys! I love you!" She threw her arms around my neck, nothing but exuberant our Meg, and gave me a big smacking kiss. "You saved me!"

"Well, no, not really." I was embarrassed by this show of affection, though it said much for my recent isolation that I endured it. "I didn't think he'd do it."

"You are so full of shit, Maralys." She punched me in the shoulder and we grinned at each other, then she cocked her head. "He's cute."

"Mmm. In a way." I sauntered down the aisle, taking advantage of the opportunity to turn my back on her. Meg knows me too well.

"So why'd you come?" She was right behind me. "Checking up on him?"

I snorted. "Hardly. I need something wow."

"How wow?"

"Really wow." I spun and snapped my fingers, as if I was remembering the idea which I'd just had. What was a celebration without other people? It wasn't as if I didn't have space. "Which reminds me. I'm having a party in two months and you're invited."

"What's the occasion?"

"Tax freedom. The official elimination of the fiscal burden of Neil."

"Awesome! Oh, I'll be there!" Meg pursed her lips and considered her inventory. "But now we need two wows."

"Did James bring any women's stuff?" So maybe I *was*

checking up on him. Or maybe I was just tempted by the prospect of a good deal.

There would have been something weird about buying one of my sister's castoffs, and I doubt I would have done it, but I was wondering, you know?

Meg was on a roll again, fingers trailing over her stock. "Yeah a few things brand-new like you said and of quite recent vintage but I took them because they'll move easily and they did some are gone already though I don't think you'll like any of it since it's kind of conservative for you and not your size." She was back in her usual mode, brow furrowed. "This designer stuff is hell to alter all those linings and flat-felled seams to pick out and replicate and it's not worth it unless you just can't live without the piece here let me show you."

She pulled out a cocktail dress, and we both grimaced.

"Who knew they made fabric in puce?"

Meg clicked her tongue. "It's called soft salmon, Maralys."

"How do you know that?"

She flicked the label. "It's from that snotty boutique on Mass that's so bitchy about returns that they won't make any so I take their stuff here and actually have a few people who come looking for it because they like the merchandise but hate the store."

I knew the place she meant, though I'd never set foot in it. I had a sudden image of James, in that boutique, talking earnestly about Bolivian cockatiels, and I started to laugh. Damn near spilled my coffee, too.

"What's so funny?"

"Nothing. Well, nothing that I could explain easily anyhow." Meg kept giving me That Look. "Okay, I didn't warn him about that place. Maybe I owe him an apology."

"You owe him my thanks in a big way and hey if you're going to see him will you take a check along? I owe James Coxwell some major money and he said he was moving soon so I don't have an address."

This seemed most unlike our boy. "What did he tell you to do with it?"

"He said he'd come back in but I wasn't expecting to sell so much so fast and he might want the cash."

I looked at the cocktail dress and remembered his assertion that Marcia and I shared a genetic ability to tick him off. "You'd better stick with his plan." I grinned. "Now, come on, I need a knock-out dress."

"I'm going to *give* you a dress for sending me this business so pick a good one."

"Oh, that's a smart move, Meg."

"What?"

"You're on the verge of bankruptcy so you're going to give stuff away. You know that I will pick the best dress you have."

"You probably will. You have great taste."

"And I'm prepared to pay for the dress. I've saved my pennies and all, so don't even go there."

Meg eyed me for a long moment and looked suspiciously as if she might cry.

I flung out my hands. "Where would I shop without you? Nope, this is a purely selfish decision on my part. I *need* this store."

"You are full of it, Maralys," she said with undisguised affection. I, amazingly, did not get a hive. You must be able to work up a basic immunity to this mushy stuff. Meg surveyed me skeptically. "But I will find you the very best dress. What color is your hair going to be on May 15?"

"Whatever color it needs to be. You can choose."

"I like that." She smiled and set to searching.

It was hours before I got out of there and hours after that— in the wee hours of the morning, in fact—that I got cold feet about the party. Dozens of people in my cave, touching my things, thinking they were my pals. Easy, sport. Who else should I ask?

Who *shouldn't* I ask?

Ah, yes, what about The James Question?

Fact was, I kind of missed the incisive commentary. He tended to call my chips as fast as I called his. Maybe it was a sparring of equals that I craved.

He certainly didn't duck and run like Neil had. Good old

Neil. I wondered whether he was still in Baja, then wondered whether he had managed to incur as much new debt as what I was coming close to paying off. Yep, big-sucker move there to go for a joint partnership. That's how the IRS got my number—that's how I got left holding the proverbial bag.

I wondered whether some unfortunate chick had just realized that she too was holding a bag of debt, courtesy of Neil, who had suddenly departed to parts unknown. It was as ancient history as James's Romans to me, though.

And James, I knew, was not the kind to leave anyone to do his dirty work. You had to like that in a guy. A woman like me really had to like that in a guy. Still, if I called him, it would be showing a weakness. Not my style. I launched an aircraft carrier's worth of paper airplanes—all with exceedingly excellent design—while I waffled. The fallen glowed in the light from the monitors, a fleet of indecision all over the hardwood floors.

Then, as so often happens, the phone rang and Fate decided what was going to happen next.

"Hello?"

A long silence was my only response.

I turned down the stereo, the hair on the back of my neck prickling like crazy. "Hello? Is anyone there?"

"M—" It was just a hoarse whisper, but I would have known it anywhere.

"Dad? Dad, what's happened?" Hysteria had me by the short hairs and was giving me a shake. "Are you there? Are you all right?" I was scrambling for my coat and praising cordless phones all the way across the loft. "What's happened? Dad, talk to me!"

"I fell." The words came in an exhalation, a single helpless and hopeless sound that made my blood run cold.

No, no, no, this was not the script I ordered up.

Make it stop.

Make it stop now.

"Okay, Dad, listen up. I'm coming. I'll be there in ten. Don't move, don't do anything, don't answer the door. I've got my keys. Understand?" He didn't answer, I could barely hear him breathing over the sound of my own heart. Deep breath. Time for levity, Maralys. Being freaked will just freak him.

"Are you there, Dad?" I asked sternly. "Because if you are, you'd better tell me that you won't do anything stupid, like start tap-dancing on the tables like you always do. I want to find you snoozing comfortably by the phone when I get there, okay?"

A little sound that could have been a laugh. "Okay."

Okay. It was going to be okay.

I didn't believe it for a minute. That was why I ran like hell. I ran right in front of a cab—they aren't anxious to stop in this neighborhood at such a time, and my erratic behavior didn't reassure this guy.

"My dad. He's old, he fell, I gotta get there." I shouted at his window. He unlocked the back door, persuaded by my entreaty or my possible insanity, I don't know.

But he moved. He squealed the tires and rocked, before I even had the door closed. You've got to love a stranger who runs a very red red, just for you.

"You call 911?"

I balled my hands in my pockets and watched the vacant windows of the sleeping city fly past. "It might not be that bad," I whispered. The cabbie flicked a look at me in the rearview, and I knew that my manner betrayed that fleeting hope. "It might not be that bad," I said again, then closed my eyes.

Right, Maralys. And the moon is made of green cheese. Why not serve yourself up a slice?

The wise cabbie handed me his cell and I dialed.

Subject: teenage girls

Dear Aunt Mary—

My daughters are driving me insane. They
won't listen to me. They won't do what
they're told. They dress like sluts and
stay out half the night. What am I going to
do—besides scream myself hoarse every day?

At the end of the rope

Subject: re: teenage girls are aliens

Dear Rope End—

In a supreme sacrifice to this advice
column when it was no more than a gleam in
her eye, Aunt Mary had her reproductive
organs removed and burned, purely to ensure
that she could gather a wealth of
experience regarding sexual relations
without ever having to learn a thing about
kids. This I did selflessly for all of you
that you might reap the benefits of my
wisdom.

Which is a long way of saying—you're on
your own.

And you owe me.

Aunt Mary
***
Uncertain? Confused? Ask Aunt Mary!
Your one-stop shop for netiquette and advice:
http://www.ask-aunt-mary.com

So, I was sitting in the waiting room at Mass General, wondering what the hell I was going to do. Truth is that I'm not crazy about hospitals, and Mass General is my least favorite. Bad memories in a major way. It gave me the crawls just to cross the threshold.

But what choice did I have?

Dr. Moss had been in the hospital and had come 'round to see my dad. I didn't ask what she was doing in the hospital in the dead of the night, much less why she looked pooped, just listened glumly to her prognosis.

Dad had chipped his hipbone when he fell and though it wasn't broken, it would be painful in the healing. She didn't think he should live alone anymore. I thought it would kill him to lose his independence.

Stalemate.

She suggested all the usual options of nursing homes and senior facilities, but I knew the only way he'd leave that house would be in a box. I couldn't articulate it, though, because I was still all jumbled up from finding him crumpled on the floor of the kitchen, as frail as a bird, the phone clutched in his hand.

The ambulance had been right behind me, a damn good thing because I wouldn't have remembered the number to 911 right then and there. Your health-care dollars at work, God bless them.

Thing was, I could understand the old bugger. If we put him in a home, we'd be telling him that he wasn't fit to be an adult anymore. He'd die of that as much as anything.

I could appreciate his desire to go down swinging, to die with his boots on, as it were. His dignity seemed like such a small thing to grant him, yet at the same time, something protective within me wanted to shield him from his own frailty.

From himself.

Clearly, anyone with a speck of independence would find that sentiment insulting. I was insulted with myself for even having it. So I sat there and worried over it.

Dad was sedated now and sleeping, the morphine having ended his flirting with the nurses and his insistence that he was fine. It was over, but I couldn't make myself go home, so I sat vigil in the hall, sorting through my own tangled feelings. They didn't even have any magazines there, which was worse than having just bad ones. There was no escape from my thoughts.

I had dug in there deep, so I jumped into the stratosphere when James suddenly sat down beside me.

"Hi." His composure was perfectly unruffled, as if we'd run into each other at the supermarket, instead of in the geriatrics ward at 3:45 on a Thursday morning. He looked tired, I noticed, though he smiled a little bit for me.

My heart took a lunge for my mouth. It didn't help when his thigh bumped against mine. He was wearing jeans again and a shirt that looked as though he'd picked it up off the floor. He'd combed his fingers with his hair and those details, as well as the concern in his eyes, told me why he was here.

The man was sexy enough to eat. I can't resist men who do the right thing, especially when my guts are strewn on the tiles all around me.

"How did you know?"

"They called me." He sighed and exhaled. "Is he okay?"

I shrugged. "Chipped hipbone, wounded pride. He'll get over it, but they don't want him to go back to the house alone."

James watched me carefully, no doubt reading all sorts of nuances in my answer. "They said they called because there was nobody here with him."

"What? Right! Who did he call when he fell?" I laughed, though I sounded a bit hysterical. My voice rose with each sentence. "Who picked him up off the floor? Who called 911?

Who rode in the goddamned ambulance with him? Am I that fucking invisible?"

James put his hand over mine and squeezed hard. He said nothing.

I took a deep breath, closed my eyes, and enjoyed the sense of not being all alone for a heady moment. Then I shook off his grip and wrapped my arms around my chest. I was amazed to realize that I was shaking, but I put a bold front on it. Surprise. "I mean, bureaucracy is one thing, but that's ridiculous."

"Oh, I think the nurse meant well," James said. "Your father told her that he was alone and directed her to my phone number in his trousers. I'd called him last night to give him our new address."

"Ah." I stared at the opposite wall, a hard knot in my gut. I ought to be getting used to this story by now, but it always shocks me.

"He's probably confused, Maralys," James said gently.

"Confused, my ass! He called me, he knows damn well that I'm here. I'm just not good enough for him, though I'll do when he's in a jam." I got up to pace the corridor and let my bitterness show a bit more than usual. "It's the same old shit."

James said nothing. Maybe he knew I was right. Maybe he thought it didn't matter whether I was right or not, because I wasn't in a mood to listen to alternative views.

Whatever. I stalked to the end of the hall, stared out at the city with my hands shoved in my pockets. I fought back my tears, called myself a weeny, then paced back. I sat down beside him with a thump.

I was glad to have some company, and though he didn't look inclined to move, I wasn't quite ready to scare James away. I tried to make conversation.

"So, you moved then." I wasn't going to be disappointed that he didn't tell me about it, because I'd said I didn't want to know and admitting that I did indeed want to know would make him leap to false conclusions. I *didn't* want to know, even if I forgot that part sometimes. So Johnny could have peace of mind. That's all."

James smiled a crooked, exhausted kind of smile. "Well, sort of."

"What does that mean?"

He shook his head, grimaced, and looked very boyish. "I had no idea we had so much crap in that house."

I smiled despite myself. "Good thing you're gainfully un-employed."

He chuckled and leaned back, closing his eyes as he stretched out his legs and crossed them at the ankles. "I could sleep for a week. Muscles hurt that I forgot I had."

"Ah, it's good for you."

He smiled, his eyes opening just enough to reveal a bright slit. "Just playing that 'anything that doesn't kill you makes you stronger' theme song, are you? Do you know any other tunes?"

I resisted the urge to smile back. Barely. "No, I don't. How'd the returns go?"

He shook his head with concern, and for a moment I thought my advice had tanked. "Did you know that there's a shocking shortage of Bolivian cockatiels in this city? It's in-credible."

I couldn't help but laugh. "Damn. And that's the only thing that she wanted for her birthday. What's a guy to do?"

"Yeah, it's no wonder she left." We chuckled together, though I was surprised that he could kid around about my sis-ter's departure. I concluded that things really had been dead in the water there for a long time.

And yes, I was glad. It was quite nice sitting like this. Easy but slightly electric, too. I felt much better than I had just a few minutes before, though nothing much had changed. Okay, a handsome man was flirting with me. That had changed. And yes, I'm woman enough that I enjoyed it.

"You owe me, by the way," James said, his voice deli-ciously low.

"For what?"

"For not warning me about that store on Mass Ave."

I fought my smile. "Bad?" I asked with all the innocence I could muster.

James gave me a look that told me he wasn't fooled. I grinned but he shook his head, solemnity personified. "They could make a fortune, bottling that hostility and selling it to trial lawyers."

"Is that a joke?" I studied his features, but there was no hint of laughter. Still, I was thinking of that mouse and had the definite sense that he was messing with me.

"Can't be. It's a matter of record that I have no sense of humor." The man turned a smile on me that was as dazzling as sunshine after a storm. "Gotcha!" he whispered, his eyes twinkling.

"You didn't fool me."

James snorted. "Big talk, Maralys. What are you going to do when someone finally calls your bluff?" He slanted me a glance that set everything in me to sizzling, and I couldn't think of an answer. I couldn't think of much but him, as a matter of fact, and whether he intended to be the one to do the honors.

Never mind what the heck I'd do then.

I tried to make us both remember the link between us. "Has anyone heard from Marcia? Is she okay?"

James smiled. "There you go, protecting your own again."

"I am not!"

"You certainly are." He leaned his elbows on his knees and watched me. "Come on, admit it. You're worried about Marcia, aren't you? Is there a little chink in your armor there? Some vestigial concern for your own blood? Go ahead, 'fess up, Maralys. Your secret's safe with me."

"Well." I fidgeted. "It's a big scary world out there. Lots of sickos. Who wouldn't be concerned?"

He nodded once, then looked away. "Well, don't worry. She's apparently been calling your dad."

Hmm, I wondered how James felt about that. No matter how dead things were, it had to be insulting that she talked to her daddy instead of her husband. No less that she was probably wanting to know about her kids.

Why wouldn't she call *them,* at least? I remembered how concerned Johnny had been and felt a new surge of anger at my sister. "So, where is she?"

James shrugged. "I don't know. I don't ask. She's fine evidently, she's made her choice, and we're all moving on."

I stared at him, amazed at his noncommittal tone. I touched his arm gently. "It really stunk, didn't it?"

"It always stunk, Maralys." He spoke with a heat that surprised me, as if he felt cheated. "It stunk from the day we exchanged our vows, maybe it even stunk before that. I tried, I really tried, you have to believe that I did. Marriage is *important.* But my trying never mattered. It was never enough. I was never enough. I always thought things would get better, that they had to get better with time."

"But they never did."

James shook his head once, firmly. Case closed. Soliloquy over.

"Then why didn't you want to get divorced?"

He heaved a sigh. "At first, because I thought marriage was supposed to be for keeps."

"For better or for worse."

He nodded. "Then there were the boys."

"You didn't find them under a cabbage leaf."

"Maybe we thought children would make things easier between us. Maybe we thought that was what was lacking."

"And?"

"They made life busier, that's for sure. And they added obligations, which made it harder to think about splitting up, for me at least. I thought it would be better for the boys to have us together. The illusion of a normal family, at least. I wanted them to have a sense of security, if nothing else, no matter how it screwed up my own life. I made my choices, after all, and I was ready to live with them."

"Hero sacrifices all chance of happiness for children's self-esteem."

"You can joke about it all you want, Maralys, but it's important to me. The most important thing anyone can do is raise their kids well."

"Even at your own expense?"

He shrugged. "That seems to be how the deal works out. And you know, you don't mind surrendering something yourself to give them a better shot. Maybe that's part of good parenting. Trying to leave something lasting in your kids. The world's tough enough without worrying whether your parents are behind you."

"Guess you've lived that."

"Mmm. You have to remember that I grew up in a family that looked good on the outside but was a mess on the inside. Maybe I assumed that was how it had to be."

"Liar."

There was that smile again. "Okay, maybe I thought we were better at hiding the truth from them than we were."

"They're smart kids."

"Don't I know it. At least there's that blessing in all of this." There was a flicker of pride in James's voice.

"You left them alone tonight?"

"No, even though Jimmy is itching for authority. Philippa and Nick were over, helping us with the move, and decided to stay the night."

"Your sister?"

"Yes. She's pregnant and fell asleep on the couch because she was so wiped out. Nick didn't want to wake her up to drive back to Rosemount."

"You like him." I could hear it in his voice.

James shrugged. "I judged him by appearances for a long time, but he's shown me the weakness of that strategy. He's good to Philippa, and she's happy. That's what really counts." He sighed and wove his fingers together, and I guessed that Nick had not been a family-endorsed marital choice. It said a lot for James that he was trying to get past that preconception.

I changed the subject for him, trying to inject a lighter note. "Jimmy wants authority? What, he figures at ten that he's all grown-up?"

James grimaced, then tapped his pocket. I saw the outline of his cell phone and the dim glow of the On light. "He's fed up with recounting the cell phone number. He's too cool for such parental details. And I think he's fed up with me."

I smiled, remembering my own rebellions too well. "You're probably a tougher sell than Marcia was."

"It's change. I have to remind myself that he's rebelling against change and I'm just the messenger in the way." He leaned forward and I knew it wasn't an easy thing to remember sometimes.

"It can't be that bad."

"Really?" James turned that bright gaze on me. "The worst part is that I know I'm not helping. Every time I say something to my boys, I hear Robert Coxwell in my voice. Every time I try to discipline them, every time I say 'no' and get attitude, I'm afraid that I'm repeating his errors, shaping them into men that they don't want to become, men that *I* don't want them to become."

He folded his arms across his chest, venting parental frustration. "It doesn't help that they challenge me on every little thing and push push push to find my limits. Reminding them to wear socks is a global crisis prompting the launch of nuclear warheads. Telling them to get to school on time makes me the evil overlord and the worst father alive."

He pinched the bridge of his nose, and I realized just how stressful recent events had been for him. James made it look easy, and it was too simple from the outside to forget the magnitude of the changes he'd shouldered his way through.

"There are mornings," he admitted unevenly, "when drowning Jimmy in his Cheerios looks like good financial planning."

"Huh?"

"One less college tuition."

"You wouldn't."

"No, I wouldn't." James took a deep breath. "But it frightens me, Maralys. It frightens me to see any echo of my father's harsh attitudes in myself."

"He's not technically your father," I felt obliged to remind him.

That impatience flashed again. "Robert Coxwell raised

me. He instilled values in me. He paid for my education, my clothing, and my housing, he used his connections to get my career started and to keep it building. Whether or not he's technically my father is immaterial—he's the only father I've ever known."

"Can you learn from his mistakes?"

"You'd think so." James looked at the floor. "But so far I can only be the tough guy and the disciplinarian."

We sat in silence for a moment. I understood, but I really didn't know what to say to him that would make it easier. It's not as if I have a graduate degree in parenting. This was seriously out of my league.

I touched his hand though as we sat there, sympathizing with the challenge he faced. We sat there in silence for a long time.

"Do you ever think," he asked softly without looking at me, "that the people who find it tougher to say what they're feeling are the ones who feel things more intensely? As if they're the ones who really understand what it means to love someone? As if they have to keep their defenses high, because they care too much and have too much to lose?"

And James turned suddenly, studying my features, his gaze searching for some hint of comprehension in my expression. I couldn't look away. The entire world dropped away from us, and there was nothing, no one, but James and his question.

I knew exactly what he meant. Surprisingly, in this moment, I had no urge to deny it. That was a good thing, because I suspected that he could read the truth in my eyes.

I'd worry about that later.

"The softest hearts always have the toughest shields," I whispered.

We studied each other, two tongue-tied souls who couldn't admit the truth.

"Or maybe the biggest chickens cluck the loudest," I added, pulling my hand back and making a joke in an attempt to break free of his spell.

James snorted and looked away, folding his arms across his chest. His shoulder still bumped mine, still sent a tingle to my toes. He glanced toward my dad's room before I could think of anything else to say. "When are they sending him home?"

I seized the change of topic like a drowning woman cast a line. "They don't want to. The doc wants him to go from here to a nursing home or to some kind of supervised care."

"Well, he can't go live with you." James spoke as if there was no question of that happening.

Even though I agreed, I was insulted by his tone. "You think I can't even take care of my own father?"

"He'd never manage that elevator, he'd hate the neighborhood, he'd be away from his cronies and his doctors. You're on opposite schedules, so you'd get no work done." I started to argue, but James held up a finger. "And last but not least, you two would kill each other if left together in a confined space for any length of time. Be realistic, Maralys. Can you afford the kind of care they recommend? Can he?"

I stared at the toes of my boots. "I think the house is pretty much the only asset there."

"That's what I thought." James frowned and stared at the opposite wall now, thinking. The cogs they were a-turning.

I was seriously tempted to let him solve this, which said a frightening thing about how much I trusted him. I mean, I usually solve everything myself because I know then that it will get done right.

But James was showing a remarkable ability to get things done in a reasonable way, and with a minimum of fuss. He'd lost his job, his inheritance, his marriage, his money, and his house, but other than some understandable frustration, he seemed to be doing just fine.

A nurse came by, her shoes making a squeaky sound on the linoleum, one that echoed loud in the quiet. She spared us a thin smile, then wheeled a cart into my dad's room. I glanced at my watch—they were checking his vitals every two hours.

We said nothing, both clearly aware that my dad's future wasn't going to be resolved easily. The nurse left, moments later, her smile prim, and continued to the next room.

"So, what else is new?" I asked, ready for a change of topic and feeling the weight of the silence between us.

"Nothing, other than that I stink at parenting. We've been over that."

I gave a very glum James a playful punch in the shoulder, recognizing that he was due for another kick. "Don't be so hard on yourself. You've only been doing it for a couple of weeks."

James snorted in surprise, then turned to look at me. "Aren't you a bit old to still be kissing the boys and making them cry?"

"Peter Pan syndrome." I grinned at him, noting that his dimple was making an entrance. "I'm never going to grow up. House policy."

"Bull. You're more of an adult than any woman I've ever known."

It didn't sound like a compliment. "And what is that supposed to mean?"

"That you take care of things. You expect nothing but you give a lot. You slip in, get stuff done, and disappear." He shot a sidelong glance my way. "It's disconcerting that you're so self-sufficient, if you want to know the truth."

"What? I'm supposed to be one of those Victorian heroines, wailing 'save me, save me'?" I rolled my eyes. "Puhlease."

He chuckled to himself. "I'm having a hard time imagining that."

"And what's the matter with being self-sufficient? You're better at it than I am," I retorted without meaning to make any such confession. "Look at all the stuff you've gotten done. Look at all the changes you're making, just as easy as one-two-three."

"Someone had to do it."

"I didn't think you'd make so many changes so fast. I didn't think you could."

"Me or just anyone?"

I shrugged. "Either way."

"You do what you have to do. If anyone understands that,

t ought to be you. I followed your advice, made my list, and checked it twice. It seems to be working out pretty well."

"Just like I know what I'm doing."

"Just like." Our gazes locked for a long, hungry moment. I licked my lips without meaning to do so, and he watched. I swear his eyes were more green when he met my gaze again.

"I saw your suits," I whispered.

James shrugged and spread his hands. "What do I need them for?"

"But you're used to having them." I brushed his cuff, needing to touch him, however briefly, but not wanting to explore why. "This is not your look, at least it hasn't been."

Impatience flicked across his features. "It's just stuff, Maralys. Stuff comes and stuff goes and the only thing that matters in the end is who you are inside, what you do, and what mark it leaves on the world."

"Oh, do I smell a midlife crisis? The timing would be about right."

"Maybe a midlife course correction." He slanted a bright glance my way. "Or maybe you're just not used to men who are adults."

"How so?"

"That jerk you married wanted a mommy, not a partner." He turned to look at me, his gaze slipping over my features like a touch. "You're very independent, Maralys, and very clever. Most men wouldn't know what to do with you, though they might find you attractive." He touched the corner of my mouth with a fingertip. "That mouth and all."

"What's wrong with my mouth?"

"Just what comes out of it. You spit barbs, Maralys, just to keep everyone at bay."

I grimaced. "Doesn't work with you."

James chuckled softly and the sound made my heart go thump. "You've got nothing on what I've faced in court." He settled back beside me and I sensed the tension in him. He was going to say something I wouldn't like. "Maybe you should date a man for a change. An adult."

"What difference does it make to you?" I knew damn well

what he was implying, and the prospect was a whole lot more interesting than I knew it should have been.

"Lots." James leaned closer and bumped my shoulder with his. We were both sitting with our arms folded across our chests and our legs stretched out, crossed at the ankles. A passing observer might have thought us old pals, but there was a distinct crackle of awareness between us.

His hands were tanned now, even the mark left from his wedding ring faded to just about nothing. James has great hands, have I mentioned that? I've always thought them very sexy. I stared at them now and let the buzz come to life in my gut. His legs are long, too. There's something great about tall men.

In a drawer far, far away, Captain V was getting jealous.

"When was the last time someone listened to you, Maralys?" he asked softly. "Really *listened* to you, as if you knew things worth knowing?"

The answer was never, and he knew it, so I admitted nothing.

"The last time a guy did what you asked?"

I held my tongue.

"Or solved his own problems instead of waiting for you to do it? When was the last time you dated a man who didn't need you to tie his shoes? Come on. Admit it."

"Never, and you know it! What the hell difference does my taste in men matter?"

"Hey, maybe you prefer men who are really little boys. Maybe you like being in charge. Maybe you don't want to lose control by trusting someone." James turned to face me, his expression avid. He was challenging me, and I was ready to take his dare. "Maybe you're afraid that you might meet your match."

"Not likely," I snapped, but the words didn't have nearly enough zing. James smiled in a predatory way, and I couldn't look away from him, as much as I would have liked to.

His gaze dropped to my lips and he whispered. "Was that kiss really as hot as I remember it being?"

My mouth was dry. "You have an active fantasy life, clearly."

"Oh, I do," he mused. "And there's a consistent theme. Maybe I should say, a consistent character." He watched me for a minute, maybe waiting for me to say something or move. I didn't. James dipped his head, brushing his lips lightly across mine.

It was an exquisite kiss. Tender and demanding and so delicious that I wanted more. A lot more.

And I wanted it now. I started to sit up and give back as good as I got. James turned in his seat, both of us forgetting where we were and why, forgetting *who* we were.

My father fixed that.

"I'm thirsty!" he cried, a feeble version of his usual tone, then coughed. "I'm *thirsty!*"

I broke the kiss with a jerk and stumbled to my feet. James stood and reached to steady me with his hand on the back of my waist. I think he said my name, but I raced away from him. I lurched into Dad's room like a drunk, I was in such a hurry to put distance between us.

There were too many memories there. And I was shocked at how easy I found it to just lean into James's kiss and forget everything else around me. It was dangerous stuff, to be able to lose yourself in someone else, especially someone else whom you weren't supposed to be kissing, someone whose motives you didn't really know.

Nope, I had to get the moat dug and the gates closed ASAP.

I found the cup of water and lifted the straw to Dad's parched lips, my hands shaking as though I was at ground zero of a nuclear blast. He was paler than usual, his pupils dilated from the painkillers. The light was dim in the room, or maybe I'm just making excuses for him in hindsight.

Because he smiled at me, really smiled at me, and my heart just had time to clench hard with gratitude that he was okay before he ruined it all.

"I knew you'd come," he whispered, stretching out one hand for my face. "Tell Mary Elizabeth to go home. You stay with me now. You're all I need."

He must have seen my shock. But he smiled at me, as be-atifically as an angel.

You've heard about the proverbial straw breaking the camel's back. This was more like a two by four, that's what it takes for me to get the message. It didn't matter whether he'd mixed us up or not—he wanted my sister, not me, and the drugs brought the truth from his lips.

I put the cup down on the side table, turned, and walked out of the room.

Enough was enough. I was out the door and on my way.

"Maralys!" James shouted from behind me, but I didn't care. I wasn't turning back for anyone. Not now. Not ever. The gates were up and double-bolted, the island inviolate.

I snagged my jacket without losing a step and flung it on. I walked down the hall, past the nursing station, not really seeing where I was going, unshed tears blurring it all. I was on autopilot, heading out of my father's life. I was numb, at least long enough to get to the elevator.

Then, as I stood there, waiting, I started to shake. I'd been incredibly dumb, thinking that I owed him anything, thinking that anything I did might change anyone's mind, thinking that people owed each other anything out of respect and/or out of blood.

The age-old simmering stew came to a boil, a red-hot frothing boil, spilling over the side of the pot and sizzling when it hit the flames.

"Maralys!"

To hell with them all. I was going back to Osaka.

The elevator was too slow, and I could hear James's foot-steps, so I impulsively dashed for the stairs. I ran down them faster and faster and faster with each floor, my heels slamming against the tiles. It felt good to flee, to feel my blood pumping and my lungs working, to peer over the railing and know that I could slip and plunge to my death.

I liked the taste of my own mortality.

I don't know how long it took me to run down those stairs. I don't even remember how many floors up we were. But that run made me more determined to live each moment to the fullest, to take what I wanted and to hell with the rest of them. No more duties, no more obligations, no more worrying about the future.

I'd thought for years that that was what I was doing, but it was all a lie. A lot of talk, as James said, because my actions were those of a dutiful daughter.

I was indeed the good Catholic girl that I'd never persuade anyone that I was, no matter how hard I had tried. Oh, it was bitter, acrid even, to face the fact that my father would never ever love me for what I was. I faced it and I hurled the truth of it out the window and I ran as fast as I could toward my new life.

I hauled open the steel firedoor at the bottom of the stairs, out of breath and damp with my own perspiration, and stopped cold. James stood there, cool and composed, his eyes snapping. He was big enough to make a good roadblock.

"I'm giving you a ride home," he said in a most parental tone.

"Wrong. I'll take care of myself, thanks." I made to brush past him but he snagged my elbow. I fought him, thinking that a scene would change his mind, but there were very few people around, and none of them were interested. I called him a few choice names, and he didn't even blink.

In fact, James snagged me by both elbows. He marched me to the door, his grip resolute and his expression grim. "You're going to lose this one, Maralys, so you might as well give it up."

"I am not going anywhere with you!" I kicked and I bit and he gave me no quarter.

"Got it in one. You're going home. I'm just your means of transport." He shoved me none too gently in the direction of the parking lot.

"It's a matter of principle," I snarled. "I'm not going to owe anyone anything ever again."

He was undaunted. "Fine. I owe you for picking up the boys the night Marcia left. This evens the score."

"The contract revision evened the score."

"Then I owe you for the advice on getting rid of the shopping." James stopped beside a motorcycle and briskly unclipped a pair of helmets. He handed me one with a look that brooked no argument.

I stopped dead, incredulous. "You've got a bike?"

"I've had it for twenty years."

"Get out of town."

A smile touched his lips, then was banished. "That was the point."

"I never knew."

"It's been stashed in the back of the garage. Your sister hated it, but I couldn't get rid of it." He glared at me, belligerent as I'd seldom seen him. "Call me sentimental and you can walk."

My mouth opened and closed. I was lost in a major way. It was an old bike, but lovingly maintained, its chrome gleaming.

"Why did you bring two helmets?"

"Just thinking ahead. I knew you'd be here." James put on his own helmet and got astride the bike. He kicked off the stand and started the engine, balancing on his heels as if anxious to go. "Helmet or no ride." This was clearly a limited-time offer.

I pulled on the helmet and seized the moment. Truth be told, the bike suited my mood perfectly. We roared out of the quiet hospital lot and rocketed through the quiet streets. I could feel the tension in James, both in the aggressive way he drove and in the tautness in his muscles. That kind of thing is tough to miss when you've got your legs wrapped around a guy.

The wind bit at my face, the air salty from the sea. There were a thousand stars in the sky and a million lights in the city. It was magical, it was perfect, it blew the old skin of me away and buffed the new me to a sheen.

"Faster," I whispered.

I don't know whether James could hear me, but he kicked it up on the straightaway. I could feel his heartbeat beneath my fingertips, my breasts were pressed against his back. I tightened my legs around him and leaned into the curves with him, loving the sense of moving together toward a common goal.

And when we rolled to a stop in front of my building and I got off the bike, it seemed perfectly natural to catch his chin in my hand and kiss him hard. I think at first I just meant to thank him, thank him for picking up the slack, for bringing me home, for blowing away the dust and giving me a new view. For not asking questions or making demands, for understanding that I just am the way I am.

And maybe for liking me that way.

But he kissed me back with a hunger that I knew was mine alone. This wasn't about my twin, it wasn't about loneliness, it wasn't about anything but the lightning bolt that hit every time his lips touched mine.

"You should bring the bike up to the loft," I said when we finally parted, our breath steaming the spring night. "It might get ripped off around here."

James looked at his watch. "An hour and a half, max," he said, his voice tight. "The boys will be getting up for school." His gaze searched mine, trying to read my response to that, letting me see how much he wanted to come up.

But I knew James had kids, and I knew that he took his responsibilities seriously. It was one of the things I admired about how he'd handled all of this. It was hardly a news flash.

"What's the matter? Did your sexual performance really peak at twenty-one? Is it really going to take that long?" I taunted, then kissed him again. He pulled me into his lap and there were no performance issues, I've got to tell you.

I don't know how we got upstairs, really. We were kissing the whole way—no, we were just about devouring each other—I was half on the bike and half off of it. The helmets rolled across the loft floor, my shirt was undone, and James had his tongue underneath the lace edge of my bra. He whispered my name, then teased my nipple as he picked me up, cupping my butt in his hands. I had my fingers in his hair and my tongue in his ear, my legs wrapped around his waist.

And things only got more enthused from there. The first

time was frenzied and demanding; it culminated in a mutual orgasm that left us both shaking.

The second time, we took it slow, savoring each other, peeling off the last of our clothes and tasting every increment of each other's flesh. We shared a long slow kiss as we came, James cupping my jaw in his hand, and my orgasm lasted at least a week. We fell asleep then, and lo, my girly girls, I was pretty much glowing in the wake of the best sex I'd ever had.

Oh, yes, Captain V was definitely out of a job. There ain't nothing like the real thing.

Subject: what am i doing wrong?

Aunt Mary—

all my friends are getting married but i'm
not. even the ones not getting married have
found mr. right. i've looked high and low
and can't find him. :-(what now?
lonely

Subject: get a grip!

Dear Lonely—

Change your world view. No woman needs a
man to make her life complete. Marriage
only works when someone (i.e., the woman)
sacrifices her life at the feet of her
partner. You can be married and miserable,
or single and self-determining. There are
no Mr. Rights in our postmodern world—just
(if you're lucky) a long line of Mr. Right
Nows. The old rules no longer hold true.
You wouldn't make yourself choose just
chocolate or vanilla for all the rest of
your life, would you? So, with men. Take
the man of the moment, enjoy, then move on.
Work your way through all thirty-one
wonderful flavors, then start over again.

Aunt Mary
***
Uncertain? Confused? Ask Aunt Mary!

Your one-stop shop for netiquette and advice:
http://www.ask-aunt-mary.com

I woke up when James's weight shifted on the bed. The light
was heading to pearly, that gray of a morning thinking about
dawn. I had been sleeping on my stomach, and James kissed
between my shoulder blades, then the back of my neck. He
shoved a hand through my hair, letting his fingers linger.

"Evening Aubergine," I mumbled, hearing the silent question.

He laughed beneath his breath. "Purple to the rest of us."
He lay on top of me, lacing his fingers with mine. I could feel
his chest hair against my back and something else a little farther south. I smiled into the pillow.

His whisper was warm against my neck. "What color is it
really?"

"I don't know."

"How long since you've had a look?"

"Mmmm, I've been coloring it since forever."

James ran his tongue along my earlobe. "I'll bet it's the
exact color of melted chocolate. Bittersweet chocolate."

It was, more or less, but there was no need to tell him as
much. I turned into James's kiss and took a chance. "You
must have been hell-on-wheels when you were twenty-one."

His eyes gleamed, a split-second warning that I had mis-
calculated. "You should know." He winked and slipped
quickly from the bed, whistling as he headed for the bathroom.

I sat up, fully awake now. "What?" I actually squawked. It
wasn't a pretty sound. That's what I get for invoking the wrath
of Bolivian cockatiels by naming their species in vain.

"You know what." The man sauntered, untroubled, dead
certain that I would follow him.

I swore. I hate being predictable.

Then I bounced out of the bed and ran after James. "No.
NO! You *tell* me what it means." I swung around the bathroom door, the only door in the place, and gripped the frame

so tightly that my knuckles went white. I was breathing hard. "What exactly did you mean?"

James took his damn time. I did take a small look, just because I was there, and had all my earlier suspicions confirmed. It had been dark in bed, too dark to *look*. He was in good shape, great shape really, and completely comfortable in his own skin. He moved with a kind of grace that was imminently masculine. Sure, he was thicker around the waist than he had been in his younger days, but the jeans had told no lie.

He slanted me a glance now as he washed his hands, one so bright that I jumped a little.

Or at least my heart did.

Then he reached out with one fingertip and touched the mole beside my left nipple. The nipple tightened like a raspberry, and I tried not to shiver. He looked me in the eye and spoke too softly. I knew he'd say something dangerous as soon as I got a hint of that tone.

"I've been looking for that mole for twenty years, Maralys O'Reilly. You're not going to get rid of me now."

My heart stopped. I felt the blood drain from my face, but then I chided myself for being surprised. I always knew he was too damn smart. "When did you know?"

"I suspected for a long time, but didn't know for sure until now." He washed his face with that methodical thoroughness that only men can show in a time of total crisis. I was having a meltdown of my defenses, and he was checking the growth of his whiskers. "Remember that theory of mine?"

"This was your theory?" I could have started shrieking like a harpy here. I was furious that he had taken so long to say anything, that he'd hidden his suspicions so well from me even though I'd been trying desperately to hide the truth from him.

Okay, I wasn't at my best. Imagine Scotty, down in the hold: "She's crackin' up Cap'n. I dinna know how long I can hold her together." Chunks were falling off my walls, the moat was being drained, the portcullis was suddenly rusted right clear through.

James *knew*.

James had always suspected.

The game was up.

"I didn't suspect at first, not until it was too late." He gave me another hard look. "And when you finally came home, I thought we'd get it straight. But you made sure that what I saw had nothing to do with what I was looking for, didn't you? You're as responsible for this as me."

My anger found an outlet. "This is not my fault!" I shook a finger at him, enraged by his attitude. "You are not going to lay this at my door! You're the one who married my sister."

"Only because I was looking for you!" James turned and propped his hands on his hips, his fierce expression revealing that he was far more angry than I had suspected. "Perhaps you've noticed that you two are *twins*."

"Liar. You were not looking for me."

"You don't know that."

"I gave you my phone number." I spat the accusation I'd held back for twenty years. "You never called. Not once."

"I took the wrong coat from the bar. I never got it back."

"A likely story."

"A true story." James shoved a hand through his hair in exasperation. "Do you know how many weeks I spent prowling campus, hoping to catch some glimpse of you?"

That nonexistent Twinkie in my gut was thinking of heading north again. "And you found my sister." Oh, it was just too horrible to be true.

"Except I didn't know that she had a sister, not then. I thought I'd found you."

"What a bunch of self-serving crap," I said, feigning indifference even though my heart was racing like I'd been running a hundred miles an hour. "You're the one who keeps saying that no one could mix us up."

"What did I know about you then, Maralys? I didn't even know your name, or else I didn't remember it."

"We were so drunk." I dropped the lid of the toilet and sat on it, burying my face in my hands. "It's ancient history, James. It's got nothing to do with anything."

"It has everything to do with everything, Maralys." James

squatted in front of me and pulled my hands away from my face, his unexpected gentleness making me want to cry. Wouldn't that be slick? "I was looking for you when I found Marcia, and I thought she was you. I courted her and married her because I thought she was you."

"Ooops."

I peeked just in time to see his expression harden. "You did nothing to persuade me differently. You hid out until after the wedding, then you showed up years later looking like a punker queen and pretending not to know me from Adam. What was I supposed to think?"

"What did you think?"

His gaze was rueful. "Just what I suspect you wanted me to think. That you were the family slut and you didn't even remember sleeping with me."

Our gazes held and I had the urge to hide from his searching look. "But you should have known," I whispered, clinging to my ridiculous romantic assumption. "You said it stunk, right from the start."

"It did." James sighed. "I couldn't reconcile how she was with what I remembered of you. I rationalized it a thousand ways. We'd been drunk that night, but she wouldn't drink when we were dating. I thought maybe she was embarrassed"—he laced his fingers with mine again—"because I remembered how shy you were once we were alone. She wanted to wait for our wedding night, and I thought it would be fine then. I thought I would get her drunk the next night if it wasn't. I was sure I could make it work. I was sure that it would all be fine in the end."

"But it wasn't."

"Marcia never liked sex, which was a whole lot different from what I remembered of you." His quick glance made me blush. "I knew she wasn't faking, but I was dumb enough that I didn't figure it out right away." James grimaced. "It didn't help when I asked why she had her mole removed."

"Oh, Jesus." I hung my head. Marcia knew damn well that I had a mole there—we used to play compare-and-contrast when we were little, maybe because we were both so desperate to find a hint that we weren't exactly the same. I laid my head on my knees and begged the nonexistent confection to stay put. "If it sucked, then why were you so determined to marry her?"

James shook his head. "Because I was enough of my father's son—or so I thought at the time—that I was determined to make things right. I thought I was supposed to marry her. You were a virgin, Maralys. I thought it was my responsibility to marry you after what we'd done."

"That's a lousy reason to get married."

"It's been good enough for a lot of other people through the ages. And there was something between us that night."

"Your dick."

"Besides that. A lot more besides that." He squeezed my fingers so tightly that it hurt, but I didn't so much as flinch. I sure didn't look up because I knew I couldn't hold his gaze. "Where the hell were you? If you'd made one single appearance while Marcia and I were dating—one show, Maralys— everything would have been resolved." His voice rose slightly. "Why the hell did you have to run away to Japan?"

I sighed, all my careful reasons at the time now seeming as substantial as dust. "I'd been thinking of going anyhow. And then you never called and I never saw you again. I figured that the cliché had come true for me, that you'd only wanted one thing from me and disappeared once you'd gotten it."

"I would never do that."

"How was I supposed to know that?"

"It's the kind of man I am."

I cast off his grip and pushed him away, getting to my feet with undisguised impatience. "Puh-leese! We were *drunk*! We barely knew each other! We didn't even know each other's *names*!"

Now I was getting angry again. Thank God I have no neighbors because if I had, they would have enjoyed over-hearing this show.

"What was I supposed to think when my sister showed me a picture of her dream date? What the hell was I supposed to think when she rhapsodized about the special bond between you? What was I supposed to do when she insisted she was going to marry this guy and live happily ever after?"

"She had a picture of me?"

"Who the hell else? There it was, in living technicolor. You and my sister were as happy as two clams, holding hands and the whole nine yards. It was, if you must know, sickeningly sweet."

"You could have made one appearance," James insisted. "You're twins, Maralys, you have to be used to being confused with each other."

"This is not my fault!" I roared. "How was I to know whether it was true love or not? Marcia was happy about it. My parents were happy about it. You looked happy about it. What right had I to destroy her engagement?" I jabbed my thumb at my own bare chest. "Who was *I* to step into the happy scenario and say, 'Hey, I've done it with him and he's okay.' Can you even begin to appreciate how much trouble that would have made?"

"No, but I'm starting to get the idea."

"We were *Catholic*, James, not Catholic the way it is now, but dyed-in-the-wool on-your-knees-every-morning and confession-once-a-week Catholics. Marcia and I were supposed to be virgins until our wedding night and only tolerate sex after that so that we could do God's will in making more Catholics."

I forced myself to take a breath. I was shaking, but it might as well all come out now. "Nice girls were not supposed to be so curious about sex that their virginity was lost on a whim. Nice girls were not supposed to get drunk. Nice girls were not supposed to stay out late with friends. Nice girls were supposed to put others before themselves." I paused for emphasis, letting James see the fullness of my hostility. "Nice girls did not get pregnant out of wedlock and left alone to deal with it."

With that, I left the bathroom, aware that I had probably shocked James for the first time in his life. His jaw had practically bounced off the floor with that last one, but I didn't care.

Everyone wanted truth? Well, they'd better fasten their knickerbockers. I had lots of truth to share around. The casualties had only themselves to blame for asking in the first place.

I started to get dressed, I don't know why, because I wasn't going anywhere. Maybe I just needed some kind of protection between myself and this man.

Ha. A little "protection" would have saved me a lot of trouble some twenty years ago. I moved jerkily, having trouble with the simplest things, like getting one foot into my undies at a time.

But wasn't keeping your undies on always the problem, Maralys?

"Pregnant?" James came out of the bathroom, looking dazed. "You were *pregnant*? From that one time?"

I gave him a scathing glance. "Spare me the slut lecture. It was from that one time." I turned my back and zipped up my jeans, thinking how stupid it was to be shy in front of this man who had already seen so much of me. But I did it anyway.

I heard him coming across the floor, cautiously, as if I might lob another Molotov cocktail at him. I expected an outburst but apparently had shocked him beyond that.

James caught my shoulders in his hands and bent his head, touching his forehead to the top of my head. It wasn't the reaction I expected from him. It was almost . . . tender.

You know that kind of shit throws my game. I stiffened but didn't turn, even though my heart was starting to skip again. Tears pricked at my eyes. I couldn't bear it if he was going to be decent about this.

James's voice was thick. "What happened to the baby, Maralys?"

I shouldn't have been disappointed that he asked that, shouldn't have been surprised that he was more concerned with his unknown progeny than with me. Nope, no "Gosh, how did you cope?" but "What did you do with my baby?"

But I could have slugged him. Really. I gritted my teeth and tried to shake off the weight of his hands. No luck. "It doesn't matter," I said viciously, fighting his grip in earnest.

"Well, yes it does." James spun me around to face him. "You owe me the truth."

"Fat chance!" I was ready to fight, but James disarmed me yet again.

He spoke very gently. "Is it so reprehensible that I want to know about our child? I know I'm late to the party, and I know that I can never make it up to you, whatever you went through. But tell me, Maralys, tell me what happened. Please."

It was the "please" that got me. Nothing like good manners to melt my reserves. Guess one of my mother's many lessons hit home after all.

I looked away as my tears welled. "It died."

"It?" Now he was annoyed. "Boy or girl?"

"Who knows? What difference does it make?"

I might have walked away, but James tightened his grip and gave me a shake. "Don't you know?"

I met his gaze angrily. "How very flattering that you think I didn't even bother to find out the baby's gender. I *miscarried*." I spat the word. "At fourteen weeks, in a hotel room in Osaka. The gender of the child was as yet not easily discerned by the layperson, particularly a young stupid layperson under duress."

I stared at him challengingly, letting my tears fall, as if they were as much an accusation as my words. "I was alone. In a country whose language I did not speak, without medical care, without a friend, without anyone I could even call."

To James's credit, he didn't look away. In fact, he seemed to be becoming as angry as I felt. "Your family . . ."

"Would have shunned me if they had known. Trust me. That wasn't an option." I shook my head. "I think sometimes that my father does know, that he somehow guesses, because that certainly would explain his attitude toward me." I stepped away, knowing that I was going to mourn my lost child once again and wanting to be alone to do it, as I'd always been alone. "Don't you have to go somewhere?"

James wasn't budging. "So, that's where you got that chip on your shoulder."

I spun on him, furious and weeping and damn near losing it. "Don't make this sound trite! I lost a child! I lost *my* child! And I lost everything with it. I lost my innocence and my conviction that there was anyone or anything I could rely upon!"

"And you were cheated." He stepped closer. "We not only lost our child, Maralys, but we lost something precious that we found for just a moment."

"Don't you show me sympathy now." I shook a finger at him and backed away, "You are not the hero here."

"No. You never gave me a chance to be. What's the matter, Maralys? Still afraid someone might live up to your expectations, if you give them a chance?"

"No. There's no chance of that."

We glared at each other. James stepped even closer, but he didn't touch me this time. I could smell his skin and feel his heat and a part of me wanted very much to have his strength wrapped around me again.

But I fight my own battles, thanks very much.

He watched me, as if reading my thoughts, then his eyes narrowed. "One of these days, Maralys, you'll either admit that you might need someone else, or you'll self-destruct."

I folded my arms across my chest, hugging myself since no one else was going to get close enough to do the honors. "Let's just say that I'm selective with my trust."

James looked pointedly around the loft. "Selective to the point of exclusion."

"What time is it, Mr. Wolf?" I said challengingly, knowing one good way to be rid of him. "Time to go home to your family yet?"

James looked at his watch, swore, then reached for his jockeys and jeans. He dressed quickly, his gaze dark and fixed on me. "This isn't done, Maralys."

"It *is* done, James. It's been done for a long, long time."

"No, it will never be done." He closed the distance between us with quick steps and caught my chin in his hand. He put his thumb over the wild flutter of my pulse, then lifted my hand to the thrum of his. I was surprised to discover how quickly his heart was beating. "It's never going to be done,

Maralys, because this spark that started it all is never going to die."

"You don't know that."

"Yes, I do. It brought us together once . . ."

"Too much cheap beer and rampant teenage hormones brought us together once."

"Cheap beer made us able to hear this, even in a bar packed to the roof with rampant teenage hormones." He folded his hand over mine, trapping my fingers against his heartbeat. "This is what it's all about, Maralys, and you know it as well as I do."

"No." I tried to step away, but his certainty stopped me. "I don't agree with you."

"Message received," James whispered. "That's why I'm going to have to change your mind." And he gave me another one of those soul-scaring kisses before I could get away.

He was way too persuasive. I pushed him back and it wasn't easy to do—either because he was bigger than me or because that kiss was awfully good stuff. But I wasn't going to be something else to be made right, something else in his life he could fix.

"I'm not another duty left undone, James."

"That's not what I'm saying."

"Yes, it is. Go home." I was rubbed raw and bleeding all over the floor, so many emotions finally cut loose that I couldn't think straight. "It's over now, as it should have been over a long time ago. Now you know and we can both move on."

"Bullshit," he said flatly and framed my face in his hands.

"Truth," I challenged.

James smiled, ready to prove me wrong, but I ducked out of his grip and retreated. I'd been angry with James for so long, with life for so long, that it didn't seem fair to suddenly find out that he had tried to make it right. Talk about losing my pointer.

It was imperative that James not make an appeal to me now, in my weakened and vulnerable state, because I might screw up and agree to something that I would regret later.

Hell, I already had screwed up.

I put my hands up when he started toward me. "Go home."

James shook his head and kept on coming. "Where does it say that you get to make the rules, Maralys? This is important!"

"It's not important to me!"

"Liar!" James's words came out in a little growl. "Maralys, I've spent my whole life living up to expectations and fulfilling duties. This is about following instincts. This is about recognizing something good and not letting it go. . . ."

"I won't be your midlife crisis!" I backed away. "Get out and get out now."

James scowled and raised a finger to argue more. I had to admire that the guy didn't back down from a fight, even if it was seriously pissing me off in this particular instance.

The phone rang before he could speak. I leaped for the receiver and knew damn well that James would interpret my gratitude for an interruption as a victory for his side. "Hello? Hello!"

"Where the hell is Dad?" Marcia demanded, without so much as a do-you-mind. "I've been calling him all night and there's no answer. What have you done with him? What have you done to him?"

On impulse, I pivoted and chucked the cordless receiver at James. "It's for you," I said with an innocence of manner that made him look wary. He caught the phone instinctively, though, and I left him no choices. I headed for the shower.

Saved by the bell.

Sort of.

The problem with being in the shower was that I couldn't eavesdrop. But then, I'd only want to eavesdrop if I had some kind of vested emotional interest in the success or failure of James's marriage, and that I didn't have.

Right.

I scrubbed and I showered and I even damn well whistled, knowing very well that there was a dangerously attractive beast of a man loose in my apartment and trying hard to forget it. I turned off the water when I couldn't stand it any longer, but there wasn't a sound.

No argument.

No mumbled masculine agreements.

Nothing. Not even the complaint of the elevator, much less the purr of a motorcycle engine fading away.

The silence made my imagination run wild. I stood in the stall, dripping, and wondered what James was up to. He was a wily type, much more unpredictable than I had long believed.

You gotta love that. I decided that standing here was stupid, as well as cold, and flung open the shower curtain.

And just about had a heart attack.

James was standing perfectly still not two feet away, holding the towel. Waiting. He was fully dressed and clearly on the verge of departure. I willed my catapulting heart back where it belonged and reached for the towel as calmly as I could.

James held it farther away, just slightly out of my grip. "I'm going to call you," he said as if he expected a fight about it.

He'd called that one right.

I shrugged. "Save your quarter. Now give me the towel."

"Nuh-uh." His jaw set. "Maralys, we're going to talk about this, whether you like it or not."

"No, we're not. We have talked about it and we're done." I snagged the towel, knowing that I'd only gotten it because he let me get it. That annoyed me beyond reason. I wrapped it determinedly around myself, then looked him in the eye. "How's my sister, by the way? You know—your wife?"

"My estranged wife," he corrected without a ripple of emotion. "My soon-to-be-ex-wife. She says she's fine."

"Where is she?"

He shrugged. "I don't know. I didn't ask." Once again, I watched him close the book on something that was no longer of interest to him.

It was a bit chilling.

James turned and gestured in the direction of my kitchen. "I've left our new address and phone number on your fridge, as well as my cell number." Then he looked back at me, a knowing twinkle in his eye. "If you suddenly feel the desperate need to talk to me, you'll know where to find me."

"I'm not going to call you."

"Then it's a good thing I'm going to call you." He swooped, kissed me hard enough to make me shiver, then headed out of the bathroom but quick.

"You're always doing that," I complained as I trailed behind him. I wiped at my mouth as though I was removing a stain.

I should have known that he'd take that as a challenge.

James paused beside the bike and glanced over his shoulder. His voice was low. "You want me to stop?"

"Well, yes." A lie, but one for the greater good. I lifted my chin and gave him my full-force glare.

Of course, he took the bait. James was back in two long strides, my chin in his hand and his lips just a smidge from mine. "Bullshit," he whispered, then kissed me even more possessively than the last time.

And oh, yes, I kissed him back. What a wimp.

He knew it, too. His tongue made a major move, which reminded me all too well of the things we'd done the night before. His fingers slid into my hair and I started to melt. I was just getting ready to surrender—or drag him back to the bed—when he lifted his head again.

There was a gleam of anticipation in his eye, and he rubbed his thumb across my bottom lip with a gesture that could only be called proprietary.

"Later. Count on it," he murmured.

"It's over, James. Cathartic sex has done its thing."

He arched one brow, unconvinced. "Then explain why there's still a sizzle, Maralys," he whispered, and kissed me again. Then he was gone, leaving me sizzling in the chilly solitude of my loft.

I closed my eyes and listened to the elevator descending, then the throaty purr of the bike's engine. It revved in the street in front of the building, rose to crescendo, then began to fade away.

I stood there, tingly, and took inventory. The incredible fact was that I was feeling reasonably good.

Somewhat against the odds, I would have thought. I opened my eyes and looked around, thought about it again, and came to the same remarkable conclusion.

I felt good. Without coffee. In the morning.

OTOH, I had just dumped a load of garbage that I'd been dragging around for an awfully long time. No wonder I felt a bit frisky. And finally, after many moons of yearning, I had gotten James Coxwell out of my system. I'd said all the things I've always wanted to say to him—and then some—and dragged the biggest nastiest truth right out into the sunshine so everyone could see it.

Huh. No surprise that I felt like Wonder Woman. I took a deep breath, ready for a new, unburdened beginning to my life.

I threw on some sweats, made some coffee, and watched the windows do their painterly thing with the first glimmers of light. Lo, it was good. My loft felt cozy with the smell of coffee brewing and the sight of the rumpled sheets on the futon—never mind the memories of what had happened there so very recently.

There's something to Lydia's theory of good sex being the perfect stress-buster. I was totally devoid of anxiety.

Well, except when I thought about my dad. I did myself a favor, reminded myself that all was good as long as he was in the hospital in capable care, and gave myself the morning as a gift. Besides, he'd sent me away, hadn't he? Maybe it was time he had some time to miss the ol' punching bag.

There's also something therapeutic in surrendering secrets and letting a lot of old bitterness loose. This fury of injustice that had driven me for so long was diminished, as was my sense that I'd been dealt a lousy hand in the game of life. I'd made my choices, I'd borne my burdens, but I'd chosen to let my frustration fester.

Until now. And it wasn't all bad to know that I'd thrown

my anger at the one person most responsible for my unhappiness, however unwittingly he had done so. I sipped my coffee and eyed James's note on the fridge, liking his resolute handwriting.

He was tough. I respected that.

I liked knowing beyond the shadow of a doubt that James would not crumple into a sorry mess because I'd yelled at him. I liked knowing that he wouldn't end up in counseling for the rest of his life because I'd dared to show him an ugly truth. And yes, I liked that he wasn't afraid to tell me that I was wrong—whether I agreed with him or not. I liked that I didn't have to protect him from me.

Hell, he kept coming back for more. I couldn't be as bad as my PR maintained.

I could even deal with the fact that he was right in one thing. I *had* dated a lot of little boys. I'd even married one. But James gave as good as he got. He was willing to rumble; he was willing to go after the truth. He was willing to face the ugly stuff to get it out of the way. I liked that, I liked it a lot.

And I knew right then and right there that I would have a hard time scaring him off now. I was going to have to think about his defense for the past. Had I played such an active role in what happened? I hadn't thought so, but maybe I had sat back like Penelope in Peril and waited to be rescued.

Hmm. It's so much easier to point a finger than to take responsibility yourself, isn't it? Maybe it isn't so simple as this person's fault or that one. Maybe we make up the dance together, as we go along, and no one knows what the result will be.

I was going to have to mull on that.

```
Subject: a question                        •

  Dear Aunt Mary—

  Is it true that you can find anyone on the
  Internet?

  I miss my mom.

  Calypso II
-----
```

Ah, the reappearance of the small adults. Or at least one of them. Armed with a knife to jab in my heart.

Great way to start your day. That's what I got for booting up.

```
  I miss my mom, too. Tough noogies.
```

That was the first thing I typed, but then I erased it. The kid didn't need to be having nightmares on my account about his mom being dead.

Maybe this was synchronicity. I needed a reminder that doing a repeat performance of last night with James would be complicated like I needed a hole in the head.

Not that I had any thoughts of going back for more. Nope. Not me. Let him keep his sizzle to himself.

The man had KIDS. Not just any kids, but kids who were the biological product of my sister's womb. Major EWWWWWW factor there. Note the billboard coming up on the right:

OTOH, I had to feel sorry for Johnny. I remembered his concerns about his mom finding them after they moved. I knew what it was like to suddenly be without your mom. Of course, I had been older and theoretically wiser, but it had still stunk.

How could Marcia do this to the boys on a whim? Hadn't she phoned them yet? The prospect that she hadn't made me see red.

I wondered then whether Jimmy had just been acting tough when he didn't seem to care about Marcia. Wouldn't your mom skipping out on you and your whole life going to hell shortly thereafter potentially leave a chip on your shoulder?

Not that I could understand such strategy, no sirree, not me.

Maybe Jimmy just shared his dad's view that they were better off without someone who wasn't going to really play on the team.

Ah, but Johnny was so much younger. Only two years, but it seemed like a thousand when you compared the two boys. He was quieter, too, maybe more sensitive of a kid.

What was I going to say? I thought for a bit about my reply—there was no question of my leaving one—because the bulletin board is public, open to the view of many eyes. I knew that some spammers and opportunists snagged e-mail addresses off the board, it's inevitable, and job one was shielding Johnny from snake oil salesmen.

```
Subject: re: a question

Dear Calypso II—

It might be true, but it's certainly a fact
that there are lots of scam artists who
```

will promise to find someone, take your
money, and disappear into the ether.

Trust that your mom has a good reason for
what she's doing. I'm sure she'll come back
to you as soon as she can.

Aunt Mary
***
Uncertain? Confused? Ask Aunt Mary!
Your one-stop shop for netiquette and advice:
http://www.ask-aunt-mary.com

Lame, lame, lame. But the only other solution was to head out
there and find Marcia. I wasn't sure that it could be done,
and, okay, for purely selfish reasons, I wasn't in a hurry to see
her again.

All the same, I called Gwen. She greeted me with the
cheerfulness that meant she was having a bite of a day at the
phone company.

"How you doing?" she asked.

"Better than expected." I gave her a moment to laugh, then
cut to the chase. "Can you get me something on the QT?"

"Drugs, men, Viagra, what?"

"A phone number."

"Boring, Maralys, really boring. I'm used to more interesting requests from you."

"Yeah, well, I must be losing my touch. Someone called
me Wednesday night, well, early Thursday morning."

"Last night?"

"Yep. There should only be two calls incoming on my
main line—one from my dad and then the one that I want to
find out about." I gave her my number and my dad's number
and heard her scribbling.

"Stalker?" she asked hopefully. Gwen has a theatrical
frame of mind. She looks for high drama in all of life's mun-
dane corners.

"Sorry, not this time. Just my AWOL sister."

"Kidnapped?"

"Avoiding kitchen duty."

"Oh. All right." I heard both the disappointment in her voice and the clatter of her keys. "I can do that right here." She hummed as she scrolled and typed. She repeated my dad's number. "That one was first, right?"

"Uh-huh." I was tapping my toe, impatient with the waiting.

"There's only one more that night, you popular creature." She gave me the number and I wrote it down. I didn't recognize the area code.

"Any idea where that is?"

"Well, the area code is in New Mexico. . . ."

"New Mexico! Are you sure?" For some reason, I hadn't expected Marcia to go very far. I blinked a couple of times and considered that I had totally underestimated her sense of adventure.

"Computers don't lie, my love."

"Except when they're given the wrong answers. Garbage in, garbage out, you know."

"Whatever. These ones don't lie. They don't have time."

New Mexico. Huh.

Gwen tapped and hummed, then clicked her teeth. "Sorry, Mar. It's a phone booth."

"Shit! Can you give me an intersection?"

"I'm sorry, madam, but that information is not available to me at this time." A supervisor had come by, right when things were getting good. Just what I needed.

"Oh, well, thanks a lot."

"It's our pleasure to serve you, madam." Gwen's tone was dripping honey. "Have a nice day."

"Right."

"See you tonight," she whispered before the line went dead.

I hung up without paying much attention, then sat and looked sourly at the screen, fixated upon the sister issue. Then

I logged on to one of those reverse telephone look-up sites and punched in the phone number.

And thar she was, my maties, an intersection in Santa Fe. Of course, it was a piece of cake to come up with a map of the town and roughly locate the phone booth in question.

The issue was what to do with the information. A phone booth is hardly a final destination. Gwen had said the call came in at 5:03 local time, which was Eastern, which meant it was 3:03 Mountain time. I think.

I checked the map of time zones on the phone company page and drummed my fingers. Marcia could conceivably be staying near this phone booth, because I couldn't imagine her just wandering around aimlessly in the middle of the night.

OTOH, she could have been just driving past it on her way to somewhere else. I idly called up the city maps and hotel guides and apartment listings and realized that there was a wealth of possibilities for accommodation in the vicinity.

Which meant that I had effectively found out nothing, beyond the fact that Marcia was in New Mexico on some wild adventure while I had been doing the wild thing with her husband.

Sordid, Maralys. Really sordid.

On the upside, I doubted that Marcia cared. I did wish, though—belatedly it's true—that I had heard what James had said to her and what she said to him this morning.

The bell rang while I was musing, and some guy shouted up the elevator shaft that he was a courier running late. I went down and took the clipboard dutifully, not thinking twice about the box or what was in it.

I was too disappointed, if you must know, that it wasn't a FedEx guy. Have you ever noticed that they hire all the hunks? I swear, it's a marketing strategy.

Think about it, it's brilliant. After all, women control the courier business. You think not? The vast majority of receptionists, personal assistants, and shipping clerks are—you got it—women. Young women, too—these are, by and large, entry-level positions.

Lotsa hormones on the loose.

Is it any surprise that those FedEx boys break out their shorts early? Some smart cookie in biz development came up with that strategy, you can bet your last buck on it. Every woman in America must have fantasies about her FedEx dude. We give them business just to see our friendly neighborhood Mr. Gorgeosity-and-Yum again and again. So, yes, I made it to the lobby in record time.

This guy was just your usual bike courier type, boo hoo, in need of a haircut, tattooed and enthusiastically pierced.

"How do you blow your nose?" I asked and he gave me a quizzical look. "I mean, if you have a cold, doesn't the stud get in the way? Don't things, uh, cling to it?"

He grinned, a real charmer. "It's not so bad." He pulled back his nostril, more than ready to show-and-tell. "See? It has a flat back."

"This is seriously more than I needed to know."

Again with the smile. "Just think of me as an emissary from the land o' stud."

"Uh-huh. Well, your work here is done, Mr. Ambassador," I muttered and signed.

"Hey, anytime!" he shouted as I scurried back into the elevator and slammed the door. Talk about distracted—I didn't even notice that the package didn't have a return address, not until I was back upstairs. I opened the box, peered in with a certain measure of suspicion, and saw the seashell inside.

A huge seashell. Too weird.

I hauled it out, then peered into the box, unable to fathom why anyone would send me such a thing. There was just a small slip of yellow paper on the bottom, so I hauled it out. The handwriting there was the same as that on the note on my fridge.

Aha. Okay, I smiled. I'm a sucker for unpredictability.

The Chambered Nautilus Nautilus pompilius *(also known as the Pearly Nautilus) contains numerous successive chambers by which the Nautilus controls its ascent and descent through deep tropical waters. The*

Nautilus is of the class Cephalopoda, the most highly developed mollusks.

Cephalopoda—which include octopus and squid—are distinguished by highly developed eyes, differentiated sexes, and the ability of the female to generate a shell as protection for her eggs. Unusual in the class, both male and female Nautilus create shells with multiple chambers.

It is interesting to note that despite their impressive defenses and carnivorous diet, neither male nor female Nautilus is toxic.

J

The man got points for creativity. Who knew James had it in him? It made me smile to be considered nontoxic.

And the shell was nice. It was big with a lovely pearly finish, but then I guess pearls come from shells, don't they? I liked the weight of it—it wouldn't make a bad weapon if the skillet wasn't at hand—and the smoothness of it.

I stood there and thought about him holding it in those elegant hands. I stroked its surface without meaning to do so. Marcia was always complaining about their annual struggle to find an all-inclusive in the Caribbean that met her standards for luxury yet was within range of a good diving site.

Had James picked this up from the bottom of the sea?

Either way, it was beautiful. And I marveled that anyone would send me such a treasure.

Against my every instinct, I put it on my desk where I could see it, or reach out and touch it. Oh, yes, I was in big trouble and trying desperately not to hotlink to BigMistake.com.

The shell made me think. Gwen's comment clicked in a bit late, and I checked my calendar, uncertain what she meant. Tonight was the monthly meeting of the Ariadnes, much to my astonishment, and it was to be here. Gee, what could have made me forget that? I made a note to stock up on chocolate this afternoon.

We were going to need lots.

I probably haven't told you about the Ariadnes, have I? Well, you are in for a treat. Get some chocolate yourself and get cozy. I'll fill you in on all the pertinent details.

Of course, I had nothing to do with the founding of this group. Me and social clubs? You can work the probability of that out all by yourself.

Well, I had nothing to do with it beyond the pungent expression of dissatisfaction at the inaugural meeting of yet another group founded purportedly for the advancement of women in high-tech industries. Sooner or later, all of these orgs decide that they need membership dues, and the more you pay, the less you seem to get. It's amazing how often it's some guy getting rich over supposedly helping women to network.

I said as much, in pretty blunt terms—imagine that—and thus became the unofficial (and unwilling) focus of seething discontent. They expected me to solve it.

Whence came the monthly meeting of a group of like-minded folk of the feminine persuasion, all of whom figured that they didn't need a man to fix their careers for them. This eventually distilled to eight diehard souls, each willing to host every eighth meeting, in exchange for chocolate.

The name certainly wasn't mine. That credit goes to Tracy. Ariadne—James probably knows this but I had to learn it—was that mythological babe who helped Theseus find his way out of the Cretan labyrinth, a quick-thinking gal who helped a dude in distress. She found their way back out of the maze by unraveling a ball of string or wool on her way in, then following it back out.

You can work out the association between threads, and we web-spinning techno chix. Antonia, our token Wiccan, loves to expound upon the sociological implications of Ariadne the Moon Goddess being dropped in rank by the Greeks to just some girl. It gets complicated, lots of paternalism and subordination and seeds-of-centuries-of-abuse stuff, but that's a whole 'nuther story. I have to admit that I don't listen really closely.

As for any speculation about Theseus being really a handsome prince who swept Ariadne off her feet forever—or for a while, anyhow—and what that subliminally reveals about what we eight clever independent women really want, do yourself a favor and put it right out of your mind. We've got a couple of frothing feminists who will gleefully feed you your own liver for such a suggestion. Seriously, they make me look like a complacent ol' puddy-tat. Don't even go there.

I'm just thinking of your welfare, you know?

So, Ariadne was the babe with the ball of twine and the plan. And the objective of the group is to share contacts and connections and help each other succeed in what is pretty much uncharted territory for women.

Let's get one thing straight before I tell you about everyone—this is not some touchy-feely super-pal kind of girly group. We don't read books. We don't moan about men and weep on each other's shoulders. We don't talk about our relationships. Well, *I* don't talk about my relationships, and everyone is cool with that.

Got that? It's really not very complicated.

So, let's meet the Ariadnes before they all show up and start hoovering chocolate. (See, we bring chocolate to the hostess, then proceed to eat it all in the course of the evening, hitting a sugar buzz by midnight that will carry us through a good twenty-four hours post-Ariadnes with a dull glow of well-being.)

Gwen: Affectionately known as "Doctor-doctor," Gwen is our resident physicist and Ph.D. She's known for not playing by the rules and regularly shooting herself (with perfect accuracy) in the foot. Metaphorically, of course, as she's an antiviolence protester. (Work that out by yourself. I never have.) God only knows how she managed to get her doctorate, because there's nothing more mired in making nicey-nice than grad school. And Gwen is incapable of nicey-nice.

My fave theory is that she was admitted in a clerical error, promptly won a fat scholarship (that part's true), so they couldn't kick her out, loss of prestige being a major academic motivation. They put her on the fast track to graduation in-

stead, reasoning that it would either kill her, drive her away,
or she'd graduate but quick. Any of the above and they'd be
rid of her ASAP.

In a particularly galling development to anyone who might
have been an instigator of such a plan, Gwen not only survived, she thrived on the pressure and graduated magna cum
laude. (Hey, that's Latin. And I even know what it means.
With greatest honor. Kewl.)

She, of course, never got a T.A. slot or even a teaching position at her alma mater post-grad and refused to grovel to get
that changed. These days, Gwen works at the help desk of the
phone company. She says she's fed up with academia, but our
consensus is that she's just mustering artillery.

That's a joke.

Gwen has a passion for melodrama, at least in other people's lives. She's a perennial volunteer at the opera, where
she's known for terrorizing subscribers into donating more
generously. She's constantly seeking the seamy underbelly o
the existences of those around her, maybe out of curiosity,
probably out of a desire to live vicariously.

She's got nothing but nothing on me.

Khadija: A gorgeous petite dynamo, Khadija has the
charm of a queen and a South African accent that melts the
butter in the fridge. Our own steel magnolia—she didn't
know the expression but liked it when she heard it—Khadija
is not to be underestimated. Meg would make much of the
fact that she's a Scorpio. She's elegant and soft-spoken, but
even when you say no to her and think you've stood firm, you
realize later that she's somehow gotten what she wanted out
of you.

It's a gift.

But she doesn't use her talents for the dark side—she's to
busy, busting her fingies for a cause. *Her* cause. Khadija host
a medical info site and support network for parents of children with spina bifida. She's a force to be reckoned with whe
it comes to fundraising for research. That's what brought he
out to the networking group in the first place—she assume

that she'd find women in that group not only willing to spread the word, but to donate to the cause.

Khadija was right. She's got us all taking our folic acid every day, just in case we get knocked up. One less potential issue to deal with, as Khadija tells it, and she knows what she's talking about. She's not a tech queen in her own right but learned what she had to learn for the cause of her heart. Khadija's first daughter had spina bifida and died young after much suffering—we know this from her site, but she doesn't talk about her daughter much.

She has her moat dug deep and that's fine with me. I've written some kicking code for her *gratis* a couple of times, not because I'm a soft touch or anything. I just respect her. Hey, it's for the cause.

Lydia. Queen of the Theories. A blonde Valkyrie, she's equipped with an explanation for damn near everything, one that may not be the truth but often sounds better than truth ever could. She's also not technically a tech person, just one drawn into the Web, so to speak, after she met Khadija. We had a vacancy—one of our few rules is that we have eight members—and we liked her.

Similarly impassioned about healthy babies, and about wanted babies, Lydia is a public health nurse. She's got our nightstands full of more free condoms than any sane mortal could ever need, and often does spot checks of expiration dates in the bedroom of the current month's hostess with the mostest. An ounce of prevention is worth a pound of cure and all that. Maybe seven or eight pounds of squalling cure.

Lydia might be a lesbian. I don't ask, but there have been a couple of clues. It's not my business, though, you know? You start delving into people's lives, and sooner or later they think it should be a reciprocal agreement. That's not my game. I take the condoms because she doesn't give us a choice, and ritually destroy enough of them before hosting a meeting that she thinks I'm a safe cookie.

Ha. Got to remember to do that this afternoon. James and I only used two.

Phyllis is fifty and fabulous. Really. I want to be a silver

fox like Phyllis when I grow up. She's our most ardent femi-
nist, a lean, mean fighting machine, with twenty years' service in the military behind her and a handgun license to call
her own. She's a certified member of the NRA and big on responsible use of firearms. Know your weapon and all that.
You can believe that she and Gwen have gone a few rounds
now and again.

(We have another rule—no discussion of personal politics—created after Gwen got bopped in the nose and bled all
over Khadija's new ivory rug and Phyllis broke her knuckle
doing the honors.)

Phyllis's husband screwed around and dumped her after
twenty-five years of what she thought was nuptial bliss for
both parties. We do not ask what happened to the boy, by the
way, or whether he sustained any injuries beyond the emotional ones. Some things are better left unexplored.

Phyllis sat up, looked around, decided high tech was the
way to forge a future (her phrase, not mine), moved to Cambridge, got her computer science degree as a mature student,
and took on the world. Along the way, she discovered that she
was a great motivational speaker, probably by cheering the
troops before exams.

Now she runs the best cache of contract code cowboys on
the East Coast, cuts a tough deal for their services, and is
practically printing money in her basement. She has, in case
you haven't guessed, an extremely low bullshit tolerance
level. She also has some major shields mounted to defend her
personal space. We're talking NASA-issue next-generation
Kevlar. It's impressive.

I like Phyllis, a lot, and not just because she gave me some
contract work when I needed cash desperately. I respect how
hard she worked to climb her way back and that she did it
alone. One of these days maybe I'll have enough work to give
her some.

Krystal is affectionately known as the Fashion Cop. This
girl can shop. Zowie kazoo. Hitting a sale with her is an education. We used to call her the great pink hunter—she's gaga

for fuchsia—but then she started picking on our taste in clothes and helpfully (?) remaking our images.

Okay, we have a few members who are, or were, kind of indifferent to appearances. That hasn't lasted. Krystal accepts no excuses, being of the "if you're looking good, you're feeling good" school of pop psychology. She's earnest enough that you halfway think she just wants to make the world look better, maybe to improve the view.

Aptly, she's been working on the most miserable beast of technology meeting femininity—an online fitting utility for a jeans manufacturer. At first glance, you might think that this would be relatively routine—the potential customer punches in her measurements, maybe you conjure up a bit of 3-D modeling to make it jazzy and show the stock jeans on the virtual model before the customer orders.

The problems are, of course, nearly infinite.

First of all, women come in all shapes and variants of shapes and jeans fit to the skin. Waist, hip, and inseam measurements aren't nearly enough to guarantee a good, much less a flattering, fit. The jean company wants to *guarantee* the fit of jeans ordered online, to instill customer confidence. That objective is terrorizing Krystal.

Second, although you could ask the potential customer to measure more elements of her own body, each request increases the probability that she will either give it up or measure incorrectly.

And last but not least, we women lie about our measurements with breathless ease and unparalleled audacity. Especially the span of our backsides. Especially to a computer program that can't actually see us. Nightmare city—do you add a fudge factor and risk not fitting the people who do measure accurately? How much should the fudge factor be? You can't exactly ask people whether they're lying or not, and if so by how much.

Krystal has bagged a no-winner here. I just hope she gets paid for all the time she's logged on it.

Tracy, although the child wonder, was one of Krystal's first victims. The Coke-bottle glasses had to go—everyone knew it but Tracy. She's all of twenty-two years old and frighteningly brilliant—well, in some ways.

She works in a lab associated with the university, working on artificial intelligence development. She's specifically working on little investigative modules that you swallow—they collect data all the way through the digestive tract, then pop out at the end of the ride, not only with pix but analysis and suggestions for treatment. Shades of *Fantastic Voyage*.

That's the part that's close to market that we're allowed to know about. Next up, they've got a plan to shrink these modules down and make them proactive. She hasn't told us more, but I'm guessing that the plan is ultimately for a patient to knock back a cup of cell warriors to take on their bad guys on a cell level.

(Hmm. James would have too much fun with the potential liability there. What if the good guys turn bad? Is it the fault of the creator of the good guys, or is each warrior self-determining? This is starting to sound like theology. Never mind.)

We have had some serious talks about the potential misuse of such powers and germ warfare. Phyllis is a conspiracy theorist par excellence and insists that AIDS was a weapon that got away from the development labs, so you know she's latched on to this one. Tracy is young enough to be utterly idealistic—but even though she doesn't work for the Feds directly, she does have some kind of security clearance. That's enough to give the anarchist in me the major creepies.

And yes, I have wondered just how much she tells anyone else about what we discuss.

Finally, there's *Antonia*, Wiccan and high mistress of twisting technology to suit her needs. No, she doesn't cast spells or tell fortunes—she's a performance artist and uses high-tech stuff in unpredictable ways. The purpose here is to challenge our conceptions of ourselves and our ever-changing world while echoing the unsustainability and fundamental tenuousness of our grip on reality.

I got that from her Web site.

We actually went to school together, all those many moons ago, when she was just a plain old repressed Catholic girl like me. We lost touch when I went to Japan. We hooked up a few years ago when I went to see one of her performances, which was blasted in the techie newspaper, thus feeding my curiosity.

It was weird.

Over the course of three hours, in a warehouse with a concrete floor, with dimmed lights and jungle sounds in the background, Antonia hunted computers. She wore a fake-fur outfit à la Wilma Flintstone and a bone in her hair, and had roboticized the boxes so they could move. Their erratic—and thus evasive—paths were the result of random number generators picking their changes of course and speeds. Several had a robot arm fitted with razor blades on the "fingers" that they periodically swiped through the air, thereby making Antonia both predator and prey.

The whole thing was unprogrammed and unchoreographed, except that the robots slowly sped up and that they vastly outnumbered Antonia. The audience had to move as well to evade the uncharted courses of the robots, making us part of the experience of the hunt. There was real panic in the air at one or two points.

One by one, the primeval hunter eliminated her foes, leaving some stalled and some smoking. When she took down the biggest and thus "meatiest" one, she dragged it across the floor, lit a fire, cracked its back, and scooped its inner cabling out like spaghetti. She eviscerated it, then began to roast bits of it over the fire, making grunting noises of anticipation as the warehouse filled with smoke.

I loved it. Having had more than a few moments when I've wanted to gut a computer, I found the show irresistible. Antonia hooked me on performance art too, that moment when the audience realized that they were part of the show having been just too delicious to forget.

So we connected again, though the Lost Years—as we've come to call them—remain pretty much unexplored, by mutual choice. We're both single now and that's all we need to know.

You know, of course, all you need to know about me, member #8.

Feeling somewhat sepulchral about life, the universe, and everything, I dressed for the evening in full Goth glory. Black leather pants that fit more tightly than my own skin these days, a plum crushed velvet fitted tunic and a white poet's shirt with a good six-inch-deep ruffle of lace at the collar and cuffs.

Rice powder is the trick to that pale pale Goth face. And concealer underneath to smooth out the hues of your skin. I followed with a catty Cleopatra eyeliner look in midnight blue, which made my eyes look sapphire and upstaged the shadows under my eyes. I chose a purple lipstick named, aptly enough, Deadly Nightshade, and decided it was coming together well. I moussed my aubergine hair and tousled it up, telling my reflection that this could be a hellish night.

The Ariadnes—a wickedly perceptive bunch—might guess that something was wrong. They might want to know. They might demand that I dish, after all their various sporadic dishing over the years. I was the only one who had never surrendered a personal tidbit. Surely I couldn't lose my touch now. I shuddered with foreboding, then slipped into a pair of beaded black mules with stiletto forever heels that I had nearly sold my soul to own. I was ready.

In the Nick—ha ha—of time.

Lydia arrived first, as usual, as befitted one unanimously acknowledged as punctuality princess. She brought a box of Godiva truffles, the big box, angel of mercy that she is, and about a hundred Day-Glo condoms.

"You'll know where he is," she said by way of greeting, pushing a dozen into my hand.

That made me smile. "I've a new theory for you."

"Oh, good, I could use some cheering up."

I didn't take the bait, not wanting to encourage confessions too early. "Golf is God's plan for a universal contraceptive in America."

"Not bad. It's the plaid, isn't it? I mean plaid is one thing, and not a very good thing in quantity anyhow, but those southerners get hold of it and suddenly it's tangerine plaid."

"Knickers," I added and we both faked a convulsion.

"If only they would wear kilts."

"Then it wouldn't be a contraceptive."

"True. I like it." She shook a finger at me. "My newest plum theory is that the popularity of the soulpatch is utterly responsible for the sudden outbreak of chastity among post-pubescent women."

Discussion was curtailed by the arrival of Khadija, with three big Cadbury Caramilk bars "from England," and Tracy, with a box of Turtles. Phyllis wasn't far behind, toting her usual no-nonsense contribution of a Black Magic box of assorted.

"It's half milk chocolate and half dark," she explained as she always explained. "Something for everyone." They had all been there often enough to find their way around—and really, you'd have to be blind not to be able to find your way around a big damn-near-empty box like my loft. I started pouring soda waters and the usual symphony of diet beverages.

I know. It makes no sense. Gorge on chocolate but drink diet soda. Leave us our illusions, please.

Cellophane was torn off the boxes, which were arrayed on what passes as a coffee table in my place—two monitor boxes, shoved together, tablecloth overtop—and they fetched chairs from every corner. The Caramilk bars were broken. It was dark outside, the sky pushing hues of navy and purple against the glass bricks. I lit about a thousand candles, then answered the bell again.

"I want those mules," Krystal said when the elevator disgorged her moments later.

"They're mine, all mine."

"Then let me know when you get tired of them."

"Manolo Blahnick." I modeled them just to feed her envy. "I will never get tired of them."

"Then put me in your will, dahling." She grinned and

sailed into the room. "Thank God none of you are wearing jeans."

Tracy was with her—they sometimes shared a ride—and smiled shyly as she passed me a sock of Hershey's Kisses. Krystal contributed a box of some Belgian seashells, then waved to everyone else as she moved into the loft. Tracy trailed right behind her, like a quiet shadow who found us slightly intimidating.

Goodness knows why.

Gwen shouted up from below, demanding the elevator PDQ as she needed to use the facilities. I laughed and closed the door so it would descend, imagining her tap-dancing down below. She was tap-dancing when she got out, too, taking just a moment to drop the Ferraro Rochers into my outstretched hand before making her beeline to relief.

Antonia was last, no surprise, an enormous bag of M&M's under her arm. "Goodness, but I love this place, Maralys. Anytime you need a roomie, you let me know."

"In your dreams."

"Don't I know it."

"I'd never know what you'd do to the place while I was asleep. I could wake up in the middle of Art."

"That's part of the adventure."

"Adventure I can live without."

She smiled briefly, then her gaze searched mine and her smile faded. "You okay?"

"No. But thanks for asking. Come on in." She left it there and so did I, the chatter of the others quickly filling the loft. Antonia was watching me, though, and I knew that she'd come back to her question when she decided the moment was right.

I tried to get those damn shields up fast.

Antonia's moment didn't take that long to turn up. We had talked about Khadija's trip to the U.K. for a conference— she was flushed with the flattery she'd had on quality of information on her site—and commiserated with Krystal that her most recent ex-boyfriend was indeed a rat. I had brushed off inquiries in my direction quite diligently, I thought, until I noticed that Antonia was getting that laser-eyed look. I was starting to squirm.

That had nothing on my full-throttle squirming when the phone rang.

I realized too late that I'd left it in the mode where you can hear whatever message is being left. I was going to get up, but Antonia had a catty little "Aha!" smile, so I sat back down, hoping for the best.

"Maralys, it's James."

So much for hoping. I lost.

There was much laughter after that, everyone trying to do the polite thing of talking loud enough that they couldn't hear the message.

Even as they were straining their ears to do just that.

"Nice voice."

"Umm-hmm. What does he look like?"

"As if that's important." I felt myself blushing despite my will to the contrary.

"Give me a call if you have a chance," James continued, then chuckled under his breath. "He suggested optimistically."

"Oh, he's got your number."

"And about last night . . ."

Eight women were as silent as mice, straining their ears for every nuance of sound. We even froze. I was looking for that gaping hole in the floor to open up and spare me from mortification but knew it wouldn't happen.

And I did want to know what he said.

"I think you should let your father miss you for a few days. I went to see him this afternoon and he's doing well. They're cutting back his drugs, and Dr. Moss wants to send him somewhere other than home alone by the end of next week. I've got an idea about that, and we should talk before they check him out." There was suddenly a smile in his voice. "Yes, Maralys, that would be both some slack and a deadline. Take care."

And with a click, he was gone. The Ariadnes exhaled as one, then looked at me.

"Anything you want to talk about?" Antonia asked quietly.

I could barely catch my breath. "Me? No. Why?"

They passed a glance around like a hot potato, then all looked at me again. Antonia seemed to have been silently appointed spokeswoman, because no one else said a word.

She leaned forward and held my gaze. "Look, Maralys, we know that you're a really private person. We all managed to pick that up and that's okay. Everyone here has shared a story, except you. . . ."

"Keeping score?"

"No. We just want you to know that it's okay. We're here, whenever you need us, even if you don't need us. The choice is up to you. We just want you to understand that we understand, either way."

My breath was coming in big shaky chunks. Because it's true—if you don't invest anything, if you shelter yourself from the world and other people, then you've got nothing to lose. You are nothing but alone. I've been there and done that, and the view is really hell.

Maybe it was time to make the trust club a little less exclusive than it had been to date. Maybe I didn't have to think that I had to save the world—and defend mine—all by myself. I knew what I had to do, I knew that this was a safe place to put my trust, but still. Old habits die hard.

"You know already that anything said among us goes no further," Antonia added.

"Absolutely," Phyllis said with force.

They were all watching me and not trying to hide that. They were the most honest and trustworthy group of people I'd ever had the good luck to know.

And I'd never told them so.

Antonia seemed to guess that I was on the verge. She eased out of her chair in that catlike way she has and picked up the golden Godiva box. She offered it to me and smiled. "Take one for fortitude."

I picked a truffle and bit into it, meeting the steady gaze of each Ariadne in turn. "You'd better all take one. This is a helluva story."

They did and when the box was back on the table and the chewing was done, I took a deep breath and began. The first words were hard, and the ones I chose surprised me when they fell out of my mouth.

Later I realized that they were exactly perfect. Maybe it was the only way I could have told the story.

One thing was for sure—I had the best audience anyone could have hoped to have. That scene with the candles flickering and the ceiling out of view, me surrounded by seven women attentive and concerned, will always be etched in my mind.

It was the night I told the Ariadnes about James and Marcia and the baby and me.

It was the night that I let the Ariadnes *really* be my friends.

"*Once upon a time, there were two sisters who looked exactly alike. Pearls fell from the mouth of one and frogs from the lips of the other. . . .*"

You see how it is. Twos fare badly in the language stakes. Twosomes exist to draw attention to contrasts, not only to identify but to add a moral judgment of opposing ends of the spectrum. You can even look at the words themselves to see the truth of our bias:

Bipolar disorder. Double trouble. Two-faced. Terrible twos. Double-dealing. Two left feet. Two-timing. An odd couple. Two-time losers and two-bit lawyers, neither of which you want to date. A two-edged sword makes for a tough choice, with neither one a winner.

Once bitten, twice shy.

Duplicate: a copy of an original, the implication being that the copy is inferior by the very fact of not being the original. How else could duplicity mean deceptiveness?

Duodenum, a particularly horrible place to get cancer. But then, I suppose there are few good places to get cancer. Perhaps there are places more successfully treated than others, but good and bad? It's not that easy.

Twos get the same kind of bad rap in the realm of folklore and fairy tale. Every good sister has a wicked one. Every fairy godmother requires an evil stepmother. Every wish is matched by a curse. Every hero needs his villain. You have to wonder, in the end, why the good guys are so insecure that they need a foil to show themselves to advantage.

Opposites may attract, but we certainly don't give them much chance even to get together. We define qualities with extremes, one end of the scale or the other. Black and white. Extrovert or introvert. Tall or short. Angelic or demonic. Up and down, in and out, north and south, positive and negative, heads or tails.

It seems that we love contrast.

What we really love are simple answers. Simple parameters make for simple choices, and often for simplistic solutions. Because if life were simple, we'd all be a lot better at making our choices. There would be a lot fewer of us screwing up the game of life so brilliantly, if there was always a right answer instead of just a best—or even a less bad—answer.

But we cling to our preconceptions, allowing only black or white in defiance of our experience. Is she nice? Is he handsome? Are they good kids?

Worse, we cling to this in direct opposition to our daily experiences, despite the data streaming back to us that says it's wrong. There are countless shades of gray in our hearts, in our bodies, and in our lives. There are hues of all the colors of human qualities within each of us: some in greater quantities and some in lesser, it's true, but none totally present or totally absent.

I can switch my computer display from black and white to 64,000 shades of gray. A flick of the wrist and I'm closer to the truth.

It's all those shades of gray that complicate things, that make the game more nuanced and more interesting. I argue in favor of shades of gray—no good children or bad children, but children with both good and bad in them, but in varying proportions. Better children and worse children, maybe. Children more or less inclined to make a good choice over a bad one, even better.

Dr. Jekyll and Mr. Hyde are alive and well, but not in their wild opposition. It's all their subtly differentiated cousins, who are tenants within each and every one of us, who really run the show.

Even the most angelic children have a bit of wickedness inside them.

Or they should.

Because anyone who appears totally good is probably hiding something from the casual gaze. Something more dreadful that might be assumed. Nature abhors simplicity, though we address this inconsistency again with the extremes of twos.

Dopplegangers and body snatchers, the double that isn't really a double deep down inside. The understudy. The body double. Literature is full of characters who aren't what they seem to be—and so, in fact, are jails. We don't want to know that the surface can be deceptive, for that would make our world not only more complicated, but far more dangerous.

Light and dark. Day and night. Sunlight and shadow. Shhh, there are some things better left alone.

And so it was that I won Whore by default, because Madonna had been claimed by Marcia. There were no other roles being cast; it was one or the other. You can't have two Madonnas, either in the religious or the pop culture sense. It's unthinkable. You can have lots of whores, but that's another issue altogether.

I have been the bad apple all my life, from the moment I made my first yell. I was louder, badder, rougher, and wild. I was the demon seed, the rebel, the nonconformist, the one who dropped out of college, the one who got pregnant at the wrong time, then didn't get pregnant at the right time. The one that my mother's friends shook their heads over. "Isn't it too bad? You know, she's always been the troublemaker."

The one my mother didn't recognize at the end.

I was the one who fled the country, the one who made bad choices, the one married to a charming loser who ought to be in jail, the one who found herself within a hair of bankruptcy, and then the one who occupied a hot seat down at the IRS. I am the one who cannot be redeemed, the one who is going to hell, the one who causes nothing but disappointment. I am the one who has fulfilled every dire prediction of my future, the one left to sink or swim.

I am the one who knows better than to ask for help.

I am the one who has picked up the pieces, the one who does not deserve to be thanked, the one with no expectations, the one who has learned to rely only on herself, the one who had become convinced that love and happiness are things bestowed upon other people.

People who are not wicked. Or perhaps, people who snagged the better role early and held on to it for dear life.

I have my flaws, but I am not the evil twin. I may have dressed the part, but you should be smart enough to not take everything at face value.

I am not the whore. I am not the bad girl. I am not the troublemaker. I am not the one beyond hope. I am not the one who got what she deserved or the one who made her own bed. I am not the one unable to take responsibility. I am not the one who is a burden upon others. I am neither the selfish one, nor the shameless one. I am not the insensitive one. I am not the wicked one.

I am not the evil twin.

I am not the evil twin. Say it twice and make it so.

I ended up somehow on the futon, my face wet with tears, Khadija on one side and Krystal on the other.

"Make the world a better place," Krystal suggested, then handed me a tissue. "Lose what's left of your eyeliner."

"Got it." I did as I was told. Krystal had her arm around me, and everyone was silent, coming to terms with what I'd confessed. Lydia passed the box of truffles, insisting that I take two.

"That sucks," Gwen said and we all nodded agreement. Phyllis sighed, then pushed to her feet. She strode off to the kitchen and came back moments later bearing a mug of tea.

She plunked it down in front of me with a stern look. "This is the sum of my maternal instincts. Consider yourself hugged."

"Thanks, Phyllis." I picked up the mug and wrapped my hands around it, even though I didn't really want it.

Antonia sat opposite me. She had her feet curled under herself like a cat, her unswerving gaze also reminding me of a curious feline. "She must have known," she said abruptly.

Phyllis barked a laugh. "His asking after the mole would have been a big clue."

"No, no." Antonia unfurled herself slightly. "Before that. I bet she knew from the beginning."

"You're joking," I said, but there wasn't much indignation I could muster up.

"Think about it! What would he have said when he met her? Something like 'Oh, it's great to see you again' if not a mention of your night together. Marcia knew you were twins, even if James didn't. She must have done the math right from the beginning."

I stared at Antonia, hating how much sense it made.

"Ewww!" Tracy shuddered. "You mean she tried to steal her sister's boyfriend? That's so mean!"

Antonia rolled her eyes. "Be serious. Women do it all the time." She snapped her fingers at me. "Didn't you think it was weird that you never got to meet the boy wonder?"

"No. I was too busy barfing my eyes out every morning, while trying to be sure that my mother of the bionic ears didn't hear what was going on. When I wasn't barfing, I was praying that James would call. When I wasn't praying that he'd call or barfing, I was trying to figure out what the hell I was going to do." I sipped my tea. "You could say that I was kind of distracted at the time."

Antonia leaned forward, eyes gleaming. "Don't you remember, Maralys? When we were kids, we called Marcia 'Little Miss Gimme'?"

"I haven't thought about that in years."

"Maybe you should have. I sure remember. She wanted everything you had. I don't know how many times I heard her explain that she was born first and that you two weren't supposed to be twins, as if you'd taken a wrong turn somewhere and belonged to another family."

"There are no twins in our family that we know of. We used to tease my mother that she got too close to the heavy water in the lab."

"She was a scientist?" Tracy asked helpfully.

"She was a cleaning lady." My friends chuckled, but I didn't. "It was less funny when she got sick."

"Cancer?" Lydia asked quietly.

I nodded, not really wanting to go there.

Antonia was on a mission and didn't mean to take a detour. Good and bad. She was practically hanging out of her chair. "I'll bet Marcia made sure there was no chance of you answering the phone and talking to James. What did Marcia look like when she showed you that picture?" she asked. "Can you remember the expression on her face?"

I closed my eyes and sat back, comforted despite myself by the warmth of the mug of tea. I really didn't want to consider that Marcia had played a big role in this, despite all the things we've said to each other over the years.

But I remember exactly what Antonia suspected.

"I remember wondering why she was so pleased with herself, then figured it was because he was such a good catch, as my mother liked to say."

Antonia eased back. "A good catch, if your sister had snagged him first. A particularly tasty one if Ms. Gimme stole him from you. He can't be a dope, Maralys. She must have deliberately tried to snag him. She must have lied."

"Then why was she so angry about the mole?"

Tracy cleared her throat. "Maybe it started out badly but she really loved him and thought he really loved her when they got married."

"That would be a cruel blow," Gwen suggested, and we all nodded.

Antonia shook her finger at me. "But you ran away. You big wuss, Maralys! I never thought you had it in you. I always thought that you had the balls to fight for what you wanted."

"I was young and pregnant and confused!"

Antonia lit a cigarette, which she knows I hate, took a long draw and exhaled. "Then what's your excuse now?"

"What excuse? We've aired our differences and can move on. Phew! I'm glad that's behind me." I reached for the chocolate.

Antonia started to cluck like a chicken.

"What's that supposed to mean?"

"You're still chicken."

We glared at each other across the room. The others had never seen us annoyed at each other and it had been years, but

Antonia couldn't poke around with my nerve endings to amuse herself. "You're just trying to stir me up."

"Enough to react, yeah. Afraid to be happy, Maralys? Afraid to fall in love?"

"No, I . . ." I began furiously, but Antonia cut me off.

"You are afraid to fall in love because you're afraid to lose control. You don't really trust any of us, Maralys, and you really don't trust James." She dragged and exhaled again, her gaze knowing. "But if you spend your whole life managing everything yourself, then you're going to spend your whole life alone."

"Maralys was married!" Tracy protested, defending me in her naïveté.

"To a little boy who wanted a mommy," I corrected quietly. "I could control him and fix his life—well, I thought so anyway."

"And when you couldn't save him from himself, you paid his debts anyway." Phyllis's tone was hard.

"I should have seen it coming!"

Antonia bowed low, her hands stretched out in front of her. "Oh, touch me with your infinite wisdom, omniscient Maralys."

I should have been insulted, but it all made too much sense. "This is really not fair," I grumbled. "I've worked so hard to keep you from knowing all about me, and so you've gone and made up a bunch of stuff. It's true that James and I had history, it's true that we had to vent, but it's also true that it's done now. Over and out. Case closed."

Antonia grinned, unpersuaded. She smoked and watched me, and my heart skipped around like a wild thing.

I swallowed, then took a scalding sip of tea.

"We often have to sacrifice something to gain something greater," Khadija said quietly. She squeezed my shoulders and I looked into her dark eyes, seeing all the sacrifices that had brought her to her current success. Here was a woman who had lost her child due to the lack of a simple preventative measure. One that she had not known about and evidently neither had her doctor.

"You never talk about your daughter."

She smiled and shook her head. "Maybe next time." Tears welled in her eyes. "But I would have been very happy never to acknowledge what had happened. Her disability and sub-sequent suffering were at least partly my fault. I had to find some goodness in what she went through, if just to ease my guilt. Preventing even one baby from developing that disease is all I ever wanted."

I was humbled by her bravery. "Do you talk to your other daughters about her?"

Khadija smiled and one of her tears slipped free. "All the time." Her voice was hoarse. "I think every day of what she might have become. And then I wonder whether there was a divine plan for what happened."

She shook her head, marveling. "We have raised so much money for research and spread the word of prevention to so many expectant mothers. All because I said 'my baby died' when I would rather not have done so. I never imagined that out of grief could come such success." Her grip was urgent on my shoulders. "Take a chance, Maralys, and you may be sur-prised. Life is too short to cower."

Life is too short to cower. I liked that. I looked at each of them in turn, their expressions expectant, and I loved every one of those women with painful intensity. I knew that they would be there for me, that they had always been there for me, even though I had never had the grace to trust them before tonight.

Even though they'd twisted what I said into something it wasn't. They meant well and I was touched by their concern.

"All right," I said, then spoke more vehemently. "That's enough advice for Maralys. I'm new to this stuff, so go easy on me. And please, don't tell me that we have to have a group hug."

They laughed and we had a celebratory gorge of chocolate, chattering like magpies all the while. When they left in the wee hours of the morning, carefully carpooling so that no one was on the evil streets alone, each one hugged me tightly.

Individually.

"Call if you need me," Antonia said and nearly broke my ribs.

"I will." And to my amazement, I meant it. "Hey, wait a minute, wait a minute. I forget to tell you. I'm having a party and you all have to come."

My dream came again, the next night, but then I had half-expected that it would. I'd been fretful since the Ariadnes left and that—or the consumption of melted cheese right before sleep—always conjured up that airline terminal. I was stewing about James and his deadline, my father and my life, as well as getting this software delivered brilliantly and on time.

Nothing else, all right?

The dream was every bit as upsetting as all the other times I'd had it. And it was exactly the same.

Except that it didn't stop. When I was pounding on the glass, watching my Cashin bag go around, a woman came through one of the doors marked NO ADMITTANCE. EMPLOYEES ONLY.

But this woman didn't look like a ramp rat. I pressed my face to the glass to see better. She was wearing a ghastly green hospital gown and white terry-cloth slippers. She was on an IV drip and pushing that little rolling rack ahead of herself, leaning on it for support. She headed straight for my bag, charting a course to intersect it with the least amount of walking for her.

And she plucked it off the conveyor. She flashed some cheek when she went for it, and I saw how thin she was. I swallowed, maybe sensing what was to come. Even in a dream, it was incongruous for a woman like this to be in a place like this and even in my dream, I knew it.

Something important was going to happen.

I stood and stared, my fingers clenched, hoping against hope that she wasn't taking my bag for herself. She slipped it onto her shoulder, the one without the IV, confirming my worst fears. Then she turned slowly, as if it pained her, and looked straight at me.

I gasped and took a step back. You see, I knew who she was, though I hadn't recognized her at first. Maybe I hadn't wanted to recognize her.

But how could I not have known my own mother?

I remembered that I hadn't recognized her when I first got to the hospital, all those years before. She had lost so much weight, she had been pale, and her hair had fallen out. She had been a faded unfamiliar specter of my mother and you had to look for the truth in her smile. You had to hide your shock.

Not that she would have known the difference. Oh, yes, my father was not the only one to fail Mary Anne. I came too late and too changed for her to remember who I was.

And now, this specter danced for me again.

Or more accurately, she hobbled across the cheap linoleum tiles of my nightmare airport terminal, as if she might demand an accounting for my failures. I went to the sliding door, prepared to accept whatever she doled out to me. Repentant, head bowed. Forgive me, Mother, for I have sinned. She opened it from her side by stepping on the thread, a whish of air, then nothing happened.

I looked up tentatively and realized that she held the bag out to me. An offering from the other side.

But it wasn't what I wanted.

I tried to take her hand, tried to speak, but she shook her head. "This is all you need," she whispered, her words like a wraith in the wind.

She offered the bag again, and this time I took it.

She waited, expectantly, so I opened it. The bulge in the bag was a ball of wool. I pulled it out and stared at my mother.

"Don't be afraid, Mary Elizabeth," she said in that same soft voice, then blew me a kiss. I leaned forward, welcoming this almost-touch, expecting to feel the impact of that air kiss, wanting some contact before she left again.

Instead, everything went black around me. The terminal disappeared, my bags were gone, my mother had faded without a trace. There was only darkness and impenetrable shadows, the kind that put a primal part of me on full alert.

The ball let off a faint glow, and when I looked, I saw that I held only one end. A string unwound from the ball and snaked off into the endless darkness, faintly luminescent for as far as I could see it.

"Don't be afraid," my mother had said. I've never been afraid of the dark, but this dark was different. It was darker. Brooding.

Breathing.

That was when I realized that I wasn't alone in this void. I heard a stirring of some great beast far behind me. It snorted and I thought it pawed its feet.

Unfathomable depths ahead and a nameless threat behind. I made my choice but quick.

And I swear to God that as I began to run, winding the string as quickly as I plunged into mysteries I could not name, I felt the steam of the minotaur's breath upon my butt.

I woke, sweating and panting as before, my loft looking like an alien landscape to me.

"Don't be afraid." The whisper clung to the edge of my consciousness like a cobweb in the corner of the ceiling. And like that cobweb, it drew my attention over and over again, taunting me to get rid of it, even though it couldn't easily be reached.

Afraid. Not a word I associated very often with myself, but there it was. You have to give some credence to the wisdom of dreams and to your own mother.

Afraid. Hmm. Okay, I was afraid as to how it might look if James and I had any kind of relationship beyond the usual sister-in-law/brother-in-law one (sordid), and what people would think (slut steals twin's hubby). Then there were the questions of why James was so determined to pursue me (sex sex and more sex; convenience), what effect it would have on the boys (incapable of committing to a pair bond ever in their lives), and the big whopper—whether it would really work out in the end or my heart would get ripped out and stomped flat under those perfectly polished Italian oxblood oxfords.

There you go. I had to catch my breath. A whole army of fears flushed from the woods. Who'd even known they were there?

Cluck, cluck, cluck. I've never looked good in red.

As in "Little Red Hen." "Chicken" for those of you hand-shaking at less than 56K baud.

I exhaled and swung my feet out of bed, shoving my hands through my hair.

What I needed was a good strong coffee. Espresso was the ticket.

I waited until Sunday, so he'd had a couple of days without the pleasure of my company, but then I went to visit my dad. James's assurances were all well and good, but I needed to see the wounded leprechaun myself.

He was staring out the window when I arrived, so I took the chance to have a look before declaring myself. There was no one in the other bed now, and the rubber-covered mattress was stripped bare. The sunlight came through the big industrial windows and touched my father's face, making his skin look as fragile as rice paper.

The sky was a giddy blue, the same hue as the rubber mattress cover and my dad's gown. It made his eyes look tired and faded, instead of the vibrant hue they usually were. He was paler and thinner than I recalled, and looked as likely to blow away on a whiff of wind as a dandelion seed.

It shook me, if you must know. Guess I'm kind of used to having him around. A regular sparring partner and all that.

"So, how are you feeling?" I asked, not quite as antagonistically as I would normally. He turned and looked at me, his eyes bright in his face. They must have been giving him something, because his pupils were small, but he seemed alert. We stared at each other for a long time, and I wondered how much he remembered of the other night.

He turned back to the window, his gaze following the swoop of a couple of seagulls. "I have been talking to your mother," he admitted quietly.

The hair prickled on the back of my neck, but I sauntered into the room as if untroubled. "That's a helluva trick. She's been dead a long time."

He flicked a glance at me. "I've not forgotten that, Mary Elizabeth." His tone was not accusing, and we eyed each other again, somewhat uncertain how to proceed.

It seemed that we were both shaken by his fall.

"Sounds like you have. I warned you not to go expecting me to remember all your stuff as well as mine. I'm already low on RAM cache."

My father ignored this in a most uncharacteristic way. I wondered, if you must know, exactly what kind of little prezzies were in the IV drip to keep him mellow.

His brow tightened for a moment, his gaze on those birds again. "Perhaps I've been dreaming of her in this place."

I perched on the side of the bed. "Is that different? Don't you usually dream of her?"

His gaze fixed on me. "Do you?"

It seemed pointless to dodge the question. "Yes."

My father seemed intrigued by this. "What does she do in your dreams?"

I didn't know how the heck we got onto this, but it didn't seem as if we would get off it soon. "She talks to me, sometimes." I shrugged. I wasn't going to treat him to the full buffet of bizarre. "Sometimes she doesn't. Sometimes she smiles, as if everything is going to be okay."

My father smiled. "Is it?"

"Hardly ever."

We both smiled at that.

My father sobered and turned his narrowed gaze on the birds again. "No, it hardly ever is. But then, your mother always had such faith."

"What does she do in your dreams?" I asked when he looked troubled. "Here. Lately."

My father shook his head minutely. "She's just here." He looked around the room then, glancing at the stainless gizmos and the pastel painted walls, the functional furniture and handrails and monitoring equipment. It was as if he sought a glimpse of her in these surroundings while he was awake, maybe as proof that she could visit him at night. "She didn't want to die here, you know."

I leaned forward, bracing my elbows on my knees. "I didn't think she had a lot of choice."

Now he was stern, the disciplinarian I remembered from

my childhood. "We all have choices, Mary Elizabeth, and we had best do our best to make good ones. We have to live with the choices we make." His vigor faded and his voice faltered. "Even the bad ones."

I waited but he didn't continue. "What bad choices?"

"Your mother didn't want to die here. She was quite insistent. She wanted to go home."

"I don't remember that."

"It was between the two of us, as all such discussions should be. Two became one when we made our vows each to the other. We made choices together. We stuck together." He sighed and again, the heat left his voice. He looked beaten, which isn't how I'm accustomed to seeing my dad. "Except that last time."

"You wanted her to stay here?"

My father frowned, the birds clearly fascinating him. "I didn't know there was a choice. There was less talk in those days of home care and counseling and such. The doctors thought she should stay here. I guess I thought they could fix it, that they could heal her."

"Even cancer?"

"Especially cancer. They seemed to have the most tools to use against it." He shook his head. "You have to remember, Mary Elizabeth, that in our youth, there were not so many hospitals. Certainly not for poor people as your mother and I were, all those years ago, back in the villages of Ireland. Babies were born on kitchen tables and the sick died in their own beds. Many suffered and many died young. You cannot blame us for believing, after all we had seen, that this modern way was best."

There was nothing I could say to that.

"At the end, though, we all become the child we once were. All she wanted was to go home, to die in her bed as was right and proper. Maybe I was afraid. Maybe I was hoping she'd recover. Maybe I thought that the only salvation for her was in this place of miracles." His lips tightened. "Maybe I still thought that a gracious God would answer my prayers."

"Dad . . ." I reached out to touch him, sensing the storm, but he sat up, outraged.

"It was not fair!" he shouted with surprising volume. "It was not right!" He was crying openly as he bellowed at the injustice. "My Mary Anne was kind and sweet and loving, as good as an angel. I was the troublemaker, I was the rough one, I was the one careless with his words, the one who hurt others and never looked back. It was not fair that she should be the one to suffer so."

His voice broke on the memory that still tore me up as well. I took his hand and he clung to mine. "And oh, how she suffered! It ate her away from the inside, that evil disease. She told me once that she could feel it, gnawing away at her."

My father took a deep gulping breath, shaking his head when I might have interrupted him. "And there was not a thing I could do about it. Not a thing. Me, the man of the household, the one she relied upon. I could not do a thing. Even my prayers were insufficient to save her, so great a sinner was I."

"Dad, I don't think—"

"And was that the worst of it? No! I even denied her the only thing she asked of me in the end." He shook his head. "I was not even here when she died, Mary Elizabeth. I did not even have the grace to hold her hand while she slipped away, even knowing as I did that she was afraid."

He shook his head and his tears fell on his hospital gown. "I failed her in every conceivable way. What kind of gratitude is that for all the gifts she brought me? No, I was never fit to be her man. I was never good enough. I failed your mother as I had no right to fail her."

"Dad, she was in a coma at the end. And you had to sleep. She couldn't have known . . ."

"Oh, she knew, upon that you can rely. But as she always did, your mother forgave me. She was a far better person than I could ever have been. That's why she's here, to tell me that she's forgiven me. She's waiting for me, to help me, because she knows that I am not as strong as she. I never was."

He took a ragged breath. "And the shame of it is that still

I know the truth. I know that in her place, I could never be so gracious. I could never forgive someone who denied me something so simple, something so clearly within their power." He looked at me, his gaze clear. "What have I learned in this life, Mary Elizabeth? What kind of sinner am I that I learned nothing from such a woman, nothing from such a tragedy?"

"Dad . . ." I reached out and touched his shoulder. He was shaking.

My touch seemed to make him crumble. He buried his face in his hands, looking smaller and more frail than ever before. It terrified me.

"I'm afraid to die, Mary Elizabeth," he whispered through his fingers. "I am afraid to die and face an accounting of all I have done. And I'm just as afraid to die in this soulless place as your mother was." His voice broke. "I don't want to live alone any more. I don't want to *die* alone."

Then my father, for the first time in my experience, wept like a child.

Without another thought, I caught him in the hug that he seemed to need so desperately. He sobbed, the tears coming from deep within him in great shaking gulps. It was as if something had torn free within him and was being spewed out. He clung to me. I'd never seen my father so devastated.

In fact, I remembered how stoic he had been at my mother's funeral. He hadn't shed a single tear, and for a long time I had thought it evidence that he did not care. There had been a time when I had hated him for that.

But now I finally understood. He'd been afraid to begin to weep because he hadn't known whether he'd be able to stop.

You would have thought that I of all people would have gotten that.

I rocked him and I whispered to him and I wondered what the hell I was going to do. After a few moments he composed himself and pushed me away slightly, though he still kept a grip on my sleeves. "Where have you been?"

"You sent me away. I did what I was told." I smiled at him. "That must be why it confused you."

He didn't smile. "What is this?"

"You told me to leave."

He blinked, uncertain. "I did?"

"Just after we came here. You called out and I came and you thought I was Marcia." My voice hardened. "You said to tell Mary Elizabeth to leave."

His brow knotted in confusion. "No, Marcia is not here. She hasn't been here at all. She has left us all." His gaze brightened as he looked at me. "I did tell your mother to send you home. She was here to take care of me, and you needed your sleep."

I stared at him and my own tears rose. He'd thought I was my mother.

I shook my head. "I don't look like Mom."

"No, no, but there's an expression you get that is the very image of her. You have it now again. Stop it!" He spoke gruffly, embarrassed by his mistake, and fiddled with the sheets.

Crisis over, I moved to the visitor's chair, an orange vinyl confection of considerable vintage. I knew my moving away would make both of us more comfortable.

My father cleared his throat eventually and frowned at the floor. "Marcia phoned me yesterday." He grimaced then, his disapproval clear. "From wherever she is with her *lover*. What need has a married woman of a lover, Mary Elizabeth?"

You can bet I wasn't going there. Because the corollary is that a married man doesn't need one, either. I shrugged.

"None, *none* is the truth of it." My father took a deep breath and straightened, annoyance, as always, billowing his sails. "What right has she to take a lover, to leave her children and her husband, to run away to who knows where? I would have thought her incapable of such selfishness." My father watched me, his gaze shrewd. "You've nothing to say about this. It's not like you."

"It's not my business."

He almost smiled. "That has never stopped you before."

An aide came sailing into the room then, carrying a tray.

"Are you hungry, Mr. O'Reilly?" The music of the Caribbean was in her voice.

"Of course I'm hungry!" My father harumphed. I guessed that this woman had served him before and he liked her. "How can a man not be hungry when all he's given to eat is broth and Jell-O?"

She smiled, untroubled by his attitude. It was mutual then. "You didn't finish your breakfast, so you can't be that hungry."

"It was too salty! I thought this was a hospital. Why, for the love of God, must everything be so filled with salt? Have you empty spaces in the cardiac ward to fill?"

She laughed and pushed the wheeled table toward the bed. "Oh, Mr. O'Reilly, I'll bet you charm all the girls." She winked at him, which startled him to silence long enough for her to leave.

My father lifted the dish over the entrée and poked at it, his expression grim. "What have they done to this excuse for a meal?" he muttered with disgust. "And Jell-O for dessert. Again."

"Looks like chicken potpie."

"You always were the imaginative one."

"It'll be worse cold. You'd better get at it."

He muttered a complaint and dug in, doing it enough justice that it couldn't have been that bad. He insisted, of course, that starvation would drive a man to eat near anything.

I was just happy to see him back in fighting form. If he was scrappy enough to complain, then he was probably going to be okay.

This time. That little truth made me doubly determined to do what he'd asked, preferably without James's help.

```
Subject: a hearing

  Dear Aunt Mary—

  She's turned me down flat, but I know she's
  just playing hard to get.
  Should I send roses?
  A singing telegram?

  James
-----
```

| sat back, astounded. I'd just been pinged.
| By James, of all people.

Just fyi, when you don't know whether a remote server is online or not, you send it a test message and see whether it responds. That's called a ping.

It was Wednesday, almost a week after the meeting of the Ariadnes, and clearly he wanted to know whether I was dead or alive.

I'd show him.

I got on the phone to Tracy, she who almost went for comparative mythology, and begged a favor. The girl ante'd up in spades.

```
Subject: re: a listening

  Give it up, Jimbo. Knowing "what she really
  wants" has been the rationalization of
  every stalker and rapist since Zeus nailed
  Leda. You'll recall that Leda ended up as a
  mute swan.
```

A *gentleman* knows that no means no.

Aunt Mary
***
Uncertain? Confused? Ask Aunt Mary!
Your one-stop shop for netiquette and advice:
http://www.ask-aunt-mary.com

I had about five seconds to be proud of my classical mythology reference before the reply boinged onto the board.

Subject: re: not listening

Dear Aunt Mary—

Fat chance. Persistence is the key to success—and if you knew the lady in question, you'd know that she talks tougher than she is.

"Jimbo"

It was really odd to know that James was online at the same time as me. I logged off quick and got back to the work at hand, fending off the warm fuzzies.

I hadn't had a whole lot of luck, either restoring my schedule to match my circadian rhythms, or finding a solution for my dad. He needed to be on or near his own turf—I mean, he'd lived in that house for the better part of fifty years—so I started there every day.

It wasn't as if I had anything else to do. Work all night, nap a few hours, go play Primary Caregiver. Each morning at the house, I cleaned out the junk mail and the flyers, put the real mail in the kitchen—there wasn't a lot of that, other than a few bills—then combed the neighborhood, taking a different direction each time. At noon I chucked it in.

There are some scary nursing homes out in the world, you know? Oh, there are good ones, too, I'm sure, but I just had to picture my dad there to know he'd run screaming out of each and every place. I visited my dad at lunch before going home for a bite, a nap, and more work—he accused me of only stopping by to ensure that he was eating, which was partly true—and updated him on the hunt. He had a few suggestions and a lot more opinions.

Even the comparatively nice ones were emotionally desolate places. It was depressing just to cross the threshold and see the vacant-eyed souls just sitting where they had been left. The nurses seemed resolutely chipper in those places, and I was always glad to escape.

My dad wouldn't be able to escape, though. That gave me the creeps.

I found a couple of hospices, or group homes, that were vigilantly homey. There seemed to be a real lack of privacy in these places with their determination to be one big happy family. Or to avoid the liability of someone hurting themselves while they weren't supervised. I don't know, but I figured my dad would go bonkers in about a week. It would be going from one extreme to the other.

I was running out of options. My dad had insisted that he wasn't going to live here, which made it easier for me to defend my sense that it wouldn't be a good fit. James had made good points about that, too.

Besides, I was crazy busy. Not only had the client signed James's amendment to the contract, but the job had spiraled into a thousand smaller add-ons. Of course the deadline stayed the same. Phyllis called it "scope creep," but I didn't much care. I had work to do and not enough time to do it, and even less time to bring someone else in and train them to do some of it. I kept my nose to the keyboard.

James was persistent in his reminders, though. I was developing a shell collection, and if you don't think that's seductive, then you don't know beans.

Besides, there's something really male about knowing what you want and going for it. Um-hmm. Very sexy.

And he *had* surrendered the chinos.

His e-mail message left me yearning. It was, for those of you with your minds in the gutter, as much for the great sex as for that wonderful feeling of not facing the entire world alone. I could trust James, with some things at least, and I knew my dad's welfare was one of them.

I mean, don't get me wrong, I'm still a commitment-a-phobe intending to die with my shields up, but a little human contact once in a while isn't all bad.

Let's be blunt. Sex would be good right now. Really good.

Besides, James had said that he had a possible solution for my dad's living arrangements. That was all the excuse I needed.

I was ready to make a deal. Sex for the paternal solution. I'll take door number three. Cue Monty Hall and the screaming masses in their wild costumes. Another rationalization, we all know that, but I was there. I snagged my fake leopard swing coat, the address off the fridge, and sailed out the door.

I'd dressed with some care, but then you expected as much, didn't you? Suede slim pants as soft as butter and the color of caramel. A butterscotch sweater with a turtleneck that came up to my chin and clung to all my curves. Movie star shades, of course, and cowboy boots with pointy toes of alligator hide—or something that looked like it.

I've got to tell you that this was one hot look, especially now that my hair was jet black. Red lipstick, red lace bra and I wished like heck I'd had time to paint my nails red, too.

Sex was seriously on my agenda, and I wanted no mixed messages as to why I'd come. Stress busting was something I could use big time.

And no, you can't get from needing something big time to BigMistake.com. You just can't get there from here. Understood?

The new Casa Coxwell was the oddball on the block, the last clapboard one to be seen. The area had been reborn a couple of times since this place had been built. It looked to be a hundred years old or so, its farmhouse style a definite eyecatcher. On either side of it were postwar brick bungalows, resolutely similar except where they had been demolished and replaced with three-story upscale joints that went from lotline to lotline.

James's house was not upscale. In fact, it ran closer to ramshackle, but had a certain charm all the same. The fence was in rough shape and due for replacement, the porch was big but sagging on the south side.

"Handyman's special" was practically written over the front door. I'd never pictured James as a fix-it kind of guy, but maybe he intended to learn. The bell didn't ring audibly, so I opened the storm door and pounded my fist on the wooden door.

Jimmy answered, complete with a whopper of a black eye, and immediately looked disappointed that it was just me.

"Expecting someone else?"

"Pizza," he said sullenly and turned away to leave me on the doorstep.

Undaunted, I stepped into the lion's lair. "Nice shiner."

"Who asked you?"

"Oh, got an attitude upgrade, did you?"

Jimmy rolled his eyes and stalked away. I remembered being the bad kid a bit too well to let him win that easily.

"Used to be you couldn't act like that until you were officially a teenager!" I shouted after him, then slung my coat over the newel post as just about everyone else seemed to have done. Cocky? You bet. I was looking forward to this. There was a definite spring in my step. "Used to be that thirteen was the magic number."

"Yeah, well, sh—*stuff* changes, doesn't it?"

"'Bout time you figured that out." I got a glare for my trouble, then he slouched off toward the tinkle of activity from farther down the hall.

I strolled after him, taking a good look on the way. The house had a casual layout, the bedrooms clearly up the massive staircase on the right. The living room was full of small boxes. The bookshelves from James's study at the old house stood empty against the far wall, and the couch and chair from the old family room were parked in the middle of the floor. The smallest of their many former televisions held the place of honor, the VCR light and time indicating that essentials—as defined by males—had been wired up.

What must have been the dining room was devoid of furniture, empty boxes and packing materials from elsewhere littering the floor. But then, that solid mahogany dining room suite would have fetched a good buck, even used. Marcia's cleaning lady had polished it religiously, and it was a good-looking ensemble.

Not that I care about such things. Really. I can think of better things to do with twenty or thirty thousand bills.

The kitchen was enormous, real farmhouse style. I liked it a lot, despite the avocado green and harvest gold color scheme. It screamed "Welcome to 1974," not a real selling point, but there were good bones behind that. Besides, I love vintage and this was vintage squared.

There were miles of counter space, and a dutch door led to a porch along the back side of the house. The cupboards were those old wooden ones with vertical lines of beading. It had high wainscots and enough room for a huge slab of a table by the back door. Some of the upper cupboards were open, presumably to display preserves and such, though they were empty now.

All of the cabinets and wainscotting had been painted Ghastly Gold, and was grimy, too, but I bet it was real wood underneath. Solid as new stuff never was. It might be worth stripping. There was truly hideous carpeting on the floor, also very dirty, though it can't have been attractive in the first place. It reminded me of one afternoon that I had been foolish enough to baby-sit newborn Jimmy—as soon as his parents were out the door, he had promptly barfed up his puréed turnip and peas.

You can bet that I didn't get suckered into doing that again. Just the memory made me shudder. Yet, here I was, hunting down a man and prepared to jump his bones, despite the presence of two small adults in his life.

Go figure.

James and Johnny were bent over a bunch of newspaper spread on the counter, the spring sunlight touching both of their heads. Jimmy kept on going to another room and slammed the door behind himself. The others didn't even look up.

James and Johnny were wearing jeans and T-shirts, their hair was rumpled, and they were both wearing sneakers. James was explaining something to his younger son with a patience my father had never shown, though I couldn't hear the words, and Johnny nodded periodically. He was more fair than James, his hair tending more towards Marcia's brown than James's auburn.

And yes, I wondered for a moment what that long lost baby might have looked like, what color its hair would have been, if it had lived. I try to leave the past behind, but every once in a while, it sneaks up and jumps me from behind.

They were so utterly engrossed that they didn't hear me come in, so I had a moment to compose myself. They even ignored Jimmy's stormy return, which told me a lot about that kid's recent moods. When James moved, I saw the metal parts all over the newspaper and the blackness of their hands.

Auto repair. Isn't that what kitchens were made for? The top of the dutch door to the yard was open, a waft of something very nasty carrying into the house. Both James and Johnny had grease-covered hands and—like big dogs—were clearly in their element with the muck. I could smell bacon fat.

I spied the frying pan on the stove and smiled. What's morning without bacon and eggs?

"Nobody drop a match," I declared, pausing in the doorway to survey the very masculine detritus of their lives. "There's enough testosterone in this place that the whole city will blow."

They both jumped in a most satisfactory way, but I was already prowling the room. I felt James watch me, and I knew he was smiling that slow smile that made me tingle. I peered at the congealed bacon fat, then touched an empty pizza box with my boot toe.

"Remind me never to eat in this bistro. You must have roaches the size of my fist."

When I dared to look, the back of James's neck was turning red. "We're just barely domesticated," he drawled. "But we're working on it. Want to offer some tutorials?"

"Not my style. Sink or swim is what I say. Survival of the fittest and all that."

"We're fixing the motorcycle, Auntie Maralys!" Johnny informed me, looking a lot happier than he had when I saw him last. He was as yet immune to the very adult zing of sexual awareness. "We're cleaning the carburetor like usual, but the engine is running rough, so Dad said we should figure out why."

He held up some grimy bit for my perusal. "Look! One of the pistons is cracked. See? Right there. I saw it first. That's the problem and we're fixing it."

I moseyed closer, pretending I could make sense of all the nasty little metal bits arrayed on the counter. "Ah, a male bonding moment. Just like a Hallmark card, but dirtier."

"There's not much for it if you want to fix the engine." James nudged Johnny. "And we're having fun, right?"

"Yeah!"

"You know what we need? Remember that crescent wrench that we left in the garage? I think it would be really good for putting this part back together."

"I'll get it, Dad." And Johnny was gone, scampering out the door in his haste to help.

I watched him go, knowing that James was watching me. I had a big stupid lump in my throat, who knew why, and I wasn't ready to look straight at him yet. I had the funny sense that he'd know what I was thinking, and I didn't want to explore that again. "He looks happier."

"Yeah. We've been spending some time together." James shook his head. "I didn't realize fully what I was missing. It's good for both of us."

"Does he still worry about Marcia?"

James nodded once. "But she's started phoning the boys."

"Change of heart?"

He almost smiled. "You could say that."

"What did you do?"

"When she called at your place, I told her that she'd better do some serious thinking. Reminded her that no judge would believe she was much of a concerned mother if she couldn't even phone her kids and that that would have a serious impact on her ability to secure visitation rights. She phoned them the next night." He sighed. "Their relief was enormous. It's easy to forget what active imaginations they have."

"I thought you were ready to cut her out completely."

"I was." He looked up at me. "But the truth is that she's their mother and they have a right to see her and to know her. It's for their good to have time with both parents, regardless of my feelings on the matter."

"Losing your edge?"

He smiled slightly. "Trying my damnedest. The man I thought was my father sees everything in black and white, right and wrong. I'm trying to not be as hard on my kids as he was on all of us."

"Most of you seem to have turned out all right."

"Because we were terrified to defy him. Except Zach, of course. But I think that kind of harsh thinking has affected our relationships. It forces us to make harder choices. I'd like for the boys not to grow up with that burden."

"Well, I've got to give you credit for trying." I admired him. And I respected that he put his kids before himself. I stood beside James and inhaled deeply. He smelled of sun and wind and that cologne. My toes were tingling. "You did some serious downscaling here."

He nodded, untroubled. "We each picked one thing to keep and sold as much of the rest as possible."

"And went for the handyman's special."

He grinned and looked surprisingly boyish, especially after his solemnity. "The price was right. Not much else was right but the price. Oh, and the location. We're car-free but it's close to transit."

"It seems big."

"But it had been empty for a year, and the owners were getting a bit desperate to have something out of it before it rotted into the ground. The raccoons weren't impressed that they had to move out."

"Are you good at fixing house stuff?"

"Not that I know of, but there's lots of time to learn."

"Oh, the confidence of the uninitiated," I teased and we both grinned. "How'd the math work out?"

"Not as bad as I feared." He grimaced. "A job would be a timely addition to the mix, though."

"You're looking."

"Of course. Working all those old connections. Something will come up in time."

"I thought unemployed people were supposed to have a crisis of confidence."

James looked up and smiled, his gaze sweeping over me in open appreciation. "I'm good at what I do, Maralys. Everything else may have gone to hell, but that's the one constant. And really, a lot of other things seem to be falling into place. I feel good about where I am now and where we're going." He flicked a glance at the closed door where Jimmy had retreated. "Mostly."

That wasn't my problem so I steered clear of childraising issues. I gestured to the disassembled engine. "Did you do stuff like this with your dad when you were a kid?"

He laughed. "That's a joke, right?"

"No, actually it wasn't."

James sobered immediately and his gaze met mine. "No, I never did. My father didn't play with children, roughhouse, or help with homework. He had more important things to do with his time."

I could tell by how crisply he said the words that he was repeating a refusal he had heard over and over again. "He's not your dad," I said quietly because I felt he needed the reminder.

"Technically."

"What about your real father?"

James looked surprised. "I don't even know who he was."

"I'll bet your mother does."

He shrugged, clearly not interested in pursuing this. "Maybe."

I, though, was intrigued. "Why don't you ask her whether he was the kind of man who would teach his son to do something?"

"I wouldn't want to hurt her feelings by dredging it up again."

"News flash, James—it's already been dredged up. If I might prompt your memory, that was how you got in this mess. Your mom might even *want* to talk about it. All anyone's getting to hear is Robert Coxwell's side of the story."

"Why would I be interested in hunting down a man who didn't care that I was his son?"

"Maybe he didn't know."

"Maybe it doesn't matter."

"Maybe it does. Maybe you'll find that you had something in common with him, something that you don't have in common with the man who raised you. It's environment and genetics that determine the outcome, you know. Maybe you'll find a guy who has a different style of parenting, so you have some other models to use."

James considered me for a long moment, and the air started to sizzle between us. Then he smiled and shook his head, carefully nesting one engine piece back into another. "And you wonder why I miss you when you're not around. You're the broom that sweeps clean, Maralys. You go after all the preconceptions, shake them up, and make me look at them again."

"Nobody ever thought that was a good thing before."

"I think it's a gift. You're a creative thinker, and you don't accept that anything is the way it is, just because somebody told you as much. I like that, Maralys." He leaned closer and my breath caught. "I like you, Maralys."

He bent quickly and brushed his lips over mine, once, twice. He pulled back only slightly, his gaze searching mine. "I've missed you," he whispered. "Welcome back."

I might have leaned into the next kiss, but James's parental instincts were on partial alert. He stepped away and turned to the door.

There was Johnny, one hand on the knob, his expression uncertain. "Dad? Is this it?"

"It is. Thanks."

"Maybe I should go," I said, but James put his hand on my elbow. It was a proprietary gesture, very masculine, and neither Johnny nor I missed its implication.

"No, it's time we had this out in the open." He smiled and his son relaxed. Johnny came closer to give James the wrench, though he still looked confused. "Thank you. Maybe you could get Jimmy and we'll have a talk."

Johnny nodded and skipped toward the other door. He raised his hand to grab the knob, then James called a warning. The boy looked back, and James wiggled his greasy fingers, making a face that a month ago I would have thought him incapable of making.

Johnny laughed and knocked with his elbow. "Hey, dope, come out. Dad wants to talk to us."

"Do I have to?"

"Yes!" James shouted.

Jimmy came out, his expression mutinous, and plopped down at the table. Clearly he had a thousand better things to do. Johnny washed his hands, then slid into a chair, his expression open and curious. James wiped his own hands dry with care, his brow furrowed as he thought. He was probably constructing his argument. Then he sat down opposite me, braced his elbows on the table, and tented his fingers together.

It really is all in the way you present the information. I listened and I learned. I certainly wasn't going to say anything because there were a lot of ugly little bits to this story and the truth might not be entirely welcome just yet.

"It's time we talked about your mom leaving," James said, his tone temperate. He met one boy's gaze, then the other's. "I didn't do it sooner because I didn't know what was going to happen. I thought she might change her mind."

"Is she coming back?" Johnny was anxious.

"I don't know. I don't think so. Or at least, I don't think

she's coming back soon. She didn't say anything about it when she called you guys, did she?"

Johnny shook his head and looked crestfallen. Jimmy's expression hardened.

"So we need to think about Mom not coming back here to live, even if she comes back to Boston."

"Is that what's going to happen?"

"We're on our own, guys. What I want you two to understand is that this had nothing to do with you. You didn't do anything wrong. You didn't make Mom so mad that she left."

"Did you?" Jimmy asked, accusation in his tone.

"In a way, but I didn't do it on purpose." James glanced at me, silently asking me to bless his version of events. I nodded. He knew the kids better than I did and knew how better to present the sordid facts.

"A long time ago, I met your mom," James said, conveniently leaving out the twin thing. "And I really liked her and she seemed to really like me, and we went out more and more, until one day we decided to get married."

"And you did."

"Yes, we did." James drew a circle on the table with his fingertip. "But you know, we were pretty young when we got married, and I wonder now whether we even knew what we wanted, how we wanted to live, where we wanted to go. We were still figuring out exactly who we were, still becoming who we were going to be. I wonder sometimes whether we got married because we thought that was what we were supposed to do next.

"I finished school and passed the bar and went to work for your grandfather. I worked a lot because I wanted to succeed. My father always worked a lot, so that was the way I thought it was supposed to be. We didn't notice it right away, mostly because I worked so much, but your mother and I were changing and growing apart. We had some fights about things, different expectations mostly, but we both thought that married people fought sometimes and didn't think too much of it.

"Then you guys came along." He smiled at each of them. "And there wasn't a lot of time to do any thinking about anything other than diapers and toys that could be swallowed and ear infections and ten thousand other things that new parents face on very little sleep."

James cleared his throat. "After you guys were in school and things settled down at home, or so I thought, my job got harder. Your grandfather became a judge, so he left active practice and I had lots of cases to pick up. I worked even more, but we had more money and I thought your mom was happy. Clearly, I was wrong."

He frowned and paused for a moment. "I guess the biggest mistake we made was not talking enough, but we had both come from homes where people didn't talk a lot. Our parents just kept their mouths shut and kept on going, whether they were happy or not. I want to try and change that in this house. Kind of make a new beginning here."

He gave them each a hard look. "I want you both to talk to me about things, even when it doesn't seem as if there's time. Okay?"

They both nodded, though Jimmy was a lot slower.

"I know it's hard right now and there have been a lot of changes in our lives. But I want you to try to respect your mother's decision to make her life be the way she wanted it to be. It can't have been easy for her to leave, especially to leave you guys, but she made a hard choice. She's probably hoping that making a sacrifice like this will give her the chance to really be happy, and that's a pretty noble thing."

I thought it was pretty noble of him to give my selfish sister so much credit, but I knew what he was doing. Like it or lump it, she was the boys' mom and they'd be seeing her again. I appreciated that James was taking the high road in an effort to minimize the emotional scarring on his sons' lives. It wasn't an easy choice, and I hoped like hell that it worked.

"Wasn't she happy with us?"

"She wasn't happy with *me*, Johnny." James squeezed his son's hand. "I'm partly to blame for that. I'm trying to do better at talking about things and having more time at home and letting people know what I think and feel. It's a big change for all of us, but I hope you two know how much I love you both."

"What about Auntie Maralys?" Johnny asked.

"Well, your aunt and I had a big fight years ago, and we were really mad at each other for a long time. But I don't think that we're mad at each other anymore." James looked at me and I shook my head. He held my gaze. "I like your Auntie Maralys, and now that we're not fighting, I think she's decided that she likes me. She might be around a bit more than before."

"So, are you dating?" Johnny asked.

James smiled at me. "Something like that."

Jimmy rolled his eyes and looked away.

That was about as much commitment as I could take without leaping in to correct him, and it did give me a little glow of pleasure that James understood me that well. Maybe he did get it that Marcia and I were different—she's always been a fan of guarantees until Doomsday, everything in triplicate, signed, sealed, and delivered. I like my options open.

The boys looked between the two of us, and I wished like heck that I could have kept from blushing.

"Do you wish you hadn't married Mom?" Jimmy asked.

James thought about it for a minute. "No, no, I don't. If I hadn't married your mom and lived with her for those years, I wouldn't have learned the things I did from her. I wouldn't be the person that I am today, and I certainly wouldn't have had the successes I've had without her help. I don't regret it, not just because I can't change it, but because it's part of who I am."

James studied his sons. "And if I hadn't married your mom, then you two wouldn't be here." He leaned on his elbows and his voice turned hoarse, his gaze suspiciously bright as he looked at his kids. "And that's something I can't even imagine. I think maybe that everything that happened between your mom and me was just so you two could come into the world. Into my world."

Awwwwww, time for a big family hug. Wipe away that tear. We're all reconciled around the kitchen table, just like nature intended.

Or maybe not.

Subject: argh!

Dear Aunt Mary—

My friend has all the best stuff and she's
so lucky! She's got a great guy and a fab
apartment and makes gobs of $ at her kewl
job. Even tho I love her to bits, I'm
starting to hate her, too.

:-(

Should I dump her?

Green-eyed Girl

Subject: re: argh!

Dear Jealous Jane—

Face it. Green's not a good color on women.

Put your envy monster on a diet and maybe
then you'll be able to shake him off your
back. Meanwhile, take care of yourself.
Hate your job? Find another. Hate your
apartment? Move. You should be getting the
drift of this now. It's easier to blame
someone else for your troubles than to
solve them yourself. Get some good stuff in
your own corner and you shouldn't be so
worried about keeping score.

If you are, you've got bigger problems than
I can solve.

Aunt Mary
***
Uncertain? Confused? Ask Aunt Mary!
Your one-stop shop for netiquette and advice:
http://www.ask-aunt-mary.com

Johnny squirmed from his chair and went to James. James kissed his son's temple and hugged him close, ruffled his hair, then looked at Jimmy.

That son's expression was hostile.

"What a bunch of crap," he snarled, then fled to his room. He slammed the door hard behind himself, and James was on his feet in a flash.

"I've had just about enough of this attitude," he muttered, but I stopped him with a gesture.

"Let me. I'll enjoy it." It was an impulsive offer, if one surprising to all of us.

In fact, I got as skeptical a look as James could conjure. "You're always saying that you don't do kids, Maralys."

"But I had attitude when I was one. Believe me, I know how to get through to him in a way a Goody Two-shoes type like you would never understand."

James gestured to the door and bowed slightly. "Then, by all means, be my guest."

I didn't think of it at the time, but later I wondered whether I had some unconscious urge to prove that I had something to contribute.

Nah. Why would I want to contribute? It may be that no man is an island, but this woman has been an island for a long, long time. And it's going to stay that way. With occasional diplomatic conferences in the land of wild sex.

It was just a chance to show off. Right?

I crossed the room and kicked open the door, a healthy

measure of my own attitude on display. "Hey, you!" I shouted as the door bounced back against the wall.

Jimmy jumped and cast an alarmed glance over his shoulder before he went back to his handheld electronic game. It was one of those units that you load up with different games, about the size of a television remote. "Go away. I'm busy."

"And I'm getting too old for this kind of garbage."

"I don't have to listen to you."

"No, you don't." My agreement clearly surprised him, so I let him worry about it.

I sauntered into the room, which was a pit of chaos in the time-honored tradition of boys everywhere. Moving was only a temporary excuse. The big Pentium box was in the corner, with the monster tube that had made me salivate when James bought it for the boys two years before. I guessed that this was the one thing Jimmy had insisted on keeping.

But I had my suspicions about that handheld gaming toy. It beeped and bopped as he played. Closer perusal confirmed my suspicions of its model and recent vintage. Jimmy was trying desperately to ignore my presence, but he was edgy.

Too edgy.

And I knew why. I had been there, done that, read the book, and popped eight bucks for the movie. Jimmy was angry that factors beyond his control were shaking up his life. Fine. The black eye and the attitude were just the tip of the iceberg. Fine, again.

Theft wasn't fine.

I had been joking about a Goody Two-shoes not knowing where to begin, but this wasn't funny anymore. James probably didn't even suspect. I wouldn't have suspected anything if Jimmy had flashed that gaming gizmo around their old house. But he had it stashed away, and I knew that pricey acquisitions were seriously on hold.

Sometimes it pays to have a nastily suspicious mind in the quest for truth.

I eased up behind Jimmy and he edged away—trying to pretend that he intended to move that way all along—but he couldn't get far. He'd parked himself in a tight place, and was still trying to hide the device from the doorway. And his dad. Wasn't that telling? He was winning the game, though, and probably couldn't bear to put it down.

I'm wily. And I'm fast. He was going to lose the game with me.

I snapped the fingers of my left hand, Jimmy looked up, I swooped with my right and snagged the toy. He shouted and jumped after it, but I backed away, holding it high. James hovered in the doorway, watching, clearly not certain where I was going with this but trusting me. You've got to like that. Johnny's eyes were as round as saucers at this unexpected household drama.

"Where'd you get this?" I asked quietly.

"It's mine!"

I held it up toward James so he could see it. "Did you buy this?"

"I don't know. All these games look the same to me."

"Trust me to find that last living Luddite in the Greater Boston Area." I rolled my eyes, then flashed him a smile. "Tell me you have a Palm Pilot, at least. Restore my faith."

James shook his head, bemused by the question. "A leatherbound daily planner." Just thinking about how tactile he was could have distracted me in a major way if I'd let it. But he looked at Jimmy, challenging him. "Did I buy it? Did your mother?"

Jimmy tried to squirm free by acting bold. It works sometimes and I gave him some credit for trying. "Well, duh."

James caught his breath and I knew he was fighting his father's demons. No doubt he would have been flayed alive for challenging Robert Coxwell so boldly when he was this age.

Jimmy stretched out his hand, but I held the game away. Then I gave James some ammo while I held Jimmy's gaze, daring him to argue with me.

"This is brand-new technology. Next generation. Very, very cool and very, very coveted. In short supply, in fact. You can play interactively offline or on the Net. There's an infrared in the head of it so the competitors can boing stuff back and forth in the same room." I paused.

"Cool," Johnny whispered, eyes round with awe now.

"It's only just shipping." I spoke to James. "You would have to have bought it in the last two weeks or so."

"I haven't bought anything lately."

"Oh, you'd notice this baby on your Visa bill, even if Marcia had picked it up." I named a price and James turned into Granite Man with Eyes O' Fire. "Then there are the games, at a hefty price per pop." I waved it at Jimmy. "What have you got on this, twenty games? That's some kind of inventory."

"Where did you get it?" James demanded of his son, and it was clear from his tone that the math was all nicely tabulating to the same answer I had gotten.

Jimmy faced him defiantly. "My friend gave it to me."

"Which friend?" James demanded in the same moment that I said, "Bullshit."

Both boys stared at me, shocked that anyone would use such a word in their home. But this was serious stuff. Jimmy was only ten, so there was a chance to keep him off the slippery slope.

Someone snagged me by the scruff of my neck when I was twelve, and I figured it was my job to pass the favor along. I'm a big fan of civic responsibility, you know.

I shook the toy under Jimmy's nose. "You stole this. 'Fess up."

But he was unrepentant. "So what if I did?"

James looked like he was going to blow, but I held up one hand. "So, you're going to make it right."

"Oh, please." Jimmy rolled his eyes. "Only stupid people think that's how the world works."

Boom! I had no chance to say anything more.

"What in the hell is that supposed to mean?" James started across the room, eyes flashing.

"Oh, come on, Dad! You get crooks free all the time!" He mimicked his father. "And you're so good at what you do."

James faltered, caught in his own inconsistency.

"Some bitch, having smart kids," I muttered, but no one was paying any attention to me.

James's composure had clearly been shaken, but he recovered in record time. "Is that what you think I do?"

"Mom said. You just went to California to get Uncle Zach out of jail. Didn't you? *Didn't* you?"

"That was different!"

"Bullshit!" Jimmy shouted, picking up my word with gusto.

James shoved a hand through his hair, then sat on the edge of the bed. He wrassled the demon of Robert Coxwell—who I suspected would have horsewhipped a child for challenging him so boldly. Either that or James and his siblings had all grown up so terrified of what their father might do that none of them had dared to challenge him.

James won his battle against repeating his own experience, took a deep breath, then bent his attention on his son. His words were very controlled, but I don't think any of us were fooled. "What I do is ensure that people have a fair hearing."

"I don't think so. . . ." Jimmy retorted, and James's anger flared again.

He pointed at the desk chair. "Sit. Shut up. Listen."

Both boys sat.

Hell, I sat.

You could have heard the roaches breathing from the kitchen. James took his time, making us wait for it. And wait we did.

"We have a system of law which is intended to keep innocent people from being punished for what they haven't done," he said finally. "It's a check and a balance to the authority of the state and of the police. Innocent until proven guilty. That's the fundamental tenet, the right of every one of us who is a citizen in this country. And if the guilt can't be proven, then the accused is found innocent."

"Even if you know he's guilty." Jimmy wasn't going to let this one go.

"You can only *know* guilt for sure if you can *prove* it," James snapped. "People lie and facts are obscured all the time. Truth is tricky. Our system demands that guilt be proven beyond a shadow of doubt or else we have to let the accusation drop."

"It's all a game."

"No, it's not a game," James retorted. "It's a cornerstone, *the* cornerstone, of a free society. The right to defend yourself against false charges, the right to a fair hearing, and the right to a defense attorney are fundamental to our liberty."

James spread his hands, warming to his theme in the face of Jimmy's obvious skepticism. "That sounds very lofty, but there are a lot of places in the world where people don't have those rights. Because you have grown up here, you don't appreciate what you have. In many parts of the world, someone could walk into this room, say that your Pentium was stolen, arrest you, lock you up, and throw away the key. No one would ever see you again, or even know what had happened to you. And they would be afraid to ask, in case they joined you."

"But it's not stolen!"

"But in those places, you would have no chance to say so." James leaned forward and held Jimmy's gaze. He'd gotten through the first barrier of hostility and both boys were listening to him. "You would have no chance to defend yourself against malicious and false charges."

"What's malicious?" Johnny asked.

"Something mean or unfair. Something someone does just to be nasty to you." James turned back to Jimmy. He wasn't talking down to the kid at all, but his explanation was easy to understand. Even I was getting a better grip on why he did what he did.

Who would have guessed that James Coxwell was an idealist? I was glad I was sitting down, let me tell you.

"The system only works if both sides fight hard to bring out the truth," James continued. "Truth plays hard-to-get sometimes, so the legal system errs on the side of the innocent."

"Guilty people can get off." Jimmy was a devil's advocate par excellence. Obviously it was a dominant Coxwell gene.

"If there isn't sufficient proof of their guilt, yes," James admitted. "But the flip side of that is that theoretically an innocent person could never be found guilty of something he or she didn't do. There wouldn't be enough proof to prove their guilt. You see? Sometimes guilty people get off, but that's to make sure that innocent people don't get convicted."

He looked between his sons, both of whom were watching him avidly, checking that they understood. "What I do, or what I used to do, was make sure that the state had done their job properly. I found the holes in their arguments or the mistakes they'd made in their procedures. I found the places where there was reasonable doubt or where they had broken the law themselves or not respected someone's rights. Rules only work when everybody follows them."

"But crooks don't follow them," Johnny said.

"No. And in a way it's not fair. But you see, the cops and the state and the good guys have to follow the rules, otherwise they'd be no better than the crooks. In a lawless society there is no justice for anyone." The boys thought about that for a moment.

"Have you ever helped a crook go free, Dad?" Johnny asked.

James looked at the floor, his expression dead serious. I thought he might lie, or at least gloss the truth, but he was straight with them. "The hardest cases I ever had to defend were the ones in which the defendant was clearly guilty, but the police had not followed the rules in gathering the evidence they had against him."

"What does that mean?" Johnny was clearly intrigued.

"We have a law that the police can't just search your home because they feel like it. They have to get a warrant first, and they can only get a warrant if they have some good reason for needing one. They have to have some proof that there's something in your house to find."

Johnny moved to sit on the bed beside his father. "What if they don't?"

"Then what they find doesn't count."

"Even if it's bad stuff?"

James nodded. "When they don't follow the rules, the evidence can't be admitted to court. It can't be used as proof."

"Why don't they just follow the rules all the time then?"

"Because most cops really want to catch bad guys." He smiled at his son. "We all forget the rules sometimes when we're sure that we're right about something. Or when we get excited and think we have to act fast. But the law says that even bad guys have rights."

"That's dumb." Johnny was disgusted by this.

"You wouldn't think it was dumb if someone said that you were a bad guy."

"But I'm not!"

"Exactly. Because of the law, you'd have a chance to say so. Innocent until proven guilty. My job, as well as that of all the other lawyers and judges, is to make sure that we don't forget to follow the law, even when we think we know that we're right. It's not a perfect system, but it's a very good one and it's worth defending."

Johnny thought about that. Jimmy, who had been watching this exchange, folded his arms across his chest defiantly. "What about Uncle Zach?"

I had to like the kid's gusto. He went right for the heart of it and didn't flinch. I was feeling pretty simpatico with this small adult.

James nodded, unperturbed. "You're right. Uncle Zach was guilty and I knew it."

"But you still got him off?"

James nodded again.

"See?" Jimmy's triumph was short-lived.

"I do see. You're right that I should never have helped him. I should never have gone to California. I was wrong, Jimmy, and I made a mistake. Thank you for making that clear to me." The boy regarded his father warily and rightly so. James smiled slightly. "You know what happens next?"

"What?"

"I learn from my mistake and I don't do it again."

Jimmy worked the implications of that out but quick. "That's not fair!"

"Yes, it is. That's the issue here. What's fair? What's law? What's right? Your point is a good one. Everyone has always saved Uncle Zach from himself. And you know, it's never done him any favors, I can see that now. He just gets into worse trouble all the time, because he doesn't think any of it matters. Zach always figures someone else will fix it." James eyed his son, leaning forward to brace his elbows on his knees as he dropped his voice. "Just like you're doing right now."

Jimmy folded his arms across his chest and tried out a glare on his dad. It wasn't bad, but he was going to have to improve it to intimidate the shark.

"Maybe if somebody had made him understand that he was wrong the very first time, Zach wouldn't still be getting into trouble," James continued quietly. "He'd know that no one was going to fix it, because no one ever had. He might have to fix things himself."

"You're not going to fix this," Jimmy said, his hostility clearly rising.

James shrugged. "No, you are." He looked toward the kitchen. "Now, where do you think our pizza is?"

James stood up to leave and Jimmy lost it. He leaped onto the bed, looking a very furious ten years old now, and screeched at his father. "How can you do this to me? How can you be so *mean*?"

"Sometimes you have to be cruel to be kind, or so they say."

"Liar! Liar liar liar!" He stomped up and down the bed, in full tantrum mode. It was a telling reminder of his age. "I hate you and I hate this house and I hate having no trip and I hate having no stuff. I wish Mom had never left! She loved me! She would have bought me this. But she wasn't here and you don't love me, so I took it! I fixed it myself!"

James said nothing, just watched his son until Jimmy was red in the face and his tears were rising. "Maybe that's the problem, Jimmy. Maybe it's time someone said no to you."

"Maybe it's a lot of things," I added, knowing from my own experience that no one person could ever be responsible for the choices a teenager makes.

The kid turned on me. "What do you know about it?" Jimmy sneered. "You just want to boink my dad. Maybe it's your fault that Mom left."

"Now, just a moment here . . ." James started to argue.

But Jimmy was furious. He turned his wrath loose on the one most obviously responsible for his woes. Me. "It's you, it's your fault. You made Mom leave, you made my dad mad at me. You've ruined everything, you, you, you SLUT!"

Oh, I wanted to hit him. My fingers twitched. If he'd been a man, I would have.

But James moved fast. He snatched Jimmy up by the collar of his sweatshirt, lifted his toes off the floor, and gave him a shake. "Apologize. Now!"

"No!"

"Apologize to your aunt and do it quickly." Well, there was some of Robert Coxwell in James. He gave Jimmy a look that must have curdled the kid's blood.

But Jimmy lifted his chin, matching tit for tat. "Will you fix it?"

James smiled a cold courtroom smile. "You are not in a position to plea bargain."

"Fix it and I'll apologize."

"I'm not going to negotiate with you." Something in that steely gaze made the kid realize he was losing, and he changed his tactics.

"You have to fix it, Dad!" Begging. It was worth a shot.

"If not in the way you expect me to."

Jimmy's expression turned wary. "What does that mean?"

"Apologize."

"I'm sorry," Jimmy said without a shred of sorrow in his voice.

James shook his head and gave Jimmy a shake, too. "Try again. You're going to learn right now that you will never call any woman by that name, and that you will never insult your aunt again. Once more, with feeling."

Jimmy took a breath to argue, but James interrupted whatever he might have said. "I strongly advise you to not push me any further, Mr. Jimmy Coxwell. Perhaps it would be timely to remind you—who did you call the night your mom left? Who did you call when you were afraid? Who dropped everything and took care of you?" He gave the boy a smaller shake, a chiding one. "You owe your aunt better than this and you know it. Don't blame the person who caught you for your own crime."

Jimmy blinked. The fight went out of his posture, and he slanted a rebellious look at me. "I'm sorry," he mumbled.

James put him on his feet. "Again. Clearly."

Jimmy looked up at me, his expression finally contrite. "I'm sorry, Auntie Maralys."

"I guess now you are," I said.

Before anyone could get too cozy, James put a hand on Jimmy's back and guided him to the door. En route, he plucked the toy from my hand. He was all business. "Now, we've got something to do. Get your coat, please."

"Where are we going?" Jimmy asked, but he did what he was told.

"You're the one who wanted it fixed."

"Where are we going?"

"To wherever you got this." The kid might have argued, but James gave him a death glare. "Time to learn how to fix things properly."

"But—"

"No *buts*. Move it!" There was a pounding on the front door, and James opened the door as he shrugged into his coat. He paid for the pizza, then passed it off to me. "Mind waiting for us?" His gaze flicked tellingly to Johnny.

"No, I'm starving. And I need to talk to you anyway. As much fun as this is, I didn't come 'round for the show." I nudged Johnny and went for the light comment. "You guys had better hurry or we'll eat it all—right, Johnny?"

They marched out the door, determined dad and the rebel who had lost his cause, then Johnny and I headed back to the kitchen. I found plates and pop and glasses and paper towels, made him scrub his hands, then we settled down for a feast. Things were quiet, but I was thinking about James's defense of his own choice of career.

I looked up to find Johnny staring at me, his eyes full of questions. He looked remarkably like a small version of his father. He chewed and swallowed, then tilted his head. "Are you really boinking my dad?"

I bit back a smile. "Do you even know what that means?"

He shook his head, blessedly mystified. "Is it like kissing?" He made a face that expressed his view of that.

"Kind of."

"Gross! Why do you do it?"

"Well, people have sex—which is what you really call it—when they really like each other."

His head tilted as he considered me. "Do you really like my dad? Even after that big fight?"

And because there was nobody else around to hear it, I made my confession. It wasn't even that painful. "Yes. I really do like your dad."

"Do you wish you hadn't had that fight?"

"Well, fights are no fun, but your dad's right. I'm kind of getting used to having you guys around."

He smiled a smile that could light the city. "I like you, too, Auntie Maralys." Then he gave me a puzzled look. "Am I going to have to boink some girl one day, just because I like her?"

"No." I laughed at his evident relief. "You should do it with someone who you like a lot, like your partner or your wife. You'll know her when you meet her." Leaving out the details and benefits of serial monogamy for the moment, I leaned across the table to snag another slice of pizza. "Trust me, one day you'll meet a girl and when you think about kissing her, it won't gross you out."

Johnny rolled his eyes and used the tone all kids save for the particular stupidities of adults. "I don't *think* so, Auntie Maralys."

Jimmy and James came back, both quieter and less angry. James went into the living room and came back with a sheet of ledger paper. To my surprise, Jimmy still had the toy.

I understood when James wrote a hefty sum in the debit column of the ledger sheet, then put Jimmy's name at the top and put the paper on the fridge door.

"You're going to work this off, just like we agreed," he said firmly. "In the real world, we save our money to buy things we want. You've done it backward, but you're still going to pay for your toy."

Jimmy looked up. "How?"

"By doing chores."

His eyes lit. "I'll take the garbage out for a hundred bucks."

"Fat chance. This is a good opportunity to learn the value of money. You'll take the garbage out for twenty-five cents and you'll only do it once a day, after dinner."

Jimmy rolled his eyes and sat back, not so displeased with his circumstances that he could stop himself from running a hand over the toy. "It'll take forever."

"Pretty much," James acknowledged. "I'll type up a list tomorrow of chores, including what they're worth and when they need to be done." He scored a couple of slices of the chilly pizza and popped them onto plates, sliding one after the other into the microwave. He gave one to Jimmy, then sat down and bit into his own. I got them each a pop.

"Is this what Grandfather did when you wanted something?" Johnny asked.

"No," James said. "He went with a flat-fee allowance. We got a quarter a week each and had to do anything we were asked. If we bought anything that cost more than five dollars, we had to ask for his permission first."

"I'm guessing he was a pushover," I said. James smiled at me across the table. My dad was not a lot of fun when I was a kid, but he couldn't touch the senior Coxwell for being a control freak. The kids missed the import of this exchange.

"What about me?" Johnny demanded. "I want one, too."

Ah, the spoils of crime were tempting.

James looked at his younger son. "You're right." He got another sheet of paper and put Johnny's name on it, putting it on the fridge beside the first one. It had no opening debit. "You can buy whatever you want with what you earn."

"Cool!"

"That's not fair!" Jimmy argued.

"It's more than fair," James reported. "You're very lucky that the storeowner didn't want to press charges. He didn't have to be so understanding."

"I'm going to do every job *first*," Johnny said, sticking out his tongue at his brother. "And by the time you've paid for yours, I'll have enough money to buy a *new* one and you'll have to start over again."

"Fine! Then I won't let you play with this one!"

"I think," James said firmly, "you could negotiate an agreement here, among yourselves."

"I'll rent it to you," Jimmy suggested.

"Kid's born to be a lawyer," I muttered.

James fixed his attention on Jimmy, as if he hadn't heard me. "No, you will not. You will share. If you don't share, then I'll take it away completely."

They ate in silence, Jimmy scowling at his father.

"Aren't you feeling lucky?" I asked the boy with the attitude.

"I don't *think* so," he muttered, adding an eye roll for emphasis.

James gave the kid a hard look, and on some inexplicable impulse I leaped in where angels would clearly fear to tread. "Don't you have spring break?"

"It's over." Jimmy kicked the table leg. "And we didn't even go to the beach, like Mom promised." He was working it for all it was worth. "All my friends got a tan and where was I? Not scuba diving, like Mom promised, nooooo, I was packing boxes and now I'll be taking out the garbage for twenty-five effing cents."

"Hold it right there." James started to get to his feet, but I lifted one hand.

I did my best Cruella de Ville voice. "Give him to me." I smiled as if Jimmy would make a tasty lunch, and the kid inched away, uncertain what to expect. His bravado faded.

Ah, he was still young and tender, and his talk was a thin veneer. I smiled wider and he folded his arms across his chest.

He looked worried. I like that.

"You sure?" James asked, glancing between the two of us.

"I'm sure. A week from Saturday will do nicely."

"I'm not sure!" Jimmy said with a last try at defiance.

I laughed, my best evil-empress-with-plans-for-world-domination laugh. The kid bolted. I popped another piece of pizza into the nuke, well pleased with myself.

"I want to learn to play, too!" Johnny shouted, looked to his dad for approval to leave the table, then bolted at James's nod. The boys settled into meaty bickering about who would play when. James left them to work it out themselves.

Frankly, it reassured me that they seemed to have some issues with each other. It's just not natural for siblings to adore each other. And a little competition prepares them for the real world.

James started to clean up. I picked up plates and glasses as the boys disappeared into Jimmy's room to figure out the nuances of the game. Periodic bellows of outrage gave assurance that they were alive and not fatally wounded.

"I'm surprised that you leaped in to volunteer," James said. "I thought you'd be just about done with all this family stuff."

"My warm-fuzzy tolerance has been exceeded," I agreed, though I hadn't really thought much about it until now. I checked surreptitiously for hives, or at least I thought I was discreet, but after finding none, I found James smiling as he watched me.

"Fatal dose?" he asked with undisguised amusement.

"I must be working up a resistance."

"As long as it's not an immunity."

I heaved a heroic sigh. "I do owe you, after all, for sending you into the reptile lady's shop without fair warning."

James's smile flashed. He glanced toward Jimmy's room, then stepped closer. "I forgot. Good thing someone's keeping track." He had a gleam in his eye, as if he had been thinking of other terms of reparation.

So was I. My pulse took a predictable leap, but I had to

cover what I'd come to do. "Before we get to the bonus round, I've been looking at care options for my dad and they all stink. You said you had an idea and I'm listening."

James leaned his hip against the counter right beside mine. "I was thinking he could move in here."

"Here?"

"Yeah. I could evict the crown prince from his lair. . . ." He gestured to the room Jimmy had claimed, and I shook my head.

"Good luck."

James looked grim. "It'll happen, for a good cause. There's a bathroom back here that your dad could have for his own and another room there that he could use as his own living room when he wanted to escape us. He wouldn't have to get rid of much furniture, he'd have his own stuff, he'd have everything on one floor, company when he wanted it, and privacy when he didn't."

I was startled by the generosity of this offer. "There's no money for him to pay rent, you know. If he sold the house, he'll have some money from that—"

"But it should be invested in case he gets sick. I don't want his money, Maralys." James folded his arms across his chest, clearly prepared to fight me on this. "I think we're close enough to his neighborhood that he could keep his doctors and still meet up with his pals. It wouldn't be that big of a change for him."

"No, it wouldn't." I looked around the space, seeing what a terrific idea it was. Then I did the math. "Daycare," I said flatly, looking at James.

"It's true that this could be mutually beneficial. Another set of eyes would be welcome. The boys are getting old enough that they could look out for your father, and I'd feel better knowing that he was looking out for them."

"Planning to run away from home?"

"Planning to get a job, Maralys." He plucked a series of envelopes off the windowsill. They were of fine stationery, clearly business letters. They were hand-addressed in James's handwriting but just with the name of the recipient.

Résumés.

"Can't you apply electronically?"

He smiled. "We lawyers tend to be a bit old-fashioned, or at least I am. I like good stationery. I like the look and the feel of an elegantly presented résumé. It's about networking, too. I'm delivering them all in person, having lunch here and there, making contact with friends and acquaintances."

"Any nibbles?"

"There are always prospects. I'd like to find something that's a little less demanding, but having your father here would definitely ease my mind. I think it would be good for him to have more than his own company, too. Do you think he would like it?"

"I think he'd love it." It was true. "The boys are the center of his universe. Are you sure that you want him here?"

James's smile widened. "He and I don't have the same kind of relationship that you two do. I like your father and I respect him. I think we'd get along just fine."

"And if not, you can each retreat to your own caves."

"Something like that." He eyed me, genuinely uncertain. "Does this make sense, Maralys, or is it a stupid idea? Am I muddling or solving?"

How could I resist that? I reached up and eased his frown away with my fingertip. "I think you're becoming a great dad, James. I admire that you're trying to do it your own way. You're right, having my father around would be good for everyone. He was a pretty good dad, a different kind of dad from yours, and could give you both support and suggestions."

"A good dad? Despite the way you two fight now?"

I smiled now. "We're too much the same, and we both know it. And I've done my share of provoking him."

He feigned shock. "Not you?"

I punched his shoulder playfully. "I'm not that bad."

"No, you're not. Your heart's in the right place, Maralys." He looked toward Jimmy's room and I saw the cogs start to turn again. "Give me a few minutes to get the bike back together and I'll give you a ride home. The boys probably can't burn the place down in half an hour."

"Don't count on it. I'll snag a cab." A lie—I'd take the bus, as it was cheaper, but what James didn't know wouldn't hurt him.

He didn't tend to believe me though. "No. It's getting too late."

I liked his concern. I liked it a lot. It made me shiver a bit. It had been a long time since anyone worried very much about me, and I was getting used to James's concern. There is something to be said for Cave Man protecting his vulnerable babe, even if I don't buy the women-are-by-nature-vulnerable premise.

I caught the back of his neck in my hand and stretched up to kiss him quickly. James caught his breath, surprised, so I did it again. This time he leaned into the kiss, wrapping his arm around my waist. Talk about great stuff. Forget pizza—I could live off this man's kisses.

Which must have been why I said what I did. It was bold, even for me.

"You're a smart guy, James," I whispered. "Your kids go to school. You're unemployed. I work nights. You know where I live. And like you said, I owe you." I kissed him again, did a little tongue fandango that put a rise in his Levi's, then sailed out the door.

My heart was pounding and my skin was tingling. I ran to the closest T stop and wasn't even out of breath when I got there.

I felt *alive*. Tonight I'd write some hot*hot*hot code. Guaranteed.

Subject: lurking

Dear Aunt Mary—

Is it rude to lurk in a chatroom or on a listserve without contributing, or even admitting that you're there? My pals say it's wrong, I think it's interesting. Who's right?

Listening Lee

Subject: lurking before you leap

Dear Lee—

Oh, what big ears you have!

Since every Net chatroom or listserve has its own dialect and tolerance of plainspeak, it's always prudent to lurk before you leap in with a contribution. You are within your rights to simply listen and learn, however it's rude—if not illegal—to repeat whatever you "hear" or observe. Many groups (like your friends) won't appreciate your silence, especially if intimacies are being traded.
When in doubt, check with the moderator or listserve owner as to the rules governing the group and/or their expectations of members.

On the other side of the coin, you can
never be sure who will read your post in
such a situation. As a general rule, if you
wouldn't say it to someone's face, or if it
isn't something you would want an
acquaintance to know about you, don't post
it to a listserve or chatroom.
Play nice, boys and girls, and we'll all
have a better time.

0:-)
Aunt Mary, who has evidently been sainted
for her generous dispensation of kindly
wisdom

***

Uncertain? Confused? Ask Aunt Mary!
Your one-stop shop for netiquette and advice:
http://www.ask-aunt-mary.com

So, I can't say that I was shocked when the elevator ground
to life the following Friday and stopped at my floor. I mean,
I invited the guy.

I turned in my chair and watched while James stepped out
of the elevator.

He was suited up in fine style, looking impeccably European in a suit of grayed green wool. French cuffs on the cream
shirt, small gold cuff links, and a brassy gold tie. His raincoat
was Burberry, painfully predictable, but nice enough. He was
the power lawyer once more, in charge of his universe.

He made me a bit nervous, reminded me of how he turned
things to his advantage over and over again in the courtroom.
I'd hoped for the jeans, as I felt more a part of the same world
when he dressed down. This look made me edgy, aware of all
the dark tunnels to unknown destinations as well as the dead
ends of the labyrinth.

Somewhere, a minotaur bellowed.

"You look expensive," I ventured.

He smiled fleetingly. "That was the point."

"How goes the hunt?"

His gaze flicked to the screen, then back to me. "I need to talk to you. Got a minute?"

It wasn't an answer and it wasn't why I'd hoped he'd come, but I nodded anyway. James came across the loft, not wasting any time on technicalities. He looked remarkably stressed, more so the closer he got. He sat down in my other office chair, balanced his elbows on his knees, and took a good look at me. I looked back, striving to appear indifferent to his presence when every cell in my body was on full alert.

I was, in case you're interested, wearing a pair of old jeans that are the most comfortable things I own and a huge faded red sweatshirt that I had always loved and Neil had conveniently forgotten. Maybe because I had hidden it from him when he started packing. That man had no ability to hunt. These days it was holding together by will alone, because it had been washed so many times.

And now I faced a consummate hunter, the very look of him making me salivate. There's something to be said for being in a predator's sights, at least for the adrenaline thrill of it. I wished that I had had the foresight to wear my little La Perla black lace underwire number, but no. I was swinging free.

"What's up?" I asked.

Typically, James didn't mince words. "I've been offered a job, and I don't know whether to take it."

"Money is always welcome."

"True enough." That half-smile flickered and faded. James got to his feet and paced off the length of the loft. It was a lot of space and it took him a while, but not long enough that his restlessness eased. He looked, to my amazement, indecisive.

"So, what kind of horrible job is this?"

"It's not the job."

"Crap pay?"

"Nope. Pay's fine." He shoved his hands in his trouser pockets and stared at the glass block windows. He must have been watching the patterns shift, because you sure couldn't see out of them.

"You're worried about the boys?"

"Some. I think I could telecommute a bit, but it would still be a change, even with your dad around." We'd worked the details out midweek, as my father was amenable to the idea and his doc liked it a lot. Dad was checking out of the place with the pastel walls tomorrow, and James was taking the K to do the deed.

Sadly, with boys, patient, and driver, there was no room left for me. Boo-hoo. You know that broke my heart, to miss out on the dirty, uh, duty work.

"Look. I don't have all day to play twenty questions." I got up and marched toward James. "I don't even know why you're here. Spit it out and let me get back to work."

"Ah, Maralys, always cutting to the chase." James spoke with amusement. Then he looked at me hard. "I'm here because I don't know what to do and I respect your advice."

"Damn, I thought you'd come for sex."

James laughed then. I was a bit disappointed that he thought it was just a joke. I didn't look that bad.

Did I?

James smiled crookedly at me. "You're good at taking things apart, Maralys, and evaluating the merit of each choice. That's one of the things I love about you."

Love? Who the hell put the L-word on the agenda? I took a step back, but James was thinking and barely noticed.

Love? Whoa, Nellie. Lookit those hives.

Surely that was just a figure of speech?

James's smile turned rueful. "I'm not good at separating emotion from rationalization, and this is a doozy."

I folded my arms across my chest to watch him. Love. Hmm. "Your father wants you to come back?"

"Not a chance. Worse."

I gave him a skeptical look. "What could be worse than toiling for the Dark Side again?"

"Come on." James led me back to the chairs, his fingers light on my elbow. He claimed his chair again, then pursed his lips, linked his fingers, and looked across the loft. He was going to get logical and legal on me. This was not a contact sport.

Too bad.

"You know that the reason my father didn't want me as a partner any longer is that I am not biologically his son."

"Even though he raised you and treated you as his son for forty-two years," I couldn't help but comment. "We could do the nature versus nurture argument here."

"We could, but it's immaterial. My father has decided. And I decided more or less simultaneously that I didn't want to continue to work in such an environment. So we're done."

"Doesn't he have to buy out your partnership?"

"Well, yes. The price is still an issue, but our lawyers will work that out."

"You just breed work for each other, don't you? It's like a kind of self-fulfilling ecosystem. Lawyers hiring lawyers to do lawyer-things to other lawyers."

"I'm not suing him."

"Is that a point of pride?"

"I could."

"All right, so maybe you have a soul after all."

"Maybe?" James had that combative gleam in his eye, and his tone turned harsh. "He wants to pay me virtually nothing for all my years of building this practice, all the years in which I was virtually his equal. You're right, I could just stand aside and let him do that."

"But you're not going to."

"Of course not. He's not going to rip off me or my kids. I worked hard for that, we all made sacrifices, and I won't let him make it virtually worthless." Then James shrugged and smiled. "It's not as if I don't know any good lawyers."

"I'll bet you've found a good divorce lawyer."

"Mmm. Maybe." James waved off the issue of Marcia as being immaterial—that cheered me enormously, though this love thing was still making me twitch. Surely it had just been a slip of the tongue?

James leaned forward, focused on his own issue. Mind in

the gutter here was thinking about where else tongues might slip. "The issue is this. Remember when you questioned the merit of defending known criminals?"

"And its value to society? Sure. So did Jimmy."

"Well, the opposite team wants me on board."

"Who's that?"

"The DA's office."

I couldn't understand why he didn't look very pleased. "That's great, isn't it? You'll be back in the courtroom, slicing, dicing, and making julienne fries out of witnesses, but doing it for the good guys this time."

"True." James looked steadily at me. "Except there's a particular case that the DA wants me to win."

I sat back, suddenly seeing the issue. "Let me guess."

James nodded once, curtly. "The Laforini case."

"The one that your brother Matt is supposed to cut his teeth on." I watched James, realizing that this was a problem but not understanding exactly why.

Sibling rivalry I could understand, but he was really torn up about this. "Don't you think you can win the case?"

He was impatient with the very suggestion. "Of course I can win it! The evidence is impeccable. The guy's guilty and the cops did everything by the book. It'll be a cinch to win."

I tilted my head to study him. "Would you have won if you defended him?"

James grinned, his roguish expression making my heart skip. "Probably. It would have been tougher."

"But it's all in how you present the information."

"It's what I do, Maralys."

I could imagine. James had this edge and it wasn't just charm or intelligence. His mind was agile and he could turn things in a heartbeat to appear to his own advantage. I'd seen it a thousand times. I respected it and admired his confidence in what he could do, but I was also wary of his ability.

"I don't know your brother Matt well," I said. "What's he like?"

"He's quiet. He's a nice guy." The implication of comparison was clear. I didn't argue with him, because I knew what he meant. No one would ever call James a "nice guy." Nice guys finish last, as they say, and last place wasn't where anyone with a brain looked for James Coxwell.

He pushed to his feet and walked, hands shoved in his pockets. "Matt's done real estate law for years. It's not glamorous, but he likes it. He likes researching titles and finding out obscure trivia about the city. He's been working on a history of Boston for years. He's let me look at it once or twice, and it's fascinating."

James made a gathering motion with his hands, and there was admiration in his voice, as if his brother's wonderful gift was an alien marvel. "Matt's good at taking lots of little bits and discerning the overall pattern in them, pulling them together in a cohesive whole. His wife is a history professor, you know, and they have that ability in common."

"Why doesn't your father take the case himself?"

"Conflict of interest. He's a judge and can't directly represent people himself. He does, though, give copious advice. He's intending to coach Matt through it, but it's not what you say in the courtroom that counts . . . "

I finished his thought. " . . . so much as how you say it."

"Exactly."

"So, Matt's the next best option, but he doesn't have your courtroom flair."

James shrugged. "He has no experience in the courtroom. I'm not sure he *wants* any experience in the courtroom. Matt's not . . . " He gestured, seeking a word to describe the difference between them.

"He's a gatherer, not a hunter."

James turned to me with surprise. "Well, yes."

"And if you do this, you're going to eat his lunch on his first day out there on the savannah."

James grimaced. "Someone is going to eat Matt's lunch." He sat down heavily and rubbed his brow. "What I'm worried about is how much worse it will be for him if it's me."

"How so?"

"My father always held me up as the example, he always measured Matt against me and itemized all the ways Matt failed. Matt didn't fail. He's different. We're all different, but my father has never been interested in that." James looked at me, his brows furrowed. "I don't want to compound that experience with my choice here."

I gave him a moment. "Well, break out the quiche. Maybe you should host a men's retreat, you know, where you can all play drums and indulge your inner tenderness."

"Don't mock this, Maralys." His expression was fierce. "It's too important."

"And Matt can't be a dope. He's got to know that he's going to lose."

James raised a brow, considering this, and listened.

I tapped him on the knee. "He might not care."

"What? He has to care!"

"You would care, but you said you're different. The man couldn't have survived forty years of being on the wrong side of compare-and-contrast if it really bothered him. He'd have run away from home ages ago." I leaned closer. "Consider that Matt is probably used to slipping under your father's radar, so to speak, nodding and mumbling, then disappearing to do whatever the heck he wants."

James smiled. "That's Matt."

"He's got to hate the scrutiny he's under now. I'll bet you that he'll be relieved to get the loss behind him, so that he can get on with his life. Maybe he wants to lose a case, the bigger the better and do it PDQ. You've got another brother, haven't you? Maybe Matt is looking forward to passing the torch down the line."

"You are not saying that it's my duty as his older brother to facilitate this." James was smiling outright now.

"No. I'm saying that it's really nice of you to worry about him, but that I don't think it's as big of an issue as you do."

He sobered, weighing my arguments as he obviously rolled through them one more time. "You might be right."

"In a pinch, you could actually ask Matt."

"I guess I could. You eaten yet?"

It was just about one, though I hadn't noticed. "No, why?"

"Obviously because I'm going to buy you lunch as a gesture of gratitude for talking this through with me," James said. He leaned down and I thought from the wicked look in his eyes that he meant to steal a kiss. I was thinking that would be just fine, but he spun my chair instead. "Let's go. I suddenly have a craving for a piece of quiche."

I didn't move. "Jeez, and here I was thinking we could celebrate by having wild sex instead."

James stopped cold. "Is that an invitation?"

"Well, duh." I got up and sauntered toward the elevator, making no secret of my disappointment as I found my coat. "You might be used to the monogrammed and embossed variety, but—"

I got no further than that. James snagged me from behind and scooped me up in his arms, swinging me high. He gave the futon—now neatly folded away—a scornful look, then met my gaze. "You've got to get a real bed."

I smiled and kicked my feet. "Convince me. Oh, and snag one of those little envelopes from the drawer. I think the yellow Day-Glo would match your tie."

"I wasn't planning to wear my tie," he growled. That was the last thing anyone said for a while.

I've got to tell you that James Coxwell is one persuasive piece of work. His argument for a furniture upgrade was presented in a very compelling fashion, and I was just about convinced . . . until we ended up in the shower some time later.

Then he made a big mistake.

Or I did. I'm still not sure.

Surely you've noticed that showers are awesome places to do the hokey-pokey, and no I don't mean the dance. It's the water, the way it beads on muscles and makes everything slippery smooth, the warmth of it on your skin. It's the sound of the water, too—close your eyes and you're in the rainforest, doing the wild thing in the wild.

And I think it's the creativity required, frankly. You have to think about sex in new and different ways—missionary position is not going to work without someone drowning in the process. Although that might turn on some people, I don't tend to partner with them.

So it was that I had my legs wrapped around James's waist and was doing the shimmy on his electric-blue-clad hardware (I made an iMac joke which was not appreciated, by the way) when the fateful moment came. And after that came a really bad one.

"I love you," he whispered as we slumped against the cold tiles, still tangled up in each other.

"What?" I braced my hands on his shoulders.

He blinked. "I love you."

"Oh, no, we are not going there." I tried to struggle free, but I was at somewhat of a disadvantage, in terms of making an escape. James immediately backed me farther into the shower corner and grabbed my thighs so I couldn't put my feet down.

"Why is that a problem?" he demanded, still hot inside me, his eyes narrowing.

"Because this is sex. Pure sex. Pure pleasure. No strings attached."

"It is not."

"It is so."

He grabbed my waist and lifted me up, then put me on my feet. His expression was grim as he retreated from the shower, and he dried himself off roughly. "I don't know where you come up with this garbage, Maralys," he muttered. "Normal people make love because they're in love or falling in love."

"First comes love, then comes marriage, then comes Maralys with the baby carriage," I chanted. Goodness knows where that came from, but I felt like an idiot as soon as I said it.

James gave me a look. "So, is this about love, marriage, pregnancy, or all of the above?"

"It's about sex. We're having sex because we like having sex with each other. Someday one or both of us will change our mind about having sex with each other and we will stop having sex. As long as no one confuses sex with love, this will be a fairly painless transaction."

He was incredulous. "You don't believe that?"

"Yes, I do. It works." I got out of the shower and dried myself off, feeling cheated of another whopper orgasm. "Trust me."

"Even though you don't trust me."

"What?"

"You don't trust me. That's what the issue is here." James glared at me, then marched out to the loft.

How could I trust him? Did he have any idea what he was asking of me?

I padded after him, and found him dressing with record speed. "You're leaving," I said, making a brilliant deduction.

"Well, duh." James was really angry. He knotted that tie with a vengeance, his gaze boring into mine. "I don't have just sex, Maralys. I'm not going to have a secret affair, and I'm not going to court a woman in front of my sons unless there's a good chance that she'll be around for the duration."

"There are no guarantees."

"No, but if we have mutually exclusive conditions, there's no point in even beginning something. I always thought that you were waiting for the right relationship. I guess I was wrong."

"There is no right relationship," I retorted, not happy that he was making this look like my fault. "Everlasting happiness is a lie, and one that serves men particularly well."

He stopped cold to look at me. "You don't believe that."

"I do. Better, I *know* it! Marriages only last for the duration when one person supports the other so completely that they sacrifice their own dreams and objectives, and just become a support network."

"It's not that simple—"

I shouted to interrupt him. "What was Marcia, other than James Coxwell's wife?"

James flinched and we stared at each other in silence.

There it was, my big boogeyman, forced out from under the bed and splayed out on the hardwood floor between us. It would be too easy to sacrifice everything I was, everything I had become, for the greater good of a relationship with James.

Oh, yes, I know that slippery slope all too well. I try at least to make new mistakes, instead of repeating the old ones. I'd given too much to Neil. He'd hardly been worth it and he hadn't asked. James was ambitious and demanding.

I needed to know that he wouldn't ask that of me.

No, I needed to trust him to never ask me. And I didn't.

"That was her choice," James said finally.

"Maybe, maybe not. The point is that it's not my choice."

His expression hardened. "Sex is your choice. Just sex, no more expectation from your partner than that. It's a pretty meager deal, Maralys."

"It works. It's realistic." I folded my arms across my chest, holding up the towel.

"Really? Is that why Neil left? Because your marriage—or your sex with no commitment—was working out so well for both of you?"

Ouch. "I don't have to explain myself to you. . . ."

"No, you don't. And that, I think, is the bottom line. You've been burned. Well, welcome to the club, Maralys. But instead of going back into the fray and looking for something or someone better, you're withdrawing from the game. You don't want to risk anything at all, which means you're not going to get anything at all. You don't want to take any chances." He shrugged into his suit jacket. "You're the last person I thought would give up everything just to play it safe."

I was getting angry, though it's tough to make a compelling argument wrapped in an ultramarine bath sheet. "You don't know anything about me. You don't know what I want—"

"No, I guess I don't." James hauled on his raincoat, then crossed the floor to me. He didn't touch me, but he spoke with such intensity that I felt as though he was reaching in to give my heart a squeeze. "But let me tell you what I want, Maralys."

I couldn't look away from his gaze. The vigor of his words bored right into me, tattooing itself on my innards so I couldn't forget. "I want a partner. I want a wife and a friend, not just a lover. I want to spend my life with someone I can trust, who also trusts me."

"I can't be that person," I managed to say. "I don't want to be that person."

James smiled. "You're wrong, Maralys. You're just afraid to try."

"I'm not afraid of anything!"

"So you say. All this talk of sipping from the cup of life and taking chances and feeling alive, yet you won't risk getting hurt. You're all talk, Maralys O'Reilly." He shook his fist in front of me. "This is the good stuff. How can you not see that? How can you not want it? This is the brass ring and you're too afraid to reach for it. Consider your bluff called."

He pivoted to leave, but I went after him. "You just want things your own way. Wouldn't it improve your plea for custody if you had a wife and a nice family setting?" It was a heinous thing to say, but I was angry enough to let the words keep falling out of my mouth. Maybe I had to know for sure. "I don't know a lot about this stuff, but I do know that Daddy doesn't often get custody when Mommy wants it, too. Isn't that how it works?"

James stared back over his shoulder, shock clearly etched on his features. I knew that I had crossed a line.

And I knew that I was wrong.

He composed himself quickly, his features setting to stone, but there was something in his eyes that I had put there.

I almost wished the words back, would have wished them back if I hadn't needed to know the answer so badly.

"That you even have to ask tells me all I really need to know." James spoke with quiet determination, then turned and scooped up his briefcase as he headed for the elevator to leave.

No! This wasn't how it was supposed to happen! He was supposed to answer me. He was supposed to be impervious to anything I said. He was supposed to give as good as he got.

He wasn't supposed to take a fatal hit.

I panicked. "Where does it say that you get to make up the

rules?" I cried. "Where does it say that you get to decide which questions are answered and which ones aren't?"

He spun quickly and came back after me, fire in his eyes. I wasn't afraid of him, though. I knew that James only fought with words.

Which wasn't to say that he was harmless.

"I don't," he snapped. "But I play for keeps, Maralys, and you know it. All or nothing. Love, marriage, and *trust*, or nothing at all." He glared at me, daring me to take him up on that.

But I couldn't. I wouldn't. I shouldn't.

"Stalemate," I whispered, folding my arms across my chest.

James's gaze searched mine for a long moment. "Do you really think I'm using you?"

"I don't know." I took an uneven breath. "I hope not."

The annoyance faded from his expression and he sighed. He came to me, lifted one hand, then let it drop before he touched my cheek. I was trembling.

"Then I guess it is a stalemate." He sounded defeated, and I felt the same way.

There was a huge lump in my throat as James pushed the elevator call button. The silence between us was oppressive, filled with hurt and disappointment. I knew who had conjured that up. I thought I might vomit, but I knew I was right.

Wasn't I? Someone has to ask the tough questions, don't they?

The elevator arrived with a groan of gears, and James didn't even look back. He was closing the book on me, exactly as he'd closed it on Marcia. And it hurt, oh, baby, it burned.

"My dad?" I asked, sounding whiny and weak just when I wanted to sound strong and independent.

I got a chilly look for that. "I keep my promises. You ought to believe that at least. He's still the boys' grandfather."

"I keep mine, too," I insisted. "I'll be there a week Saturday for Jimmy, like I said."

"Suit yourself." James shrugged and swung open the elevator door. His glance was piercing. "But then you always do, don't you, Maralys? Maybe it's better to know that now than to have expectations later."

I will never forget the look on his face when he turned back to face me. There were so many things mingled in his expression—yearning, disappointment, and yes, love.

I almost went after him, but this was about self-preservation. I was old enough and wise enough not to stick my finger into 220V and expect to survive unscathed.

Which didn't explain why I wanted so very much to cry. I had done the right thing. I had ensured my own emotional survival. I had learned from experience.

But a little voice in my head taunted "cluck, cluck, cluck" all the same.

Subject: getting burnt

Dear Aunt Mary—

What's flaming? What's a flame war? Where's
the fire?
I don't get it!

Net Newbie

Subject: smokey says

Dear Newb—

Flaming is one of the rhetorical arts of
the Internet, a tradition of speaking your
mind without holding anything back. I mean
"anything"! It's part of the culture and
lo, it is good.
Flame wars, however, are not good. By
fanning the flames, so to speak, and
responding in kind to a flame on a
chatboard, thus starting a heavy exchange
of hostile fire, you waste everyone's
connect time. How rude. How petty. How
juvenile.
So speak your mind, but take your fights
into *private* chat. To learn more about
online do's and don't's, type "netiquette"
into your search engine.

Remember—only you can prevent forest fires.

Aunt Mary
* * *
Uncertain? Confused? Ask Aunt Mary!
Your one-stop shop for netiquette and advice:
http://www.ask-aunt-mary.com

Nobody called.
No deliveries came.

No one demanded my help.

I worked away all that night and the next, then all the next
week through, knowing I should be damn glad to finally have
some peace and quiet.

I wasn't. Instead, I felt surrounding by an endless vacuum.
It was privacy. Silence. Safety. Solitude.

Loneliness. I took it like penance and told myself I liked it.

At the end of the week, I gave the last tweak to the contract
job and installed the code remotely on their server. I gave it a
poke and checked it out, e-mailed the contact person to let me
know how it worked. I'd tested it backward, forward, and
sideways. It worked like a charm.

I told you that I'm good—at writing software anyway.

I printed my invoice and mailed that sucker off, then paced
the loft for the ten thousandth time. It was late the following
Friday, and the phone was eerily silent.

Maralys without a date. Huh.

My imagination kicked into gear. No news was good news,
right? I supposed my father had gotten settled in well enough.
I supposed that James had engineered the transition well. Of
course he had. He was nothing if not organized. Competent.

He didn't need a mommy. He didn't need me. I shivered
and put on a sweater.

We'd decided to leave most of the furniture and such in my
dad's house until it sold, though James had planned to pick up
my father's bed and dresser so he'd feel more at home. He
was using the K, which delighted my father to no end.

I stared out the glass blocks at the sunset fading quickly into night. Marcia was probably getting some right about now, somewhere under a desert sunset.

The way I felt right now, I'd be about a thousand years old before I let a man between my thighs again.

It's not often that I get depressed, and I wasn't going to stay that way without a fight. Next morning was my day with Jimmy, and I was going to get through to him, one way or the other. I got on the phone and made some deals.

Actually, I didn't have to give up that much. I was surprised. I've never asked the Ariadnes for anything, but they don't drive tough bargains. More than one of them said they were glad I was finally asking, and they had some good suggestions. And it was good to hear their voices. Antonia I called just for fun and her offer of sharing dinner just about made me weep. I didn't go—I have some pride left—but it made me feel better to be asked. I went to bed at midnight, a full day booked and then some.

I could still smell James on the futon, even though I'd washed the sheets twice. That did just about nothing to push me off to dreamland. Neither did the awareness his scent brought of the orgasm I hadn't had. I dug out Cap'n V and apologized for being inattentive.

Here's a first—I stared at the ceiling while my faithful consort slaved away. Nada. I shifted around and tried again. Zip. It did look as if there could be a watermark in the far corner of the ceiling though. I trotted over with my flashlight, certain that the threat of water on my wiring was what was distracting me.

It was just an illusion.

I settled in, finally found a reasonably comfortable position, and tried again. No luck.

I sat up and punched the pillow before flopping down one more time. It was this futon, I decided in frustration. It reminded me of James too much and might do so for a long time. In the game of compare and contrast, this mechanized gizmo lost big time.

What I needed was a new bed. That would bring back the romance between my studly Captain V and me. A change of scene. A new venue. Yeah, that would work.

Guaranteed.

Ha. It had been James's idea that I get a new bed, and I'd never be able to look at one without remembering the glint in his eyes when he swore to convince me.

I had the sudden realization that I had moved in to Big-Mistake.com without even realizing I'd packed.

Now what?

"**B**rat pickup and delivery service," I said cheerfully the next morning when Jimmy answered the door. His shiner had moved into the yellow and mauve zone of the spectrum with some greenish highlights just for fun.

He blew through his lips with disgust, then sauntered back toward the kitchen. "I don't want to go."

"I don't blame you." I moseyed after him and shut the door behind myself. I was dressed with attitude myself, a biker chick in leather. Sadly, I have not yet put studs in my face. "That yellow is really not your color, and the whole world will laugh once they get a look at it."

"Thanks a lot."

My father was holding court in the kitchen, looking perky if a bit thinner than before. I gave him a kiss on the cheek, said hi to Johnny, and finally looked at James.

He gave me a cool considering look that wrenched my heart, then turned when the toast popped up. "Want anything to eat?"

His indifferent tone cut me like a knife. "No, I'm fine."

My father, sensing nothing amiss, expounded with relish on his chosen theme. Clearly the tea was good and strong today. "Do you know that when Mary Elizabeth and Marcia were born, their mother had the idea that we name them differently?"

I stiffened, not really wanting to hear about my mother right now. Johnny was intrigued.

"Differently?"

"Yes, one for the new world and one for the old. One good Irish Catholic name for the sake of tradition, for our roots, and one American name for the sake of our new beginnings, for our future." He chuckled to himself. "We thought ourselves quite clever in finding names that both began so similarly."

"Marcia and Maralys." Johnny grinned at me, his innocent delight easing my tension a bit. I smiled back.

"Marcia and Mary Elizabeth," my father corrected, then he chuckled and shook his head. "But since those babies looked identical and had yet to utter a word, a single word, we got their names exactly backward."

"How so?" James asked tightly. I was surprised he got involved.

"Well, Mary Elizabeth was always the tomboy, the one to defy any instruction, the one to push the boundaries over and over again. Mary Elizabeth was so untraditional that she couldn't even use her given name. She had to change it, to make it sound like what it wasn't, to make it suit her modern ways."

My father's disapproval of those ways was more than clear. I looked at my boot toe, not really up to a public battle. Jimmy watched the exchange with undisguised interest.

"While Marcia, she with the American name, was always a good girl. She's the one who did well in school and had nice friends, and got into no trouble at all. She's the one who married and married well, and gave me grandsons, too." He smiled at the boys, and Johnny smiled back at him.

Well, at least I knew where I stood. No surprise there. "You ready?" I said to Jimmy.

"I think you've got it wrong, Connor," James said tersely. Everyone stopped. James looked right at me. His eyes gleamed and I knew that this wasn't just a casual comment. "I think you named them exactly right, because what's on the outside isn't as important as what's on the inside."

"And what is that to mean?" My father was turning indignant, because he didn't take well to having his rhapsodies corrected.

James held my gaze and I felt very warm. "Maralys is the one you can count on. She's the one who doesn't promise anything she can't deliver, even if you'd rather hear otherwise. She's honest, which is more than most people can say for themselves."

He glanced at Jimmy. "Maralys is the one you can call. You know that no matter when you ask her for something, or what kind of a jam you're in, or how much she grumbles about it, that she'll come through for you." Jimmy bit his lip and looked down. "And she expects nothing but maybe a little courtesy in return." Jimmy's neck turned red.

I had a huge lump in my throat at this defense of my character, but James wasn't done. He turned to my father. "She'll sacrifice her own time to be sure those she loves are safe and get good care. She'll drop everything for you, just because you ask. She'll check up on those she considers to be beneath her care. She'll spend days and days of time she doesn't have looking for a solution to please the most capricious of tastes." My father colored and dropped his gaze. "And she'll never blame you for it."

James met my gaze again and a smile touched his lips. "Maralys will give anything she has for someone she's protecting. She'll even pay his tax bills. Maralys is the one who keeps her word, which has to be the most traditional value of all. I think you and your wife, with all respect, got your daughters' names exactly right."

I'm not used to men defending me. I stared at James, completely tongue-tied, and the other three stared at us. My father started to say something, then just cleared his throat and fell silent again. Finally I smiled and tried for a joke. "Maybe. Maybe not. I guess it's all in how you present the information."

James shook his head and his smile faded. "No, Maralys. *Res ipsa loquitur.*"

I remembered that one. The matter speaks for itself. James was looking at me, hard, as if he'd will me to say something or to believe something that I wasn't nearly ready to process.

"Come on, Jimmy. Get your coat and let's move it. Time's a-wasting."

"I said that I don't want to go."

"You lose. Come on. We've got an appointment." Without any further explanation, I waved to the lot of them and strode back down the hall, feeling James's gaze follow me the whole way.

I smiled two minutes later at the sound of sneakers behind me. Curiosity killed the cat. The kid and I were two of a kind, just as I suspected.

I had this small adult's number.

We walked first to my dad's house, to meet the realtor. He lived in the neighborhood, albeit in one of the stuccoed new monstrosities built where old houses like this one had been torn down, so he knew both the house and the area.

My dad had signed the contract that the realtor had dropped off the week before, so we finished the paperwork. We walked through the house to review a few things, then he headed off to pound in the sign and make the listing.

I stood and had one good look around, probably the last look, seeing my mother in a thousand places.

"Is this the part where you tell me how rough you had it as a kid?" Jimmy asked.

"No, but since you mention it, let me show you something." I marched him to the back of the house and a very pink room. "Your mother and I shared this room until we were eighteen."

There was still a Magic Marker line down the middle of the floor, and Jimmy looked at it with a frown. "Is that the boundary?"

I smiled. "It was. I did it when she took something of mine, and I nearly died for my creative expression." He clearly didn't understand. "Magic Marker on the floor. Big sin. Right up there with tape on the walls and thumbtacks in the door."

He looked around. "It's not that big."

"You said it, not me. I just hated the pink."

He smirked, then laughed. "Mom loves pink."

"I know. She loved this room. I think it scarred me for life. I can't even chew bubble gum because of the color."

He laughed again, then watched me a bit uneasily.

I smiled at him, deciding to keep him worried. "Come on. We've got things to see, people to do." And I headed out of the house, locking the door behind me and taking my memories of my alive-and-well mom with me, thank you very much.

We walked down the street, and I could nearly hear the neurons firing away next to me. Jimmy was looking at the neighborhood, really looking, perhaps imagining Marcia and me growing up here. We covered a lot of turf before he spoke up.

"What's it like being a twin?"

There was no reason to be ambiguous. "I always thought it sucked. Everyone thinks you come in a pair and that you're interchangeable with each other. That you should dress the same and look the same and talk the same way. It gets old."

"And that you should share your stuff," Jimmy added. I glanced at him in surprise. "That's what Mom said once. That I should feel lucky that I don't have to share my birthday with anyone else."

"You feel lucky yet?"

He grinned, knowing that I was teasing him. "No."

"Why not?"

"We were supposed to go to Jamaica this winter. It's not fair!"

"My heart is bleeding for you here."

"Dad always said I couldn't learn to scuba dive until I was ten."

"Ahh!" The light went on. "And you're ten this year, but you aren't on a beach with a bunch of scuba-diving pros. I get it."

"It's a big deal, you know." He trudged along in his unfastened sneakers, hands balled in his pockets. "If we don't go next year, either, then Johnny and I could be learning to dive at the same time, which would be so lame."

"You like to be first."

"I get to be first! I was born first! It's not fair." He kicked stones along the sidewalk beside me, glowering all the way. "Besides, all my friends all went somewhere cool. It's like totally unfair."

"Poor baby. How many times have you been to the Caribbean?"

"We go every winter. Except this one."

· "And I've never been. Trust me, kiddo, I've seen a lot more Marchs than you have."

"Don't tell me I should feel sorry for you."

"I wouldn't dream of it. I lived in Japan for three years and that, my short friend, is luck."

"Did your dad pay for that?"

I laughed. "Right! I worked there. That's what paid for it. Remember that moral about paying for what you want?"

He made a dismissive noise, but I wasn't expecting much else.

"Here's something else for you to think about. Your mom and I are twins, which meant that neither one of us was technically older."

"Mom always said she was born first."

"Yeah, she did. It's not like she remembers."

He snickered at that.

"But here's the thing. You get an easy tag. You'll always be the older one, no matter what happens. Your mom and I didn't get any easy tags. Neither of us was older or taller or prettier. We were exactly the same. People mixed us up. It really bit."

"I bet."

"So, you end up having to find something that makes you different from the other one. Something not so superficial as being more blond or being older or even being smarter."

Jimmy was interested now, though he probably didn't want to be. "Like what?"

"Well, like the good one and the bad one. That was what we went with. It has a certain simplistic elegance."

Jimmy grinned. "I know who was who."

"Well, duh. So did everybody. But you know, as a distinction, being the bad one has no legs."

"Huh?"

"It can't take you far. It's cool as hell when you're a teenager, but you get into your twenties, and it's not so cool. You either have to get really bad and take crime as your career choice, or you have to fake being bad, which starts to look pretty stupid. Either way, you end up with bad choices and fewer opportunities. See, I've been there and I've done that, and I think that a smart kid like you could come up with a better choice than being the bad one."

He was skeptical. "Like being the good one?"

"Puh-leese! Think outside the box! What about being the artsy one? Or the technogeek? The history buff or the mechanic who can fix or build anything? What do you want to be? What do you want to do?"

"How do I know?"

"You don't have to have the final answer. You just need a place to begin." We walked along and I liked the sound of his furious thinking. This was a good start.

"The astronaut," he said, nodding firmly.

"And what do you need to do to be an astronaut?"

Jimmy blinked. "I don't know. Go into space."

"*Before* that. How do they pick who's going to be an astronaut?"

He looked up at me, expecting an answer, but I shook my head.

"You've got an Internet connection at home. Find out. Why should everyone just give you the answers on a silver platter? Do you think astronauts have no initiative?"

"What's initiative?"

"Taking things into your own hands. Doing what needs to get done without being told to do it."

He got the same look his father has when he's thinking hard. "I could go to the NASA site," he said carefully. "Maybe they say what you need to do."

"Maybe they have links to the biographies of the astronauts in their program. You could look for the things the astronauts have in common." He was busy with this one, and I knew I'd gotten my foot in the door.

But I wasn't nearly done yet. We were going to slam this

lesson home, hard. "Let's go talk to my old pal." I caught Jimmy's shoulder and steered him into the police station right beside us that he hadn't even noticed we were passing yet.

Flaherty, of course, was waiting. He tried not to look as if he was waiting on us, but he failed miserably. He loved doing this trick. He'd told me on the phone that it was his contribution to society.

There's a reason why Flaherty's still a beat cop. He's a good-hearted guy, but he is incapable of being unobtrusive. He's great on the beat, dispensing breezy greetings and quelling glares. He's also good at being underestimated, something that serves him well.

He was getting older and heavier, so I figured he was still scoring doughnuts somewhere. His hairline had receded, but his eyebrows were as furry as ever, if not more so, and now gray. They seemed to move independently, like caterpillars desperately trying to escape some sticky stuff that had been applied to his forehead.

"Mary Elizabeth O'Reilly!" he boomed. "And is this not a surprise!"

It wasn't, but Jimmy didn't seem to realize as much. On the other hand, Flaherty made an impressive sight as he rolled toward us, buttons nearly bursting. The kid seemed a bit taken aback. Flaherty is tall, too—there's a lot of this cop to like. He gave me a quick wink, loving that he was going to fake out a kid on my express request, then scowled at my outfit.

"Did you learn nothing in all these years?" he demanded. "What is it that you're doing to make your living these days, hmmm?"

"I'm a webmistress." He blinked so I elaborated. "Computer stuff." He took a breath to expound upon his view of the high-tech industry, but I leaned closer and dropped my voice confidentially. "But you were right all those years ago. Bad blood will out, no doubt about it."

"Yes?" He did his squinty-eyed cop look, the one that used to terrify all us kids and which now nearly made me laugh.

"This is my nephew, Jimmy."

"Marcia's boy!" Flaherty shook Jimmy's hand with great

ceremony. The kid had a tolerant look on his face that I hoped wouldn't last much longer.

I shook my head sadly. "He steals, Flaherty."

POP! The boy was shocked. "Auntie Maralys!"

"This fine boy? Well, it takes all kinds, that it does. What'd you steal?"

Jimmy stammered then named the toy.

Flaherty put out his hand. It hadn't even occurred to me that Jimmy might have brought it along, but he pulled it out of his jacket and surrendered it.

Looking daggers at me all the while.

Before Jimmy could say boo, Flaherty had spun him around and handcuffed him. It was no accident that he had a small set at the ready, though I was impressed by how quickly he still moved. "Come along, young man. There's only one place for a thief."

"Auntie Maralys!"

"Hey, what can I do?" I shrugged and leaned against the counter, apparently indifferent to Jimmy's fate.

They had some really lousy magazines in the waiting area, bad enough to make me wonder whether people who couldn't be dentists became cops.

Flaherty came back whistling a few minutes later and perched on a chair beside me. "Scared him crapless," he said with satisfaction. "We'll give him half an hour."

"Thanks. Thanks so much for this. I know it isn't legal."

"But it ought to be. Can't put the fear of Jesus into anyone anymore, and you've got to get them early even for a fear of the law."

I fanned my magazine and chucked it back in the pile. "You've got some crummy magazines, here, you know?"

"Well, it's not the library, is it?" He grinned. "Besides, we don't want to encourage the lawyers to hang around."

I laughed with him, then hunched forward. "Do you know who his dad is?"

Flaherty shook his head, then a light came on. "Wait a minute. Marcia married a lawyer. What did you say the boy's surname was?"

"Coxwell."

Flaherty grinned, even as he looked amazed. "No shit? One of them in here." He whistled through his teeth. "I would have made more of a show of it if I'd known."

"James Coxwell is his dad."

"Well, doesn't that take the prize. Was this his idea?"

"No, mine. I'll never forget this place."

He squeezed my hand in a paternal way. "But it steered you straight all these years."

"It did. I never wanted to see the inside of a cell again."

"Crude but effective, that's what I say." Flaherty nodded and looked around the station. "James Coxwell, you say. Now there's a family of legal eagles. Is he the one said to be going to the DA's office?"

I nodded. "News travels fast."

But Flaherty was remembering something. "He took me apart in court once, had me wondering whether I even knew my own name. He's good, dangerously good—it's fine news to have him on our side. He's tough about people following the rules, and there are those who don't appreciate being told their job, but it's the respect for the law that marks the good guys."

Before I could comment, he leaned forward and tapped my knee with a heavy fingertip. "Here's another thought for you. You take that boy to see his father in court one day, especially now as he's on the right side."

"That's a good idea. I'll do that."

"It's an education."

"I'll bet."

"All right then, Mary Elizabeth. I've got to walk my beat, but it was a delight to see you again. You ever need my help again, you let me know. And you give my best to your father." He stood and smoothed down his shirt. "You still remember the way?"

"Oh, yeah."

"Larissa will go down with you. Let him out when you're ready." He gestured to a statuesque black woman in uniform, who glanced up at the sound of her name and smiled at me.

"Maybe I'll go down now," I said, sparing a glance at the clock. What a soft touch I'm getting to be. It had been barely twenty minutes.

Flaherty touched my shoulder. "You never get another chance to make a first impression, Mary Elizabeth," he counseled quietly. "Let him wait the full thirty."

I did.

Larissa walked down to the lockup with me, then hung back, letting me talk to the kid more or less alone. He was the only guest of this particular hotel of the State of Massachusetts at the moment, either because the streets had gotten less mean or because it was early in the day.

He looked small and young.

He glanced up when I strolled along the corridor, then looked down at his shoes. He was clearly relieved to see me and just as clearly determined to hide that relief. I leaned against the opposite wall and let the silence stretch long.

"When I was twelve," I said finally, "I stole a lipstick."

There was a flicker of interest from the boy behind the bars. "Lame," he whispered and I smiled.

"You bet. I took it from the nickel-and-dime store at the corner. It's not there anymore. I not only had no money, but I wasn't allowed to have any makeup until I was thirteen. But I wanted that lipstick. I was sure it was just the right color for me, maybe even that I deserved it. I thought it would be cool to steal something. I was sure I'd never get caught."

"But you did."

"Not by the store. They never had a clue."

He looked up, curious despite himself.

"Someone ratted on me." I spared the kid the detail of who that person had been. You can work it out—I painted that line down the middle of the bedroom right after I got out of the big house. I'm sure my parents despaired of me then. "And Flaherty came to the house. I thought he was visiting my dad, but he zipped those handcuffs on me just like that. And then he walked me all the way here. I thought I would die because all of my friends saw us."

Jimmy turned to face me, interested now.

"They left me there all night."

"All night?" he squeaked.

"It was a different time, Jimmy. We thought the world wasn't nearly as dangerous then as we do now, and lots of people thought kids needed tough lessons." I crossed the corridor and leaned against the bars beside him. "And I wasn't alone."

"You were in here with crooks?"

I smiled. "A pair of old hookers. Prostitutes. They talked about a lot of stuff that I didn't understand but maybe you would. One of them fell asleep, and then the other one came to talk to me. I was scared, but I wasn't going to let her see that."

He watched me avidly.

"She told me about her life, about her father raping her, and about getting kicked out in the street when she was nine. She told me about searching for food and being alone and being cold and selling her body to get something to eat. She had this voice that was all gravelly, from cigarettes and who knows what else. She told me a lot of things she'd done, most of them illegal, and then she took my hand." I shook my head, remembering. "I thought she was about a thousand years old, you know, and she smelled."

He shuddered. "I wouldn't want her to touch me."

"I didn't, either, but I didn't want to act like I was scared." Jimmy nodded, understanding. "So I let her, and her touch was so gentle, even after what she'd been through. Even though she talked so tough. She said to me"—I coughed up my best impression of that voice—"'I bet you don't feel too blessed tonight, do you kid?'"

"When I said no, she smiled and squeezed my hand. 'But you are and don't you ever forget it. I wish someone had loved me enough to snatch me back from the edge.'"

Jimmy stared up at me for a long moment before he looked away. "Am I supposed to feel lucky now?"

"Don't you?"

He didn't look up and he didn't answer me. I beckoned to Larissa, content with incremental progress, and she unlocked the door. "Don't you let me see you back here again," she said sternly to Jimmy as he walked free.

Jimmy didn't say anything, but he was thinking about it. He retrieved his toy from the front desk and gave it a hard look before he tucked it away.

The first class at Maralys U was making headway.

Next stop was Meg's to check on progress for The Dress, of which there had been none. She had prominently displayed the last of James's suits, on my request, with not just the price on the tag but James's name on it. Jimmy noticed—the kid was literate, after all—but said nothing. His eyes did widen at the price, and he stayed quiet long after we left.

"You buy used clothes?"

"All the time."

"Isn't that kind of gross? Knowing that someone else wore it first?"

"Well, it's been cleaned. And what's the difference between your cousin's hand-me-downs and someone else's?" I held up a hand. "Wait, don't tell me, you never got hand-me-downs."

He shook his head.

"Trust me, they're awful. Picking what you want is way better."

He smiled at me and I thought it was time for a break. We passed under the golden arches, which pleased him no end. "How come we never go to your place?" he asked when we were eating.

"Bite your tongue." I stole one of his fries. "You think I'm going to let someone with sticky fingers into my cave? Wrongo, *Calypso*."

"I'll bet you have cool stuff."

"Very cool stuff. Repent from your wicked ways, and we'll talk about it."

Even lab rats get the occasional piece of cheese, or at least a whiff of it, right? We went to see Tracy, who'd lined up the nickel tour of the lab just for us. They didn't show us the really hot stuff, but it was enough to intrigue technically-inclined Jimmy. Phyllis walked him through her contract operation, talking to him as if he was a potential recruit, which thrilled him no end. She reminded me of a beta test she wanted me to help with later in the month.

"Mind your p's and q's," I told Jimmy, "and I might let you help with the beta-testing."

"What's that?"

"The last test of software before it's shipped. We try to break it, to find the mistakes and weaknesses in the code."

"Cool!"

"As long as you're not the one who has to fix it. That can become a bit of a drag." I gave him a steady glance. "I'd have to pay you, of course, but I don't hire crooks. Nobody does."

He looked at me hard. "Do I get a chance to do better?"

"There's always a chance to do better. Hurry up, we're late." We went from there to a seminar that Lydia was helping to organize. It was part of a program associated with one of the hospitals, which did a lot of facial surgery on children. The idea was to help kids look past the deformities of other children, and thus to be less aware of their own. I guess it's supposed to build self-esteem. Lydia had suggested that we drop in, but I really wasn't prepared for the children.

No. What I wasn't prepared for was the sight of their ravaged little faces.

It broke my heart. There is a nasty little impulse that lives on in all of us, maybe a residual of the reptile brain that's still wired in. It makes our guts jump when we see another of our species that isn't within bounds of tolerance of mutation. It makes us understand why sparrows will peck the sick one to death. It's an ugly urge, all the more so because you can't just cut it out and be rid of it.

It's not civilized, but it's still there. It will probably always be there, lurking in all of us.

I was surprised at how hard it lunged for my throat. So

many kids, so many anomalies. We arrived when they were taking a play break—as planned—and, like kids everywhere, they were making a heck of a racket. All the same, I had to sit down and mentally wrestle my reptile.

Jimmy was silent.

I watched the kids and realized that they were either freed of the ugly urge or had gotten over it. Maybe looking in the mirror every day at a cleft pallet in the process of repair or an inoperable tumor gives you greater tolerance. Maybe we could all get past it if we tried. I looked hard and saw the way they smiled as they played, the way they shouted and ran, just like all other kids, and focused on that.

Lydia came over as soon as she saw us, wearing a great big smile. "Oh, it's going so well," she enthused. "Here's my new theory—we need to be reminded once in a while that we're not alone, in order to be better people."

"Works for me." I shared my FedEx theory—well, with some editing for little ears—and she thought for a moment before she nodded.

"I like it. It has potential."

Jimmy scanned the room, then looked up at me. "What are we doing here, Auntie Maralys?"

I smiled and lied. "I thought you might want to play with some new kids."

He held my gaze, assessing me in a startling echo of his dad's manner. Then he nodded and looked back at the kids. I swear he thought I thought he'd buckle, and he was determined to show me wrong.

The kid had pluck. Jimmy marched right up to a small boy, the only kid not bouncing around. The boy just sat hunched over alone in the middle of the floor. I saw the portwine birthmark that covered most of the boy's face.

What Jimmy saw, I realized a moment later, was that the kid had the same handheld toy that Jimmy had stolen. He was alone, not because of the mark on his face, but because he was playing that game with such concentration that it excluded everyone else in the room. I was humbled, because I had overlooked what Jimmy thought was the most intriguing quality of this kid.

Lydia and I exchanged a glance, then sidled closer.

"Is that one of those new ones?" Jimmy asked, then named the model.

"Yeah," the other kid said, not even looking up from the game. His attitude was dismissive, as if Jimmy's presence might affect his game. "My dad bought it for me."

"It's supposed to let you play interactively."

The kid shrugged, attention fixed on the game. "Yeah."

"Does it work?"

"I don't know. I don't know anyone else who has one."

"Neither do I," Jimmy said. The other kid looked up, and Jimmy pulled his toy out of his jacket. "Wanna play? That is, if you feel lucky." They grinned at each other, then the other kid sobered as he scanned Jimmy's face.

"So, what's wrong with you?"

Jimmy gave me an impish look. "I have an attitude problem."

"Me too."

They giggled together as if this was the funniest thing in the world, then put their heads together. No doubt they had to load up the same game, then get the units to acknowledge each other. They worked diligently at it, pointing out things to each other to get it done ASAP.

I had a humongous lump in my throat.

In no time at all the two forgot everything except what fun they were having. They were squared off like stormtroopers, firing away at each other. They frowned in concentration, they bit their lips, they shouted with glee when they made a hit, and they laughed.

Some of the other kids gathered around, and Jimmy passed his toy to another kid when it was time for a new game. The other boy did the same, and the kids formed organically into teams, Jimmy and the first boy telling the current team captains how to play. They didn't even look up at each other, or stare at each other's faces.

The game was everything, it broke down barriers and brought them all together.

You've got to love technology. Those barriers were down because Jimmy marched out there and shared. I had to look away. I was so proud of him, so touched by his choice.

He'd trumped my ace, that kid, gone one better in showing me what he was really made of. I thought my heart was going to explode it was pounding so hard.

Lydia gave me a hug from behind, and I held fast to her hands, not trusting myself to speak. "Hey, Maralys, time for a new theory."

"What?"

"You're a natural, girly."

I looked back at her. "A natural what?"

"A natural mom. You reached inside that kid and"—she reached out with a fingertip—"you touched him, Maralys. You really touched him."

She smiled at me and I smiled back, feeling like a great big sap. I wondered then whether I really could do this parenting thing. I wondered then whether it wasn't a given that I'd let James and the boys down, sooner or later.

Because that's what I was really worried about. I had a zen moment of utter clarity there. I was afraid that I would fail them because I didn't know how to do kids and marriage and all that stuff.

On the other hand, James had some experience. And he'd been pretty accommodating of my slips thus far.

I wondered whether my worst enemy here was myself. Maybe I controlled my environment so carefully to ensure that I was never really tested. Maybe I made sure that I was never faced with a challenge that I couldn't conquer.

Maybe it was time I took on some new, untamed, unpredictable peaks.

Someone called Lydia and she headed back to work with a big thumbs-up. I sat on the sidelines and watched, working through my own reactions to these children, who were just kids after all. And my heart skipped along as I wondered and thought and hoped.

It was with great reluctance that Jimmy eventually came back to me. He had only a couple of minutes to introduce me to his opponent, whose mom trailed behind.

"Steve lives right near us," Jimmy said, Steve nodding with enthusiasm. I realized that they probably hadn't met because they went to different schools. James had kept the boys in their private school. "I know his house. Do you think he could come over?"

"I don't see why not. But ask your dad when we get home."

"Okay."

"Maybe you guys should swap phone numbers," Steve's mom suggested, her smile telling me how pleased she was. She leaned closer to whisper to me. "All he does is play that game. I thought I'd never get him to play with other kids."

"At least they can play the game together." I had a pencil and paper in my pocket, so the ritual was done, then Steve was called back to a seminar. His mom gave me a smile and waved as she steered Steve toward the conference rooms.

Jimmy put his jacket back on and looked at me expectantly. "Now what?"

"Now, I dunno."

"I thought you had everything planned."

"I did." I looped my arm around his shoulder, and we headed for the door. "I had this great big scheme to teach you the wisdom of the ages in seven easy steps. Or at least what I know of it." Jimmy harumphed, but I gave his shoulder a squeeze, and he looked up.

"I wanted to make you realize how lucky you are, Jimmy, but it turned out you knew a few things already. I brought you here to teach you a lesson, but instead you taught me one."

"Really?"

"Really. You did a good thing there. I'm proud of you and I'm glad you made a new friend."

He shrugged. "I just went to play, like you said."

"I know. That's what's so great about it."

Jimmy gave me a skeptical look, à la Coxwell. "You feeling all right, Auntie Maralys?"

"I feel great. Come on, *Calypso*, let's return to base. Our work here is done." We headed out of there with one last wave for Lydia, snagged a bus, and worked our way back to the house.

When we were walking up the street, about a block from home, Jimmy looked up at me. "I thought today was really going to suck, Auntie Maralys."

"It started out kind of rough, didn't it?"

He smiled. "You know it. But I had fun with Steve. I'm glad we went there." He gave me a quick hug, embarrassed by his urge, then ran toward the house.

"Hey!" I shouted after him. "Tell me where you got the shiner."

Jimmy paused on the porch, wary again. "Do I have to?"

I climbed the steps. "No. But I'd like to know."

This kid could do suspicion in spades. "Are you going to tell my dad?"

"Depends. If you don't want me to, I won't."

"I don't."

"Okay, I won't."

"Promise?"

"Absolutely."

He sighed and looked across the street with a frown. "When we were changing for gym, Louie said that Mom left us because Dad is an asshole."

"Ouch."

"He said that everybody knows it, and that his mom heard it from my mom." Jimmy watched me, his expression fierce. "I couldn't let him say that about my dad. It's not true."

I hunkered down in front of him. "No, it's not true. Did your dad ask you about your black eye?"

"Well, yeah. The school told him that Louie and I had a fight, but not why. I couldn't tell Dad that people say he's an asshole. Could I?"

I smiled. "I think he's more used to it than you think. People say that a lot about lawyers."

"Well, they shouldn't. It's not true."

"I think you could have told your dad what happened.

He'd probably tell you not to listen to the garbage that other people say."

"You think?"

"I think you should ask him yourself. I mean, you may have noticed that not only am I not your dad, but I'm not a guy." We grinned at each other. "Locker room politics is not my forte. There's got to be protocol for such things, but we chicks don't get the rulebook."

"What would you have done?"

I shrugged. "Probably made a joke at Louie's expense and stayed cool."

"Like—it takes one to know one."

"Something like that. Or, is that why your mom left?"

"Oh, yeah!" Jimmy bounced. "His parents are divorced too!"

"I'm glad you're all so well-adapted."

"Stuff happens, Auntie Maralys." Jimmy shrugged, insouciant as ever. "You just have to deal with it and move on."

I stared at him. "Are you really ten years old? Or are you some kind of impostor? A body snatcher, an alien, who's really a hundred and ten years old but trapped in the body of a child? That must be it! Do you have the end of a watermelon vine where your navel should be?"

"No!"

I snatched at him and tickled him, purportedly feeling for something that would reveal his alien status. Jimmy laughed and squirmed and we eventually made it into the house, looking flushed and rumpled. James was on his way out the door, going to take his mom to her AA meeting, and my father was grousing about dinner, though they looked up at the ruckus we made.

"Remember, *Calypso*, our mission was top secret," I whispered and Jimmy nodded with satisfaction.

"Roger, Houston. Over and out."

I do think everybody knew that we'd had just too much fun.

Subject: men!

   Dear Aunt Mary—

   So, where are all the good ones? Every guy
   I date is such a loser. Things start out
   well enough then go straight down the
   toilet. I've dated quiet ones and rowdy
   boys, doctors and thieves—everything from
   soup to NUTS. What kind of genetic mutation
   is this? Where can I find a keeper?

   Looking for a Hero

Subject: men . . . and you

   Dear Lost Girl—

   What's the common variable here? You. The
   issue may be that your behavior is showing
   repeatable results. Which is another way of
   saying—life is too short to make the same
   mistake twice.
   Or learn from others' mistakes. Life's also
   too short to make them all yourself. Take a
   hard look at your own choices before you
   blame half the world for your woes.

   Aunt Mary
***
Uncertain? Confused? Ask Aunt Mary!
Your one-stop shop for netiquette and advice:
http://www.ask-aunt-mary.com

Much, much later I heard James come in, the front door closing with a click that echoed through the slumbering house. I stayed right where I was, though my heart started to pound.

I heard the deadbolt shoot home, then heard him walk down the hall to the kitchen, the hardwood floor creaking with every step he took. I closed my eyes and pictured him moving through the house, checking locks and windows, ensuring that my dad was fine.

I smiled at his protectiveness. James wasn't there long, but then, I knew my dad was already asleep.

The house breathed gently of all of our presences, even as James's careful steps creaked on the stairs. I heard him pause at each boy's room, heard his whispered "good night" go unanswered. I heard him sigh as he headed toward his own room and smiled to myself, knowing that he envisioned another night alone.

I do love surprising him.

James didn't turn on the lights, but the blind was still up and the light from the street touched him as he moved through the room. He shed his shirt, his jeans, his socks. He folded his jeans over the only chair in the room, threw the rest into the laundry basket. He paused to look out the window before drawing the shade, and the harsh light made his features look careworn.

Tired and burdened.

My heart squeezed and I sat up, bracing my weight on my elbows. He spun at the unexpected sound and just about jumped through the roof when he saw me.

I smiled. "You're going to have to lift your game, Coxwell."

James smiled and drew the shade down against the night. "I thought you'd left." His voice was low and velvety, the sudden darkness in the room making me shiver in anticipation.

"Dad fell asleep. I couldn't have abandoned the fort and left it undefended."

The mattress squeaked as he sat on the side. Even in the darkness, I could feel his gaze on me.

"I owe you an apology," I admitted. "I'm sorry I said what I said. I was wrong."

He nodded, apology accepted. "Is that the only reason you're here?"

"Nah. I thought I'd try out a real bed, see if it was worth the investment."

James half laughed, then his hand landed on mine. "Really, Maralys."

I sat up and reached for him. I found his shoulder, then discerned his silhouetted face. I eased closer, dropped a kiss on his shoulder and wasn't pushed away. "I had to tell you that you were wrong."

"How so?"

I heard him inhale deeply, as if he was as intoxicated by my scent as I was by his. He didn't move though, just waited for my explanation. Any other guy would have rolled me to my back and asked questions later. Not James.

All or nothing. I had to respect that.

And I understood that maybe I wasn't the only one afraid of the intensity of my feelings. I ran my fingertips down his cheek to his chin, feeling the stubble of his beard, then caressed his lips. He felt all new to me, he was new in my realization of what was between us. I could have touched him all night, explored him, gotten to know all of him.

But James caught my hand in his, his words hoarse. "Tell me."

"You said I was afraid," I whispered. "And I am. But it's not all about taking a chance. Mostly I'm afraid of letting you down."

"Maralys!"

"No, it's true. I don't know how to do this family stuff. I'm afraid that I'll miss a cue, that I'll screw up and the boys will be scarred forever."

The strength of his fingers was in my hair, cupping my nape and drawing me closer. "We all make mistakes, Maralys," he whispered, his breath fanning my lips. My eyes were getting used to the darkness, and I could see more of him with every passing moment. He was so intent upon this, and I wanted so much to believe him. He smiled slightly. "But you're the most reliable person I know. You'll do fine."

"I don't know. . . ." I started to argue, wanting to make sure that he understood.

James's thumb slid over my lips. "No, but even when you don't know or you don't understand, you try so much harder than anyone else."

"I want to try."

"It's all any of us can do."

"Even if it's not enough?"

"We'll make it be enough, Maralys. We'll do it together." He was watching me, waiting for my agreement.

I smiled at him and slipped my arms around his neck. "Now, can we get to the celebrating part?"

James grinned and swooped down for a kiss. "You're going to love this bed," he murmured. I was happy enough to let him deliver on that threat.

It was a huge concession, you know.

We awoke to a day bursting with the promise of spring. Birds were singing and the sun was just peeping over the horizon. The sky was devoid of clouds and it was going to be gorgeous. The last of the snow was already receding, as I saw when I opened the shade. James stretched, looking like a big contented lion, the way he smiled when he saw me just adding to the analogy.

"Where are you going?" He whispered and so did I.

"Down to the couch, while there's still time."

He sat up but quick then. "I'm not going to hide the truth from the kids, Maralys."

"Well, I fully intend to hide it from my dad."

"You can't be serious. If anyone in this house is going to figure out exactly what's going on, it'll be your father."

"Wrong-o."

James rolled out of bed and came after me. We argued in tense whispers as I tugged on my undies and sweater.

"Maralys, you're not a little girl anymore. Your father has probably noticed."

"No, but I am the eternal virgin."

"What? You were married!"

"Oh, now here's a boy who doesn't know his doctrine. There are three reasons to get divorced in the eyes of the church." I held up my thumb. "One is consanguinity."

"You and Neil were not cousins."

"Clearly." I held up my finger. "The second is that you were never really married in the first place. It never happened."

"A legal technicality."

"Right. But my father was in that church and he saw me get married. He knows it happened—he paid for the reception. He saw the legal paperwork being done, so he knows that I was hitched without a hitch."

"So to speak."

I held up my second finger and wiggled it. "You know the third possible reason?"

James shook his head.

"That the marriage was never consummated."

I got a skeptical look for that.

"Oh, yeah, my father knows it was, but he prefers to think that it wasn't. The alternative—that I am sexually active although unmarried—just isn't thinkable. We both participate in this charade, and trust me, you don't want to mess with this particular cornerstone."

"Then you'd better move it," James said, a wicked gleam in his eye. "I go running at six and Johnny sometimes goes with me."

"Jimmy?"

"Not yet, but I keep asking."

It was five to six. Yikes. I gathered my stuff but quick and made to head out, but found James in my way when I got to the door. "You are not going to sleep on the couch until we're married," he muttered.

I grimaced. "Don't even say that m-word."

"The whole enchilada, Maralys." I got the steely-eyed look and knew I wasn't going to win this one. "You know that."

"Let me ease into this. Please." I stretched up and kissed him, an entreaty if ever there was one.

"You're lucky you're so cute," James growled at me. "I'd never let another woman take advantage of me like this."

"Is that a joke?"

He grinned.

His kiss was reassuring, as it was probably supposed to be, and I leaned into it. I considered coaxing him back to bed, but then, Johnny might be coming around to check on his dad. I had to get used to having small adults more or less constantly underfoot.

Well, I didn't have to get used to it, strictly speaking. I could just walk out the door and leave them all behind.

As if. I kissed James back, hoping to tell him by touch that he was stuck with me. I'd get the words out sooner or later.

I left before things got so interesting that we forgot pertinent details. I tiptoed past the boys' rooms and scurried down the stairs, sticking to the edge of each step so the wood creaked less.

I had no sooner settled onto the couch in the same pose as the night before and hauled up the afghan, than James noisily erupted from the bedroom upstairs.

"Johnny? You with me this morning?" I heard James rap on the door, then a mumbled answer that I assumed was a no. "Jimmy?" Another rap and another mumble. "Then, don't make your grandfather crazy. I'll be back in an hour. I've got the cell."

Then James was pounding down the stairs. He burst into the living room and I opened one eye, surprised despite myself to see him not only in his sweats but looking wide awake.

"Maralys!" he declared in apparent astonishment. He looked on the verge of laughter, as well as bright-eyed and bushy-tailed, and I could have swatted him. Why did sex leave him looking like Tigger and me feeling like Garfield? I'm going to have to talk to Lydia about refining that theory. "I didn't know you stayed over."

I sat up, and felt decidedly rumpled in comparison to his fresh appearance. I treated him to a skeptical survey. "Do you iron your sweats?"

"No, why?"

"There's something unnatural about looking so good so early in the morning."

"Is that a compliment?"

"Don't push your luck," I muttered. "I'm not a morning person and you know it. It's vulgar to flaunt your advantage." I lowered my voice. "I think we should go back to bed and wake up the old-fashioned way." I winked at him and he smiled, but didn't take the bait.

"Come running with me," James said instead, as if he would challenge me. "It'll be good for you."

"Fiber is good for me." I thumped the pillow and collapsed on the couch again. "I'll have a bran muffin instead."

"Come on, Maralys. It's a perfect day." He dropped and did a dozen push-ups, just too damn energetic to be believed.

I snuggled back down and closed my eyes. "Wake me up when the coffee's ready."

I felt him lean closer and knew he was just a couple of inches away. "We don't usually make coffee in the morning," he whispered, pure devilry in his tone. I kept my eyes squeezed shut. "But I have a secret stash."

My ears perked up.

"Jamaican Blue Mountain, dark roast."

I opened one eye. "Beans or already ground?"

James scoffed. "What kind of heathen do you take me for? We were *yuppies*, Maralys—we had a German-made electric coffee bean grinder before anyone else even knew what one was." He did some stretches. "They're really oily beans. Fresh. Perfect."

I sat up. "I'll find them while you're gone."

James smiled. "Good luck." He bent and checked his laces, then turned to go.

"You wouldn't leave me here, fantasizing about coffee. That would be too cruel."

"Watch me." He was in the hall in the blink of an eye. I

heard the door open and James take a deep breath of the morning air.

Damn him!

"I've got nothing to wear!" I wailed, the lament of women everywhere when faced with men making impulsive, intriguing invitations.

James ducked back into the doorway and grinned. "I'll lend you some sweats."

"Shoes. I need shoes."

He pointed to a Rubbermaid tub in the corner. "The last dregs for Goodwill. I think there's a pair of tennis shoes in there that I found in the crawlspace on moving day. Get a move on, Maralys, daylight's a-wasting."

And so it was that we were running, at 6:05 A.M. on a perfect Monday morning. It was still chilly, and our breath made little white puffs in the air. The streets were quiet, the sun just thinking about rising. (Kind of like I would have been, without the kindly encouragement of my running mate.)

The sky was brightening, the lights in the city towers standing out like stars against the sky. There were a few people walking their dogs, all bundled up against the chill, and a few diehards heading off to work already.

Even in the evil city, people are more friendly in the morning. Other runners nod, dogwalkers say good morning. We acknowledge each other as neighbors in a way that we don't once the city really gets rolling.

Now, don't get me wrong. I like running. There was a time when I used to run every morning, when I used to take an hour to myself before school and work, etc. That was B.N.: Before Neil. Before I joined the geek culture and became a software nerd, just like all the other boys. Before I inverted my life and went vampiric, burning the midnight oil every night and sleeping while the sun doth shine.

Thank God I never went for the diet—that is, nothing that doesn't come out of a vending machine is worth eating. Neil

was a health food freak—because he was impossibly vain—
so I have him to thank for my affection for whole grains and
obsession with whole foods.

I've always loved to run, although it's hell to get started.
You go for the moment, that transcending moment when running changes from something to be endured to something
magical. You hear your blood pumping and feel your muscles
flexing, you become more aware of yourself and your place
in the world. You feel the air on your face and smell the city
and hear the pound of your feet on the sidewalk and you know
that you could run forever like this.

I ran beside James, following what was obviously his established route. We didn't talk, just the beat of our shoes and
the puff of our breath enough. Of course, his neighborhood
now was the one I had grown up in, so it was a tour for me
that brought back a lot of memories.

I noticed where buildings had been demolished and new
ones built, shops that had morphed into restaurants, parks that
had disappeared, trees that had grown. When you run—or
when you walk—in a city, you're closer to it than when you
zip through it in a car, or zip under it in a subway. A great part
of Boston is still built on a very human scale: Its streets and
townhouses are proportionate to people, approachable, appre-
ciable.

I ran and appreciated.

"I didn't know you ran in the morning," I said finally.

"I used to go to the gym." James smiled. "Not so long ago,
I'd be at the office by now, catching up on my paperwork. I
was out the door before the boys were even up."

I watched him. "You seem amazed by that."

"I did it for years. I'm amazed that I could have been so
fixed on one goal to the exclusion of everything else. I remember coming home, finding the boys in bed, and sitting on
the edge of their beds to watch them sleep. I remember being
astounded that they had grown so big. It seemed only yesterday that they had been born."

"Ten years is a lot of yesterdays."

"Yes, it is. I was a lousy father."

We turned into a park, our footsteps crunching on the gravel pathway. "That's a pretty tough call."

"It's true. I worked all the time. And when I wasn't working, I was ensuring that I'd be able to work again. I went to the gym. I networked. I ate. I slept." James's eyes narrowed and it wasn't because of the sun. "Marcia was right. It wasn't sustainable. I was on the fast track to dying young or burning out."

He cast me a sidelong smile. "And you know, no one would have missed me. In all my effort to make a mark, I wasn't making one that counted at all. I was so intent on succeeding and getting the trapping of success that I failed in the most fundamental ways."

I didn't say anything, because he seemed to have plenty to say himself. We ran a bit more before he continued.

"Marcia threw me back, for being a lousy father and a lousy husband, and she was right."

"Helluva wake-up call."

"It was the only one that would have worked."

"You don't sound so bitter about her leaving."

"Well, I guess I'm not. I guess she did what she had to do."

"You're getting soft in your dotage."

He smiled again. "The boys are Marcia's kids, too. Although the primal urge is to keep them from her, as a kind of punishment, that would be my father's solution."

"And yours?"

James frowned. "They need her. She's their mom. Nothing is ever going to change that. There are things that Marcia knows and Marcia does for them that I can't. There's a reason why parents come in teams. We can better offset each other's weaknesses that way."

"Are you going to teach me the words to *Kum Ba Ya*?"

James chuckled, then shook his head. "The thing about running like this is that you have time to think."

"Running away?"

"Running through. Working through. Sorting out."

"Unemployment is good for that, too. Great time generator."

He nodded in acknowledgment. "I've been thinking, a lot. I owe Marcia for this. She had the guts to take a stand. She had the guts to get off the roller coaster. I don't agree with her way of doing it, but I was ready to keep on going for another twenty years, to hell with the consequences."

"You wouldn't have lasted that long."

"I couldn't see it then, though I see that now. Our marriage was crappy, but I helped with that. I didn't listen to Marcia. I didn't talk to her. I didn't invest in the relationship the way I should have. It's no wonder there was nothing left, or even anything in the first place. One person can't make a marriage work."

I was not at all convinced that my sister had been trying so hard, either. "I don't think it's all your fault. . . ."

"No, but it's not all Marcia's, either. I may not have been the architect of my misfortune, but I was certainly one of the major contractors. I owe her for setting me straight. I owe her for doing the only thing that could have made me pay attention to what was important."

He paused, then continued more softly. "I owe her for what's happening between me and the boys. This is new stuff for me, and although some of it is tougher than I imagined, most of it is more rewarding than I imagined parenting could be."

"You're doing pretty well."

"But it wouldn't have happened without Marcia forcing my hand."

Well, that was probably true. I wasn't so sure that my sister's motives were that altruistic, but I wasn't going to argue with him. What did I know?

"What about you?" he asked, and I looked at him in surprise.

"Me?"

"You and Neil. What came out of that for you?"

"Debt." I grimaced. "Credit purgatory. Healthy skepticism. A long-standing immunity to men and their sweet-talk."

"No, really, Maralys."

"No, really, he left me in a hole. More like a gaping pit

with no discernible means of escape. I really do have a friend at the IRS."

"No one is arguing that Neil pulled a fast one in making his escape to Mexico. But you must have had a role in what happened—nothing is ever one partner's fault entirely. And you must have learned something from it, something maybe about yourself."

"Like I'm a sucker for a great butt?"

James gave me a cutting-to-the-chase look. "Would you have started your own business if you hadn't had one with Neil first?"

I had to think about that for two blocks. It was a good question. "No. I never would have. You're right. I didn't agree with the way he ran his business, but I would never have had the audacity to go out on my own. I saw him do it and screw it up, and that was when I knew I could do better. Before that, I thought that only the truly brilliant could make a business work."

"Why'd you pay his bills?"

"Well, we were partners, so technically they were also my bills. And I didn't pay any attention to them. I was so busy writing code and having a blast with that, that I assumed the nitty-gritty business stuff would take care of itself. I signed where I was told to sign and went right back to work."

"You're giving me hives here, you know."

I laughed. "Another joke. I'm going to have to reassess my opinion of you, Mr. Coxwell."

We smiled at each other, though my thoughts were still whirling around the axis of Neil. "I guess I figured it was partly my fault for not asking questions or even listening."

"What happened to the code you wrote? Surely there was value in that?"

"Well, yes and no. It was operating system stuff, a very neat concept at the time which has now been completely eclipsed by other developments. It might have been worth something, if it had worked completely. Now it's virtual dust in the wind and nothing more than a learning experience for me."

"What about the marriage? Do you still think that failed just because of Neil?"

"Jeez, I thought this run was going to be fun."

James grinned, but I wasn't off the hook and I knew it.

"Well, his flight to Mexico from bankruptcy, incidentally leaving me holding the bag, certainly didn't help things any. But you're right—as much as I hate to admit it, it wasn't all his fault. It wasn't even that we wanted different things from marriage, but that we didn't talk about those things very well. We stunk at communicating and though we met for sex at regular intervals, we just slipped further and further apart."

James let me think now as we turned back toward the house.

"When I think back about the fights we did have, they were always about the same thing. He said I wanted control, which I did, even if I didn't exercise it. I didn't trust him and that drove him crazy. I couldn't trust him, because then I wouldn't be in control and only being in control of all the variables would keep me from getting hurt. Or so I thought."

"Then what happened to the financials?"

"Ah, I trusted the consultants. The so-called experts. And they trusted Neil, who was sure that there was a big IPO in our future and truly could sell ice to the Innu. Maybe he's selling sunshine to the Mexicans these days."

"He had a line, I'll give him that."

"They were all counting on a big influx of cash at some future point, and I guess, so was I. I just didn't know how far things had gone until Neil was gone."

We turned back onto James's street. "So, do you blame him for the failure of the business and marriage?"

"Ah, the million-dollar question."

"Bingo."

"No. I can't." I frowned and turned to James as we walked the last block to cool down. "You're right. I was a participant, and I guess acknowledging that means that I can learn something from it and move on."

He smiled at me. Evidently I'd gotten at least a B on this exam. "We're where we are because of where we've been,

Maralys, and because of who we've been there with. Things would have been different if you and I connected again all those years ago, but they wouldn't be the same because we wouldn't be the same."

"Things might not have been as good between us," I dared to suggest. "It doesn't say anywhere that it would have been better."

"No, it doesn't." James had no chance to elaborate. We were approaching the back porch and my father's voice carried from the kitchen.

"Put another teabag in that pot. They're not made of gold—"

I had no time to wonder who he was talking to, because the boys wouldn't be making his tea, before a familiar voice answered.

"And a man's got to have some pleasures. I know, Dad, I know."

Marcia.

James looked as amazed as I felt. He bounded onto the porch and opened the door, though whether it was because he was dying to see her or because he had to see it to believe it, I didn't know. (I spent a good bit of time thinking about that later, btw.)

All I saw was that my father's face was lit up like a Christmas tree. The boys were glowing, too. And in the middle of this little triangle of love was none other than sister dearest, looking like a million bucks.

Give or take.

She'd always been a morning person, damn her. She'd lost some weight on her sojourn and had obviously been pampered. She looked sleek and expensive, turned out and subtly made up. She was tanned and thinned, and I wondered fleetingly whether she'd had a nip and tuck, because she looked so much younger and more serene.

Is that all she'd left for? A little restorative work in the desert? I wouldn't have put it past her to at least upgrade the hardware before heading back out in the marriage market again.

Maybe she came back because her Amex card was declined.

My sister turned with a smile, her response souring when
she saw me. Her gaze flicked between James and me, and oh,
yes, I knew that I wasn't welcome.

Nor could I compete with that roses-and-sunshine look. I
stood, perspiring and unshowered, hair snagged up in an im-
promptu ponytail, red-faced to be sure, dressed for success in
her husband's faded old sweats. You've got to love the contrast.

"Mary Elizabeth," my father said. "I didn't realize that you
stayed the night."

"It was too late to go home. I slept on the couch."

My sister's eyes narrowed.

"Well, perhaps you'd best head home now," my father suggested with false cheer. "This looks to be a family moment."

That he included himself as family, but not me, shouldn't
have hurt as much as it did. "Good idea," I said brightly, then
headed to the living room and my stash of clothes.

"Maralys," James said from behind me, and I felt them all
turn to watch as he pursued me. "Thanks for yesterday," he
said carefully, his eyes filled with a thousand things he
couldn't say. "Thanks for everything."

Did that sound like a brush-off, or what?

I peeled off the running shoes and chucked them back into
the Goodwill box, still smoking. "We aim to please," I said
and he flinched at my tone.

Well, good! How dare he *thank* me as if I was hired help?

"If you'll excuse me, I'll change and get out of here." I
gave him a look that could have stopped nuclear torpedoes
cold, but James held his ground. He wanted to say something,
but didn't want to do it in front of the current audience.

Well, he was the one who didn't want to hide anything. I
reached for the hem of the sweatshirt and hauled it up. I was
spitting sparks, let me tell you.

When I pulled it over my head, they were all gone.

I could have offered to launder his sweats but wasn't feeling particularly charitable in the moment. I couldn't tell what

James was thinking, I didn't know how far his gratitude to Marcia extended, and I wasn't going to take the opportunity to ask.

I was mad.

I didn't even say goodbye, just headed out the front door and slammed it hard enough to rock the crockery in the kitchen. I replayed the conversation I'd had with James this morning, seeking clues that he had known of Marcia's pending return, or hints of what he would do when faced with that eventuality. All I had was that he was less angry with her now.

That he felt indebted to her.

Great. That was very reassuring stuff.

I got halfway home before I cooled down enough to think straight.

If Marcia had left because James wasn't being a good enough father and spouse, she was going to love James v2.0. He even had a swell job again, so the cash would be flowing like milk and honey soon enough (though obviously putting crooks in jail wouldn't be nearly as profitable as keeping them out). My father's beaming countenance spoke volumes, and I knew the boys had to be thrilled that their mom was back.

It had all just been a bad dream. Go away, Maralys, you've outlived your usefulness.

If nothing else, it would be much easier to just continue on the same path. I didn't think James was the kind of guy to take the path of least resistance, but then, he'd faced a lot of obstacles lately. He might be ready to just get on with his life.

Maybe I had been a rebound special. Galling thought.

Maybe I was the only one who thought that I could do this family stuff, after all.

Yet I, with my characteristic brilliance and spectacular sense of timing, had not played the only card I had. The man had said that he loved me—granted, it had been a few days ago and before I had insulted him royally—but he had *said* it. And James wasn't the kind of guy who said stuff like that, then changed his mind.

Was he? Gut-writhing time. Surely he must have told Marcia that he loved her, at least once in all those years. And yes,

I had confessed love to Neil, many drunken moons ago, but that had nothing to do with this.

I reminded myself that the man had said that he only wanted to get involved if our goal was marriage and eternal happiness. He could very well think that I wasn't interested in his long-term plan. James could easily think that I'd come back for the sex the night before and said what was necessary to get it.

We hadn't talked that much, after all.

But I hadn't gone back just for sex. I was in love with James Coxwell. I was determined to work for what I wanted.

Too bad I hadn't said so, flat out.

Because now I wasn't going to get the chance to strive for what I wanted. It was another repeat of every time Ms. Gimme swooped in and took what I had, what I wanted, and got away with it.

No. Not this time.

I damn near went back—until I realized that I was now officially in a no-win situation. If I called up and told James now that I loved him—or worse, went back and humiliated myself in front of them all—it would look as if I was competing with my sister. Like I was trying to one-up her. Like I wanted the goodies, just to keep her from getting them.

Gee, not like we've seen that game played before, huh?

I trudged back to the loft, which seemed to have become a big echoing hole in my absence, and treated myself to a long hot shower, trying to figure out what to do.

I studied myself in the steamed mirror afterward, welcoming the harsh light of morning. I usually shunned it and it was not friendly on this day.

I was just as harsh on my appearance as the light. Black might have been a good hair color for me once, but on this morning, it contrasted too much with my fair skin. All the little lines were made more evident by the contrast, as were the shadows under my eyes.

Okay. I was tired, but still. And I generally look good for my age. But sixteen is gone, honey. Long gone. In this moment I looked about as alluring as roadkill. I had become what all women love to mock.

The woman who dresses as if she's younger than she is. The woman who has outgrown her look.

I did not look like the kind of woman that a prominent lawyer should have lunch with, unless she's a client. I certainly did not look like the kind of woman he should be seeing over the breakfast table every morning for the rest of his life.

Surely, you didn't think I was just going to roll over here, did you? No. It was time to defend my turf. I might lose, but I'd go down with everybody knowing what I'd wanted to win and why. I needed heavy artillery.

Remember that song "My Boyfriend's Back"? I started humming it, liberally changing the lyrics to suit my circumstance. Go on, make your own words to it.

My sister's back and she's making double trouble....

The thing was that I knew it wasn't just about Marcia and me. James would make what he thought was the best choice for his sons, even if it meant less of a good choice for him. I could lose him on a technicality.

And I wouldn't love him any less because of that. I liked his sense of honor and responsibility. I liked how serious he was about protecting his sons.

I took a deep breath and considered my reflection. It was time to grow up, whether or not I ended up with James. It was time to pick up all my emotional baggage and make my way out of the terminal under my own steam.

"I yam what I yam" and all that, but I looked like what I had once been, not what I'd become. I needed to look like an adult. Not just any adult, though, not just any successful entrepreneur who could be trusted with the secure handling of your deepest employee secrets. Not just the kind of woman who could win James Coxwell's heart and keep it.

I needed elegance with edge. Edge, I understand. Elegance was tougher.

Fortunately, I knew just the person to ask for help. You know, this asking for help thing really does get addictive, even when you do know that somehow, someday, in some way, you'll need to reciprocate, though probably not exactly in kind. I'm starting to like this network of connections. I picked up the phone, reached out and touched somebody.

Shay la, shay la, my sister's back.

Subject: pearls to swine

Dear Aunt Mary:

My son is an A-student, good-looking, and athletic. He's got everything going for him, but he insists on throwing himself at the most trashy women alive. How can I persuade him that he can do better?

Worried Mom

Subject: re: pearls to swine

Dear Mom:

Give the boy my phone number.

;-D

Seriously, maybe he sees something in these chix that you don't. Maybe you have ::ahem:: an elevated idea of your son's many charms. Maybe he's depriving some village of an idiot. Tough to tell from here.

No matter how you slice it, no one can save people from themselves. Unconvinced? Type "Darwin Awards" into your search engine. Some of these stories *have* to be urban myths . . . don't they?

Aunt Mary
***
Uncertain? Confused? Ask Aunt Mary!
Your one-stop shop for netiquette and advice:
http://www.ask-aunt-mary.com

Which is how I ended up at the city's most exclusive spa-salon on the following Saturday, with an appointment at a most coveted time. You know the place, the one where you have to sleep with some rich and famous muckity-muck even to get in the door.

That, come to think of it, was more or less what I'd done. Beverly Coxwell took me, so I was under her patronage, so to speak.

She'd had only one question when I called her up, even given my fairly remarkable request. "What are your intentions toward my son?"

I'd jammed the phone under my chin, not really comfortable telling James's mommy that I wanted him hook, line, and sinker. "Aren't you supposed to ask him that?"

She laughed. "I know what James's intentions are. You're a wild card, though, Maralys, and I don't know you that well. What do you want with my son?"

I took a deep breath. "I'm in love with him. I want to find out whether we can make it work."

"There are no guarantees, Maralys," she said softly, and I remembered that she was in the midst of a divorce from James's father. Well, not his father. Robert Coxwell. "Even with James."

"I know. But some things are worth trying for."

"For whatever it's worth, I think you're wrong, Maralys."

"What?"

"I don't think that how you look will make that much difference to James, or he wouldn't look the way that he does when he talks about you." My heart went skippity-bump at that. "But if it will help your confidence, I'd be glad to help you. We women are often a bit short of the confidence we need to achieve what we want to achieve."

"Thank you."

"Wait until I'm done before you thank me," she advised, a smile in her voice. "Let me phone my salon and get back to you. Is any time particularly good or bad for you?"

So there I was five days later, in the swishy salon, in the front chair even, within the domain of the great man himself. I was thinking, not about the cash flow of this place—though that would have made for some interesting math—but that no one had called me again this week. It proved my theory that I had to tell James what I felt or lose it all.

Without calling the house, lest Marcia answer.

I would not give a message to his mommy, thanks.

Adrian was running his hands through my locks while Beverly consulted with him. He had that way of grabbing your hair that gay hairdressers always have—a possessive caress that leaves you wondering whether you just get to borrow the hair for those three or four weeks between appointments.

"It's wonderfully thick, very healthy despite the obvious abuse." He surveyed my ends, his expression adequately conveying his opinion.

Beverly stood slightly behind me, her arms folded across her chest. Both she and I were wrapped in terry robes so thick and swish that I was wondering how I could nick one without anyone noticing. "I think it's too heavy for her face."

"Oh, yes, it's definitely in need of shaping."

"She has such lovely cheekbones."

"Great blue eyes." Adrian twisted my hair up in his hands, studying my reflection in the mirror as he mocked different lengths of cut. He pulled a few strands free, arranging them over my brow. "Maybe we should take it to the shoulders, work in some long layers to get rid of the bulk, give it some swing. Maybe a few long bangs." He plucked and pushed my hair around, showing what he would do.

I found it interesting that "we" apparently didn't include me.

"That would draw attention to those eyes," Adrian continued, fixed on his vision. "Then, we could sweep it up for formal occasions." He did just that, baring my neck.

"We want something elegant," Beverly said firmly. "Gracious and graceful."

Adrian arched a brow. "Yet easily maintained."

I could have been insulted at his assumption of my prowess with hair care, but then, he had pretty much nailed it. I color my hair, I trim the ends bluntly with a pair of kitchen shears. This is the sum of my hair-care regimen.

I guess it showed.

"*We* have to be able to make a ponytail," I insisted, and Adrian nodded, barely listening to me.

He was too busy grimacing. "But the color . . . " he began, unable to bring himself to finish. He rubbed my hair between his fingers and tsk-tsked.

"The black has to go," Beverly concurred. "It's too harsh."

"How about my natural color?" I interjected. They both looked at me as if they'd forgotten I was there, a curious thing since the man's hands were full of my hair.

"What is your natural color?"

"It's golden brown," Beverly said, then faltered. "At least if it's like Marcia's."

"Beverly, we all know how many luscious shades come out of bottles," Adrian chided gently, and Beverly lifted one hand to her own lusciously silver coif.

"It's brown," I said with a smile. "The exact color of melted chocolate."

Adrian studied my roots and the hue of my brows, looking for confirmation of what I said. "It could very well have been," he conceded finally. "How long since you've seen it?"

I shrugged. "Twenty years, give or take."

He leaned closer, his expression puckish. "I hate to break it to you, darling, but your natural color might be gray."

I laughed, because he was probably right, and he grinned at me in the mirror. Then he pushed my hair around more aggressively. "All right then, we're going to make some highlights, subtle ones in reddish hues to draw attention to the face." He patted me on the shoulder. "You'll get your ponytail, but you'll look stunning with your hair up or down." Then he snapped his fingers and called for his girls to gather around.

"A pedicure and manicure, too," Beverly said with a smooth authority that had the staff bobbing their heads. At my expression of surprise, she smiled.

"Don't worry, Maralys. This is my treat. I find a certain appeal in spending part of my pending divorce settlement from Robert on you."

We actually did lunch, which was a first for me, but in the rosy glow of having been fully pampered at the spa, anything less would have been unthinkable. It was a late lunch, given our efforts of the morning. I really liked my hair. It did swing and the color was something I could never have achieved on my own. Not quite natural, not boring, yet not outrageous, either.

I looked expensive. Got to love that.

We zipped down to visit Meg, to check on her progress in the Great Dress Hunt. She was smiling. "I just left you a message, because it's here and it's wonderful, like some kind of cosmic justice, Maralys, it's the most *perfect* thing for you, no one else could possibly wear it the way you do and check the color! Your hair will go perfectly with it now, I was a bit worried because the dress has a certain attitude and it could have so not worked, but obviously this was meant to be."

Beverly looked momentarily alarmed by this soliloquy.

"She breathes through her pores," I explained when Meg disappeared into the back. "She's been doing it for years. You'll get used to it."

Beverly began to nod, then her eyes fell out of her head. I turned to look and gasped myself.

"It's fantastic!" I lunged at the dress, marveling at its details. It was a flamenco dress, probably the real thing judging by its ruffles and frills. It was literally the hue of flames and quite possibly had been worn on stage. Surely there was no other reason for it to be orange, red, and hot pink.

It was hard to look straight at the dress.

One look and I was smitten. I *wanted* this one.

"Try it on, try it on. I hope it fits, Maralys, because it's just so you and the only reason I took it on was because it made me think of you. It was worn by a dancer who passed away and her daughter brought it in, such sentimental value, they want a fortune for it, but look at the workmanship! It's lined, the seams are French-finished and look at the handwork in the hem . . ."

I was peeling off clothes in the middle of the shop, which wasn't as outrageous as it sounds. The place is so packed with clothing racks that it's hard to see two feet away, let alone glimpse anything from outside the store. Both Beverly and Meg had seen everything I have, and I wanted to get that dress on my back ASAP.

It gaped through the bust—surprise—but Meg was busy pinning and tucking before I could even comment on that. She said the darts were divine intervention because they were exactly where they needed to be for her to make them deeper and adjust the dress for me. The length wasn't an issue, as it so often was, as the dress had a train. It perhaps had less train on me than on its original owner, but who was to know?

I did a fakey little flamenco dance, liking the feel of the dress very much. It was heavy in the back, which made you sway your hips in a very seductive way, but was cut high to show leg up to the knee in front. The back of the bodice dived to almost the cleft of my bum, what there was of the bodice hugging my curves. Meg would make it fit like a second skin.

It was glamor, writ large.

Beverly alone appeared skeptical. "Where in the name of God would you wear such a dress?"

"I'm having a party. You should come." I gave her the *Readers' Digest* condensed version of the sad saga of Neil and the disappearing money, and my resulting joust with the IRS.

Her eyes narrowed as she considered the dress. She walked around me, considering. "It does suit you. But you'll need some kind of support and a bra won't do."

"What about those cups that kind of stick on your skin?" Meg suggested.

"I'll swing loose." I lifted my arms over my head and wiggled, letting my breasts rock.

Beverly gave me a stern look. "I thought you wanted my advice."

"I do."

"Hookers swing loose. Sixteen-year-olds swing loose. You are neither. You will show no nipples, which in that dress means you need support. You also will refrain from wearing castanets."

It was galling to think that she'd seen through me as far as that. I'd thought the castanets would be a surprise. "If I'd known you were going to be such a spoilsport . . ."

"No jewelry. It will just clutter the look."

"I'd thought something gold . . ."

"No. Simplicity is the key with such a dress." Beverly pursed her lips. "The shoes will make or break it," she concluded. "They must be the perfect height and the perfect shade of red. When is this party?"

"Next Friday."

"Then we don't have much time. We have to shop for shoes and we have to do so immediately."

I grinned at her. "Now we're speaking the same language."

I t was six when Beverly dropped me off at the loft. We had indeed found the right shoes, after much searching, and they had even been in the markdown bin. Meg had given us a snippet of fabric from the bodice dart that was doomed to get bigger. I had a newfound and healthy respect for Beverly's shopping abilities by the time she returned me home. I was bagged, too.

I had already decided to introduce her to Krystal, though the two might change the face of the world forever if they shopped together.

"I don't know how to thank you, Beverly. I never expected you to help me so much."

"You needed it," she said wryly, and we both laughed.

"You'll come Friday?"

"I'll be delighted to. Here?"

I looked at the sleek leather interior of her car as I nodded. "Maybe you should take a cab."

"I will."

"And bring a friend, if you like. There's lots of room."

She sobered then and sighed. "I don't think there's much possibility of that, Maralys."

"Then maybe you'll meet someone here."

Her smile was thin. "I doubt you know any old men."

"You might be surprised."

She studied me. "Yes, I might be. You seem to be a woman with a full store of surprises." She tilted her head. "Thank you, Maralys."

"For what?"

"For a day so busy and so interesting that I forgot all about needing a little encouragement in the middle of the afternoon."

She looked so careworn that I reached out and touched her hand. "How is it going?"

"Oh, it's appalling. You sit with strangers and they expect you to confess all your secrets and urges." She shuddered. "I was raised to keep my thoughts and feelings to myself. I find it quite distasteful to know as much as I do about these people. There are people I have known for decades without knowing a tenth of what I have learned about these troubled souls."

"Does it help?"

"I don't know." She was impatient with the thought. "I suppose that they are right, in that you cannot solve a problem that you haven't faced. They are right that you must understand why you drink to stop drinking. And they respect that none of this is easily done."

"Maybe some kind of private counseling would be easier."

"Oh, undoubtedly. But I'm not certain that it would be very effective. I can't help thinking that my urge to keep sordid matters private while presenting a good face to the world is a part of this, and a part that I need to address. This compels me to a kind of honesty, which is not easy and not pretty and not even entirely welcome. I think, though, that it's healthy." She shrugged and smiled. "In my good moments, at least."

"And in the dark ones?"

"I wonder why the hell I bother. The problem, of course, is that I have always drunk when I felt isolated or lonely. My life right now, in the midst of this divorce, is being played almost entirely in that key."

"You miss Robert?" I was incredulous, and she must have heard it, because she smiled again.

"I miss the sound of others around me. I miss knowing that I could go downstairs and talk to someone else, even though I know that I never did. Condos, although neat solutions, are often chilly." She sighed. "And I miss the habits of Robert. It has been years since I loved him, but he was familiar and there is comfort in familiarity. It is frightening to face the world alone at my age, no less because the world has become obsessed with youth and wealth." Beverly toyed with the stickshift. "I lack one and, if Robert has his way, will soon lack the other as well."

"I thought he wanted the divorce."

"Oh, he does. He also wants the money." She shook her head. "It's very ugly, Maralys, and not worth discussing further. Essentially, Robert's pride is at stake, and he is determined to not let it go cheaply, regardless of the cost to me." She glanced up. "He has retired as a judge, you know."

"No, I didn't know."

"He's astute enough to see the writing on the wall. He's a great tactical thinker, Robert is."

"I don't understand."

"Robert is what used to be known as a hanging judge—his supporting vote comes from the conservative right. These are not people who will be particularly compassionate that he was cuckolded, or that he is divorced, when next they go to the polls. He has retired, rather than face them, though his official reason is to rebuild the practice of Coxwell and Coxwell in James's absence."

She looked suddenly so tired and defeated that I felt like a jerk for not inviting her up sooner. "Do you want to come up for a cup of tea or something?"

Beverly smiled, my question restoring her gracious mask. "No, thank you, Maralys. But I will see you on Friday. And I may call you on an afternoon when I feel a weakness, if you don't mind."

"I'd like that." I smiled at her and she smiled back.

"One day at a time," she said, then smiled once again. "Thank you for this one. Now, please remember, no castanets." She winked as I got out of the car.

"How about finger cymbals? Belly dancers have some really cute ones."

She smiled and waved, revving the Jag as she drove away. I stood on the pavement and watched her go, feeling tremendously sympathetic to her. I could have become someone like Beverly Coxwell, my shields so secured into place that it would take a nuclear blast to get them down.

Well, she was in for a surprise. I have some big guns at my disposal. Whether or not James and I worked things out, I was going to reach out to Beverly—even if she nipped at my fingers once in a while.

I figured I was the only one with the credentials to understand.

I managed to wait until 9:32 on Monday morning before calling James at his new job. The receptionist had a bit of fun hunting him down, as it was his first day and he probably wasn't on the roster yet. I tapped my toes.

"James Coxwell," he said crisply, and I jumped even though I'd known he'd answer eventually.

"Hey, sailor. Thought I'd congratulate you on your new job."

"Maralys!" There was warmth and pleasure in his tone, enough to soothe my fretting.

I interrupted him before he could continue. "Look, I wanted you to know something. I respect you to make the best decisions here, but you need to have all the facts."

"Such as?"

"I love you." I spoke fiercely, not wanting to be distracted from what I had to say. "I love you more than I ever thought I could love anybody, which is pretty scary stuff, but I know that this isn't easy."

"Maralys . . ."

"I want you to know that. And I want you to understand that I'm trusting you here. You might remember that I stink at trusting people and not drag it all out too long."

He laughed under his breath. "Thank you, Maralys. That means a lot to me."

I was a bit shocked that he didn't reply in kind, even though he was at work. "Well, it should. I don't go around falling in love with just anybody, you know."

"Lucky for me."

No one said anything then. I could hear him breathing and my heart pounding. Well. This was working out wonderfully. "See you Friday? I'm having this party, and I think you should come."

"I wouldn't miss it. We'll all be there, Maralys."

Now, that was more than I needed to know. Someone spoke to James and he excused himself, probably a relief to both of us, and I was left holding the receiver, vastly dissatisfied with the result of my bold foray into the land of sweet confessions.

So much for that.

Look, Ma, I'm getting stronger by the minute.

Now, you know that I could have hooked up with James and probably elbowed my way into his life. I thought of it a thousand times that week. I could have seized control of the situation and made it come out my way.

But see, that was the point. I had to trust him or lose it all, even if trusting him might mean I lost it all anyhow. So, I schmoozed my client and picked up the check and rushed it to the bank like it might melt if I held it in my hands too long. Then I made a visit to my friendly IRS dude, who really is a pretty reasonable guy, and paid the last payment.

That was a good feeling. Mr. Morelli printed out my receipt and smiled as he pushed it back across the desk, weaseling it between all the pictures of the grinning Morelli familia. "You should be proud of yourself, Ms. O'Reilly. Not many people would have the stick-to-itiveness to see this through to the end. You've made a remarkable achievement."

"Thanks. You know, I'm having a party Friday night to celebrate. You should come."

"Oh, no. That's a private affair."

"Well, I wouldn't be having it if you hadn't helped me work out a payment plan. You've got to come. Bring Mrs. Morelli and all the little Morellis. Please."

He looked at me and smiled a little. He was as proud as could be of his kids, and I had a feeling that inviting them kind of turned the tide. "All right. Maybe we will. Thank you."

And I walked out of the IRS offices for the last time with my head held high. Ha.

I was dressed but still getting the mirror ball just right when the elevator buzzer rang from below. I assumed it was the caterers again and to tell the truth I wasn't in that prime of a mood. I was going to enjoy my party or die trying but was starting to think that the latter was more likely. It buzzed twice more while I stumbled down off the ladder in my spikes.

"What?" I shouted down the shaft. "Haven't you figured out how it works yet?"

"That would be a trick, seeing as I've never been here before."

It was my sister.

Marcia came up the elevator, oozing attitude, though I was glad to see that she was alone. She wore jeans and a tailored Lauren jacket, not exactly party-wear but elegant stuff.

"You're too early," I said, turning back to the mirror ball. "Come back in an hour."

"That's what I was hoping. I wanted to talk to you alone."

I turned and looked at her. "That's a joke, right?"

Marcia shook her head. "No, it's not."

"Come to gloat?"

She smiled. "No. You should be the one gloating. This is an incredible place." She wandered into my cave, not touching anything, just eating it up with her greedy gaze.

"I wouldn't have thought it would be your style."

Marcia looked back at me from some twenty paces away and almost smiled. It was like looking in a mirror—well, almost, except I had the fab dress this time. And a better haircut.

"Maybe that's the problem," she said enigmatically. She poked in her purse and came up with a pack of cigarettes. "Mind if I smoke?"

"Actually, I do."

"You'll get over it." She lit up and her smile broadened at my evident shock that she had defied my request. She blew the smoke at the ceiling.

"It's not like you to be rude," I said with caution.

Marcia was hostile. "You mean it's not like me not to bend to everybody's expectations."

"I don't know what you mean."

"Don't you? Look at you! You do what you like, you say what you like, you live how you like, and no one ever dares to question you about it. No one ever had any expectations of you. . . ."

"Right! They assumed I'd be dead in a ditch, or in jail, before I reached twenty years of age."

She poked her cigarette through the air at me. "Wrong. They knew that if they challenged you, you'd gnaw their faces off. Mom and Dad respected you. Maybe they were even afraid of you a bit, but me . . ." Marcia exhaled smoke again, and her words turned bitter. "I was supposed to fulfill every dream they'd ever had."

I blinked. I'd never thought of it that way.

Marcia sighed. "You always slipped under the wire, Maralys. I never knew how you did it, but was I ever jealous of you." She took a deep drag and glared at me, smoke wreathing her features. "I hated you for years. I *fucking* hated you."

I moseyed over and stole a butt from the pack. "Ever said that word before?"

"No." She touched her cigarette to me, lighting mine, and we both took a drag. "I mean, fuck, no."

We looked at each other and started to laugh. "I'll call Dad and he'll wash your mouth out with soap," I teased, but Marcia shook her head.

"No, you won't. You never ratted on anybody. You never did what you were supposed to do. You just defied them all, and they washed their hands of you."

"Nobody made you be the goody girl."

"But once you start, you can't stop. Every bit of praise and affection was based on my being good. On my doing the right thing. Of my not disappointing anyone. What kind of life is that? I was keeping my shoes clean and playing parentally approved games and being a nice young lady—while you, you were running through the mud with the boys having a whale of a time. You're lucky I didn't kill you in your sleep."

"Is that what good girls do?"

"No, but I had no idea how not to get caught. You were always the one with the devious mind."

"Ah, go easy on yourself. You picked pink for our room. I'll need trauma counseling about that color for the rest of my life."

We chuckled together, then I gave her the eye. "Is that why you left, to give a test drive to the bad-girl coupe?" I did not ask why she'd come back. Not yet.

"No," Marcia sobered, then looked around for somewhere to butt out.

"In the sink," I suggested.

She eyed the kitchen zone while she was there, marveling. "This is so cool. It's so you."

Was that a hands-off warning? Who knew.

"Thanks." I drew deep again, waiting.

Marcia folded her arms across her chest. "You know, the problem with other people's expectations is that you get so used to fulfilling them that you forget to stop and think for yourself. We were supposed to go to college, but not to learn anything. We were supposed to snag a man and get married and make babies." She eyed me warily. "You have to know that after all my years of being good, it really made me mad to realize that this hunky guy was only chasing me because he thought I was you."

I butted out in turn, not saying anything. I wasn't going to make this easier for her.

"So, you've probably figured out that I lied to him. I mean, why not? It started as a joke, just something to pull your chain."

"Like the picture?"

She shook her head. "That was so mean. And I loved it, you know. I loved how it ripped you up." She looked away. "I didn't know then that you'd slept with him, Maralys. I thought you'd just gone out once."

I declined to provide the details that a/ we had never actually gone out together and that b/ I had conceived a child. Some things are better left alone.

"And then, I kind of liked James. What I really liked,

though, was that he was so eligible, so handsome, plus had such a good family, such a promising future. I loved that Mom and Dad adored him. I loved that he was so determined to marry me."

"Did you love him?"

"No. But I thought he loved me, and I thought that would be good enough." She shrugged and smiled at her own youthful assumptions. "I certainly appreciated the advantages of marrying him. And besides, that was what we were supposed to do. Leave school, get married. I was living up to expectations. And I was flattered that he was so hot to trot, if you must know."

Oh, I knew what was coming. I scored another smoke and lit up, then Marcia did the same. She watched me, her eyes knowing.

"He told me about the mole," I admitted.

"Yeah. There was a rude awakening. He was still crazy for you. I was so angry. I felt so cheated. I lied and lied and lied, because I thought he deserved it. And I was afraid not only that tossing him back would make everyone angry with me, but that you might snap him up after all."

"That wasn't going to happen."

"No. Not only did you hide out, but when you came back, you blew him off. Then I wondered what the hell was wrong with him. Then everyone expected kids from us, so I had to have kids, as if that would solve everything." Marcia laughed and shook her head, blowing smoke in patterns. "Maralys, I have spent my whole life being so fucked up, I can't even believe it."

"So, what's changed?"

"Thank you very much," she retorted and we laughed together. Yeah, we're sisters still, down there deep. You just have to poke us hard with a stick to get us to admit it.

She ground out her butt in the sink. "I met this guy last year, and I knew he was all talk, but his talk was all for me. And I went for it. I was so low that it seemed I couldn't make things any worse. And you know, I wanted to do something bad for a change. I wanted to be naughty. I wanted to find out what I wanted, instead of just wanting what everyone told me that I wanted. So I slept with him. And I asked for a divorce. When James wouldn't give me one, I tried to get even."

"By spending as much money as you could."

"Yes." She took a deep breath. "And then I ran away with my lover to New Mexico."

"Where is he? What's his name?"

"It doesn't matter. I realized just after we got there that I didn't want him. It wasn't him, it was escape. It was the chance to be bad."

"Trust me, it's overrated."

"I needed the chance to make a mistake, Maralys. Look at me! I'm thirty-eight years old, and I have no idea what I want from life. I've lived the whole thing like a robot, always doing what I'm supposed to do next. Never questioning it. Never insisting on what I want. Hell, I don't even know what I want." She paused and studied me. "Except that I want to find out what it is."

"Where does that leave your family?"

Marcia smiled. "It leaves James pretty much where he was when he started. And the boys, well, they're big enough that they don't need me around all the time. Maybe it's better for them that I'm happy, or at least vital, instead of the household doom-and-gloom committee."

"Did you really want to stay home with them?"

"Hell, yes! I wanted the classic setup. I didn't want to work. I wanted the easy way out. It was a shame that it took so long for me to get pregnant, but not doing it with your husband very often can affect that, I hear." Marcia sighed. "I wanted what Mom told us we should want. I wanted not to have to work as hard as she had, and I wanted it because she said she wanted it for me."

We stared at each other for a long moment, and suddenly I had to know. "Do you dream of her?"

"All the time." Marcia swallowed. "She's in our kitchen, washing dishes and cleaning up. She's dressed like something out of a fifties fashion spread in red and white, even wearing little gloves with red bows on the back and a hat with a bit of netting. Dressed for church even though she's doing house-work. The kitchen literally sparkles. I had this dream over and over again."

She looked at me, hard, as if she expected me to challenge her on this. "And then, last summer, the ending of the dream changed. Mom opened the window over the sink, looked over her shoulder, and winked at me, even though I didn't think I was actually there. Then she lifted her arms and flew out the window. I ran and looked, but there was only a bird flying higher and higher, disappearing into the sky." She sighed. "I knew that I had to leave then. And so I did."

Marcia cleared her throat and rummaged for another butt. "I've been taking some dream-interpretation classes, in Santa Fe, and—"

I lifted one hand. "Don't tell me. I like the understanding I have of your dream right now."

"Do you dream about Mom?"

I smiled. "Yes. She kicked my ass into the labyrinth."

"What?"

"It doesn't matter. She was right. She really did know what was best for me, just as I think she did for you. What are you going to do now?"

Marcia drew heavily on the cigarette. "Well, James and I have made our deal. James has custody although I can have all the visitation I want. It worked out very amiably in the end. I haven't got much in my wallet, but I figure I rode on his dime for a long, long time. It's partly my fault that there's not much there anymore. I'm going to go back West. I like it there. I like how new and fresh it is, and how people can shape their own expectations. I don't know what I'm going to do, but I'm going to find out what I really want."

I nodded, understanding better now what had driven my sister to make the choices she had.

"I'm sorry, Maralys," she said softly. "I'm really sorry."

"It's okay." I forced a smile.

Her answering smile was just as uncertain. "I'm scared, Maralys. I think sometimes that I'm too old for this."

"You're never too old to go after what you want." I made

another one of those impulsive offers that keep drawing me deeper into the net. "You can call me if you need advice."

Marcia stubbed out her smoke, then took a step closer. "I don't expect you to forgive me, but I'd like to try to be sisters the way other people are sisters."

"I'd like that, too."

You knew we had to hug. It's the only way to end a scene like this. Although actually, it ended with the caterers shouting for the elevator and Lydia appearing with them and the mirror ball finally getting into gear.

And when I looked around five minutes later, Marcia was gone.

The question was, where was James?

Beside the fact that he hadn't called me, even though he must have known that Marcia wasn't really coming back—for which I could seriously bite him—where was he *tonight*? The people just kept on coming, all the Ariadnes and a bunch of tech connections and the Morellis and the neighbors and some artists who Antonia must have found under a rock from the looks of them.

Whatever. Put your contribution in the bar and let's dance.

The joint was jumping, and I was glad to have industrial-grade floors. The mirror ball made it look like it was snowing in there, the booze was flowing, and the cabs were already lining up outside. Nothing like a couple of hot tips to the cab company switchboards to have them sniffing for business. The caterers had laid an awesome buffet, complete with some primo sushi. A friend of Tracy's was playing DJ, the music was good, and there was serious acreage for the dance floor.

And there was absolutely no sign of the guest I most wanted to see. I trusted him, I reminded myself, and went to adjudicate a fridge allocation dispute between the barkeep and the caterer.

I felt warm fingers on my back and knew, just knew, whose they were.

"Dance?" James murmured beside my ear.

I glanced back and pretended not to recognize him. I also pretended not to be thrilled to the bejabbers to see him. "Do I know you? You look vaguely familiar."

He grinned. "The disappearing man, at your service."

I poked his shoulder. It was as hard as a rock. "So are you real, or an illusion?"

"Come and dance and find out."

"Maybe, maybe not. Convince me."

He raised his fist to his chest as the music changed to a slow romantic piece. "You're breaking my heart here. After I bribed the DJ and brought you a present, too."

"There are gifts involved?" I let myself perk up. "Why didn't you say so?"

James laughed, not fooled in the least, and it was heaven to dance with him. He was wearing his tux, no slouch, this boy, it was custom and very sexy. Mmm. There was that cologne, too. I took a deep appreciative breath and settled closer. The small adults darted by, overwhelmed by party and people and food . . . but mostly by hardware. I was surprisingly cool about this, but then they were well behaved.

"No questions?" James asked, his lips wonderfully close to my ear. "I'm surprised."

"I'm trusting you, Coxwell, and it's just about killing me. Don't push your luck."

"Time for presents, then. Look in my pocket."

I flicked a glance to his face, but he wasn't telling. I kept one hand on his shoulder, and he continued to lead me around the floor. One suit pocket crinkled, so I reached in.

There was something stiff folded there.

I was, just for the record, disappointed. "This is my present?"

"No. It's the first exhibit for the defense in the case of the disappearing man, O'Reilly versus Coxwell."

I smiled and unfolded what was clearly an official document. "It's your divorce decree." I stared up at him in awe. "How did you do this? Mine took a year!"

"I have a few connections." James winked.

"This is what you were doing." I read the damn thing, incredulous and touched as I did the math.

"I wanted to start fresh, Maralys. We've spent a lot of time cleaning things out. Now it's time for us."

Well, that was encouraging. I gave him a smile and let him see how much this meant to me. "Thank you."

James smiled and his thumb slid across the bare back of my waist. "I know that you're an old-fashioned woman deep down inside, Maralys. It's another thing we have in common. I had to see this all resolved, so that everything is in the clear."

I felt my cheeks heat. "Thank you."

He clicked his tongue and shook his head. "It's not your present, because you don't get to keep it. Fold it up and put it back." I did what I was told, then met the laughter in his eyes. "Now, check the other pocket."

I reached into his other pocket on the outside of his jacket and found nothing. James smiled and danced, content to wait. I unfastened the button and checked his inside breast pocket. "People will think I'm feeling you up."

"Let them worry about it."

My fingers closed around a box and I met his gaze.

James smiled in a decidedly Cheshire fashion. "What's keeping you?" he teased.

I pulled it out and discovered that it looked a whole lot like an antique jewelry box. It was the size made for a ring.

"I thought you were curious," James whispered when I hesitated.

I didn't have the heart to tell him that I hoped like hell it wasn't a diamond. It probably was and I was going to have to love it, just because it came from him. But I hate diamonds. They're so pale and, yes, so pedestrian.

I flipped open the lid, realized I was wrong, and didn't mind a bit. Nestled in the worn velvet lining was a gold ring, almost the entire depth of my knuckle. It was a serious chunk of gold, thick, its surface beaded in a three-dimensional pattern of two lions facing each other. There was a blood-red ruby between the fronts of the lions, a smooth cabochon pebble that had to be worth a fortune.

The color of the stone made me uncertain of his intent. I looked up, just as James leaned closer. "Do you like it?" He was anxious as I'd never seen him anxious.

"It's gorgeous. It must be old."

"It was my grandmother's. My mother's mother. She wore it all the time, and I loved it when I was a kid. It's a Byzantine piece, though it's been reworked so many times over the centuries that no one's sure how much of it is original. I was always catching heck for wanting to play with it in the sunlight."

I smiled. "Once a classics minor, always a classics minor."

He nodded and smiled, too. "Bred in the bone, I guess. Technically, it's a dinner ring, but when my mom offered it to me, I had a different idea." James took my left hand in his, then gave me an enquiring glance. It was a novelty to see him looking somewhat uncertain of himself. "I thought it would look good, right there." He touched my ring finger gently. "You have elegant hands, Maralys, and the personal style to wear such a piece."

I gave him a skeptical look. "So, you're offering it to me as a fashion statement?"

James smiled, shook his head. "Will you marry me, Maralys?"

My breath caught. "Depends on why you're asking."

"I told you already. I love you."

"Even though I said such an awful thing to you?"

James shook his head. "You were telling me that you were afraid, and why. If love disappeared when we touched the faultlines, it wouldn't be worth much, would it?"

I shook my head, so very glad James was saying what he was saying.

"I love you, Maralys, and I don't intend to stop." His voice dropped and turned husky. "Marry me."

I nodded, then put out my hand. He slid on the ring—it did look damn good—then caught me close. I touched his chin and looked into all the myriad hues in his eyes. "Because I love you, too, with or without the Byzantine queen rock. I love you, James, and I don't intend to stop, either."

"Works for me." James kissed me in a most thorough manner.

I only realized when the hooting started that not only had the music stopped, but that every single person there was watching.

"Gawkers!" I shouted and they laughed, all my friends and family. I held James's hand tightly as people gave us their congrats, and I knew in my heart that he had called it right.

This was the good stuff.

And I had the brass ring—well, the gold one—to show for it.

Subject: error code

   Dear Aunt Mary:

   What does Error Code 403 mean?

   Lost in the World Wide Web

Subject: re: error code

   Dear Lost:

   403 means access forbidden to the site,
   because there are too many users already
   logged on. The line's busy, essentially. Go
   wander the Net and come back later.

   Or, if at first you don't succeed, try, try
   again. :-)

   Aunt Mary
***
Uncertain? Confused? Ask Aunt Mary!
Your one-stop shop for netiquette and advice:
http://www.ask-aunt-mary.com

Things were pretty hectic after that, and I won't kid you that
it was easy going. I gave up half of the loft, leaving just my
biz there and renting the spare chunk to Antonia, while James
gave up the better part of the master bedroom closet. I walked
into Art sometimes, but at least didn't wake up there.

The summer was a blur of swimming on Tuesday and karate on Wednesday and Beverly's AA meeting on Thursday and soccer all the damn time. James coached Jimmy's team that year, and they made the playoffs.

Yes, it's true. By virtue of the blended family, I became a soccer mom. Yikes. You have to believe that I made a sufficiently compelling fashion statement that the other S.M.'s were compelled to lift their games. And woe to the ref who makes an unfair call against one of my boys. They flinch when they see me coming.

Insert diabolical laughter here. He he he.

I did have to retreat once in a while to the loft in the first couple of months, just to catch my breath. All that intimacy and interdependency was a bit overwhelming for the uninitiated. Some days I watched the boys head out into the big, bad world, and my fear of what could happen to them out there nearly took me to my knees.

The encouraging thing was that they all knew that I would come back—they trusted me, all three of them, go figure—and that was the most heartening gift of all. I knew they wouldn't starve to death or pine away to nothing in my absence. On the other hand, I knew that I had something to contribute.

After all, there has to be one lone female voice howling in the testosterone-infested wilderness of that household. I howl but good, in selfless service to all of my gender.

You all owe me, btw. Payment and/or offerings at the altar of Maralys can be rendered in shoes, 9B, please, and no cheap espadrilles.

Jimmy gradually lost his attitude, just in time to head into those dreaded teenage years and get a new one. He's discovered girls. Be still, my heart. I teach him some code stuff and let him help with the beta-testing—he has a taste for fancy technology now and needs the bucks to pay for it. He's planning to get a doctorate in physics to better get into space.

Johnny started showing an interest in animation. Krystal hooked him on Japanese anime flicks and Antonia takes him to shows sometimes. He's also a hardware junkie. Those nimble little fingers are almost unbelievable. I let him change my drives and upgrade my memory when it has to be done.

James took to the other side of the courtroom like a fish to water, yet he doesn't work nutty hours. Sure, there are times when he has to work late, but I have those times, too. The trick is not to have them at the same time. And to work remotely when you can. All this technology has to be good for something in the lifestyle department.

I've got James hooked on an organizer that even a Luddite can move from desktop to palm. I use the same system and wrote a jazzy little routine that updates each other's calendars automatically whenever we log online. It keeps us in sync. Let the computers do the grunt work is what I say.

My father rages anew at injustices, real and perceived, large and small. His hip has healed, so I send him out at regular intervals to terrorize the neighbors. Mrs. Carducci next door evidently does not know how to properly grow dahlias, and yet remarkably has survived to the age of eighty-three, growing spectacular dahlias, both she and they unaware of her lack of knowledge. I didn't think my father knew anything about dahlias, either, but he sees fit to enlighten her from time to time. I think she agrees with me.

Our own garden, btw, looks like junk. Maybe next year.

Beverly comes by for dinner once in a while, her battle against the booze getting easier as it goes on. She's warming up a bit, though is still tart enough to make you pucker. I like her. And I like James's sister Philippa and her husband Nick. Philippa makes me laugh with her jokes about being pregs.

My sister sent enough postcards from weird and wonderful places to cover the fridge, then settled down in New Mexico just before the holidays. She's working as a fashion consultant in some big store in Scottsdale and having too much fun telling people what goes with what. And she's taken up skydiving, which the boys at least think is way cool.

James has put a ban on them visiting her for the short term. He jokes it's until her sanity returns, but those parachutes definitely make him nervous. Just the ones that don't open, of course.

My rhythms have adjusted slightly—though I'll never be a morning person, I do go running with James every day. It's a precious time out of time for us, the only time each day that we're alone together and conscious. Sometimes we don't talk about anything. Sometimes we give the magpies a run for their money.

See, I have to do something resembling a nine-to-five business day, or at least be available during one, since my business started perking along so well. That client from last year was so pleased that they gave me some great references, and you know how it goes.

My father makes breakfast while we run, and I hang out with him for part of the morning after the "men" head out to school and work. Then I go to work and stay at the loft into the evening, doing the java jam.

And yes, the clan can feed themselves, if need be. Miracles abound if you know where to look for them. They don't even live on pizza. Praise be and hallelujah for barbecues. All four of them can cook some slab of meat dead, nuke potatoes, and steam some veg.

The wondrous thing is that no one expects me to be the domestic drudge who holds it all together. I have a business to run, an increasingly successful one, even though I do have a rep for nasty contracts. As James often reminds the boys, you don't have to be of any particular gender to pick up after yourself or turn on the washing machine.

How could I not love this man?

Sometimes James comes by and we go for dinner together; most often, he picks me up around 9 with the K (which is still going strong—another miracle. Who says the big guy doesn't have us on his short list?), the boys in the back and all fired up from whatever their sport of the night had been.

Such is the routine of our lives. It's good, damn good. I never thought humans got to be this happy.

And so it was that in the gray of February, we escaped the bounds of Boston and headed south to warmer climes. Specifically, we went to an all-inclusive in the Caribbean to tie the big knot, one that was (what a coincidence!) near some extremely good scuba diving. I intended to learn how to dive, and so did both of the boys. We took them out of school for the week for the festivities.

The Ariadnes were there, of course, some with partners and some without, all grinning like fools. I made them promise not to sing. Beverly was there, as were Nick and Philippa and their lovely new baby girl. My father came, of course, and the boys, who I suspect were as excited about going diving as the wedding. Marcia flew in with her current love, an ex-Mountie whom Antonia had instantly christened Studly Do-Right.

Of course, most of us flew down together. I tell you, we had more luggage that you could shake a stick at. The resort had to send another minivan to pick it all up. Who could believe that people could pack so much junk for two weeks on the beach?

It didn't bother me at all, though. My baggage has not only been checked and claimed, but unpacked, laundered, and put away.

It did bug me that Lesley and Matt and their daughter hadn't come—things had been strained between us over this pending court case, but I thought blood was blood. James said he wasn't surprised when Lesley had primly declined our invitation.

Robert Coxwell, of course, hadn't even replied, which was a good thing, as James didn't know that I'd asked the old bugger. I had this weird idea that maybe they could all patch it up and put it behind them, but I figured I just didn't understand how deeply it all cut. I wanted the boys to have some knowledge of their other grandfather, but couldn't force that contact upon the great man.

I thought things got strange in my family, but the Coxwells left us all in the shade. I'm never going to understand it. It was amazing how many of them were becoming reasonably normal after what they'd been through.

So, James and I got married, on the beach, as the sun rose behind us, surrounding by the posse of our nearest and dearest. New beginnings and all that.

I wore, in case you're interested, an electric-blue strappy little lace dress that was cut dead straight and came just halfway down my thighs. Meg lined the lace with hot pink satin, and it was one eyeball-melting little number. I had to get married in the islands, as it was illegal to wear something so flash for nuptials in the forty-eight contiguous states.

And you couldn't even see that I was starting to show.

Oh, yes, there will be an addition to the household this year. I'm terrified, but James knows the baby routine, and I've got the Ariadnes nagging me about my vitamins and my ultrasounds. Philippa seems to be handling the new arrival thing with aplomb. I've got plenty of sources of help and advice, as well as a newfound certainty that I don't have to know everything before I take on a new responsibility. We'll manage it together.

In a way, I can't wait.

I wasn't nervous at all when the time came for those vows. Krystal tucked a pink hibiscus behind my ear and gave me the fashion thumbs-up before I headed barefoot across the sand to James. He wore his tux, traditionalist that he is, but he was barefoot, too, with his pants rolled up so they didn't drag in the surf. The breeze ruffled his hair, and he offered his hand as I walked toward him. I smiled, remembering his own short-list of life goals.

He wanted a partner.

A lover.

A friend and a spouse.

Talk about hitting the jackpot. The man had a way of cutting to the chase. I slipped my hand into the warmth of his and looked around at all the people who had taken the time, the trouble, and the expense to share this moment with us.

I looked around at all of them and felt those first trimester hormones ganging up on me. I was going to cry. You see, I knew that I had followed my mother's ball of string into a complicated net. Or maybe I had woven it into one. Either way, I was cossetted by a network of friends and family and love, one that gave me a boost to higher heights and scooped me up when I dipped low.

I felt blessed, if you must know, and I still do. I gripped James's hand and felt my heart swell as I met the conviction in his gaze.

"Ready?" he asked softly.

"Absolutely." I smiled up at him. "I'll have the whole enchilada, please."

"Good idea." He squeezed my hands. "I'll have exactly what you're having, from now through forever."

We grinned at each other like idiots, then the priest did his thing. Johnny had been granted custody of the Byzantine queen special and provided it solemnly at the right moment. Jimmy and I were in cahoots on James's ring—which he didn't know I'd gotten. A jeweler pal of Antonia's had made it. It was gold and wider than was usual for a man's ring, subtly etched with the same lions that appeared on the ring I'd wear. It was arty, and would be a bit of a surprise on the hand of such an apparently conservative guy.

But then, it suited. James had a few surprises himself. He was certainly surprised by this, though I immediately saw in his expression that he really liked it.

As if I needed an excuse to ogle his hands.

Here's the hideous part—we got married, and pledged our love eternal, on Valentine's Day.

Ack! I can't believe I let this happen. Can you? It was the *hormones*, I tell you, the hormones ganging up on me in my weakened state.

But OTOH, it was *really* romantic.

National Bestselling Author
Katherine Sutcliffe